Jillene approached Vince's table and gave him a glance.

The dial of his watch picked up the sunlight when he held his cup. He had nice hands. They reminded her how long it had been since she'd held hands with a man.

As she neared him, her senses were heightened. Why did he have to smell so good?

A pang of loneliness assaulted her and she swiftly shook it off. She had a floundering business, debt to clear and two daughters to raise. Hadn't she told Hannah not ten minutes ago she was giving up on men?

On the other hand, she wasn't dead. She could still appreciate the sight of a handsome man, enjoy the sound of a deep voice and the scent of nice aftershave—couldn't she?

"Laced with humor and passion, Stef Ann Holm's novels tickle the funny bone, capture the imagination, and give readers 'a true sense of being there.'"

—*Romantic Times*

Watch for the newest novel from
STEF ANN HOLM
and MIRA Books

Coming October 2003

Girls Night

STEF ANN HOLM

MIRA®

ISBN 1-55166-949-8

GIRLS NIGHT

Copyright © 2002 by Stef Ann Holm.

All rights reserved. Except for use in any review, the reproduction or utilization of this work in whole or in part in any form by any electronic, mechanical or other means, now known or hereafter invented, including xerography, photocopying and recording, or in any information storage or retrieval system, is forbidden without the written permission of the publisher, MIRA Books, 225 Duncan Mill Road, Don Mills, Ontario, Canada M3B 3K9.

All characters in this book have no existence outside the imagination of the author and have no relation whatsoever to anyone bearing the same name or names. They are not even distantly inspired by any individual known or unknown to the author, and all incidents are pure invention.

MIRA and the Star Colophon are trademarks used under license and registered in Australia, New Zealand, Philippines, United States Patent and Trademark Office and in other countries.

Visit us at www.mirabooks.com

Printed in U.S.A.

TO THE GIRLS:

For the commentaries on fashions and friends.
For the jokes, *Gidget*,
I Love Lucy and all the Marilyn movies.
For slug patrol and daytime television—*Jerry, Jerry!*
And for slumber parties and
playing Trouble by candlelight.
For the bubble baths and facials.
For ruining the Stylus phonograph needle,
and for your laughter when I thought my car was
on fire, but it was the Burger King charbroiler instead.
For the Cheez-Its I find in the sofa cushions,
and for the time we set off fireworks
and ran around the front yard in our pajamas.
You girls are my life, my everything.
Thanks for your contributions and ideas.
I love you.

"You take all the credit for this book
and we don't get the money."
—alias Claire and Faye McDermott

One

All Jillene McDermott wanted was a little breathing room and the only place she could find it was in the bathtub.

Even though she wouldn't be lucky enough to have the tub all to herself before the bubbles went flat and the water cooled, she'd take every minute she could get.

She grabbed a book she'd just bought along with the latest issue of *Women ROAR* which had just hit the magazine racks. The acronym *ROAR*—Reaching Out And Rising—was a tribute to the Helen Reddy song "I Am Woman." Jillene hadn't bought the forty-five. She wasn't into roaring. Contrary to feminist philosophies, she didn't strive for empowerment or liberation. Pieces of her life were being tugged in all directions, but it didn't matter to her which side of the fly the zipper was zipped so long as she could pull things together.

She stuck the plug in the drain, twisted the faucets and gave the water a generous squirt of Tweety Bird bubble bath. Rubbing her sore neck muscles, she walked into her bedroom for her nightie and slippers. As she returned to the bathroom she heard loud giggles and music coming from her daughter Claire's room where she and her sister Faye were playing Disco Dance Studio to the soundtrack of "A Night at the Roxbury."

Jillene wished she could goof around with her daughters, but she needed to figure out how to better manage Coffee Time—a coffee bar that had been her late husband's idea. An idea that was now her only source of income. Becoming a single parent and business owner after being a housewife for so many years had meant she'd had to change her coping skills and take on the role of sole provider.

She undressed in the bathroom. The tiny space had been remodeled when she and David bought the house three years ago. Two of the walls were cornflower blue with a painted seashell border. The pine floorboards were bleached and needed maintenance. A faded spot in the wallpaper above the mirror outlined the spot where an antique lamp had once been. She'd sold it last November to pay the heating bill.

Their seaside cottage, off the coast of Washington, had been built in the forties. When she, David and the girls had first moved in, it had required fixing up, but the house was large and airy, making the gloomy winter days a little brighter. Now the rooms seemed even larger because some of the furniture had been sold, the proceeds going toward expenses. But nothing could take away the view from the front porch. She could still see the Blue Heron Beach marina and walk down to it on the wooded trail that started behind her house. At least something in her life hadn't changed since her husband's death two years ago.

A yellow Labrador retriever padded into the bathroom, shoved her tan nose in the bubbles and started to drink.

"Sugar!" Jillene nudged the dog out and closed the door. Grabbing the magazine, she sank into the tub with a sigh.

She lay there for a full ten seconds before she opened *ROAR,* hoping for some useful advice. Because she'd been in absolute distress during the first year on her own, she'd let the manager of Coffee Time continue on in his position. But eleven months ago, she'd taken out a second mortgage and let him go. When she had first bought a copy of *ROAR* last December it had inspired her to make her first big decision. That was to rename the coffee bar. In order to save it, she needed to make it hers. So Coffee Time became Java the Hut.

Lifting the magazine, she read the finance columns while making mental notes. She was supposed to keep an eye on gross profits by focusing on the cost of sales. *If it doesn't make a sizable profit, you don't need it.* She thought of the Chihuly chandelier in the store—it didn't do anything but hang and look pretty. But—Oh, how pretty it was…

If it doesn't make a sizable profit, you don't need it.

Jillene groaned. To part with the Chihuly, it would be like…. She didn't want to think about how hard that would be.

She scratched her knee, submerged her leg back into the warm water and moved on to an article about power lunching.

With a frustrated sigh, she tossed the magazine onto the floor. She'd read more later when she could think more clearly. She picked up the book she'd set on the edge of the tub. For a moment she stared at the cover photo of a smirking Satan worshiper/serial killer. *The Night Stalker: A Tale of Terror*, by Vince Tremonti.

Vince Tremonti was the local celebrity. He might not live in Blue Heron Beach, but he'd grown up here. His father owned Al's Barbershop across the street from Java, and Al proudly relayed his son's accomplishments in publishing. Al bought a coffee from her most mornings and always asked her how she was doing.

Jillene had never tried one of Vince's books. True crime stories weren't her idea of entertainment. She'd read *Helter Skelter* back in high school, but though she'd read to the end, she didn't like being in the mind of a sadistic killer. It wasn't worth the insomnia.

She eyed the lurid cover of Tremonti's book with some doubt. She'd wanted something to read other than women in business magazines, spread sheets and motivational stuff, but it had been Al's faithful patronage of her coffee bar that made her buy his son's book.

Vince Tremonti's bio on the jacket flat said he lived in metropolitan Los Angeles and was a former Seattle police detective. A black-and-white author photo took up the entire back cover. She looked at his picture, thinking he came across as intense.

She opened the book to the first chapter.

The demon struck in the darkest hours of the night, creating earthly hell and—

The door to the bathroom burst open and her ten-year-old daughter, Faye, made a beeline for the toilet and pulled her jeans down.

"Do you mind?" Jillene commented over the book's edge. "We have another bathroom in this house."

Faye smiled as she went ahead with her business. "Yeah, but I like this one."

The toilet paper spindle unleashed yards of costly squares as Faye slapped her palm across it.

"Hey!" Jillene cautioned. "Go easy on that toilet paper."

With a crinkled nose, Faye muttered, "Sorry."

While Claire resembled Jillene, Faye looked more like her dad. There were times when Jillene looked at her younger daughter and saw so much of her late husband that an ache formed in her chest. Faye's brunette hair was silky straight and her eyes were green, while Claire's hair was blonder and she had brown eyes.

In a burst of energy Claire came into the room and declared, "We're out of cotton balls."

Twelve-year-old Claire was tall and slender with pre-teen curves and small breasts that were perfectly round and pert. Faye still carried some of her little-girl body but insisted on wearing a bra like her sister.

"Funny you should mention the cotton balls." Jillene still held the book open in her hands, but hope was fading fast that she'd be able to actually read any more of it now that the girls had invaded. "I wanted to take my toenail polish off and I couldn't find any. What happened to that bag I bought last week?"

Faye stood and gave the toilet a flush. "We had to use them because we were making all the Barbies pregnant."

"At the same time?" Jillene asked.

The girls had at least forty of the dolls between them.

"We were doing a fake TV show," Claire said. "The Barbies were on an episode called 'My Man's Cheating on Me.'"

The commentary didn't shock Jillene.

Her daughters possessed uncommon imaginations. They were mature for their ages, but they still played Barbies—a pastime Jillene had promised not to talk about outside of the house. When popular boys and school activities weren't a priority for them, they dressed up in old Halloween costumes to put on dance shows for her. Claire was taking home economics in school so she liked to bake cookies on her own. The three of them used to have a great time at the mall on mother-daughter shopping sprees for fun platform shoes and perfumes and cute undies. But they couldn't afford to do that anymore. Things were so different now...

Jillene was in debt up to the Space Needle. In 1998, when her husband had sold his Seattle communications company, he'd led her to believe his investment in Coffee Time was the best thing for them. She'd known nothing about running a coffee café and neither had David. But he had assured her he could make Coffee Time work. He'd needed a change of pace and had said he would hire a savvy manager. Jillene had always trusted him.

David McDermott had been her high school sweetheart. He'd taken care of her for over seventeen years of marriage and he'd worked hard to provide for them. After being open for six months, Coffee Time hadn't evolved the way David wanted it to. Many times she had asked if they would be okay. But he'd kiss her and tell her he did the worrying in the family—and there was nothing to worry about.

But he hadn't sold his communications company for a lot of money, certainly not enough to sustain Coffee Time if things went bad.

Jillene could now acknowledge it had taken his death to make her see the reality. Their finances were awful, and she was angry with herself for not having asked more questions over the years. Now David was gone and she had to come up with her own answers.

These days she felt as if her life were a parking lot spotted with chewing gum. No matter how carefully she stepped, things always got sticky.

"Playing Barbies is fine, but the cotton balls cost money. You can't use them anymore." Jillene hated to remind them constantly that the simple things they'd taken for granted were now luxury items.

"I'll find some." Claire searched beneath the sink for a straggler cotton ball to remove her own toenail polish. She and the girls had applied Fantasy Fuchsia two weeks ago, but now it was chipping. "Yuck. There's water under here. The drain is leaking."

"Great." Jillene's sarcasm was so dry she could have toasted a piece of bread.

Coming up empty-handed without even one cotton ball, Claire rose to her feet. "Do we have any hot water left? I want to take a bubble bath."

Faye added, "Me, too."

"Nope. No hot water. I did a load and a half of laundry before the washer broke."

"Then, can we take a bath with you?" Faye asked.

Jillene eyed both girls with their bright, expectant faces. So much for reading. "Put my book on the counter so you don't get it wet."

Excited laughter came as the girls snatched Vince Tremonti's book and set it aside. T-shirts were lifted over heads and jeans kicked off.

"But—" Jillene cut in "—let's give ourselves facials while we're in here." She still had a half tube left of Estée Lauder almond mask that she used sparingly. "Claire, go downstairs and get the cucumber slices in the fridge."

"Okay! Faye, don't get in until I get back."

Claire ran out of the bathroom in her bra and panties and returned several minutes later. "The cucumber was moldy, so I used the eggplant. I sliced six pieces." She held up the purple rounds with tight clusters of tiny seeds in the middle already turning brown.

"That'll work. I guess."

Plain cotton bras were unhooked and panties slipped down two pairs of girlish legs. Purple plastic shower caps covered their hair. Then two naked girls stepped into the big claw-foot tub, while Jillene slid to the middle and sat sideways with her feet dangling over the edge. Water sloshed in a wave up the sides of the tub as the girls sank into the bath.

"Move down," Faye complained to her sister, her bony knee hitting the chrome faucet spout.

"I am moved down," Claire said, settling in.

"How come I always have to be on the faucet side?"

"Because you're the youngest," Claire told her smugly before moving on to her day at school. "Ohmygosh, Mom, you should see Amanda now that she has a boyfriend. She's wearing her makeup really bad. Black eyeshadow up to her eyebrows."

"Ooh, that's so Gothic," Jillene said as she flipped open the cap on the green facial treatment, glad to have this time to free her mind and fill it with silliness.

"Mom—it's Goth," Claire corrected. "She's not doing the dog collar, but she dyed her hair with Kool-Aid and her eyelashes are really clumpy from too much mascara."

"Ooh, Tammy Faye." She squeezed liberal amounts of the mask into each girl's hand, and the three of them began to apply the grainy liquid. The scent of almonds filled the room.

Faye stopped rubbing green onto her cheek and stared at her mother. "Did you name me after Tammy Faye?"

"Heck, no." Jillene massaged the mask over her forehead.

Claire finished smoothing in the cream. "Who's she?"

"Well, you know that Christian channel on the TV with the lady who wears the purple wig and all that caked-on eye makeup?"

"Yeah," both girls said.

"The makeup lady is like Tammy Faye Bakker. Tammy Faye got thrown off television for defrauding the followers of the PTL Club."

"What's the PTL Club?" Claire asked.

"Praise the Lord Club."

Faye's mask was uneven over her cheeks and she'd missed half her chin. "What do they do?"

Jillene snapped the cap closed. "They were supposed to be praising the Lord." She set the mask tube in the bathtub caddy. "But Tammy Faye and her husband stole money from the Lord."

"I thought God was poor." Faye's green brows lifted in question.

Jillene leaned back and pressed the eggplant slices on her closed eyes. "Yeah, He is because Jim Bakker ripped Him off."

She heard the girls slosh and wiggle as they settled in. The three of them lay there soaking in the warm water. A slow and steady drip coming from the bathroom sink made the only sound.

Claire's question broke the short silence. "Mom, do you miss Dad?"

Some days Jillene's heart broke from missing David and some days the mess he'd left her in made her too angry to miss him. "Very much."

"Me, too."

"I miss how he always watched *The Simpsons* with us."

Jillene quietly smiled with memories of her own. She missed the whispered conversations shared across a pillow at night. How he held her hand on a crisp fall day. Or feeling his strong arms come up behind her to pull her against his broad chest.

Dog toenails clicked over the wood floor as Sugar came back into the bathroom.

"Mom, when we get out of the tub can we have a girls night? It's Friday so we don't have to get up for school tomorrow." Faye bumped her knee against Jillene's as she put her legs out over the tub's side, too. "*Seven Year Itch* is on at nine-thirty."

"I love that movie," Jillene said. "Let's watch it again." They'd seen the film four times. Jillene could go for a fifth time with her girls because they always recited Marilyn's dialogue when she was in the bathtub, got her big toe stuck in the spigot and had to call for a plumber. "Girls Night" meant they'd stay up late, watch old movies or snuggle in the same bed and tell stories.

Infinitely more fun than debit and credit columns.

Sugar licked Claire's toes and she giggled as she shook her legs, her eggplants falling into the water with a soft splash. She replaced them and leaned back once more, copying the position Jillene and Faye were in—legs dangled over the tub's edge, Trix the Rabbit tattoos on each of their right ankles. The rub-ons had come in the Trix cereal box as a special promotion—buy one box, get one free—and they'd bought three boxes so they could each have a tattoo.

The noise of Sugar's tongue lapping spilled bubble water off the floor, mingled with the drip of the faucet. Jillene felt herself begin to relax. But the serenity lasted about ten seconds.

"Mom?" Faye peeled the eggplant off Jillene's right eye so she could look at her.

Jillene stared into her daughter's face, the smeared green paste giving her raccoon eyes and the plastic shower cap slipping down her forehead. The sight made Jillene smile. Faye's lips were pursed and she looked serious.

"What's a dog's vagina called?"

Jillene had to think about that one for a moment, then replied, "I believe that would be a furgina."

Two

What Al Tremonti liked most about Blue Heron Beach was that nobody had lawns. At the age of sixty-four, he hadn't fired up a Snapper in years and he sure didn't miss cutting the grass. The small beach house community used crushed shells and nautical motifs to decorate their yards. Standard stuff: skiff planters, pelican and seagull statuary, rusty anchors and ropes.

Easing his foot on the accelerator of his refurbished 1962 Chevy Impala SS—"Super Sport" for those who didn't know just how cherry an SS was—Al drove down Seaward Street running through the main part of town. Colorful wind socks waved in a breeze carrying the smells of seaweed and fish, while shell chimes hung from the eaves of curio shops. All the businesses competed for tourist money. Bed-and-breakfasts attracted nonstop summer business. But hardly anybody wanted to be out on the island for the cold, wet winter.

Late May was still too early for Blue Heron to attract mainlanders, but that didn't bother Al. The crowds would come within the month and life on the island would speed up with the fast pace of vacationers until September, when everyone left once more.

Al turned right at the corner, lowering his speed to twenty in a twenty-five mile zone, hoping to get a glimpse of Ianella Sofrone working in her flower garden. Anticipation gave him a case of sweaty palms. He gripped the steering wheel even harder as he searched for the goddess among the rosebushes that grew up against her picket fence. Her house was one of the few in town to have a lawn. For Ianella, he would push a mower.

Because he'd been in love with her for six years.

He'd known her since his grown son, Vinnie, was born. But he hadn't really noticed her until one day during Mass at St. Mary's Church, several years after his wife, Grace, died of cancer. Ianella had been sitting next to her husband, Leo the Louse, on a summer day as sunshine poured through the stained-glass mural. As the priest delivered the liturgy, the red pane in ''Jesus Washing the Disciple's Feet'' touched Ianella. The soft scarf covering her head slipped a little so the natural red in her hair shimmered like spun henna. He'd barely been able to sit still. He thought her so beautiful, he'd become dizzy. But she was Mrs. Leonardo Sofrone and nothing could ever come of him thinking she was beautiful.

Al was a devout Catholic and wouldn't have wanted Leonardo Sofrone to descend into hell, but the louse had abandoned Ianella seven years ago for another woman. Ianella had never divorced him. She couldn't and remain true to her religion. Al understood that.

Over the years they had both continued to attend the same church. Confess to the same priest. Although there were some things Al could never speak about to Father Pofelski—there weren't enough rosaries to cover his impure thoughts of him and Ianella. She became Ianella in his thoughts only after Leo left her. But he still called her Mrs. Sofrone to her face, and he still couldn't ask a married woman out to a lobster supper.

But a month ago, and about good-damn time, her sinner

husband dropped dead from liver failure. Lost time had to be made up if love were to conquer all.

The low rumble in the Chevy's engine set a beat for the racing rhythm in Al's heart. As if he had willed it to happen, her front door opened and he saw Ianella framed by the pink clematis growing wildly over the stoop.

She wore a striped pastel dress with a matching belt, her slender hands covered with floral gardening gloves. The fiery red hair he longed to bury his fingers in was hidden beneath the brim of a straw hat. He didn't have to look into her eyes to know they were brown. Wonderful brown like the chocolates in a Whitman's sampler box. She had legs better than Mitzi Gaynor's because Ianella's had a finer shape to the knees and calves.

Just when his car was even with her mailbox, she looked at him and waved. Panic stabbed through Al. His chest constricted and burned; his breath grew choppy. Christ-all-Jesus. He'd been spotted.

His impulse was to slam on the brakes, but his foot wouldn't make contact with the pedal. His leg worked in the opposite direction; he actually kicked up the speed of the Impala. He put enough pressure on the accelerator to lay some rubber on the asphalt as he sped away.

Now that Leo was in the great beyond, Al had a free and clear path to the woman of his heart. But he was a nervous wreck. In the dating department his technique was as rusty as an old can. What if he asked her out to the Lobster King and she said no?

After all those years of thinking Leo wasn't worthy of her, Al found himself questioning his own worthiness. Self-doubt had never been a problem of his until Ianella. He was usually levelheaded, he had a decent income and he wasn't too bad to look at. So why was he faltering? He couldn't stop imagining staring at Ianella across a red-

and-white checkered tablecloth, him leisurely buttering her bread, light from a fishnet candle shimmering off her lipstick.

Back on Seaward Street, the slam of Al's pulse didn't let up. He focused on the stretch of road as he traveled past the Seaview Market. He had no intention of stopping there. Connie Duluth's silver Benz was in the parking lot. She stalked him in the produce section, always asking when Vinnie would be coming up for a visit. On his left was the Thrifty Nickel Drugstore. Nothing in the store had been a nickel since 1971; the marquee was advertising St. John's Wort for $6.99.

Three short blocks down, his shop with its green awnings and barber's pole drew Al as a kind of safe haven. Many things had changed in Blue Heron over the past forty years, but Al's Barbershop was still at 521 Seaward Street.

Looking at the barber's pole made him think of how Vinnie used to wind the spring when he was little. He'd seen his son a few months ago when they'd gone on vacation together, but it had been years since Vinnie had been on the island. He traveled a lot with his work and deadlines kept him busy. Vince Tremonti was to true crime writing what Stephen King was to horror fiction. The best in the genre. Popular with readers and more successful than a dad ever could have hoped for his only son.

Slowing to make a U-turn, the Impala's tires hugged the pavement with a screech as Al angled next to the curb. Across the street, Java the Hut—the fancy coffee bar—blocked Al's view of the harbor.

Al cut the engine and leaned his head back on the vinyl seat. He slipped his black fedora over his forehead and closed his eyes. Through the vortex of thoughts and images hitting him, some stood out over the others. Ianella being beautiful. Leonardo being food for worms. Grace being made to suffer treatments and long hospital stays. Would she approve of him and Ianella? She had been gone so many years now.

A rap on the driver's side window jolted Al and he straightened, pushing on his hat. He half expected to find Officer Jerry Peck happily writing him another illegal U-turn citation.

Suddenly everything colliding inside Al came to a peaceful standstill. His face broke into a smile.

His son had come home.

The long hours driving from Los Angeles didn't seem so long once Vince saw the Impala parked at the curb. His dad jumped out of the car and stood on the sidewalk with a wide grin.

"Vinnie!"

The sound of his nickname loosened the stiffness in his muscles. His father embraced him and they clapped each other's backs.

"It's good to see you, Pop," Vince said, and he meant it more than words could express.

Alphonzo Tremonti's appearance was a respectably seasoned version of his photographs dating back to the fifties. He'd aged well. He'd always been a handsome man with black hair, olive complexion and a strong Italian nose that was on the large side. When he grinned, the nostrils had a tendency to flare. A few gray strands touched his ink-black hair, which was still thick enough to support his trademark fedora.

"This is a surprise, son." Stepping back, his father blinked a few times, then rubbed the underside of his nose. "A hell of a surprise."

Tremonti men didn't cry in public—or when their sons

came home for the first time in four and a half years. They didn't cry even when their wives or mothers died and attending the funeral pressed in like the weight of a grave stone. Words like *eternal life* meant nothing to those left behind grieving. Trying to understand something that emotional was saved for private, kept between a father and son who had both lost the most important woman in their lives.

Vince had been seven when his mom died of breast cancer, but he still remembered the funeral with an uncanny clarity. The priest. St. Mary's. The casket. Curls of smoke coming from the censer. The Eucharist. White roses. Aunts and uncles filling the house. People he'd never seen before and relatives he'd never met. The sweet wines. Plates of *asciutta*. To this day, the smell of basil made him want to puke.

Concern softened Pop's features. "You seem beat, Vinnie. How come you didn't fly up?"

"I felt like driving." Not quite true. Needing to get the hell out of L.A., he hadn't wanted to wait three hours for the next flight to SeaTac.

"You look like you drove straight through."

Vince's gaze slid to his Range Rover parked in the marina's overflow lot across the street. The bug-splattered windshield and grill were an indication of the pace he'd set getting to Blue Heron. He'd stopped for a few hours of sleep at a Holiday Inn Express, then he'd hit the road again and traveled Interstate 5 for the past ten hours. "Something like that."

"You need a shave." Al reached inside the Chevy's interior and pulled a set of keys from the ignition. "Let your old man give you one."

Vince fought against losing sight of his problem. Part of him wanted to do nothing more than forget about the

past few days, and having his father give him a shave
would be a few minutes to do just that.

With fatigue tensing the back of his neck, Vince followed Al inside the barbershop, and the familiar smells
struck him immediately. Markham shampoo in different
flavors: orange, cherry-almond and banana. No perfumed
Paul Mitchell or Sebastian. Dad believed in the old way
of barbering.

Removing his Serengetis, Vince squinted to adjust to
the interior light. Eight chrome-legged chairs upholstered
in burgundy vinyl made up the customer waiting area. On
the opposite wall was a long mirror and barber's chair, a
counter rack of scissors, a corded Oster clipper with a
variety of blades, and a narrow glass Barbicide cylinder
soaking combs. After all this time, everything was the
same. But *he* was different.

Framed keepsakes representing Vince's career hung in
various places on the walls. There was the dust jacket
portrait Annie Leibovitz had snapped of him in the L.A.
Green Line station; he sat in a hardwood executive chair,
a speeding Metro rail train blurred behind him. Photos of
him at banquets receiving the Peabody Award and the
Edgar Award. Him in a color shot standing with the som-
ber group of LAPD detectives who had assisted with the
research on the Night Stalker, Richard Ramirez. Him on
Park Avenue in Manhattan with his editor and agent on
either side of him. Newspaper clippings of the *New York
Times* best-seller list where his books had hit top slots.

Seeing everything, a raw chill clawed at Vince. Normally, he would have been honored to have the items
displayed. But after what he'd heard in the L.A. County
jail three days ago, he was inclined to rip everything
down—to break the glass and torch the papers.

The uncharacteristic rage he felt was so potent, he could

barely lower himself into the old-time barber's chair with its aqua-green leather.

For a flicker of a moment, his thoughts shot back to the day and the hour when Samuel Lentz had held his attention captive in the prison's visiting room.

You were a cop. I was a cop. We can relate to one another.

With a flourish, a black hair-cutter's cape fanned over Vince's chest. A chest where his heart pounded frantically.

Al paused, frowning. "Vinnie, are you okay?"

"Yeah, Pop." The lie was hard to swallow.

"You're letting your work wear you down, son."

His father's observation was more than precise. With each book, Vince immersed himself in the lives of murderers, rapists and child molesters, retracing their steps around the country.

Contrary to some of his literary counterparts, his career wasn't glamorous. He recalled the drab paint on walls, saw a cell door close and heard the chilling voice in his head.

Vince snapped back to the present. *Get him off your mind. Think about something else.*

Vince gazed at their reflections in the mirror. His dad looked back at him and said, "You need a vacation."

Beneath the plastic cape, Vince pushed up his sleeves. "We were just on vacation, remember?"

The two of them had been to Maui in February, and Pop still had some of his tropical tan. So did Vince, which wasn't hard to maintain living in California. Before Hawaii, his dad had come down to L.A. for a few weeks last Thanksgiving.

"Yeah, I remember, but you don't look rested. How long can you stay?"

"I'm not sure." He wasn't sure of anything.

"You need a hot shower and a decent meal." Several pumps of the chair lever jerked Vince higher. The seat went back and his father's palm caught a squirt of foam from the automated lather machine.

A soapy cream was rubbed into Vince's jaw in a circular motion with a barber's brush. His father gave him a close shave using a straight-edge razor. He wiped the excess foam off with a towel.

"While I've got you, I'll give you a trim, too."

Warm water rushed out of the sprayer and wet Vince's hair. He closed his eyes and tried to relax, just for a little while, as Markham's creme de shampoo was massaged into his scalp.

"It's not every day I get to work on my famous son." His dad's baritone turned sentimental. "It's really great to have you here, Vinnie. It's been too long since you've been back."

Though they may not live in the same city, the bond between them remained solid. Whenever Vince could manage time away, they took trips together. They'd been to Europe three years ago and had spent a month in Italy with distant relatives. If his pop needed anything, Vince always offered—but Al always declined. He was a proud man. A hardworking man. A father who had instilled in Vince not only a gentleman's manners but a strong work ethic and the need to take responsibility for his actions.

Disquieting thoughts went through him. Maybe he'd failed Pop on that one.

Vince made an effort to push the tension from his body. He took in a breath and willed the knots to release from his muscles. "I didn't recognize the ferry terminal on this side."

"It's a new dock. A barge load of Hyundais slammed into the old one. The captain was smoking grass."

"That was real smart."

"The newspaper said he was from Kent."

Kent was south of Seattle and took a rap for being populated by a dope-toking, beer-drinking, blue-collar industrial plant workforce.

Growing up on the island had distanced Vince from the influence of the sixties and seventies, a turbulent time for the country. In high school, he and his friends had tried some of Duane Bobcock's homegrown after wood shop. Aside from pot or sneaking *Playboy* from the Mini Mart magazine rack, a childhood in Blue Heron Beach had been far removed from the Watts Riots, Bobby Kennedy's assassination, Watergate, counterculture, Manson's terror, draft dodgers, hippies and *Valley of the Dolls*.

Vince's generation was the result of a nation's disregard for the Ward and June Cleaver outlook. A generation that, instead, had thrust itself into psychedelic drugs and marches for equal rights, flag burning, bra burning, brain burning. The liberated movement took the picket-fenced house off the map, and in its place came working mothers and day care. Latchkey kids. Divorce. The disintegration of America. War on the streets. Gangs. The Oklahoma City bombing. Columbine.

Vince reasoned he should have been immune to the evolution in violence. He had always thought he was. But at forty-two, he realized he wasn't. More than that, he didn't think he ever would be.

The world had adapted to the insanity of crime. People cohabited with it—they watched the Dahmers on the nightly news while eating McDonald's Big Macs. Fear didn't come easily because the guy next door was always the reserved type. Who figured that their neighbor liked wielding a knife and cutting up prostitutes? And when interviewed by Dan Rather, the killer's first-grade teacher would report he'd always been a good student in school. Very cooperative and quiet.

As a true-crimes author, Vince put himself into the minds of homicidal maniacs and psychopaths, sinking down there with the lowest of the low. For eleven years he'd been in the belly of the beast—and it was devouring him. All because Samuel Lentz, a convicted serial killer, wanted to be famous.

A tautness in Vince's leg muscles held him still. The interview tapes were in the armrest console of his Rover. He'd listened to them more than once, a sick feeling growing in his stomach each time. The stuff on those tapes had really messed him up. That was the reason he'd driven to Blue Heron—so he could get his head on straight and figure out what to do.

Vince glanced out the window at Java the Hut and commented, "I see the mayor's easing up on chain restrictions."

"No. The coffee place is an independent business. The mayor still swears he'd have his guts scooped out by a Cat before he'd ever let a Wal-Mart or McDonald's break ground. That damn building blocks my view. Lean forward." The chair's back lifted, and his dad rubbed a towel over his hair. "The city council wouldn't have approved their business license if they hadn't been from Seattle. If they were native California liberals with bad attitudes, I might still be able to look out at the harbor."

Vince may live in Los Angeles, but they always joked about it. Pop said he was, and always would be, a Washington son.

"But that's all right," his dad said. "I like Jillene

McDermott. I buy coffee from her. She's on her own and it must be tough. She's got two kids.''

"Divorce?"

"Her husband died two years ago. The guy smoked. Let that be a warning. He was only in his midthirties. I think the stress he lived with did him in. You just don't open a coffee bar in a town where you can get coffee anyplace you happen to be. For a quarter you can get a cup at the Flying Gull gas station, Mini Mart or the Quick Lube.''

"In Los Angeles, coffee's going for four bucks a cup and people pay it.''

"Not here. Which is why I think she's barely hanging on over there." Pop ran a comb through his hair. "You're wearing the top shorter. Who cut your hair?"

Vince looked at his reflection. His hair was as black as his father's and he didn't see anything wrong with the expensive cut. "A salon in Beechwood Canyon.''

"You can't go to those fancy Hollywood places and get a good cut, Vinnie. I'll smooth it over.''

Vince kind of smiled. Nobody who cut his hair would ever do it well enough. He rested his foot on top of his knee. "Sure.''

"Straighten up and keep still or I'll have to get out the Army Men.''

For the first time in days, Vince laughed. And it felt damn good. Pop used to prop him on a booster seat and drop a bucket of green plastic Army Men on his lap to keep him occupied so he wouldn't fidget. His scuffed cowboy boots would stick out from the cape as he directed the combat figures in massive wars on the chair's armrests. His summer buzz was actually something he looked forward to because that particular army guy set came with M3 tanks, 105-mm howitzers and an M41 Walker Bulldog and could only be played with during a cut, so it never lost its appeal.

"Do you still have those Army Men?"

"Most of them."

Vince watched his father in the mirror. "You know how Mom always set up the nativity under the Christmas tree? Remember when I lined up my Panzer 5's around the tree skirt and my sniper took a bead on the three wise men?"

"You gave her heart failure. She whacked you on the head with your catechism and dragged your fanny down to the confessional."

"Yeah. And you know what I never told you? Father Pofelski thought the Army Men were funny. He only made me say one Hail Mary."

The scissor blades stilled. "Only one Hail Mary? That explains it. He got broadsided by a Chem Lawn truck last year and broke nearly every bone in his body. He had casts on for months. You have to wonder about that when nobody in Blue Heron has a lawn. What are the odds? Sometimes God waits until his flock is unsuspecting—then *bam*."

Vince opened his mouth to point out that Father Pofelski getting hit had nothing to do with his laughing over Army Men, but a quiet realization stopped him.

Like a lawn service truck, he hadn't seen Samuel Lentz coming.

Three

Jillene watched as the workmen disassembled her prized Dale Chihuly wasp's nest chandelier. The blown-glass sections were shaped like gold, white and clear-colored jalapeño peppers.

She should have sold the Karmann Ghia instead because she'd never drive it. The sports car took up space in her garage. She might be able to get ten thousand for it, but she couldn't confront that decision yet. And maybe never.

So the Chihuly was being sacrificed.

Some years ago she'd received an inheritance from her grandmother's estate. Shortly afterward, she'd viewed the Chihuly at a Bainbridge auction. She used nearly every penny to bid and purchase the magnificent piece of art. The chandelier had hung in the foyer of their home until five months ago when she'd moved it to Java the Hut to add sparkle to its interior. She loved it, and seeing it come down made her feel as if she was failing. But she had to do something to improve the chances of her business surviving. David's social security checks were covering most of the monthly lease on the building, but they weren't enough.

Standing in front of the commercial espresso machine at eight-forty a.m., Jillene concealed the mixed emotions she felt. The awesome chandelier was the room's focal point—or rather, it used to be.

The last glass piece was removed. Once the workers had gone outside with the chandelier, only Jillene and Hannah remained.

Hannah had worked at Java for just over a year and Jillene had gotten to know the twenty-four-year-old as a free spirit. Her height may have been average, but her appearance was far from it. Her eyeglasses were retro horn-rimmed and she had a tiny silver ring pierced through her right nostril. Her natural brown hair was dyed Priscilla Presley black and fell to her shoulders. She used ski pass necklaces as a bracelet; their miniball links crept three inches up her slender wrist.

"I'm sorry it had to come to this, Jillene. I feel like it's my fault after what happened the other day."

"No, Hannah." Jillene shook her head. "Don't be. You did the right thing by telling me that guy came in here and harassed you. And the truth is, I knew I had to sell the chandelier anyway."

Hannah's lips fell into a regretful line. But it wasn't her fault a male customer came into Java yesterday and gave her a hard time. His behavior had scared Hannah. Thankfully he had left when he saw Officer Peck's police cruiser pull up in front of the barbershop across the street. Jillene should have had the foresight to make sure two employees were in the café at all times. With her cash flow at a trickle, she'd never hired another barista after the last one quit.

Hannah pushed her glasses higher on her nose. "Are things really that bad?"

Jillene had confided the bare facts to Hannah, but she didn't want anyone in town to know she was struggling. She hadn't even told her parents. How could she confess

her husband had wiped out their finances and that she
hadn't known about the dire state of her affairs until it
was too late? Her father would lay into her over her poor
judgment and her mother would want to send a check to
fix things. That was not the way Jillene was going to
handle this.

"Things aren't great." She forced optimism into her
tone. "But they'll get better. With the money I get from
the Chihuly, I'll hire another employee. A college boy.
I'll call the *Times* today and place a help-wanted ad."

"I could take a pay cut," Hannah offered.

"No way. Without your help I'd have to make arrange-
ments for my girls after school. Because of you I'm able
to be at the house when they get home. That means a lot
to me."

Until Faye had entered the third grade, Jillene had always been a stay-at-home mom. She'd volunteered in the
girls' classrooms helping out with art projects and field
trips before she worked in the cafeteria. It had really been
an ideal setup because she was gone only when the girls
were gone and she had the summers off.

"Don't worry about your job." Jillene's smile carried
a spark of humor. "Besides, if I didn't have you, who
would enlighten me on the single life?"

Hannah heaved a sigh. "Being single is hell. If you're
not dating it can really be bad."

"Even if you date someone it can be no good," Jillene
countered. "I did have a date last month—that guy who
said he was a marine biologist."

"That's right. But really, he maintained the aquariums
at dental offices. It's a good thing I needed a filling and
busted him. I caught him arm-deep in a saltwater tank
with a net in his hand."

"I asked him about that. He said he really was studying

to be a marine biologist and the fish tanks were a side-line.''

''Uh-huh. I can see how cleaning algae would be help-ful.''

''I know. That's why I'm not dating him—or anyone else.''

''So you had one bad experience.''

Actually she'd had at least three. The plastic surgeon who wouldn't open a car door for her because he was afraid he might hurt his hand, and the guy who sold used cars and told her how he rolled the odometers back. But Hannah didn't need to know about the other men. Because Jillene was trying to forget them, and there would be no more.

She hadn't realized how really horrible the dating pool was. Why had she even considered getting her toes wet? Some grown men were so screwed up. Juvenile minds in six-foot-tall bodies going through their second and third divorces. Chronic liars. Exaggerators. Or momma's boys.

David had been the love of her life, and that only happened once. She would be okay on her own. She had her girls. And Sugar to sleep on the bed with her and keep her feet warm.

One of the workmen returned and shoved a clipboard at Jillene. ''Sign here for the release.''

She took the cold metal board, gripped a pen that felt even colder, then boldly wrote out her signature on the line. Done. A plan of action established and followed through on. The chandelier was going to an auctioneer. She'd make a respectable percentage after paying a commission, and the proceeds would keep her head above water for a while until she figured out her next strategy.

When the workman left, Hannah said, ''If you don't

want to go through the hassle of dating, use the Internet and surf porno sites.''

Jillene gave a choking laugh. ''Good God, I could never have artificial sex.''

''It's called cybersex, and I'll bet half this town is getting it that way.'' Hannah tidied the coffee sleeves. ''Haven't you noticed how happy Harry Newton has been these days? He just got a computer.''

''That's not why he's happy. It's his Viagra.''

Hannah's eyes went wide. ''How do you know?''

''Edith Schlichting.''

There was only one pharmacy in Blue Heron Beach and the druggist was Edith Schlichting. Built like a fire hydrant, she wore rhinestone glasses and red canvas Keds. She spoke with such a smoker's baritone that, on occasion, its deepness put her gender in question. When you got a prescription filled, everyone in the store knew exactly what you were getting because her voice carried all the way to the deodorant aisle.

Hannah poked a stray black hair into her ponytail elastic. ''If Harry's doing the wild thing on his Craftmatic adjustable bed, I know who he's doing it with. Wanda VanHorn. I always see them together at the Oyster Shell Lounge on ladies night, even though she's got to be twenty-five years younger than him. I read that Viagra can make a man salute for hours—if you know what I mean. And it doesn't matter how old he is.''

Jillene didn't know anything about the pill's potency. She hadn't had sex in two years.

Admittedly, she missed intimacy. Kissing. Touching, and the feel of naked skin against her body. Being stroked and caressed. Feeling so weak from need that she was drawn to the height of passion.

But more than just the physical act, there were moments

when she longed to be embraced and to rest her cheek on a masculine shoulder. To have a man read the Sunday paper with her. Somebody who would squish a spider crawling on the kitchen floor, then ask her if she wanted a refill on her coffee while he was up.

Hannah tossed her dishcloth in the stainless-steel sink. "Viagra and Harry Newton is too much for me. Can you imagine them doing it?" With exaggeration, Hannah fluttered her eyelashes closed and cried, "'Harder, baby! Do me harder, oh-h-h-h yes, yes, yes!'"

"Can I get a cup of coffee?"

The two of them whirled around, startled to find a man wearing aviator sunglasses standing just inside the door. Jillene quickly halted the laughter she'd been on the verge of spilling, while Hannah blushed a bright pink and escaped into the back room on the pretext of counting paper cups.

The man's amused smile echoed in his voice. "But I would change my mind if what she mentioned is being served." He made a short study of the wide menu board above the bar, then his gaze fell back in line with Jillene's.

This time she blushed, making his smile widen. "I don't see it. Guess I'll take a Caffe Americano. The largest you serve."

With an easy motion he removed his sunglasses and tucked one of the temples into the placket neckline of his shirt.

He was beyond good-looking. Handsome in a way that would grab the attention of female shoppers during the half-yearly shoe sale at Nordstrom. He had neatly cut black hair. There was an inherent strength in his face. His eyes were an extraordinary color—a smoky blue-gray. His mouth was strong and sensual. But it wasn't only his appearance that made him attractive. He had an innately captivating presence.

If she were to guess his age she'd say early forties.

The knit of a black V-neck pullover defined broad shoulders while his hard and muscular legs filled out a pair of wash-faded jeans in a way that should have been illegal. She could have gotten a ticket for staring so long.

From everything about him it was obvious he wasn't a local, though somehow he looked familiar. He was tanned. Since the sun was so limited out on the island, people in Blue Heron never got a tan that naturally beautiful, even when they paid for it at the tanning salon.

"Can I get you something to eat, too?"

"What do you suggest?" When he stepped closer to the counter she could smell his aftershave. A warm and clean scent she didn't recognize.

"Scones."

He laid a worn ten-dollar bill on the counter. "Okay."

Using a pair of tongs, she reached for a blueberry scone from the glass case, then hesitated. "Would you like it on a plate or in a bag?"

"Plate's good."

She rang up his order and he paid, dropping his change into the tip box. After making the shots of espresso mixed with steaming hot water, she put the Americano up on the hand-off station.

"Thanks." He selected a fork and napkin from the utensil bar and chose a seat by the window where a rare wedge of sunshine spilled across the table. He looked out at Seaward Street, then back at her.

She fought the unexpected urge to smooth her hair that was up in a faux-tortoiseshell hair claw. When she wore it down, the ends rested at the band of her bra and she usually kept it parted in the middle.

She grabbed a damp cloth and walked out from behind the bar to wipe tables. She told herself they were full of crumbs and needed her immediate attention.

Pushing in chairs, she looked at the photographs of Italy découpaged on the round tabletops. She'd refinished them all herself and had chosen hunter-green cushions and backrests to complement the birch-frame chairs. Six easy chairs in taupe leather angled cozily where the window light was best for reading. Lace café curtains and black and white floor tiles finished off the decor. Java didn't resemble much of the old Coffee Time, even though she'd redecorated on a strict budget.

Jillene approached the man's table and gave him a glance.

The dial of a Swiss Army watch picked up the sunlight when he held his cup. He had nice hands. They reminded her how long it had been since she'd held hands with a man. Strong fingers curled around the side of the cup as steam rose from the black surface.

Nearing him, her senses were heightened. Why did he have to smell so good?

A pang of loneliness assaulted her and she swiftly shook it off. She had a floundering business, debt to clear and two daughters to raise. Hadn't she told Hannah not ten minutes ago that she was giving up on men?

On the other hand, she wasn't dead. She could still appreciate the sight of a handsome man, enjoy the sound of a deep voice and the scent of nice aftershave—couldn't she?

Jillene edged closer to his table. "Would you like the newspaper?" she asked.

When he raised his head, she noticed a faint scar marked the left corner of his chin. Once more, she had the oddest sensation she thought she should know him.

"I'm okay." His gaze dropped to her collarbone and the bib of her khaki apron. Beneath it, she wore a short-sleeved white spandex blouse with the top three buttons unfastened. His attention focused lower, and the longer his gaze held the more her skin heated. Then she glanced down and saw she had a chocolate syrup smear just above her left breast. Embarrassment singed her cheeks.

In an effort to look casual, she folded her arms over her breasts.

He rested his forearm on the table's edge. "You weren't here the last time I was in Blue Heron."

"We've been open for almost three years."

"I meant you. I would have remembered seeing you before."

The statement somehow made it difficult to think. This kind of thing didn't happen to her. Customers rarely flirted. Perhaps she sent out signals for them not to. She was at a loss over how to reply without looking like she was encouraging him.

But maybe she should.

Maybe she shouldn't.

With her indecision, she could feel the fine hairs at the nape of her neck tingling.

Catching a bite of the scone with the edge of his fork, he brought it to his mouth. She watched as the blueberry pastry disappeared. Then he withdrew the fork, keeping his lips together.

It was the weirdest thing, but she wanted to know something about him. "Where are you from?"

"Los Angeles."

Most people in Blue Heron would have offered a prejudiced opinion on the City of Angels, but Jillene's mother lived in the San Fernando Valley so she wasn't anti-Californian like other native Washingtonians.

"My mom lives in Van Nuys," she offered.

"I have a house in the Hollywood Hills."

"Wow." *Wow?* The lame word passed through her lips before she could stop it. So he lived close to where her mother did. Small world. Maybe that was it. When she'd gone down for a visit she'd seen him at Gelson's Market or on Ventura Boulevard.

Yeah, fat chance.

"So—" she picked up a discarded newspaper from one of the tables, then quickly put her arm back in place to hide the chocolate "—what brings you to Blue Heron Beach?"

Her question went unanswered as the café door opened and Connie Duluth from Island Realty came inside wearing a spring collection jacket and skirt in tulip pink.

With a breathless turn of her head, the realtor gazed in their direction as if she'd sprinted across town for a better look at something. Immediately, she removed the designer sunglasses she wore. She stared at Jillene and the man she was talking to.

"Ohmygawd—Vince Tremonti!" Connie's voice grew higher in pitch as the syllables shrieked across the room along with the sound of her polka-dot mules clacking over the floor. "I thought that was you." Pairs of gold and diamond bracelets on her wrists clanked together. "I haven't seen you in forever! I was so disappointed when you didn't make it to the last high school reunion, but here you are. I can't believe it."

Vince Tremonti?

The book—of course.

Jillene gazed at Vince, seeing his facial features in black-and-white instead of living color. No wonder she had thought he looked familiar. She'd been reading his book for the past couple of days. For some reason he was taller than she had thought he would be. More muscular and athletic. Definitely not your typical ex-cop and more "normal looking" than she'd expected of a man who wrote about crazy people.

She was four chapters into his book and the honest truth was that it really bothered her. The descriptions freaked her out. He portrayed Ramirez as the devil incarnate and had described him in such a way that it made Jack the Ripper look tame. She'd slapped the book closed after the second murder had taken place. She had made Sugar go downstairs with her to check all the locks on the doors. And afterward, she'd awakened to even the slightest noise.

"Hey, Connie," Vince replied, standing to greet her. "I didn't expect you'd still be in town."

"Of course I am. When did you get in?"

"This morning."

If Connie smiled any wider, her mouth would pop off her face. "Ohmygawd. Doesn't Al tell you I ask about you whenever I see him?"

"He might have mentioned it a time or two." Vince sat back down but he didn't ask Connie to join him, and Jillene was glad he didn't. She'd never particularly liked Connie. In fact, she was pretty close to hating her guts.

"Well, hey, Connie, I figured you would have gone over to the Eastside by now. Bill Gates has a lot of friends over that way."

"Screw Microsoft," she laughed, one hand on her slender hip. She gave a soft shake of her head, as if to emphasize her naturally blond hairdo with its sexy layered cut. Her perfect weight shifted, and her push-up-bra breasts stuck out.

Jillene quietly stared. Connie was flirting. Flagrantly.

"I don't need their business," Connie said with a con-

fidence Jillene had only read about in *Women ROAR*.
"My office on Main is doing a multimillion-dollar business. I'm my own broker and keeping damn busy. Did Al
tell you I'm getting divorced again?" The last two sentences ran together without a breath in between.

"I don't think he mentioned that."

"I am." She gave Jillene a slanted glance, the first time
she'd paid her any attention, then moved in closer to
Vince as if he were a prized listing she wanted the exclusive on. "We have to go out for drinks and talk about old
times, Vince. Does Al know you're here?"

"I just came from his shop."

"I'll bet he went crazy. He talks about you all the time.
I run into him at the grocery store and over the tomatoes
he tells me what a great son you are."

Hannah came out from the storeroom, saw Connie's
back and rolled her eyes. Then she started to steam some
milk.

"Gawd—" the realtor sighed in punctuated exasperation "—my ex was such a loser. I don't know why I ever
married him in the first place. He's in Central America
on one of those feed-the-poor-kids missions. He's not going to make any money doing that."

"Piccolo nonfat raspberry latte," Hannah said as she
put up the coffee.

Connie Duluth always ordered the same thing.

Connie glanced over her shoulder, then back at Vince.
"How long are you going to be in town?"

"I don't know."

"Let's get together tonight."

"Actually I'm tired from the drive. I'm going to hang
out with my dad."

"Then, we'll get something going in a few days," she
said, walking over to the hand-off counter. "And if you

want something to do in the meantime, come by my office. I have the ideal property for you. You need an investment for all that money you're making. A nice summer home here in Blue Heron Beach. You may like it so much you'll never go back to L.A." She smiled and picked up her latte, then went back to Vince.

Jillene watched in shock and amazement at Connie's aggression as she thrust her business card in Vince's hand, letting her fingers skim over his. The woman flirted and did business at the same time. Jillene doubted that tactic was in *ROAR*.

"Take care of yourself, Vince. Call me. I mean it." Connie softly shook her hair once more.

She left the store but her Aqua Net remained, overpowering the pleasantness of coffee and aftershave.

Vince tossed the Island Realty business card on the table. "Does Connie do that often?"

"Do what?"

"Not pay."

"She didn't?"

Jillene turned and silently questioned Hannah. The girl groaned. "I—I didn't even think about it. I assumed she did. I wasn't paying attention. I'm so sorry."

Damn that Connie!

Jillene should have been watching her more closely. She knew she'd try to pull a fast one. This wasn't the first time something like this had happened. On the last occasion, she'd had to ask Connie for the money twice. Her gall pissed Jillene off. Three dollars and twenty-three cents might be nothing for Connie, but it was something to Jillene McDermott.

Shoving aside her feelings, Jillene smiled pleasantly and tried not to let Vince know she'd been taken. Even temporarily. "I'll catch Connie on the next visit." Before she could stop herself, she mumbled beneath her breath, "She may wear expensive clothes but she uses cheap aerosol hair spray."

Vince's laughter was low and rich.

She instantly stiffened, regretting he'd heard her. Apparently he and Connie had a history together, having gone to the same high school. Not to mention that it was bad business to complain about one customer to another. "I shouldn't have said that."

"Hell, you could have said worse."

His words were bold and quite frank. The way he took her side made her forget to be sorry about Connie.

Jillene felt a ripple of excitement. Her heart lurched. She wished she'd spent more time on her makeup this morning and had fixed her hair better. Why couldn't she have had this kind of reaction to a man during her short-lived dating career?

Because Vince Tremonti interested her in a way that nobody else had. It was disquieting. She couldn't afford to feel like this. She *didn't want* to feel like this.

Not now.

Not ever again.

She bit the inside of her lip until she felt it throb. "Connie's right, I'll bet Al was really glad to see you." She gave one last swipe to the table before putting the newspaper in the magazine rack. "Have a nice visit."

She returned to the counter and replaced the filter on the brew machine. Then she went into the ladies rest room and pressed her back against the cool tiled wall. She dragged the hair claw from her head and let her hair spill free. Within a few seconds, she pushed away from the wall and stared at her reflection.

She used to have her hair foiled every six weeks. Now

she did it herself, but at least she'd become an expert at applying the honey-blond highlights.

Twisting on the faucet, she cupped icy water and splashed it on her cheeks. She told herself she was upset because of Connie. Or maybe because of the Chihuly.

But it was really because of him. Vince Tremonti.

She took in a deep breath punctuated by several even gasps.

With a sweep of her hands, Jillene caught her hair. By the time she put herself back together and returned to the dining area, Vince was gone.

But a five-dollar bill had appeared in the tip box.

Four

"When did you quit smoking?" Al asked Vinnie.

The father and son sat at Al's diner-style kitchen table with Fast Wok Chinese food cartons and two bottles of Heineken. Two bachelors having dinner.

"About a month ago. And it's been a long month. If I got hold of a cigarette, I'd probably light up."

"No, you wouldn't. You've got stamina, Vinnie. Good for you that you quit. I'm really glad to hear this. It means you'll live long enough to enjoy your pension from the police department. Unlike someone else we know who smokes like a chimney." As Al served himself a portion of fried rice, he mentioned the chronic smoker by name. "Jerry Peck came into the shop this afternoon. I told him you were in town."

"I haven't thought of Jerry Peck for a while. Can he still be a pain in the ass?"

"He's definitely a pain in mine. He keeps writing me tickets for illegal U-turns."

Vinnie held his fork still and uttered an indifferent observance. "Huh."

Al knew that normally Vinnie would have made a biting comment about the parking tickets. Deserved or not. Al wondered if the darkness in his son's eyes was directed at something else. Since his unexpected homecoming yesterday, Vinnie had seemed distracted.

Shaking his head, Vinnie gave a short laugh. "Jerry and I had some good times growing up, but he could be a real dick-head. Like when he blew up my '68 Ford GTO model with an M-80."

"I remember that. You boys were around ten years old. Jerry and his dad kept firework explosives in their garage and they built cherry bombs on the tool bench. You were worked up over that M-80 blast for weeks."

"Hell, yes, I was. It took me forever to build that GTO." Lifting his beer to his mouth, Vinnie remarked, "I can't believe he's still a cop. I thought he would've been bored with it by now."

"Jerry always wanted to be just like you. It killed him when you made the Seattle P.D. and he didn't."

"I know."

"I run into his wife and kids in town. I get a kick out of his boy, Timmy. He wears his hair in a side part that starts just above his ear. I'd swear he's in training for a comb-over like his old man."

"Peck's got hair left? He used to live on Rolaids. I'd've thought all the pointless anxiety he puts himself through would have made him bald by now."

"Almost. He keeps talking about making Lieutenant. He's passed the written test but never manages to pass the oral. I don't know why not—he has no problem talking while he's in my shop."

"Huh." Vinnie shrugged and ate a bite of sweet-and-sour chicken. His expression remained clouded in thought.

Al studied his son while they ate. Vince adjusted his watchband and rubbed his wrist, his gaze was remote. He pinched the bridge of his nose. Al knew something was wrong.

"Is everything all right?"

"Sure, Pop. Fine."

But things didn't seem fine. Al got to wondering if maybe Vinnie had woman trouble.

Casually, he asked, "Have you seen Sheila lately?"

Al had never really thought too much of Sheila Dela- hunt, but he had always kept his opinion of his son's girlfriend to himself. After living together for three years, Vinnie and Sheila had broken up about eight months ago. Something about two writers under one roof created too much conflict. Al hadn't wanted to pry into the details.

"No. She got married."

"That was fast." Al pushed a water chestnut to the side of his plate. "So are you seeing anyone else?"

"Nope."

"You'll meet somebody else and she'll make you for- get all about Sheila." With a grin, Al grabbed a napkin with a red dragon printed on it and wiped his mouth.

Vinnie lowered his brows and gave him a false smile. Obviously not being with Sheila wasn't what was both- ering him.

Al pulled in a breath. "How's the new book coming along?"

The beer in his son's hand slowly lowered. A flash of uneasiness lit his eyes. "It's there." A long pause held the room. "So are we going to dig for clams this week- end?"

"Sure. Sunday. Right after Mass."

They ate the rest of their meal in silence. At times, Vinnie's gaze drifted to the clock above the stove. Other times, to the telephone on the wall.

Something was wrong. Maybe with his book, but Al wasn't sure. With Vinnie you didn't push. When he was ready, he'd tell his pop what was on his mind.

Five

Instrumental pop melodies pumped through the sound system at the Seaview Market. With his mind in overdrive from lack of restful sleep, Vince pushed a grocery cart with a wobbly front wheel down the cereal aisle to grab a box of Cheerios. He'd already chosen half a gallon of whole milk, hot dogs and buns, a value pack of macaroni and cheese and two rolls of paper towels. For his sweet tooth, he found a white icing bakery cake, then chucked three Milky Ways and a Snickers on top of the clear plastic cover.

As he turned the corner, he stopped.

Jillene McDermott stood at a rack reading a magazine. She wore white canvas platform sneakers without socks. He couldn't imagine her being a widow. She looked too young.

She had her back to him with one foot propped on the grocery cart, her hip tilted to one side as she flipped the magazine pages. A coil of heat slid low inside him. His skin tightened and his muscles flexed.

Her body had curves in all the right places. Without an apron, her figure was defined in a pair of pink capris that showed off her legs and fine hips, while a white knit top fit snugly around her waist. The vaguest impression of a lace bra band was visible through the cotton fabric. From his recollection, her breasts weren't in need of one of those push-up jobs, nor were they unproportionately large for her frame. He liked her curves. She wasn't emaciated like some actresses who had no breasts or hips.

Her hair was without its clip and was not severely pulled back the way it had been before. He hadn't expected it to be so long. Or so richly thick. Most of it tumbled carelessly over one shoulder. The wealth of blond color shimmered, resembling gold and looking so soft he felt like touching it. His fingers itched. He was tempted.

The string of windows beyond the cash registers let afternoon sun into the storefront. Vince rolled his cart forward, his gaze on the sunlight shining over the warm shades of her hair.

"Hello," he said, causing her to spin around.

She slapped the magazine closed with a throaty gasp. The blush in her cheeks pulled his eyes to the cover. *Cosmopolitan.* From the article teasers printed over the model with airbrushed breasts, Jillene was either interested in the spring style guide, new ways to slim her body or "What Men Want: Ten Secrets for Hot Nights."

He kept his smile in check.

"Oh, hey—hi." Her tousled hair framed her face. The low fluster in her voice made her sound sheet-rumpled, an indication she'd been absorbed in hot sex secrets.

The pressure of heat pulling at him intensified.

Fumbling, she returned the magazine to its slot and stood strategically in front of it. An obvious attempt to hide her reading selection.

Too late. He was on to her.

His mouth quirked into the smile he'd been holding on to. "We sort of met yesterday. I'm Vince Tremonti."

A slim hand lifted to her collar and toyed with an enamel heart hanging on a gold chain. "Uh, sure. I remember. From Connie. When she called your name and

I—'' She cut herself off as if she couldn't believe what was coming out of her mouth. "I'm Jillene McDermott."

"I know. My dad told me."

The rosy color on her cheeks deepened. "You asked Al about me?"

"You came up in our conversation. He said you own Java the Hut." He had never been one to linger over small talk. He usually got the information he wanted from a person and moved on, but he was enjoying this exchange. "By the way, the coffee you served was great."

"That's nice to hear. Spread the word."

"Not a problem."

He took a fast inventory of her grocery cart. Three large bags of cotton balls with a box of cherry, grape and orange Popsicles. Some fresh produce and an issue of *Inc.* magazine thrown on top. He grew intrigued. *Cosmo* and *Inc.* Diverse choices.

Lifting his gaze, his attention fixed on her full mouth. Her lip gloss was a soft frosty pink. Sexy as all hell. She didn't appear to be the kind of woman who needed to catch up on bedroom pointers. She could get his imagination going simply by standing there.

No longer feeling the fatigue he had when he'd walked into the store, he asked, "Have you lived here long?"

"About three years."

"I grew up in Blue Heron."

"I know. Your dad has nothing but nice things to say about you."

"He's a good guy."

An awkward silence engulfed them.

He wasn't ready to end their conversation.

Vince rubbed his thumb across a blue banana label that a kid must have stuck on his grocery cart handle. "You mentioned your parents lived in California," he said, not wanting her to leave just yet. She had the nicest lips. They pulled his attention.

"Just my mom." She ran her finger over a chip in her nail polish and didn't look at him when replying. "My dad lives in Florida."

He followed her gaze to his groceries and realized he came across like the stereotypical bachelor living on protein and sugar. Strangely self-conscious about his choices, he took his thoughts elsewhere.

He knew body language and it wasn't hard to guess she was closed off about something. He'd already noticed how she folded her arms as a defense mechanism. He wondered why.

Impulsively, he said, "I heard about your husband. I'm sorry."

"I'm sorry, too."

Her words came out in a rush and he heard the sadness behind them. But whatever private memories she had just remembered only lasted a moment.

An uncertain frown stole into her expression as she began, "About that five dollars you—"

Two fair-complexioned girls ran up to her shopping cart. The taller of the two dumped in frozen macaroni and cheese, and the other brought two king-size bags of Skittles.

"We got our dinner, Mom."

Mom. Her children.

He gave them a quick study and determined the oldest looked more like Jillene, while the youngest probably resembled her husband.

"I didn't say you could have the king-size," she said, pushing her hair off her forehead with a sweep of her fingers.

"They were all out of the regular."

"Uh-huh." Her reply was skeptical and she handed the big bags back. "Go check again."

The girls glanced at him, and Jillene offered, "These are my daughters. Claire and Faye. Girls, this is Vince Tremonti."

"My mom's reading your book," the blonder of the two remarked.

Vince hadn't anticipated hearing that. To Jillene he said, "Really?"

"Yes…well. Your dad recommended it," she replied quickly, seemingly embarrassed for him to know she was reading a book he'd written. "I've only read a few of the chapters and the bio where it said you used to be a Seattle police detective."

The younger girl, Faye, asked, "How many people have you arrested?"

He confided a lesser-known secret. "Despite what you see on television, policemen don't like to arrest people."

"Why not?"

There were a lot of reasons why not. He gave one of the simplest ones. "Paperwork."

"That's cool you write books," Claire said.

He knew that being a published author made people form preconceived notions about him—very few of which were true. He didn't have a driver or a chef. And no, he'd never met Oprah. "Yeah, but I buy toothpaste like everyone else."

Jillene straightened and brought her foot back onto the cart bar. "Why did you quit the police department?"

Although it was information easily learned from any Blue Heron local, he didn't want to discuss it in front of her daughters. "I retired."

"My grampa is retired," Faye said. "He's sixty-eight. You don't look that old."

"I'm not."

"How old are you?"

"Faye," Jillene cautioned. "That's not a polite question."

"It's okay. I'm forty-two."

"My mom's thirty-eight," Faye volunteered, looking at his candy. "How come we can't have any Milky Ways? He's got some."

"You have Skittles."

"But I wanted a Milky Way, too."

Claire squinted at him. "You've got big muscles. Do you play baseball?"

"I've always wanted to play professional ball."

"What stopped you?" Claire asked.

Vince couldn't remember the last time he'd revealed something so offhandedly. "Talent."

Although it hadn't been his intent, he made Jillene laugh.

"Where are my markers?" Faye worked her hand through the items in the cart, going right to the bottom.

"School project?" he asked, motioning his chin toward all those cotton balls.

"No." Jillene lined up the giant-size bags. "We go through a lot."

As Faye continued her search for the markers, jars of chicken baby food clattered in the cart. He could see them pushed up against the side.

Why was Jillene buying baby food? Pop hadn't told him she had a baby. Who was the father if her husband passed away a couple of years ago?

Jillene inched her grocery cart forward. She seemed intent on releasing him from her company. "Well...I'll let you get back to your shopping."

Claire said, "We still need soda pop."

"And Mom has to get her Kleenex."

"No, I don't." Her reply was uttered in a hurry. "I already have some."

"Nah-uh. You used the last box up when you were watching *Emergency Vets*. Remember how you were crying about that Chihuahua's broken leg surgery?"

Jillene gave a casual shrug, but Vince could tell she'd forced the gesture. "Okay, whatever."

An image of her crying over a tiny dog touched him.

Sheila, his ex-girlfriend, had rarely, if ever, cried. About anything.

Vince had had two serious relationships in his life; the most recent with Sheila had lasted three years. Twice he'd fallen for women who shared his occupation. When he was a cop, he'd gone out with a cop. When he'd turned to writing, he'd moved in with another writer.

He'd really thought Sheila was the one for him. She was a published author so they had that in common. While he wrote nonfiction, she wrote women's fiction. One bad thing, though—she had a tendency to compare him to what she called the beta male characters she created. Men she'd named Zachary or Blaine.

Vince would never be a Blaine.

To his credit he didn't leave the toilet seat up, he held doors open and he memorized her birth date and their "anniversary." But Sheila thought he should be more spontaneous. Do more to make her happy. She said they weren't friends. Only lovers. The pressure she put on their relationship drove a wedge between them. They'd finally ended things.

"Girls, we have to go." Jillene tentatively began to push her cart, as if she wanted to say more but wasn't sure what. "Um—goodbye, then."

When she disappeared behind a potato chip display, he

slowly let out his breath. An emotion he avoided defining gripped his heart while an expected thought held him still.

He wished he was going with them.

Good Christ. Where had that come from?

The butcher announced a special through the loud-speakers, and Vince turned his attention to the magazine rack. He contemplated the glossy periodicals, searching for something completely mindless.

After a few minutes, he picked up *Wrestling Mania* then went to the checkout.

Jillene set the groceries on the counter and then noticed the blinking light on the answering machine. Because of the creditors who had been hounding her, she'd gotten into the habit of not playing the messages while the girls were in the room.

"You guys," she called to Claire and Faye as they juggled bags, "take Sugar out for a quick walk down to the marina and back. She's been cooped up all day."

They jumped at the chance to get out of bringing in more bags and buckled the dog's collar around her neck. As soon as the front door slammed, Jillene went to the machine and punched the play button.

"Yes, this message is for Jillene McDermott. This is Candis Lawlor from Seabank VISA. I'm calling in regard to your March and April payments. We haven't received them. I'm afraid if a payment isn't made, we're going to turn you over to Collections. Please give me a call back as soon as possible at our 800 number."

Standing in the silence of the kitchen, Jillene thought about giving up but fought against it. The *B* word had drifted into her thoughts last week, but she had too much pride to declare it.

The sting of frustration threatened as she lowered her chin.

Damn you, David, how could you have let this happen?

But just as the question assailed her, she was overcome with a shameful guilt and a knowledge that she wasn't completely blameless.

Six

Clicking off his corded trimmer, Al picked up a baby-fine neck duster and whisked hair from a mainlander's shoulders. The man paid using an American Express for a $12 charge and exited the shop. When he was gone, only two locals remained.

"Which one of you guys wants to go next?" Al asked, brushing down the front of his white barber's smock.

Mujid Pantankar—Mu, as he was called by his friends—owned the Laundromat next door. He never got his hair cut. Come to think of it, Al had never seen his hair. Mu kept it wrapped in his turban. But he did like his beard trimmed once a week. Not the mustache. You didn't touch Mu's ink-black *mustaccio* with the curled wax ends.

Sitting next to Mu was Sol Slobodkin who ran the video store four shops down. He'd been to the original Woodstock in '69 and he went back each year it had returned. He liked loud Hawaiian shirts with parrots and hibiscus. He wore shorts and rubber flip-flops year-round. Even when it rained.

Sol rose. "Just a little off above the ears."

"Take a seat while I sweep up," Al said, and went for the broom with its attached dustpan.

One of Blue Heron's blue-and-white squad cars pulled up to the curb of Al's with its rear end mangled. The bumper looked like it had been bashed in by a Dumpster. A barking German shepherd in the back seat of the K-9 unit went from window to window, smearing the glass with moist breath and a wet nose.

Gripping the door frame, Officer Jerry Peck spilled his overweight body out of the Crown Vic. After tucking a folded newspaper beneath his arm, he called for the shepherd to calm down while he examined the damage.

With a tuck of his double chin, Jerry entered the barbershop.

In his Indian accent, Mu said, "I don't believe that automobile is in proper operating condition, Officer Peck."

Peck slumped his shoulders. "The Captain is going to kill me. I'm a dead man."

"Dead Man Walking." Sol twisted in the chair as the patrol officer slapped his newspaper on the counter. "Sean Penn died of a lethal injection at the end."

Peck frowned. "Thanks for the optimism, Sol. I feel much better now." He took off his stiff hat, patted the ten strands in his comb-over, then sighed. "I was backing up the car and Duke started barking like he had friggin' rabies. I didn't know what set him off until I saw that Fontaine kid loitering in front of the Mini Mart across the street. Duke went on auto-bark as soon as he recognized him."

Only fourteen years old, Buddy Fontaine had six priors and was a frequent guest at the juvenile detention hall.

"Fontaine ran when he saw me, so I figured he was there to rob the store." Peck put his cap back on and tugged at its patent visor. "I gunned the accelerator to chase him. I forgot I was in reverse and I backed into Velma's LTD."

"Tank with James Garner," Sol compared.

Velma Hicks drove a '78 Ford LTD Country Squire wagon with a faded For Sale sign that had been taped on the back window since '89. The LTD was royal blue with glow-in-the-dark moons and stars stuck on the front and side windows. It was missing all its hubcaps, and a bunch of charms hung from the rearview mirror. Velma claimed she could communicate with the dead.

"One good thing—" Peck sighed "—nobody saw what happened. Velma was inside Knit Wits."

Sol kept his legs crossed, idly moving his foot and causing his flip-flop to make a flapping sound beneath his callused foot. "Where were you?"

"In the parking lot."

Nobody asked Peck what he was doing in the parking lot of a yarn and needlepoint store. But Rosie Greer did come to Al's mind. An image of Peck crocheting an afghan popped into his head and he immediately suppressed it.

Al asked, "How does Velma's wagon look?"

"Not a scratch on the heap." Peck lowered his large frame onto one of the chrome chairs. "I'm going to hang around in here while I come up with a good story to tell the Sergeant."

"That's brilliant, Peck," Sol commented. "You're a cop. You're supposed to be honest. 'To Serve and Protect.'"

Peck folded his arms over the girth of his stomach where black buttons strained against the fabric of his uniform. "Sol, don't you have to go stock *Beaches* in DVD?"

Al grinned and kept sweeping, but when he glanced out the window he froze.

Ianella Sofrone was walking past his shop carrying an enormous flower arrangement. She kept her chin held high so she could look over the mums, lilies and carnations to see where she was going. She made it down the curb and out of his view. He quickly positioned himself next to the window to watch her.

Shifting the flowers in her arm and leaning against her Oldsmobile, she stuck a hand in her pocketbook. She had to be looking for car keys. Without a second thought, Al shot out of the barbershop and was by her side.

"Mrs. Sofrone, let me help you with your car door." It was hard not to sound breathless with his heart thumping.

"Thank you, Mr. Tremonti. These are hard to manage." She gave him her car keys. They dangled on a ring with a plastic photo holder. The snapshot looked like one of her grandson in a peewee football uniform. Ianella had two married sons, Rocky and Carmine, who lived in Seattle.

Al stuck the key into the lock. "They're very nice flowers."

"I bought them for Sunday Mass. I'm on my way over to see Father Pofelski."

"He'll be grateful." Al opened the door for her and took the flower arrangement.

Ianella reached around him, her arm brushing his to engage the power locks for the other three doors. At the slight contact, he stood there with his pulse jumping in his jaw. The perfume of fresh-cut flowers filled his nose. He knew he would never smell carnations again without thinking about Ianella.

He would have set the flowers on the back seat, but it was filled with oversized boxes, suit jackets, fishing tackle and a stuffed beaver with reddish-brown fur and glass eyes.

"Here, hand those to me and I'll put them on the front seat."

He passed her the arrangement, and she leaned into the car to situate it. As she moved a shoebox out of her way, he tilted his head, noticing how the gathers in her dress draped over her shapely rear end. She was one of the rare women who still wore a dress and nylons to go into town, and he liked that. The hem of the dress rose and brushed the backs of her knees. Those magnificent legs. He wished he could run his hand over them. Down to her ankles and back again.

He pressed his lips tightly against his teeth. He had to stop thinking about her body. "That's a nice beaver you have there, Mrs. Sofrone."

She seemed to freeze for a second before she looked over her shoulder, brows arched.

He realized his mistake.

Holy Sweet Jesus!

"I meant *the* beaver." His face burned so hot he was sure he'd turned as red as his Impala.

Hail Mary, Mother of God.

"It was Leo's. The beaver, the clothing—it was all Leo's." She backed up and straightened, smoothing her dress. "He left this junk in the attic and now I'm donating everything to Saint Vincent de Paul."

The louse really must have put her through hell if she was dumping his belongings at a Catholic charity instead of turning them over to his family.

"Now…where did I put my keys? Yes, of course, you have them."

"Uh, oh." Al dropped Ianella's keys into her open palm. Her fingers wrapped around them, and he wanted to hold her hand to see if it felt as soft as it looked. He wanted to stroke her knuckles. But he lowered his arm, put out of sorts by the feelings that ran deeply through him. He loved her so much. But he hadn't said endearing words to a woman in such a long time. He couldn't just blurt out his true thoughts. A man had to win the affections of his girl. Court her, take her out for a lobster supper.

Clearing his throat, he asked, "Do you like lobster, Mrs. Sofrone?"

"I adore it."

He nodded. "That's good to know."

She smiled. And waited. And waited. But he couldn't bring himself to ask her out. He could barely swallow as she held his gaze.

Then she said the most amazing thing. "I think it's about time you called me Ianella."

A warm ache filled his throat. "You can call me Al."

"All right." A smile lingered at the corners of her lovely mouth. "I've got to get over to the church. I'll see you there on Sunday."

He hated to let her go. "Or sooner, if we have need for the confessional."

At that, she laughed. "You're very funny, Al."

She made him feel ten feet tall. He was thrilled she thought he was funny.

She got into the Oldsmobile, turned over the engine and drove off.

Al slowly returned to the barbershop, his mind not on the trim he was supposed to give Sol. All he could think about were fields of carnations. With him and Ianella walking through them, the fragrance of sweet flowers filling the air.

And them holding hands.

* * *

Vince saw Jerry Peck, the local police officer and former Blue Heron Beach high school graduate of the class of 1976, sitting in one of the chrome chairs in Al's barbershop. His eyes were glued to the weekly Sears circular.

Jerry had changed in some ways and in others he had not. Vince remembered their school days when Jerry kept torn-out pages of panty ads from the Sears catalogue pinned up in his locker. They'd been tight boyhood friends since the second grade, but the years had separated that bond and he couldn't offer an exact reason as to why. Rather than confronting it, they were sarcastic whenever they got around each other.

Vince entered the shop. "Still getting your jollies from looking at Craftsman tools and brassiere models, Jerry?"

"Hey, Vinnie," Sol greeted from the barber's chair.

"It is a long time since you came around," Mujid put in, standing and shaking Vince's hand. "Your dad told us you were back in town."

Although Sol and Mu were newcomers by Blue Heron standards, they were old regulars at Al's.

His dad stood behind Sol at the chair, scissors and comb in his hands. "Hi, son."

Jerry didn't budge his hind end, but he rubbed his nose with the back of his hand. "Vincenzo, you got some outstandings."

"You're full of it. I haven't had any outstandings since I was eighteen."

"Keep your money in your wallet, Vinnie," his pop advised. "Peck's just thinking of how he can save his butt by collecting on bogus warrants."

"He wrecked the squad car." Mu pointed out the window.

Vince had noticed the taillight on the canine unit was bashed in.

"I didn't wreck it," Jerry grumbled. "Velma's LTD got in the way."

Vince had once got in the way of one of Velma's cars when he'd been ten years old. He'd ridden his Stingray to the Seaview Market and thought he could get away with stealing a nineteen-cent bottle of paint for his model GTO. The manager had spotted him, and Vince had taken off at a run. He'd grabbed his bike and pedaled with breakneck speed—but he hadn't made it out of the parking lot. A car clipped him and knocked him unconscious onto the asphalt.

He'd come to in a hospital bed, convinced Pop would ship him off to the nearest Catholic school. But his dad's worried face hung over the bed and he'd said it would be okay. Vince had wanted to bawl like a baby from loving his dad and missing his mom so bad—it was much worse than his broken arm. Al hadn't given him a whaling, but he'd made him pay for the paint and apologize face-to-face to the manager. Vince never stole anything again.

And that '68 Ford GTO with its blue paint—the one he'd ended up getting a broken arm over—had been destroyed when Jerry got a wild hair up his ass and had blown it up with an M-80 Big Banger—along with a jar of Mrs. Peck's cold cream and a can of Mr. Peck's Colt 45 malt liquor.

Vince removed his sunglasses. "Pop, after you close up, come down to the marina. Is the *Gracie* still slipped in row A?"

"The same place. But she doesn't run. These three Dexters took her out deep-sea fishing and blew the inboard. I'm waiting for a new engine from Chrysler."

Mujid, Sol and Jerry's expressions grew collectively guilty.

"We didn't mean to do a Rambo on the motor," Sol offered. "In fact, me and Mu—"

"It was Jerry. He drank too much Bud," Mu accused, his accent pronounced. "He reversed the throttle at full speed."

"I saw a marlin! I swear to God."

Vince gave the cop an impatient glance. Peck had always been an embellisher. "There aren't any marlins in these waters, Jerry. It's too damn cold."

With those words, Vince walked toward the door.

"Okay, Vinnie," his father said, combing Sol's hair. "I'll come down in about an hour."

Vince stepped outside. He felt for his cell phone in his shirt pocket. The Nokia wasn't there. He'd left it in the Range Rover on purpose. Turned off. But it was habit to reach for it, to make calls to prosecutors or witnesses. He was always anxious to talk to anyone who could provide him with clues or answers—people who could tell him things about his subjects and their games. Self-serving. Self-amusing. It was Vince's job to put their stories together in a readable form.

To make it entertaining.

Shit.

For a moment, Vince questioned his decision to tell his dad what was going on. He wasn't great at expressing his emotions. In fact, he never liked to talk about them. He was better at doing something to change his situation.

But in this case, he didn't know what else to do.

Seven

Anchor Books smelled like paper and ink and book bindings. The scent of blackberries came from the burning votive on the cash register counter. Copies of Vince Tremonti's books were prominently arranged so all the titles faced outward in the front window display.

The store was intimate and cozy with narrow aisles and shelves so tall that one needed a ladder to reach the top row of books. The layout reminded Jillene of a homey place where people could come and lose themselves in written words for hours. Service was personal and friendly. Anchor Books didn't offer lattes or feature a Sunday afternoon guitarist. There was nothing progressive about the store, and that's how the citizens liked it. No way would the city council allow an urban chain to open on the island.

And Blue Heron Beach could afford to be picky. The National Trust for Historic Preservation had bestowed its Great American Main Street award to them.

The shop bell sounded above the door as a customer came in just behind Jillene. She held an envelope of discount coupons Hannah had made on her computer. Jillene wanted to approach the bookstore about giving out a Java coffee coupon with book purchases. Since she didn't want to discuss her proposal in front of a customer in case Anchor couldn't work with her, she waited.

She gave the lanky clerk an evasive smile, then feigned interest in a section of books. She tucked herself down the aisle and discovered she was in the human sexuality row. It was crammed full of books about relationships, body language, love words and something about 1,001 ways of kissing.

She pulled that one out when she was sure nobody was looking. The color photographs inside were revealing—literally. The models were nude. She scanned the captions. Short and to the point. Highly erotic. There were so many ways to kiss. There were lots of techniques. And pages upon pages of examples.

She felt flushed.

Slamming the cover closed, she gazed at the clerk and wished he would hurry up. But he seemed engrossed in discussing a popular title with his customer, who also appeared to have time on his hands.

Jillene looked across the column of relationship books, her mind wandering as the titles suggested a variety of ways to improve her love life. Whatever the experts said, it didn't matter. To Jillene, her choices fell into four categories.

Married, divorced, widowed or never been married.

Not that she was considering any of the four, because she could summarize, pretty quickly, why each was out of the question.

Married: No way. No morals.

Divorced: In all likelihood this one came with children and, at present, she didn't want to involve her girls in a blended family.

Widowed: Deceased wife issues likely.

Never been married: Major commitment problems.

The list was her own conception and utterly ridiculous now that she went over it. None of her theories had any clinical merit and she'd deliberately overinflated them to suit her own means. And that was so she wouldn't get involved.

She glanced again at the clerk, and was glad when the purchase was finally rung up and the customer exited. Jillene went to the counter and tried to steady her nerves.

"Hi, there."

"Hi, Mrs. McDermott."

She held out a sample coupon. "I was wondering if the bookstore could slip one of my coupons in the sales bag with each book purchase."

"What's the coupon for?"

"Fifty cents off any coffee at Java the Hut."

He glanced at the cleverly printed coupon. "I'll talk with my manager about it, but I don't see a problem. Can you leave me some?"

"Yes." She handed him the envelope. "You can have these."

"All right. I'll let you know."

"Thanks very much." She felt relief at having accomplished her mission, and optimistic that she'd have results.

"So what do you think of the Vince Tremonti book I sold you?" the clerk asked as she was turning to leave.

"Oh...well..." She lifted her brows somewhat uncomfortably. "I, um...I'm still reading."

"I thought the part where Tremonti got into the Valley murders was awesome. He can really paint a vivid picture. You can smell the blood on the walls and everything. Don't you think?"

"Well...I thought it was disturbing."

"Like how?"

"Like..." Her mind spun, searching for the right words to form her opinion. She wasn't focused on the sounds in the store and didn't readily identify the shop bell ringing.

"While I'm sure it wasn't the author's intention, that scene made me feel like I was reading about a meat processing company. Vince Tremonti writes really gross stuff. It's not my cup of tea."

"Hey, Vince," the clerk said, and Jillene spun around.

Vince Tremonti, of all people.

She drew in a sharp breath and willed the paleness to evaporate from her cheeks. *Oh, no.*

Oh, no!

Why hadn't the clerk alerted her instead of letting her go on? If there had been a hole in the floor, she would have jumped in it.

"Hi," he responded, his voice appealing. She couldn't read any emotion in his eyes. They were hidden by his dark sunglasses.

A groan thickened in her throat. Given that written words were so personal, she might as well have said she thought he was ugly or something. And that was about the farthest thing she had in her mind about him.

The opposite was true.

He projected an energy and power that aroused her curiosity, as well as her vanity. She had the compulsion to tuck her hair behind her ear and put on some lipstick.

"Hi..." she muttered. It was difficult to maintain what little demeanor she had left.

The clerk's face lit up like a holiday sailboat in the December harbor. "It's nice to have you in the store. I heard you were in town. We've got you in the window display, of course."

"I appreciate that." Vince's body seemed tense when he lifted his hand and removed the sunglasses. Had she made his muscles that taut and rigid? The question hammered her, but quickly vanished. The blue-gray color of his eyes was so virile and startling, she couldn't help but lose herself in them.

He stared back, and she was filled with expectation.

"Vince, I—" she began, trying to push away the conflicting horror pumping through her heart and the surge of excitement that tingled across her skin.

"You're one of our best-sellers, Mr. Tremonti." The clerk beamed, his skinny neck pressed against his shirt collar. He was clearly thrilled to have the hometown star in his company. "What's your next book about?"

Vince's jaw clenched, and Jillene could see the flare of his nostrils as he took in a breath with his lips firmly together. "A serial offender."

"Everyone here will be anxious to read it. I loved your last one." The clerk shook his head, nonplussed. "It's amazing that people didn't see his dementia before he killed all those people. That incident in the woodshed should have been a major tip-off. Do you think the guy will ever get out of prison?"

"He's up for parole next year."

Jillene shuddered. She hoped whoever they were talking about would never get out.

Vince ran a hand through his black hair, then down his chin. She could almost hear the rasp of beard beneath his fingertips. She noticed he must have nicked himself earlier in the morning. A cut marked the underside of his neck, just below his jaw.

"I think people noticed something wasn't quite right about him, but they didn't know just how deranged he was."

The fact that they could be standing here casually talking about killers unsettled Jillene. Perhaps it unsettled Vince as well, because with his last words he grew quiet and introspective.

"I'm going to look around," he said.

Jillene's throat felt like dust. She wanted desperately to apologize to him. "I...um..."

But he'd gone toward the back of the store.

The clerk addressed her. "So, I'll tell the manager about your coupons."

"Thank you." She stepped toward the door, then bit down hard on her lip. Turning, she went to find Vince.

He was in a far corner. The narrow aisle squeezed her in its musty clutches. She pushed herself into the deepest nook at the end, where he stood with his back to her. She wanted to die.

"Vince, I'm so sorry about what I said."

He looked at her. "What did you say?"

"Don't make me repeat it."

Vince stood close, the heat and scent of him dominating the tiny space. "It's okay."

"It's not okay. I'm mortified. I never meant it."

"Jillene, it's okay," he repeated. "True crime isn't for everyone."

"But it's not that I don't like your writing. It's the story that I..." The thought trailed. She was making a muddy mess.

"You don't like the story."

"Yes. No." She countered herself like an idiot.

She struggled to maintain her wits before they failed her altogether. His solid male body was so easily within her reach that if she exhaled, her breasts would graze his chest.

"It's not a book I would have picked, no. I bought it because I like your dad."

Vince's eyes bored into hers as his face towered over her. "That's nice of you to make the sacrifice."

"It wasn't a sacrifice."

"Jillene, I'm teasing you."

"Oh..."

"So what do you enjoy reading?" he asked.

"Anything," she blurted, wondering why he cared and wondering why she had such a reaction to him. Swift and unpredictable. Heat spreading through her in a rush as she caught herself being wistful for more than conversation. A foreign feeling of not wanting to resist came over her without warning and had her thinking thoughts she wasn't equipped to handle.

Like what it would be like to have his hand caress her cheek. Or fanning through her hair. She wondered how his skin would feel at his jaw. Warm and scratchy-rough? Or how the firmness of his heavenly mouth would feel against her throat if he kissed her there.

She held on to a groan.

The way she was going on, it was like she was after no-strings-attached sex. Or was that what she wanted? Her pent-up libido warred in her, not only in her body but in her heart. How could she do something like that? She was not the kind of woman who did such a thing. She had never. She couldn't...

Then again, he was incredible to look at. With remarkable eyes that gazed at her as if they'd seen too much of the unsavory side of life. Like he was looking for some kind of angel to see him through the darkness.

At length, she replied, "I like books with seaside settings where I can smell the wind and salt. Where people know everyone and there's this happy harmony."

"Happy harmony?"

"Yes..." Barely aware she was speaking, she asked, "What do you like to read?" The thump of her heart filled her ears. She stood motionless. If she moved, she'd brush up against him.

"Biographies," he said simply. "About great people who do good things for the world, not bad."

"Biographies," she repeated, needing to say something coherent and halfway intelligent.

"I sink my mind into enough material about nefarious crimes that I have to read about something better or I'd go nuts." From his sudden nonchalant expression, she got the feeling he'd caught himself revealing too much and was now making light of things. "Like Frederick's biography."

She hated to be ignorant, but she didn't know who he was talking about. Even though he was half smiling as if she should be amused. Was Frederick a crowned ruler of a European country? She prodded herself to inquire "Who's that?"

"The lingerie guy who invented push-up bras and thong panties. Frederick's of Hollywood."

Her head jutted forward and her brows lowered. "You read about him?"

"Absolutely."

She doubted his sincerity and speculated on the existence of such a biography.

The smile on his mouth broadened. His arm raised above her so that he practically pinned her to the bookshelves with his hip. "I'm just kidding."

"I kind of thought so."

He moved his face a fraction away from hers. With her nerves skittering in all directions, she licked her lips. An unwitting gesture on her part. She heard the hissing intake of his breath.

Was this what Hannah had meant when she said there were men she was instantly drawn to sexually and went to bed with? That kind of spontaneity had never crossed Jillene's mind.

But now it did.

She was mortified by the direction of her thoughts.

"But if there was a book about naughty lingerie," he said in a tone infused with a provocative quality, "I would read it. Especially if there were pictures."

His teasing threatened to undo her sensibilities. She could easily forget everything she was working toward. Thankfully the rational part of her mind pointed out that she had a coffee bar to improve and a life to put in order.

She hugged her waist tightly with both hands, perhaps to shield herself against the feelings that were overwhelming her. "That picture-book section is over by the door."

Oh my God. What had she just said?

The smart cells in her brain were dissolving. She'd been eating too many high-calorie foods lately and chasing them down with rich coffee.

He laughed, a low-timbered sound that caused gooseflesh to erupt across her skin. "You've been checking out the human anatomy books."

"No," she denied, her heart thrumming madly. "If I wanted to check out body anatomy, I'd look at myself in the bathroom mirror." A strangled yelp escaped her lips. She never should have said that aloud without thinking it through.

He flattened his forearm above her head. Perspiration moistened the nape of her neck.

"That would be pretty one-sided, but you've got a point."

She blurted, "I didn't mean that the way it sounded."

He grinned, but he didn't debate the issue further.

She managed to slip out from under his arm. "I have to go now."

"Sure."

With a half turn, she walked away as gracefully as she could.

Once on the sidewalk, she sucked in air faster than she could swallow it. Not until she was inside Java and making her way across the checkered floor did she become aware of something.

When she'd been talking with Vince, she hadn't thought about David once. No comparisons, no memories flaring. Just Vince and the chiseled strength of him. The way he leaned his strong arm against the bookshelf and the hint of smile tugging at his lips.

Jillene wasn't sure what she felt. Guilt? Happiness? Relief?

She shook the thought away with a snort of disgust. Clearly she was a sex-starved, nearly middle-aged woman whose hormones had run wild at the first sight of a good-looking man.

Hanging her head with a sigh, she guessed chocolate and a bubble bath weren't providing the satisfaction they once had.

Eight

Sitting at her desk in her bedroom, Faye held a mechanical pencil in her hand and pumped the little tab at the end. She kept pressing it until the lead came out too far and fell onto the carpet.

Crap.

With the mess on her floor, she didn't see where the tiny piece of lead had gone. Rather than look for it among the gum wrappers, fake fingernails, schoolbooks and dirty clothes, she inserted another length of lead into the Hello Kitty pencil. As soon as she did, she began pumping the little tab once more—because she liked to watch the lead come out.

"Are you sure the *Seattle Times* doesn't ask for money up front?" she asked Claire. "What if they do? We don't have any. Do you think you can sound mature when you make the call?"

Claire glared at her little sister. Sometimes Faye could be so annoying. "I read the classified section and it says they bill you."

Twisting a piece of her hair and pinning it back with a bobby pin, Claire thought it was a good thing she had junior high experience for this. It made a big difference to be in the seventh grade instead of the fifth grade like Faye. Those FLASH—Family Life And Sexual Health—classes had taught her a few things about boys.

Because she knew what boys liked in girls, she was confident she and Faye were going to write the perfect boyfriend ad for their mother. They both agreed Mom was upset a lot. They knew it was because she didn't have their dad to sit and talk with at the table. Dad had always stood behind Mom and rubbed her shoulders when she was upset. With him gone, she and Faye had stepped in, but they just weren't the right kind of substitute. Neither of them would kill a bug in the house or take the garbage cans out to the curb on trash day. That was a boy thing.

Giving her sister a smug look, Claire said, "Don't worry. I told you I can sound mature when I want to."

Faye made a snotty face back. She hated it when Claire acted stuck-up. "You must never want to be around me because you always sound like a sixth grader."

To be demoted back to elementary school was a put-down, even for a sister.

Claire angrily thrust out her boobs as far as she could without falling off the bed. "Oh, yeah? Listen to this. 'Hello, this is Mrs. McDermott and I'd like to take out a boyfriend ad.'"

Faye gave a yell of disgust. "Hell-ooo? You said that with a British accent. Our mom isn't British."

Claire gave her a dirty look. "So?" she shot back, knowing she could only do an adult voice if she imitated the mom from the remake of *The Parent Trap*. "I sounded like a woman, didn't I?"

"Yes." Faye lifted her hands and made air quotation marks with her index and middle fingers, *"A Brit-ish wo-man."*

"The newspaper won't know our mom isn't from England." Claire flipped the pages in her binder for a clean piece of notebook paper, then paused and turned to her sister who could be a crybaby at times. "Are you really okay with us doing this? Neither of us liked those guys who came over to get Mom and take her out. So maybe we shouldn't encourage anyone else."

"But they were stupid."

"And stupid guys could call our mom because of the ad."

"Yeah, but in the ad we're going to say what we want for her. It's like we're helping find her the perfect match. If you don't fit the credentials in our ad, don't bother to call."

Claire studied her sister, pondering her intelligence. "Jeez, Faye. I can't even spell *credentials*. Sometimes you're smart."

"I'm always smart. That's why I get straight As."

"Don't rub it in." Claire struggled to keep a high C average, and a B was like a dream come true. "Okay. So this is the plan. We're going to try and find another dad." She gave her sister one more opportunity to back out. "You aren't just going along with this because Mom is sad. Right?"

Faye thought a moment. She had loved her Dee-Doo— when she was a baby she couldn't say Daddy so it came out Dee-Doo—but he was in heaven. She remembered lots about him and she'd never forget him. But she missed having a dad who would come to school on parents' night and who wanted to go bike riding along the shore to hunt for special rocks. After a few seconds, she nodded. "No, I want to. Let's write the ad."

Faye left the chair and went onto the bed to lay on her stomach next to Claire. They put their heads together. "How should we start it?"

"I was thinking we need to draw some attention. Something interesting."

"Yeah, I know." Faye bent her legs and rubbed her stockinged feet together. "What do you have in mind?"

"How about 'I Need Some Fun'?"

Faye pursed her lips. "Okay. I like that."

Claire wrote that down, then they spent the next five minutes arguing about what else to put in the ad. Since they were both fans of the television show *Growing Pains,* they were able to put in some of the relationship stuff they'd seen in the episode where Mike got engaged.

Finally, they were done.

Faye chewed on the end of her pencil and silently read the final version, while Claire went to get the cordless phone.

I Need Some Fun! Seeking a boyfriend who is full of fun. He has to love dogs and the beach. I'm 38 and have a really cute figure. I also have two daughters who are pretty and popular and like shopping at Nordstrom. You have to have a good personality and not be afraid to make a commitment. 206-555-3958. Ask for Jillene.

It all made perfect sense to Faye, and she was certain that by this weekend her mom would be getting a lot of calls. This would make her happy. She'd been so sad since Dad died.

Once, through a crack in her mom's bedroom door, Faye had seen her, Dad's Mariners T-shirt against her nose. She was sniffling and her shoulders shook. She had some pictures and envelopes on the bed quilt. Faye thought they looked like Christmas ones.

Even Sugar moped around without Dad. She didn't have anyone to play really good tug-of-war with because there weren't any super-big tube socks in the house anymore. Her dad had had huge feet and wore huge socks from J.C. Penney. It had been funny to watch Sugar tear up the old socks when Dad got her all worked up.

On that thought, Faye wrote just in front of their telephone number: *Must have big feet.*

Nine

Seagulls circled over the marina, alternately landing on and taking flight from the pier pilings. Buoys clanged from wakes made by slow-motoring boats. The floating dock accommodated about thirty vessels. The *Gracie* was moored at the end and was the only mahogany-hulled inboard.

The 1951 50-foot Catalina from Chris-Craft was a classic hardtop. Refurbished from bow to stern, the sleeper stood out in the row of motorboats with its white cockpit and helm station.

As Vince stood on the aft of the *Gracie,* he watched his father walk down the artificial grass ramp toward the boat. He wore his fedora and Ray·Bans. A pair of Bermuda shorts showed his bony, olive-toned legs, and a loose-fitting short-sleeved shirt fitted over his chest. His pop had a smile on his face and an easiness to his walk.

When Al stepped onboard, Vince tossed him a Milky Way.

He caught it and remarked, "As soon as I get the *Gracie* fixed, we should take her out. I'll check on the part tomorrow."

Vince sat down on the red Naugahyde bench seat beside one of the half-full grocery bags with the candy and paper towels.

Al asked, "What's that for? I have food up at the house."

"I bought some for the boat."

"But we can't go deep-sea fishing until I get her fixed."

"That wasn't what I had in mind."

Frowning, Pop briefly stuck his head inside the cabin where Vince had taken his belongings. "You brought your Fender with you."

When he had packed for Blue Heron, he'd included his hard-tail strat. He loved that guitar. A prime, staggered-pole beauty made by Fender that sounded nice and hot when he fingered the strings.

"When did you move your clothes down here? What's going on? Spill the beans, son. What's bothering you?"

The questions hung suspended between them.

Vince had always been honest with his dad. But this was one of those times when he wondered if a false silence was better than truth.

He'd been able to block out Samuel Lentz when he'd seen Jillene in the bookstore. He was dealing with the hardest choice of his career, but he wasn't blind, and during that brief encounter, he had no longer felt like a crime writer with a tormenting weight on his shoulders. He'd simply been a man enjoying a woman whose nearness stirred his interest in a way he hadn't anticipated.

Pop sat down beside him, and Vince caught the scent of Brut. A cologne that made him remember nights in the Barcalounger sitting on his father's lap and listening to Dr. Suess for the millionth time.

Vince tore the edge of his Milky Way wrapper with his teeth. "I found out something pivotal about the book I've been working on." The milk chocolate overpowered the bad taste in his mouth.

"The Killer Wore Blue." Pop supplied the title. A reference to the color of an LAPD officer's uniform. Samuel Lentz had worn one before he detoured from upholding the law to slashing women. He'd had a place in the thin blue line of police officers separating the public from injustice but he'd thrown it all away. For a different lineup that came with a mug shot.

"What did you find out?" Al bit off a piece of Milky Way.

"Lentz confessed something to me."

Crumpling his candy wrapper, Vince went to the boat's stern. He looked at the water and watched the rays of sunlight reflecting off the rippled swells. Boats motored in and out of the marina.

Pop's voice came to him. "Go on."

Vince caught the smell of saltwater on the wind. Felt the breeze on his face. But then the sensation was gone. He was no longer in the present. He was being pulled someplace else.

A foulness assaulted him—the musky body odor of too many men in confinement.

In an almost trancelike state, he began to talk. He heard his voice but it sounded far away.

He relayed to his dad how he'd gotten involved with the case. Lentz had been on trial for slaying twelve women. The story was sensational because Lentz had once been a police officer. One of the good guys gone bad. Everyone wanted to know how such a thing could have happened. The media crews set up camp at the courthouse every day. The evening news headlined Lentz in ways that were reminiscent of the O.J. trial.

Vince had been finishing the first book of a two-book deal when Lentz contacted him and invited him to come and watch the proceedings. Vince had taken him up on it and stayed for the entire three months of the trial. He couldn't write his notes fast enough. This was a story he wanted to understand—to dig deep and to put together.

Last week Samuel Lentz was found guilty and given the death penalty. While he waited to be shipped to San Quentin, he got in touch with Vince again. This time he asked him to write his story. An exclusive. He wouldn't talk to anyone else but Vince.

Having the subject's cooperation was ideal. The timing was right and Vince wanted to act fast. He proposed to his editor that he write the Lentz book to complete his contract. His publisher jumped at the opportunity to have the first book out on the trial. Vince would deliver it in four months. He had enough preliminary work done and, along with the public information on Lentz and the trial transcripts, all he needed now was the interview. Details from the killer's mouth.

A boat horn blasted twice, pulling Vince back from the horror into which he was sinking. He was grateful for its intrusion. Because not even with his dad, could he show any outward signs of weakness. If Vince did, he might come apart. So he continued in a monotone, "I went to see Lentz at L.A. County last week. I've done a lot of interviews there. I followed the standard procedure and went to the visiting room. The guards brought him in with cuffs on his wrists and ankles. The expression on his face was one I'll never forget. It wasn't sinister. It wasn't smirky. It was euphoric. He looked at me like I was some blockbuster movie star and he was someone just as important. The first thing he said to me was 'Finally, it's just you and me. Now we can get to work. You don't know how long I've waited for this, Vince.' Maybe it was because he said my name like we were buddies. I don't know. But something triggered in my head and I could feel something wasn't quite right. When I turned the tape recorder on he was real happy—so anxious to get started he could barely sit still.''

Vince's mind recoiled. He could remember noting that Lentz had clean hands, and his fingernails were neatly trimmed. His features were nondescript. He was thirty-three, brown hair and brown eyes, average height and weight, clean shaven, no scars—but he was someone Vince would never forget.

''I asked him some general questions. He rushed his answers. I sensed he wanted to get to the actual murders. He didn't want to talk about his childhood. I knew he'd gone to medical school and dropped out after two years. He joined the LAPD, but never made advancement in the ranks despite his high IQ. When I brought that up, his neck flushed red. He wouldn't comment on it. I told him to tell me about the women and how he had selected them.

''He said he had no method. They were just in the wrong place at the wrong time. He didn't care what they looked like. Large. Small. Old. Young. Because none of that mattered. It was the killing that was important. He wanted to do twelve. 'It's an even dozen,' he said. 'Like a carton of eggs. After number twelve, I began leaving clues at the scene. It was time for me to be caught.'''

Pop sat quietly and listened, his eyes never leaving Vince's face.

''Then he told me to put a fresh cassette in the recorder so he wouldn't be cut off. He said the next part was too good to be missed. I got a play-by-play of the murders. He had wrapped duct tape around their wrists, telling them that if they pleaded he wouldn't hurt them. Toying with their minds was just a high for him—he raped them no matter how much they begged. Then he sliced into their bodies like a surgeon, killing any hope they had of surviving.''

Vince's muscles were numb as if he'd fallen asleep on the couch in the wrong position. But this wasn't a dream. It was a nightmare. One he couldn't wake up from. He was living it.

"Beth Conners was screaming and crying as he slit her throat. He said he wanted to remember the exact tone of her voice.'' Vince gazed at his father, steeling himself for his reaction when he said, "So I could describe it—for the book.''

"You?'' Pop said in astonishment. "But he didn't know you then. There was no book in the works between you.''

"He planned the whole thing. Those women he killed—he claims he killed them—'' The rush of anger and outrage he'd pent up unleashed as he said, "For me.''

"Christ...oh, Christ. But why?''

"Because I was a cop and he was a cop. We were two of a kind. Both of us quit police work and turned our attention to the darker side of human minds.''

"But you didn't quit so you could murder people!'' Pop yanked off his Ray·Bans, his eyes deeply troubled.

"He said he'd read all my books and followed my career. He's my biggest fan. Jesus, can we say *Misery* here? He admires me. Calls me brilliant for tapping into what makes people tick—for getting into the criminal mind and dissecting it. He even suggested that I'd wanted to be a doctor, too. He had it all planned. First he picked me. Then he picked the crime. In the end, the two would meet. Author. Criminal. Story. Infamy.''

"Son, you're going too fast. I'm not following everything.''

"He wants me to make him famous!'' Vince ripped the

words out of his lungs in a sharp exhale. "He wants people to buy *our* book and then everyone will know who he is." Vince made a fist and slammed it on the back of the captain's bench. "Fuck."

Pop didn't flinch. "This is unbelievable. My God, Vinnie. He's bullshitting you. It's all bullshit."

Vince spread his fingers and combed them through his hair. "No, it's true. I feel it. I know it. And even if that weren't so, there *is* proof to support what he said. He addressed me in a personal notice stuck in the classifieds. I checked the newspaper archives. It was there on the exact date he killed his first victim, over a year ago. A record of his intentions."

"What did it say?"

"Vince, it starts tonight with number one. We'll go to twelve and get it done."

"Holy Sweet Jesus."

In a hoarse voice, Vince continued. "Would pricks like him kill people if writers like me weren't selling books about it? I never meant to glorify criminals, but maybe that's exactly what I do. My books have been made into movies. The content fascinates and it sells. When I think about that, it makes sense that Lentz would want me to turn his story into a best-seller. I *could* make that happen."

A coldness swept through Vince's body. The dark and insidious enemy that he had privately faced was now out in the open. "I don't know how to begin to write this book," he said, vaguely aware that his hands gripped the railing to keep them from shaking. "I'm not even sure I can. The whole thing makes me sick."

But there was a reality he hated to confront. "I've been paid money for this book and I have a contractual obligation. Hell, I was the one who approached my publisher in the first place. And the fact is, if I back out of this contract I won't have a career anymore. Then what would I do? Writing is all I've known for so long, it's who I am. If I walk away, then I'm screwed.''

''Son, take some time to think it all over. Whatever you decide will be the right thing.''

Pop stood, gave Vince a man's embrace and patted his shoulder, then broke away. He was clearly affected but didn't want to reveal just how much. It was the Tremonti way.

''Please,'' Pop said. ''Come back up to the house, Vinnie. What do you want to be on the boat for, anyway?''

''I love this boat. I need to be here.'' Maybe the boat would help him. He hadn't slept more than two or three hours a night since he'd left L.A. County nearly a week ago. ''I like the feel of the water beneath me when I'm sleeping.''

Softly, his father said, ''Your mother liked that, too.''

Vince traded a knowing exchange with his father. ''I wonder what Ma would have to say if she knew I'd enticed a sociopath to commit glory crimes.''

''Don't do that, son. You're being too hard on yourself. You don't make them do squat.''

He and Pop sat and shared a silence for a long while. When Al finally spoke, it was to offer dinner. Vince declined and his father reluctantly left him alone on the boat.

The pressure of keeping everything to himself was released, but now Vince felt empty. He still had no answers, and the shadow of time was passing over him.

The last evidence of daylight sank into the farthest reaches of the ocean. All that was left in the sky were hazy streaks of orange painted across dark blue.

Opening the cabin door, Vince descended the narrow ladder steps. He grabbed his guitar and returned to the deck. He sat and propped his feet up, settling the Stratocaster on his lap.

The electric guitar was part of his life. When he was a teenager he'd played in a garage band. As an adult, he'd kept up with his music.

The night was cold and the water lapped against the boat's hull. Without amplification, he played the notes to an old Stanley Clarke tune.

But not even as he strummed chords on the Fender could he block out the inevitable.

Evildoers were preparing for a night of terror, knowing that the Vince Tremontis of the world would write about their exploits. And make them famous for all time.

Ten

Jillene sat on the folding table in Mujid Pantankar's Laundromat, dangling her bare legs while chewing on a piece of the girls' grape bubble gum. Purple bubbles popped between her lips, then she snapped the gum back into her mouth. The rhythmic hum of four-cycle washers and the heat from the commercial dryers thickened the air.

Since her washer was on the fritz, she'd accumulated a week's worth of laundry, filling seven washers. When she'd explained the problem to the appliance repairman on the telephone, he'd told her it was probably going to cost two hundred bucks to fix. She'd almost keeled over. Her washing machine was going to have to stay dead for a while longer.

The day was warm enough for shorts and a sleeveless top. Jillene wore a floral patterned tank top and straw sandals that showed her Trix the Rabbit rub-on tattoo. She'd taken her toenail polish off and applied a new color: Ruby Red.

The lyrical notes of a sitar and a lilting male vocal streamed through the Laundromat's ceiling speakers. Mu always played Indian music, and he kept a marker board up-to-date with the popular songs and movies of his homeland that were telecast on AVS cable access. Currently, *Dillagi* was the hit video rental.

Biddu was singing through the sound system. A poster of the hot Indian star hung over the change machine, and Jillene thought he held the sitar like he was making love to it.

The girls came bustling into the laundry without the movie she'd said they could rent for the evening. On Sundays, old favorites were ninety-nine cents.

"Mom," Claire said in a tone full of complaint, "Sol's not at the movie store and the boy behind the counter said we can't rent rated-R without our parents."

Popping a bubble, Jillene frowned. "I signed a release."

Faye shook her head. "He said you have to come over."

"I wonder where Sol is." Jillene jumped off the table, grabbed her purse and walked to the video shop. She paid for the girls' choice of *Romy and Michele's High School Reunion,* but they didn't want to return to the Laundromat with her.

"We're going to get an ice cream," Claire said, the video tucked beneath her arm.

Jillene didn't know if she had any money left after feeding dollar bills into the coin changer. The washers and dryers had eaten up all her cash. She opened her purse and checked for spare change at the bottom. Nothing. She'd really have to justify every purchase she made, and make serious changes in her household accounts. No more buying financial magazines. She could borrow them from the library.

Looking into the girls' faces she hated to reply "I don't have the money for ice cream."

"We don't need any money." Faye stuck her hand into the pocket of her shorts and came out with a folded bill and some pink lint. "Uncle Al gave us each a buck yesterday."

"Oh." The gesture was awfully nice of Al Tremonti, but Jillene was uncomfortable with it. She didn't want to be a charity case. But the girls called Al a sweet ol' grandpa even though he didn't have any grandchildren. They liked him a lot.

Jillene hesitated. "All right. You can get the ice cream. But come back to the Laundromat when you're done."

The girls took off to the end of the block and disappeared into the ice-cream parlor.

As soon as she returned to Mu's, Jillene hopped onto the folding table once more. Mu had set up the laundry in an organized way, with the washing machines in neat rows, the dryers against the wall and, up front, an office and a counter where he took in dirty clothes.

Leaning back on her arms, she scissored her feet and thought about the Mocha Madness idea she'd put into place. By running a special on mochas, she was hoping to interest customers who normally wouldn't buy an Italian-style coffee. Also, Anchor Books had given her the go-ahead on the coupons and already several had been redeemed.

The folding table vibrated slightly beneath her as the second washer went into the spin cycle. The bubble gum had lost its flavor and she would have gotten rid of it if she'd had a piece of paper to put it in.

The glass door opened and the gum in Jillene's mouth stuck to her back teeth.

Vince Tremonti walked in carrying a duffel bag.

He spotted her and smiled.

She politely smiled back, her traitorous body stirring in response as if it were mocking her for all those Hershey's

Kisses she'd devoured last night. Chocolate had let her down yet again.

Vince went to the counter and talked to Mu.

The knit of Vince's shirt emphasized the width of his shoulders. Sunglasses hid his eyes. Wearing an untucked polo shirt, khaki shorts and boat shoes with no socks, he looked ready to take a sailboat out for the afternoon.

Mu wrote Vince a claim ticket for his laundry. Vince pocketed it and started for the door. He stopped, and seemed to change his mind. With a turn, he walked across the room.

The beat of her heart rose a notch. There was no time to ditch the gum so she shoved it into the corner of her mouth.

"Hi," he said.

"Hi." She quit moving her legs and sat up straight.

"I see you're doing some laundry."

She wondered how he could see anything with those sunglasses on. She could never get an immediate read of his expression. It was like he was hiding behind the smoky lenses of his aviators.

"My washing machine is broken. Is Al's broken, too?"

"Not that I know of."

"Oh."

When he removed the Serengetis, the appraising look in his eyes made her feel off balance. Precariously uncentered. She couldn't explain how, but it was like she'd just received a sudden jolt of carpet shock.

He commented, "You probably have a lot of laundry with your baby. What is it? A boy or a girl?"

The question practically knocked her off the table. "Me with a baby? I don't think so."

"You had baby food in your shopping basket."

"Oh, that." She couldn't help laughing over his conclusion. "It's for our dog, Sugar. She has to take a pill every day and she won't eat it with dry food. So we hide the pill in a spoonful of chicken baby food and mix it into the dry."

"I thought you had the two girls and a baby."

"No..." She shook her head. She forgot herself and took a few short chews on her gum, then abruptly quit moving her jaw. "No baby. That part of my life is behind me."

There was something about the measure of his smile that shot through her, raising her pulse to where she felt it clear down to her painted toes.

In a mellow voice, he offered, "You're still young. You could meet somebody and change your mind."

She might have thought about that once, but that notion was no longer a consideration for her. She was done and had moved on. No more babies. No more husbands. Although Vince's opinion that she was young enough did give her pause.

How did he manage to make her indulge in dreams of yesterday? She had to be responsible for herself and her daughters. A man sharing her secrets and renewing her life as a wife were thoughts that could wear her down. But from the way Vince stood, she wondered if that was his intention.

He'd positioned himself in front of her knees. One step closer and he'd be between her legs. She smiled. Lust, she could deal with. Tripped-up emotions about babies and families and second chances, she could not.

"I'm quite happy with the children I have."

"Your girls seem nice."

"They're more than nice. They're my sweet angels."

"I could see that."

"Just like you saw your way to putting five dollars in

my tip box," she said, recalling that she'd started to bring that up in the grocery store but the girls had unintentionally interrupted her. She was bothered by that generous five. He shouldn't have covered Connie's coffee.

He didn't try to deny it. In fact, the corners of his mouth lifted in a way that was incredibly sexy. "Guilty."

"You didn't have to do that. I don't need the money."

"I never thought you did."

"Well…then, thanks. Hannah appreciated it."

Vince seemed in no hurry to leave, which dismayed her. After her less-than-stellar performance at Anchor Books, she worried she wasn't adept at small talk unless it revolved around kids or craft projects. A scattered sensation of awkwardness caused her to be self-conscious. Like a fish out of water.

Like a woman out of circulation.

Grappling for something profound to talk about, she ended up returning to a subject that had discomforted her—just to make sure things had been mended. "So, do you like being a writer?"

He shifted his weight from one foot to the other. "Right now I don't."

"Why not?" Perhaps he was bothered by his choice of subjects, too. She wondered if they ever brought him down. Depressed him or made him want to write happier stories.

After a short pause, he said, "I can't figure out Microsoft Word."

"I'd have thought that figuring out software would be a lot easier than making arrests."

"Not really."

He raised his arm, and her heartbeat pumped like crazy when his hand slipped around her ankle. His fingertips felt surprisingly rough. Callused but warm and smooth.

Fiery heat burst to life in the pit of her stomach. She hadn't been expecting his touch, and when the slow glide of his fingers skimmed across her skin, she nearly swallowed her bubble gum.

"I like your tattoo."

The contrast of his tanned hand against the lighter skin on her ankle made her go still. Fresh shivers scattered over her arms and up her calves. The exquisite sensation saturated her every pore, and she had to remind herself to breathe.

"Trix the Rabbit," he said as the washing machine nearest her clicked off.

"Yep." She could hardly talk. Hardly make sense out of what was going on between them. She needed to get down from the folding table and put her clothes in the dryer, but there was something wicked about him holding on to her ankle, rendering her unable to move. His hand felt brazen and heavy. And she liked it. Way more than she should.

The laundry door swung open and Vince let go of her ankle as casually as he'd grasped it. She sat forward on the table, inexplicably leaning toward him as if pulled by an invisible string. She had to catch herself and stop. He'd already turned away, and she worked hard to convince herself she was glad someone had entered.

Duane Bobcock walked in pushing his beat-up Schwinn over the linoleum. Duane was fifty-one years old, but the state wouldn't issue him a driver's license due to his medical problems. He rode around town on a bicycle. The saddle baskets over the rear fender were filled with *Rugrats* Tommy Pickles doll heads the size of coconuts. Why Duane had the heads was anyone's guess. But knowing him, an enterprising venture was on his mind. Jillene had read in the paper that a container ship with a load of

Tommy Pickles heads had spilled into the Pacific and were washing ashore in Washington and Alaska.

"Hey, man—does anyone have the phone number for Mattel?" Duane asked in a serious tone.

An unkempt beard and a wild mustache covered half his face. He kept his brown hair tied back in a newspaper rubber band; the tapered ponytail fell to his waistband. He always wore huaraches, GI pants, and a green scrub as a shirt. He was in and out of the VA Hospital for treatment, so Jillene supposed he liked to be prepared. Simply take off the pants and sandals and he was all set to be admitted.

The Vietnam War hadn't been kind to his mental faculties, which was a shame because she'd heard he'd been in Army intelligence. But five years in the Hanoi Hilton had rendered him unstable unless he took medication. Sometimes he didn't, and then he'd have to be taken to Seattle for post-traumatic stress evaluation.

Duane held on to the handlebars of his Schwinn and looked around. "Anybody?"

"I'm sorry, Duane," Mu said.

"Bummer. I need to get the phone number so I can collect the reward. It's going to be a lot of bread, man."

Jillene didn't think there was a reward being offered for the flotilla of migrating doll heads, but she wasn't going to be the one to tell Duane.

Looking at Jillene, Duane suddenly said, "You gave me a cup of coffee the other day. Good stuff, man. Not like the shit from the Mini Mart that tastes like boiled Himalayan Gold. Reefer is not made for drinking. You have to toke it."

She always gave him free coffee when he came in. She had a soft spot for him. Beneath the beard, he really was a gentle person. "Come in anytime and I'll give you a refill."

He scratched behind his ear, squinting in deep thought. Then he looked up and saw Vince. He came toward them, and Jillene could see the animation twinkling in his clouded eyes.

"I know you, dude! You work at Taco Juan's."

Vince shook Duane's hand in a comfortable grip. "Not since 1975, buddy."

"No way, dude. You fixed me a taco last Tuesday. Extra cheese. No lettuce."

Quiet for a moment, Vince finally nodded. "Yeah, that's right. I did."

"Far out. I knew it." He turned the bike around and headed toward the door. "Okay, man—if anyone gets the phone number you know where to find me."

Duane lived in a single-wide mobile home with a POW flag waving in the front yard. The flagpole was held steady by cables attached to cinder blocks sunk in the weedy lawn. Colored strings of Christmas lights wound around the cables, and industrial electrical cords plugged into floodlights so that the flag was illuminated at night.

"I remember when Duane came home," Vince said over the rolling drums of dryers and the *thunk* of metal buttons hitting the sides. "I was a junior in high school. He wasn't the same guy who'd left Blue Heron in '69."

"How'd he get that trailer he lives in?" Jillene asked, admiring Vince for his kindness for having gone along with Duane. "I've always wondered."

"After Saigon, he lived in a home for vets for three years but his mom had him released in her care. She died in the eighties and left him the trailer."

"You know, sometimes I see him and he's perfectly coherent. He'll come by Java and talk to me about the most intelligent things. Then other times, he seems really disoriented."

"It's probably the weed he smokes. He's been growing it for years."

Jillene knew about that. "Duane says he uses marijuana for medicinal purposes."

The Laundromat door opened and the girls came inside. They were laughing and playing their game of imaginary friends named Teresa and Janece. They would put themselves into a whole other world, carrying on conversations between the fictitious characters. Jillene heard something about Janece crashing her car on the sidewalk and Teresa dodging the cops.

The girls walked over to Jillene, giving Vince a momentary glance. At the corners of Faye's small mouth was a slight smear of chocolate. Claire had a fresh coat of frosted lipstick on her lips. She always kept a tube in her pocket.

"Did you like your ice cream?" Jillene asked, feeling less flustered by Vince now that her children had arrived.

"Yep," Claire replied. Then to Vince she said, "Your dad's nice."

"Yeah," Faye piped in. "He gave us money for ice creams."

Grimacing, Jillene wished Faye hadn't said that. It still didn't seem right.

Vince said, "He used to give me money for sweeping hair off the floor of his barbershop."

"Did you buy ice cream with it?" Faye asked.

"Sometimes." He slipped his hands into his pockets. "What school do you girls go to?"

"North Beach Junior High," Claire informed him. "And Faye goes to Sea Cliff Elementary."

Faye protested, "But I'll be in junior high in another year."

Jillene hoped they wouldn't start a fight in front of Vince, but to her surprise he smoothed things over.

"I went to both of those." Addressing her oldest daughter, Vince asked, "Does Miss Keister still teach science at North Beach?"

She nodded.

"Does she still smell like a cat box?"

"Yes!" Claire exclaimed excitedly as if she'd found a comrade in arms who, like her, thought Miss Keister was gross. "She's the meanest teacher in the whole school and her classroom stinks."

"Still has the stuffed owl hanging from the ceiling, huh?"

"Yeah, and it hangs right below the heater vent and when the heater comes on, the room smells like the boys' gym lockers."

Jillene frowned. "How do you know what the boys' lockers smell like?"

"Cynthia Stein pushed me in there once."

Not to be left out of the conversation, Faye spoke in a swift tone. "The hamster in our class escaped and it's probably been eaten by a fox or run over by a car."

Turning his attention toward Faye, Vince asked, "Do you still have the map of Washington painted on the playground?"

"Yes, but the orange section with Tacoma chipped off."

"I'm sure that makes many Seattlites happy," Vince remarked.

The easy way he conversed with her daughters caught Jillene off guard. Her girls could talk to anyone and, most of the time, they did. But the way Vince put himself into their world was something she had not expected. She didn't have him figured for the type of guy to talk about school things with children he didn't know.

With a visible hint of curiosity in her tone, she inquired, "Did you really work at Taco Juan's?"

Rubbing his jaw, Vince replied, "For three months. Summer of '75. It only took that long to realize fast food wasn't my line of work."

"Well, you picked a good place to figure that out. They make great tacos."

"I got sick of them. You can only eat so many freebies. I haven't had a Juan Supreme since I was sixteen."

"What a co-ink-e-dink," Claire said. "I *loovvve* Juan Supremes, but only if there's no green onions on them."

"Me, too," Faye added in a wistful voice. "I love Taco Juan's."

The girls hadn't had fast food in a long time. They used to be able to get it every Friday night when Jillene needed a break from cooking all week.

Faye tapped Jillene on her bare knee. "Mom, could we have fast food for dinner?"

"No, I don't think so."

"Why not?" Claire asked with a pout.

"Because I said we can't. Don't step on your lip, Claire."

"But we never have anything good to eat," Faye complained.

Jillene raised her brows. "I cook every night."

"But all your cooking is like Grandma's." Claire adjusted one of the three silver bracelets on her wrist. "We have to have a fruit or a vegetable with every meal. And half the time, we can't get our dessert because we won't eat lima beans."

"I hate chicken," Faye added.

Jillene pointed out, "You love McNuggets."

"That's fake chicken."

Vince's laugh had them all turning their heads in his direction. "Ah, what's fake chicken?"

"The dark meat in the McNuggets is fake," Faye explained. "I never eat the white ones. When I bite into one and see it's white, I throw it away. They suck because they're real chicken."

Jillene nudged Faye with her foot and glared at her. They'd had a talk about the word *suck.* The slang may have been readily used by a lot of people, but Jillene didn't like her daughters to say it because of the figurative meaning.

Looking apologetic, Faye curled her arm around Jillene's calf and gave it a squeeze. She laid her head on her thigh and looked longingly at her face. "Mommy, can't we *please* have Taco Juan's for dinner?"

"Please, Mom," Claire seconded.

Jillene held on to a sigh, not liking that were pressuring her in front of Vince. She didn't want to get into it with him standing there.

"I really don't—"

"Why don't we all go? My treat." Vince's suggestion caused Jillene to look directly at him as he added, "You girls can tell me more about my old schools."

"Sure!" Faye straightened, letting go of Jillene's calf.

Claire grew excited. "Okay!"

"No, we can't." Jillene got down from the folding table. "We have to go home and I have to...to fold the laundry." She named the first excuse that came to mind. Totally lame.

"We'll do all that for you, Mommy," Faye said, "after we get home from Taco Juan's."

"Please, Mom." Claire gave her an artful oh-Mommy-please-please-I-love-you face.

Jillene felt as horrible as a mother could feel. She wanted them to be able to go, but she didn't want to be indebted to Vince. "I...I just don't think so..."

"He doesn't look like a nerd, not like the fish tank guy," Faye said, causing Jillene to lift her hand and rub her temple. She cursed herself for telling the girls about her dinner with the marine biologist wannabe.

"Fish tank guy?" Vince asked.

"Long story," she said, hoping to put an end to it and escape.

But to her chagrin, Claire decided to explain. "The last time my mom had a date, they went out to dinner and she had chow mein and the guy held a chopstick on the tip of his nose and he put the other one in the center of his forehead. Then he grunted like a rhino."

Jillene wanted to crawl into one of the dryers.

There was a slight pull at the back of Vince's jaw—as if he were trying not to laugh. "I promise I won't do that."

"See," Faye said. "He won't do anything embarrassing."

Jillene tucked her hair behind her ear. She was cornered. Trapped. It was three against one. She shouldn't make a big deal about it. It wouldn't be a real couple date. "Okay. Fine. Yes, we'll go. But I insist on paying for myself and the girls." If she had to, she'd shake down every sofa cushion and sweep a yardstick under the fridge to find lost coins. "But we'll meet you there."

"Yippee!" Faye shouted, hugging Jillene around her waist.

"Meet you at six?" Vince proposed.

"That's fine."

"See you then."

After he left, Claire said, "I'm starved. Why couldn't we have just gone now?"

"Because I have to take our laundry home first." *So I can grab on to my common sense before I sit across a dinner table from that man.*

As warm water came out of the showerhead, Jillene rinsed the shampoo out of her hair. With water hitting the top of her head, she pressed her fingertips over her closed eyes.

She'd actually agreed to a date.

No, it wasn't a date.

But what if *he* thought it was a date?

Oh God. She was making a huge mistake meeting Vince at Taco Juan's.

She thought she heard the phone in her bedroom ring. In a second, it rang again.

Jillene opened the shower door. "Girls! Answer the phone!"

Ring.

"Damn." Jillene stepped out of the shower. Dripping onto the floor, she grabbed a towel as she ran several feet into her bedroom.

Ring.

Her heartbeat was thumping wildly.

Ring.

She wanted it to be Vince saying he'd changed his mind.

"Hello?"

It wasn't Vince.

"Hello, I'm looking for Jillene" came a male voice on the other end. It was deep and raspy.

"This is Jillene." Water ran down her arm and onto the phone cord.

"I'm calling about the ad."

Strange. Jillene had listed Java's phone number in the *Times* help-wanted ads, not the one to her residence. Hannah must have given it out. Although that didn't seem like something Hannah would do.

"Um, all right." She tugged the towel more closely around her. "Can you tell me your qualifications?"

"I wear a size fourteen shoe."

Jillene held the receiver away from her ear, then returned it. "Pardon me?"

"I have big feet, baby."

"Excuse me?" She pushed her wet hair away from her brow. "How old are you?"

He sounded creepy when he asked, "How old do you want me to be?"

"W-what?"

"I can be anything you want, doll. I'm a damn lot of fun—"

"Hey, wait a minute. Are you sure you're calling about the ad? I'm looking for someone to work for me, preferably a college student who isn't puny."

"Sweet-cakes, I'm not puny at all. I'm a solid ten inches of—"

The caller's voice buzzed in her ear as he graphically started to describe "Mr. Winkie."

Appalled and disgusted, she slammed the receiver onto the cradle.

She stared at the phone, then pushed it away from her as if it were an icky crawly thing with a dozen legs.

"Good God." She exhaled, her mind in dazed confusion.

She'd just received her first obscene phone call.

Eleven

Jillene pulled her white Altima into the parking lot of Taco Juan's. Vince had already been there for ten minutes, and as he had waited outside the door, he'd wondered if she would show up. She got out of the car with her girls following. They joined him at the planter-filled walkway in front of the restaurant.

"Sorry I'm late," Jillene said apologetically as she tucked her purse beneath her arm. Her hair was brushed into a high ponytail. She wore a yellow print sundress and strappy sandals.

Claire walked alongside her sister. "My mom got scared her car was on fire."

Color spread on Jillene's cheeks. "I'm due for an oil change."

"We thought her steering wheel was on fire again. Once," Faye continued to explain, "we were driving on the freeway to visit my grandma and smoke started coming out of my mom's steering wheel."

Jillene's tone turned unexpectedly gruff. Slightly high-pitched. "The fan belt on my air-conditioning was rubbing on something under the hood. I didn't know the dash was so airy. The smoke came inside the car. I thought my steering wheel was on fire. I panicked."

"But this time," Claire said, "her car wasn't on fire. It just smelled smoky."

"Yeah." Faye straightened. "Because we were driving past Burger Shack."

Vince failed to make a connection.

Faye responded with bright eyes. "The smoke we smelled was coming from the charbroiler cooking hamburgers, not her steering wheel. She said we couldn't come tonight if her car was broken. She even pulled over."

Rushing in, Jillene argued, "It could have been our car on fire."

"She's nervous," Claire whispered.

Walking with jerky motions, Jillene replied, "I am not nervous. Let's eat."

He wasn't convinced that car problems were what had caused her delay. She appeared apprehensive about being here. With him.

Claire said, "Mom, we didn't run for the door just like we promised."

"And it was hard not to," Faye added, then made a dash for the inside as soon as Vince opened the door.

He stood back, waiting for Claire and Jillene to follow.

The spicy aroma of Mexican food was intensified by the kitchen's heat lamps. He felt nostalgic the minute he walked inside Taco Juan's. The wall paint was still orange, red and green. Colorful parrots were painted on the walls as well. Each of the bathroom doors still had *Señors* and *Señoritas* written on them.

Jillene held back, studying the menu board. In the order line, Vince briefly touched her elbow to put her ahead of him. He felt her stiffen, as if she had been surprised to feel his hand on her skin. He wondered if maybe she was forcing herself not to react. He knew that whenever he was around her, he felt an immediate and total attraction.

"Order anything you like," he said, hoping she'd change her mind about the evening being his treat.

She didn't respond to his invitation, as she placed her order and that of the girls.

"I've got that," he said to the cashier, his wallet open, intending to pick up her meal check.

"No," she replied, practically elbowing him out of the way. "I'm paying."

A lot of coins and one worn-out and taped paper bill appeared from her purse. He held on to a comment, sure that she'd struggled to come up with the money. It bothered him that she wouldn't let him take care of the tab. She was proud, just like Pop.

As she counted the correct amount, he gazed at her shoulder where a recent sunburn had begun to fade. Since her hair was pulled up, he could see the nape of her neck. A vague tan line was noticeable from where a bathing suit top had been tied. The straps of her dress were narrow. The scooped bodice clung to her breasts, then flowed around her waist and stopped just above her knees. He liked her shoes. They were heeled and buckled by thin leather at the ankles.

When she moved on to the drink station with her girls, he took her place at the register. He could smell where she'd stood. Her shampoo, a subtle and sweet fragrance, and the powder scent of soap captured his senses.

The four of them shared a table. Excited at the opportunity to eat fast food for dinner, her daughters snagged their seats. That left Jillene and him sitting beside one another on the fiberglass swivel chairs.

Claire removed the paper from a burrito and sunk her teeth into it. A rapturous smile lit up her face. "Yum. Dad told me that when I was a baby he'd wrap me like a burrito in my baby blanket."

Faye slurped icy cold cola through a straw, then took a crunching bite of taco. "Yum. Did Dad burrito me, too, Mom?"

"Yes. He did that for both of you."

The girls were delighted.

Vince didn't expect to, but he wondered what kind of man David McDermott had been. Serious? Humorous? Had he been loyal? Devoted? It crossed his mind that David might not have left his family financially set. But it wasn't his business to question.

"I remember Faye used to call the stroller a stroller-ride." Claire looked at her sister. "Because Mom would always say, 'Let's go for a stroller ride,' so you thought that's what it was called."

"Oh, yeah."

"And how we used to listen to Disney songs on the cassette player in the park."

"Now we have CDs. Not Disney music, but popular stuff." Faye wiped her mouth with a napkin, having finished one taco. "My mom, she knows all the words to the Partridge Family songs. She sings pretty good."

He glanced at Jillene and found her gaze upon him. She quickly moved it elsewhere.

Claire asked him, "Do you like Céline Dion?"

He didn't much listen to pop music. He'd been influenced by rock and roll and the bands of the eighties. To him, nothing compared to great groups like Led Zeppelin and the Rolling Stones. "She's all right."

"We like her, but our mom doesn't."

"*Faye.*" She spoke her daughter's name with a mumbled emphasis.

"Yeah, but you said you hate the way she sings like she has marbles in her mouth."

Vince couldn't resist smiling, waiting to see if she'd contradict the statement.

Grudgingly, she dropped her hands in her lap. "Yes...when she sings *to* it sounds like *ter* and that does drive me crazy."

Vince had never gotten pleasure out of watching someone else's discomfort. But the way Jillene blushed edged his lips into a smile. Discovering her idiosyncrasies kept his struggles at bay. Listening to her was an inexhaustible source of pure refreshment.

Between bites of taco, the girls talked about their schools and the teachers they had, about the dress codes and how they didn't think there should be anything wrong with wearing shorts shorter than the ends of their fingertips when they stood with their arms at their sides.

Vince relayed some stories about the days when he had attended Sea Cliff and North Beach. While Claire and Faye were more focused on fashion styles and popularity, he and Peck had been into releasing horny toads in the nurse's office, and igniting Hot Wheels cars with short-fuse putty explosives in the schoolyard trash cans.

He observed that both girls spoke well and were more mature than he would have figured. At their age, Vince had been full of horseplay. Being a widower meant his Pop had had to reinforce manners and responsibility in him. Because his father hadn't remarried, Vince had grown up without a feminine influence, and he did get a little wild at times. Aside from the female parishioners at St. Mary's who'd hugged him too tightly after Mass, he hadn't been around soft voices and the scent of Cashmere Bouquet for a long time.

After his mother's death, her things had been removed from the closet but her favorite perfume remained on his parents' bedroom bureau. When Vince didn't think he could be brave anymore, he'd sneak into the room, hide his tears and smell the perfume in the cobalt-blue bottle with the silver cap. Evening in Paris.

The girls went to refill their soft drinks. If it hadn't been for them, there may not have been much conversation. He learned that Sugar the dog liked to eat fish food flakes. Claire wanted to get highlights put in her hair. Faye was on the track-and-field team.

He gathered that Jillene's life revolved around her coffee business and her daughters. The girls hinted she'd gone out in the past couple of months. The chopstick-rhino guy had been mentioned again, and Jillene had groaned her displeasure.

Palms on the tabletop, he regarded her. "What kind of dates do you generally go out on?"

"First," she replied, as if the answer had been automatically programmed, "that was when I tried dating. Now I don't."

"Why not?"

"I don't have time."

"You could make time."

"I'm not interested," she said flatly, then stole a glance at his face. Her brown eyes sparkled as she turned the tables on him. "What kind of dates do you have?"

"Haven't had any for a while."

"Why not?"

He pretended great disappointment, grimly smiling for her benefit. "All the good women are taken—or aren't interested."

"Hah!" Her laugh was pronounced but capricious. With a crooked grin, she shook her head. Her ponytail swayed, brushing against her neck in a way that held his attention. "That is a line if I ever heard one. I think you swiped it from a Richard Gere movie."

Claire and Faye returned with their cups filled to the brim. The four of them left Taco Juan's, the girls running ahead to the Altima.

It had been more than nostalgia that he'd felt during the meal. It had been a sense of innocence and energy. A happy display of life's fullness and the gratitude of small pleasures. Jillene's demeanor exhibited a strong pulse of determination. And there was no question her children held her in their hearts with love.

In contrast, he was a man caught in a web of hate, fear and guilt.

Jillene dug inside her purse for her keys. He took them from her to open her car door. But the vehicle was unlocked. He'd run across too many horrible things that happened to women who didn't protect themselves. As he opened the door, he cautioned her. "You should lock your car."

An awkward moment followed. "Why? It's Blue Heron. It's safe here."

"It may seem like that. But you should always be careful."

Because Vince knew otherwise.

Amy White, Beth Conners, Sarah Ford and nine other women had thought they were safe, too, before Lentz had killed them.

The girls snatched the keys from Jillene and clicked the ignition backward so they could listen to the radio.

He heard her pull in a breath. "Well...thanks for inviting us along."

"Thanks," Faye said from the back seat with Claire echoing, "Thanks," from the front.

"Sure."

"I guess I'll probably see you around."

"Probably."

Then she got inside the car, turned over the engine and backed out of her parking space. The girls waved to him. She left the lot and her car traveled down Seaward Street.

As Jillene drove away, she could see Vince in her rear-view mirror. He remained standing in front of Taco Juan's watching her drive away for a long time.

She knew she had said some silly things in response to questions he'd asked. She'd caught the touches of humor at the corners of his mouth and sometimes in his eyes. She thought he should smile more often.

Long after she'd tucked the girls in and switched off her bedroom light, Jillene was still awake. Still seeing Vince's image. The sunset playing across his hair and reflected in his sunglasses.

She closed her eyes to blot him out, but his handsome face was set in her mind. Turning onto her side, she brought the covers to her chin.

Sugar made light snoring noises from where she slept on the foot of the bed. The red LCD glow from the alarm clock brightened the nightstand. In the distance, the dull plop of the leaky bathroom sink worked its way down the hallway to her room.

Much later, Jillene was still watching the numbers change on her bedside clock.

Twelve

The morning cloud cover had yet to burn off and the afternoon moved on without sunshine. A white overcast touched the harbor waters and was reflected in the chrome boat trim. There was no threat of rain. It was just one of those Pacific Northwest days that brought more than the usual calls to Island Realty for free market evaluations. Being surrounded by sunless gray could get a person thinking crazy. Potential sellers would say that Arizona looked real good even with its retired Californians, day spas and smog.

Today's abysmal sky resembled Vince's mood.

He held the cell phone and gazed at a lone outboard cruising away from the marina. Its wake made the *Gracie* bob softly beneath him. Without looking, he dialed a number and lifted the phone to his ear.

In two rings, the line was answered. "The Herzl Agency."

"Yeah—Mel, please."

"Who may I say is calling?" the woman asked.

The tightness knotting the back of his neck muscles didn't loosen when he applied pressure with his thumb. "Vince Tremonti."

There was a startled pause. "Hold one moment, please. He's in his office."

The hold button's double beep filled Vince's ear for mere seconds, then Mel's voice resonated through the line.

"Vince—where in the hell are you?" Mel spoke with an aggressive New York accent.

"I'm up at my dad's place in Washington."

"All I've been getting is the recording on your cell, so I called your house. Don't you check your messages?"

"I haven't been."

"Nobody's heard from you in a week. What's up with the Lentz interview?"

Feeling disassociated from everything going on around him, he replied, "I got it."

"Good." Mel disregarded the incessant ring of another phone line in his office—something he rarely did. "Since you made a verbal pitch for *The Killer Wore Blue,* you need to put together a story outline right away. Your editor's called me twice wanting to know when she can expect pages from you. They're moving ahead with the back cover copy."

Vince didn't have an outline. He had yards of untranscribed tapes with Samuel Lentz's detailed descriptions of the murders, along with his rambling vision of how the story should be written.

Mel asked, "When can you get something to Gail?"

Gazing at a gray seagull roosting on the marina's bait sign, Vince replied, "I'm going to need some time. The material is complicated."

"How much time? There's a rush on this for the sales kits. It's important to get it in the catalogue." Mel's voice faded a moment as he spoke away from the receiver. "No. Wait. Put him on hold. I need to talk with him." Then, more clearly, he said to Vince, "Look, here's what I want you to do. Overnight the pages you have, and I'll tell her

to expect them tomorrow—and we can get this thing rolling. I'll call Gail right now."

"Don't do that, Mel." Vince didn't recognize the up-
tight grit in his tone. His lungs felt like they were being
choked by thick dust. He ran his hand over his jaw, feeling, but not feeling, a half day's growth of beard. "Sorry.
I just—" He inhaled the cool marine air. "Give me another week. Tell Gail I can get her something in a week."

"Good."

The second phone rang once more. There was a long
pause in the conversation and the ringing phone was the
only constant.

Mel Herzl was not a hand holder with his clients. His
attitude was straightforward—a no-bullshit approach to
negotiations. He made things happen. He didn't go soft
in rough situations. He kept his composure rock hard. So
his next words kind of threw Vince.

"Hey, uh, Vince," he said, "is the old man all right?
Is that why you're in Washington? He didn't have a heart
attack or anything, did he?"

"Pop's fine, Mel. Thanks for asking."

"All right, then. I need to take another call. Keep your
phone turned on so I can reach you."

"Right."

As soon as Vince pressed the disconnect button, he
turned off the cell phone and tossed it onto the captain's
bench. He reached into his pocket for a stick of spearmint
chewing gum. Sometimes the craving for a cigarette was
almost more than he could stand.

For a June afternoon, the marina was full of boats due
to the bad weather. The orange Unocal 76 ball mounted
on the roof of Eugene's Boat Works slowly rotated on its
axis. A Bayliner fueled at one of the old-time pumps
where the amounts were displayed on rolling counters

rather than in digital increments. Table umbrellas advertising Budweiser at the Rusty Pelican had been cranked open but the seats beneath were mostly vacant. The aroma of grilled onions and burgers overpowered the odor of motor oil.

Duane Bobcock rode his bicycle along the pier. He stopped to stare up at the large orange ball and to have a conversation with himself before pushing off and heading in the direction of town.

Vince recalled a different time when Duane used to crack jokes and ride a bad-ass motorcycle instead of a Schwinn. His long hair had been a statement against the establishment rather than unconscious neglect.

A deep-seated sense of injustice filled Vince. He had been raised with the church's belief that things happened for a reason. But it made no sense for Duane to be out of touch with reality. There were evil minds out there that should have been taken instead.

The Bayliner turned over its loud engine.

Vince's gaze fell on the cell phone. He'd had to call Mel to check in and that had been his only intent. Now he had to deliver on his promise to have an outline to his editor, Gail Castellano, within a week.

It was a promise he shouldn't have made.

Because crime cases were so horrendous, an author had to find some good in them to make them work. He had to pick an identifying person who could play the role of the hero, the rooting interest for the reader. Sometimes it was a cop. Sometimes a family member. And sometimes it was an assistant district attorney as in the Diane Downs case.

Lentz thought of himself as the hero.

There was a single absolute clarity for Vince and it had been there since day one. The heroes in his book were the victims' families. They would be the story's voice. The world would know that their daughters would not be forgotten. There would be redeeming value in this project.

But if Vince went ahead with it, he would be publicizing murders that had been executed for the sake of fame. He'd be fulfilling Lentz's plans for infamy—and that was something Vince wasn't sure he could do.

Vince went into the cabin, ducking his head as he stepped down. From a narrow cupboard in the galley, he removed several tapes. He stuck one into his player and pressed Play. The filtering of audiotape through a speaker overtook the small space, and Vince's voice came forth as he said the date, time and place.

Then Samuel Lentz began to talk.

Motionless, Vince listened.

The McDermott residence was being flooded with calls from perverts.

The phone had been ringing all morning. Jillene couldn't figure out what was going on. She was getting calls at Java for the help-wanted ad, but why were they also coming into the house? Hannah wasn't sending them here. Somebody had messed something up. These men weren't applying for the barista position. They wanted a position with *her*. It didn't make sense.

Switching her attention away from the prank calls, Jillene crammed a wrench around the drain pipe beneath the bathroom sink. She hoped she'd fixed the drip.

The cordless phone rang, making her jump. Her grip on the tool slipped and she jammed her finger.

"Dammit!"

Angrily, she snagged the phone. "Who is this?" she screamed into the receiver.

"It's your mother."

She breathed a sigh of relief. "Mom." Laying on the cool floor with her shoulders against the cabinet, she bent her knees. Thankful she didn't have to go another round with a guy who wanted to talk about his feet, she relaxed.

"Who did you want me to be?" her mom asked. "Were you expecting a man? Are you seeing anyone? Who is he? What does he look like?"

Jillene closed her eyes and rested her hand on her forehead.

Jodi-Lynn Burch had never been conservative. She rarely acted her age, which at present she admitted to being fifty-six—only a year off from her real birth date.

While growing up, most of the time Jillene thought it was great to have such a nontraditional mother. Other girls came home after school and found their moms wearing white ruffled aprons, the cookbook open and a pot roast in the oven. Oftentimes, Jodi-Lynn was found in a painter's smock painting clouds and stars on the bedroom ceiling, rearranging the living room furniture or digging up a bush in the yard to put it elsewhere. Ultimately, her unconventional ways had been too much for Jillene's dad.

A trip to the Oregon Coast was supposed to bring them together to talk things out, but they came home not speaking. The next day, her father moved out. Jillene was sixteen.

"There's nobody, Mom."

"Are you sure you aren't seeing someone?"

Unbidden, Vince Tremonti's face popped into her head. "Yes."

"Jillie, you can tell me."

"There's nothing to tell." She propped her sneaker-clad foot onto the edge of the claw-foot tub. "So, how are you?"

"Good. Did you get those fuzzy white mule slippers I sent you?"

"Uh-huh." They had come a few days ago and the girls had been wearing them in the kitchen to listen to the heels clatter over the floor.

"They were too darling to pass up," Jodi-Lynn said, "and I know that's not something you'd buy for yourself."

That was true enough, and Jillene did think they were rather a decadent treat. "They're fun to wear, Mom. It was sweet of you."

"So, how are my little girls? Are they excited to come see Grandma? Refresh me on when they get out of school."

"June twenty-second."

"I'll start checking out the price of airline tickets. My treat, sweetie."

Jillene would have argued if she'd had the leverage. She was grateful for the offer, more than her mom would ever know. Claire and Faye were going to spend several weeks during the month of July in California with Jodi-Lynn. They'd gone on the trip last year as well. It was her mom's way of making the summer special for them because they didn't have a dad to take them camping at the lake anymore. Jodi-Lynn took the girls to Disneyland and Universal Studios, to Malibu Beach, and to Mann's Chinese where the girls had snapped nearly a whole roll of film on Marilyn Monroe and Jane Russell's cement handprints.

"Thanks, Mom." Jillene looked at the ceiling where this winter's leak had made a water spot. It looked like the plaster was ready to fall down. If it did, she would suddenly find herself with a natural skylight because there was no money to patch the hole.

She debated confiding in her mom about her financial

situation. But it was too painful to admit that David had gotten them into trouble. Her mom had adored him and thought he could do no wrong. After her own failed marriage, Jodi-Lynn had always been so happy that Jillene had gotten things right with the perfect man.

Her mom lowered her voice and said, "Guess where I went yesterday?"

"Hmm?"

"Flo and I went to the Party Store in Burbank."

Jillene adjusted her grip on the cordless, remembering the big warehouse of discount party goods with its marginally racy adult section.

"We bought some naughty things. Flo got some sparkle pasties for Ralph—not for him to wear, but for her. And I got one of those floaty pens where the stripper's pants slide down his legs and he stands there naked."

"That sounds useful."

"It will be for our Scrabble tournament. My flasher pen is going to distract the other players. They won't be able to come up with anything worth a damn in points."

"You're a wicked woman."

"That's what your father—"

"Never mind." Jillene didn't want to listen to any hard feelings against her dad. That habit was too easy for her mom to slip into. "Is that your cookie timer going off?"

"I don't bake cookies. Don't be so square, Jillie."

The dated sixties expression caused Jillene to roll her eyes. She'd never considered herself "square."

For the next hour, they settled into a comfortable talk. Her mom really was great. She had a wonderful sense of humor and a generous heart. Jillene forgot about the bad calls and enjoyed the conversation. But as soon as she hung up, the phone rang again.

This time, she didn't bother to answer.

* * *

I Need Some Fun!

Jillene found the ad in the newspaper and read it. Each line brought a deeper furrow to her brow.

Seeking a boyfriend...Loves dogs...Cute figure...Shopping at Nordstrom...Good personality...Ask for Jillene...Big feet.

Well, wasn't that nice—not.

Jillene phoned the *Seattle Times* classified line to see what was going on, and to chew them out but good. They informed her that they had not mixed up her ad for a barista with that of her seeking a man with big feet. To her surprise, she was informed she had a personal ad running.

Jillene was mad, and when she found out who did this, they were going to be sorry.

The girls came into the house, dropping backpacks and heading straight for the refrigerator to get after-school snacks. Faye handed Jillene a colored picture. Jillene had learned long ago not to guess what the drawing was in case she was wrong.

"This is really nice."

"Do you like my picture of the Statue of Liberty, Mom?" she asked as she pulled apart a Ziploc bag of peanut butter cookies.

"I love it." She thought the black silhouette was a saguaro cactus. Using a magnet from the fridge, she stuck the picture on the door.

"Today," Claire said, pouring a glass of orange juice, "this boy in my P.E. class yelled 'Ow, my nuts!' every time he had to do the splits for gymnastics."

"There's this boy in my school," Faye giggled, "and—"

The phone rang.

Faye went to answer it, but Jillene stopped her. "I'll get that."

She moved past her daughter to the cordless and pressed the talk button. Rock and roll music played in the background. "Hello?"

"I'm looking for Jillene."

"She's not at this number."

"You sound like you could be a Jillene. A real sweet thang. I'm Moe."

"I don't care who you are."

"But I love dogs." Moe's voice was deep and strong. "I have three Rotties who guard my shop."

She didn't want to know what kind of shop. These calls were freaking her out. Moe's burly tone raised the fine hairs at the nape of her neck. Could he somehow track her down? She couldn't let him know she lived alone.

Cupping her hand over the receiver, she urgently whispered, "Sugar!" From her snooze spot on the sofa, the dog lifted her head. "Squirrel!"

Sugar bounded off the couch and charged to the back door barking up a storm and wanting to be let out.

"This isn't Jillene," she shouted. "*Dobie!* Dobie, you don't bite my big mean boyfriend who rides that Harley and wears black leather." She stood directly over Sugar in the line of bark-fire, letting the deep barks fill the mouthpiece. On that, she pressed the disconnect button.

She thrust her shoulders back displaying a strength that was dissolving fast. For the first time since the calls had begun, she felt like crying. If David had been here, he would have handled everything. She'd be able to go to bed tonight and not be worried about Moe. Instead, she knew she was going to lay awake and be frightened by every little noise.

Vince Tremonti's cautionary words filled her mind. *Keep your car doors locked.* She rarely did. Not on the island, where everyone knew everyone. But she didn't know a Moe and hoped he lived across the water over in Seattle.

While Sugar offered protection, it wasn't the same as listening to the comforting tick of David's wristwatch on the nightstand. Or having the smell of musky soap linger in the bathroom just before lights-out.

At this moment, she missed having a man in the house to take charge. If she had somebody to lean on—

But she didn't.

Sugar was still barking. Jillene went to the door and opened it. The dog had just about burned up the lawn on the false squirrel alarm.

She turned to the girls. They knew there had been unusual calls coming in. She might as well tell them what was going on and give them strict orders not to answer the phone.

"I don't know how it happened, but there's an ad in the newspaper. About me. It lists our phone number, and men think that I want to go out with them. It's very upsetting to me."

Claire and Faye traded glances, their cheeks growing red.

"I pulled the ad and it shouldn't be in tomorrow's paper." Jillene ran warm water in the sink and used a dishcloth to wipe away the purple Kool-Aid ring on the countertop. "Until I'm sure it's not running anymore, I don't want you to answer the phone. In fact, we'll screen all our calls and let the machine pick them up." She should have been doing that anyway, since the only people to call these days were perverts and bill collectors.

The girls whispered to one another. Faye shoved Claire. Claire shoved her back.

Jillene tossed the dishrag in the sink and put her hands on her hips. "What's going on?"

"Mom..." Claire nervously pulled on a broken fingernail. "We did it."

Faye sorrowfully added, "We didn't mean to make you upset."

Jillene bluntly asked, "What did you break?"

"Nothing. We're the ones who called the newspaper." Faye quickly added, "It was Claire's idea!"

"You wanted to do it, too!"

Jillene's mouth dropped open. "You guys ran the personal ad for me?"

Claire came forward, put her arms around Jillene and gave her a hug. "We're sorry, Mom. We know you're sad. If you went out on dates you could be happy."

Faye snuggled in and leaned her cheek against Jillene's arm. "We loved our dad. We'll always love him. But it's okay if you find us a new one."

Claire explained, "We thought you could find one in the newspaper."

Alternating between the desire to hug them to death for their misguided caring and to swat their little fannies for their recklessness, Jillene stood still. "I can't believe you did such a thing. I don't know what to say."

"Say you're not mad at us."

"But I am mad."

"Sorry," Faye mumbled.

Jillene sighed. "Thank you for wanting to help, but I don't need to find a date. It's not for me. Not now. I'm all right with just the three of us. So promise me you'll never do anything like this again."

"We promise," they said together.

"All right, then. Good."

They broke apart—Jillene relieved to have everything out in the open.

Claire looked over her limited snack selection in the pantry. "I sure loved Taco Juan's that night."

"Me, too," Faye said. "I wish we could have it tonight but I know we can't—and I'm not begging, Mom. I'm just saying that I wish we could."

"I know." Jillene tidied the kitchen.

Claire put away the orange juice carton. "Uncle Al's son is nice."

"Yeah, he tells funny stories." Faye took a bite of cookie. "He blew up Hot Wheels cars when he was in junior high. Did our dad ever do that?"

"No." She was quite certain David McDermott had never dabbled in small explosives.

"Do you think Vince is nice?" Claire asked.

Jillene found herself unable to repress the truth. "Yes, I think so."

The girls kicked off their shoes, plopped on the sofa and aimed the remote at the television. The tube warmed to a picture and what used to be the Disney Channel came in as snow.

"Aww, man. Cable's broken," Faye muttered.

Jillene shook her head. "No. I canceled it."

"What?"

"Why?"

"Because we can't afford it," she said.

Claire frowned. "We can't afford anything."

"I'm sorry, girls. We have to be on a budget."

"I don't like budgets." Faye clicked the changer and went through all six stations in less than six seconds.

"Me, either," Jillene agreed. "But let's just be thankful

that the previous owners left a television antenna on the roof, or we wouldn't be picking up anything at all.''

Jillene went down the hallway with a dull throbbing in her head. While she'd miss watching some of her favorite programs, too, the cable seemed the least of her concerns. She'd received a letter from their medical insurance company stating her policy was going to be canceled on the eighteenth because she hadn't kept up with the payments. As soon as she got back on her feet, she was going to renew it. She had to with the girls. But to get the policy reinstated was going to cost a small fortune. She couldn't think about that right now.

As she opened the bathroom medicine cabinet to get a bottle of aspirin, Jillene had the sinking feeling that everything around her was being inked with one big Cancel stamp—and she couldn't retaliate fast enough.

Thirteen

The First Bank of Blue Heron was the first and only bank on the island. Its decor dated back to the release of Barry Manilow's "Mandy," when there was a walk-up window instead of an ATM at the front of the building. Black-and silver-speckled linoleum tiles sparkled over the floor and a sand canister ashtray was situated by the entrance doors. There were three teller stations but only one teller working.

The new engine for the *Gracie* had come in yesterday, and Vince wanted to pay for it since he was staying on the boat. Pop had turned down his offer, so Vince was going to make a deposit into his dad's account. By the time Pop got his next bank statement and figured out the mysterious deposit, he wouldn't be able to do anything about it.

Velma Hicks waited in line ahead of Vince. Since he'd last seen her, she'd shrunk below five feet. The eighty-something geriatric wore knee-high hose and a daisy wig with white flower petals and yellow centers. He hadn't seen anything like it since St. Mary's youth group graduation pool party and the girls had worn those skintight rubber bathing caps.

After Velma finished her transaction, she looped the straps of her purse through her arm and gave Vince a curious stare. Recognition soon dawned on her face.

"You're Al's son. You write about rapists." Pink rouge dotted her wrinkled cheeks. "I never see you and your wife in town, Vincenzo. Only your father."

"That's because I don't have a wife. And I live in Los Angeles now, not Blue Heron."

"Los Angeles?" The lines around her mouth became more distinct. "California has all those vaginatarian women. No wonder you don't have a wife."

The door to the bank opened and Connie Duluth walked in carrying a briefcase. She went toward the notary's desk. The chair was vacant. Irritation slowed her stride. But the instant she saw Vince, her lush red lips curved into a stunning smile.

"Ohmygawd." Her designer heels echoed across the floor. The tailored lines of her suit accentuated her breasts. She flaunted that fact when she came toward him, jiggling everything she had. "Vince, I'm glad I ran into you."

He'd met her for drinks at the Oyster Shell Lounge on Wednesday evening. It had been a casual get-together to talk about old times, although they didn't really have a history aside from a one-night stand—which he now regretted.

She'd chased him throughout high school, slipping notes into his locker and calling to ask him if he liked her. During their senior year she'd bring beer to Friday night football games and invite him beneath the bleachers during halftime. The night their team played East Pine, they'd ended up sleeping together.

According to Pop, Connie was on her third divorce. She'd probably switch back to her maiden name soon. She liked having the last name Ronco. People asked her if she was related to Ron Popeil, the infomercial millionaire. She claimed he was her uncle, which was bullshit.

Velma's nostrils flared as she sniffed perfume in the

air. "Mrs. Duluth, a *splash* of Jean Naté would have been enough."

"Miss Ronco," Connie corrected. "When I get my new business cards in, that'll be the name on them."

The daisies on Velma's wig perked up. "Oh? My Veg-o-matic is broken. Can your uncle take a look at it?"

"I'll ask him."

Velma left and Vince moved toward the teller, but Connie began talking about her day. He was listening but not really hard. Connie's ego was huge and most everything she said was blown out of proportion.

Then Jillene McDermott entered the bank, and it was impossible for Vince's gaze not to stray to her. She wore black slacks, a blouse and a clean khaki apron. He recalled how attractive her legs had been in that sundress at Taco Juan's. The way the scooped neck had exposed the hollow of her throat.

That night with her and her daughters had come to mind when he was supposed to be pulling together the Lentz outline. Maybe it was because he couldn't concentrate. He would try to focus, but inevitably Jillene always came into his thoughts. Once, he caught himself writing her name on his notepad. He couldn't remember a time that that had ever happened to him.

Jillene held a merchant's depository bag. Seeing him and Connie she hesitated, then came forward.

"Are you in line?" she asked, giving Connie a cursory glance.

He sensed Connie rubbed Jillene the wrong way and that casual run-ins were probably something she liked to avoid.

Connie cheerfully informed her, "I'm waiting for the notary. I just sold a six-hundred-thousand-dollar property."

If he was reading her right, Jillene seemed to be exhausted, physically and emotionally. Her hair was pulled back in a clip with wispy strands tucked behind her ears.

"Go ahead." Vince stepped aside. He would have liked to ask her how she was doing, but as soon as Jillene stood in front of them Connie cozied up to Vince.

"I had a lot of fun the other night, Vince. We have to do it again. Only this time, you don't have to get me drunk." She laughed with a seductive sound.

He didn't remember her being plastered.

It was unlikely Jillene could have missed the remark, but her attention remained on the teller's rapid computer key input of her account number.

"When you're done here, I want you to come with me." Connie tossed her hair with a slight shake of her head. "I have a listing I want to show you. You'll love it."

The teller deposited a series of checks as Jillene toyed with the bank's pen that was secured by a metal chain.

"I've got a house in L.A.," he replied, as Jillene smoothed her hair from her face. Despite Connie's Fendi perfume, he could smell the subtle aroma of rich coffee that drifted from Jillene.

"But this one has mature trees with lots of privacy. And it's vacant, so we can take our time looking."

Sunlight pouring into the windows touched Jillene's shoulder where her blouse collar met her neck. He wasn't sure why, but it surprised him that she wore delicate pearl-drop earrings. The feminine jewelry was a contrast to the kid's Trix the Rabbit tattoo she had on her ankle.

"Come on, Vince. It'll be fun." Connie laid her hand on his arm, the gold bracelets on her wrist ringing together. "Like under the bleachers."

"That was a long time ago."

"But I still remember. *Everything.*"

Distracted, Vince watched as the teller finished Jillene's transaction by sliding a receipt to her. She was looking hard at the balance. As she turned away, dejection was set on her profile. He caught himself wanting to know why.

Jillene dragged in a dispirited sigh. When she looked at him, he couldn't read her thoughts.

"Thanks for letting me go ahead." she said.

"Sure." He wished she wasn't leaving. But with Connie here, there was nothing he could think to say to make her stay and talk.

Jillene was going for the door when Connie called after her, "I like your Mocha Madness idea, Jillene. I might even deviate from my raspberry latte to try one. It reminds me of when I had an open house at the Mariner's Tide subdivision and gave away free tennis lessons with every sale—Pay and Play."

"I'm sure tennis lessons came in real handy for all those first-time homebuyers on tight budgets," Jillene commented. She gave Vince a parting glance that was devoid of the tentative teasing that had characterized their dinner. "I need to get back to Java. Thanks again."

Vince put the money in his dad's account and left moments after Jillene. Whether it was the fire of sarcasm she'd shot at Connie or the barely disguised vulnerability that had come over her face when she'd checked her bank balance, he wanted to know her better.

He passed on Connie's insistence he see the house. She tried her high school pouting and persuasion, but he didn't change his mind. He had to return to the boat and get to work.

Long into the afternoon, he had barely added another handwritten page to the two he'd torn from his yellow legal pad. Material and notes were laid out in front of him on the deck like a layer of bilgewater.

He'd had his secretary overnight him the folders he had at home. She had access to his house and was keeping an eye on things for him while he was gone. Since his residence phone was his main contact, she'd said his message machine was filled to capacity. Only a trusted few people had his cell phone number, and his address was unlisted in the phone book. When she'd played him the messages, he had written down the names of the people he would call back. The others would have to wait.

He was tempted to call the pool service back and discuss the chlorine levels in his hot tub. A waste of time on something completely trivial. But Vince was looking for an excuse because sitting with a pencil in his hand was the worst form of torture.

He repeatedly tapped the dull point against the pad. He stared beyond his surroundings to the tree-covered hill above the marina. The rooftops of several homes poked through the canopy of pines. One of those homes belonged to Jillene.

He tried to focus on the book. He had four days left to complete the outline. That thought paralyzed him given how little he had done already. Coming up with *profound* and *gripping* was nearly impossible right now.

Vince, it starts tonight with number one. We'll go to twelve and get it done.

The outline that Vince had promised was nothing but doodles on the edges of the pages—a man's face without clear form and a series of squiggles.

Vince rubbed his eyes. They were dry and tired. He stood and stretched the stiffness from his muscles. His legs had gone to sleep; tingles speared down his thighs to his kneecaps.

He had to get off the boat and find something to look at instead of the tapes and papers and files and garbage he was writing. He put it all away.

His gaze rose to the hillside that jutted into a steep swell of land and greenery. Leaving the boat, he took the artificial turf ramp and crossed the parking lot.

He hiked up the foot-worn trail that wound through evergreens and native blackberry brambles. The prickly stems were beginning to form buds where the sun sliced through the foliage to hit them. Tree boughs whispered overhead—the sound of nature. He'd almost forgotten what that was like.

The musty scent of the woods and the warm earth filled his lungs. A woodpecker thumped in the distance. A bee flew past his ear on the breeze. He'd come here often when he was a little boy. He and Jerry had built a tree house with scrap lumber and carpet remnants. He wondered if the planks and boards were still standing.

Deciding to check it out, Vince walked higher to the residential side of the hill. Through the tree branches, he could see weathered plywood stuck in the lower limbs of a sturdy oak. A rope and tire swing were anchored to the right of a newly built ladder. Voices of children drifted to him. Girls. They were giggling.

Framed behind the bushes, Claire and Faye McDermott had spread out a bunch of doll stuff. Claire held on to a camcorder. She filmed as Faye restyled—with scissors— the hair on a Barbie doll until it was nearly bald in places with spiky pieces sticking out. A dog nosed around the long hair that had come off the doll's head, then playfully stole some and ran off. The girls were laughing so hard that Claire couldn't keep the camera straight.

"Sugar! Drop it!"

The dog darted around the girls' blanket.

"Let's start over with the camera," Claire said, the crests of her cheeks red.

As if she were doing a commercial, Faye exclaimed, "Are you tired of the same old hairstyle? Do you need a makeover? On today's show—"

Sugar ran across the blanket, the synthetic hair in her mouth sticking out as if she had a black mustache drooping on either side of her muzzle.

Faye and Claire burst into infectious laughter again. Claire dropped the camcorder and fell over sideways.

Vince didn't want to intrude on the girls' fun so he took a shortcut across the path to the edge of the woods. The fact that the old tree house was still there didn't surprise him. What did, however, was the fact that Jillene let her daughters play down here without supervision.

Even though her house was about a hundred feet away, this part of the hillside was obscure. The area could be reached without her knowledge.

Vince climbed the rail-tie steps to the back of Jillene's yard.

The last time he'd seen the house, the colors had been sand and white. Now it was painted blue. The wraparound porch was still a nice feature. He'd never been inside, but Pop had known the people who'd owned it before the McDermotts.

An explosion of colorful flowers grew up close to the windows and, in some cases, covered the glass. While they looked nice, he couldn't help thinking like an ex-cop. She was at risk. Prowlers could hide in the bushes and bust into the house through the concealed windows.

A hummingbird feeder and wind chimes hung from the back porch, where a screened door was in place but the inside door was open. Anyone could walk in.

Vince went through the backyard.

Music came from inside the house, drifting through the open windows and the back door. Patsy Cline twanged, "I Fall To Pieces" with a steady beat, and Jillene sang along. She had a nice voice, punctuating the words in a drawl.

Taking the steps, he rapped his knuckles on the screen door frame.

Jillene instantly stopped singing.

She approached the door with wary steps, a cloth in one hand and a can of Pledge in the other. Through the screen mesh, he could see the frantic beat of the pulse at her throat.

He'd frightened her.

Good.

"Vince…hello."

"I didn't mean to just drop by. I was walking and I saw your girls by the tree house." He knew his greeting contained a strong suggestion of reproach, but he went on anyway. "It's not a good idea to let them play down there when you're in the house with your music cranked up. Anybody could come along and do something to them."

Dumbfounded, she gazed at him. "My music isn't that loud and my girls are fine. I can see them from here." She looked beyond him to the woods where Faye chased Claire up the tree house ladder. "Why are you trying to scare me?"

"I'm just making you aware."

"I'm always aware."

Jillene's cheeks went pale. He'd rattled her and he was sorry. But he wasn't sorry for pointing out the truth. Society was full of sociopaths waiting for opportunities. While the chances were remote, they were there. He hated to remind her the world could be ugly, but she had to be careful.

She stood back, the screen between them a soft filter of gray. Her hair was pinned in a messy twist with pieces falling at her ears. She still wore the pearl earrings but had changed her Java uniform to jeans shorts and a slim white T-shirt with Felix the Cat across the front.

"Look—I'm sorry. I realize now that you can see and hear them. I just know what can happen."

"So do I. That's why I always check on them."

"Good." He nodded. "That's good."

Notes faded and Patsy moved on to "Walking in Midnight." The music filled the silence that fell over them. He was angry with himself for rocking Jillene's contentment with his cynicism and distrust. The cop in him was still there. He didn't look at things the same way he used to. Between police work and writing about true crime he'd become pretty hard-boiled.

His gaze went to the dusting polish in her hand. "I'll let you get back to your cleaning." But he made no immediate move to leave. Her picture-perfect house seemed so removed from the images waiting for him on the boat, he felt absolved from obligations.

Hesitation marked her brows and filled her eyes. She gave him an exaggerated smile. "Just what I'm anxious to do. The bathrooms are next."

He smiled in return, the sun warming his back.

The girls giggled and Sugar barked, as a rope swing flew in the air and a Barbie doll went sailing from the tire seat.

He'd yet to step one foot off her porch, and she moved closer to the screen.

"Um, would you like to come in? I don't have any beer, but I could offer you a glass of Kool-Aid."

He leaned against the sturdy porch post and folded his

arms across his chest, feeling an unusual flood of innocent pleasure. "What flavor?"

"Grape."

"I'm partial to grape."

She reached out and pushed the screen open for him.

The kitchen was large and bright with yellow walls. The room smelled like pine cleaner and Windex. Cleaning products cluttered the counter along with a pair of rubber gloves. The eating area opened into a small, but neat and tidy living room. A print sofa and two wing chairs were arranged in an area where a rug must once have been. He could see the faded imprint of a large rectangular shape on the white pine floorboards. The fireplace had recently been swept. A vase of daffodils had been put on the mantel beside framed family photographs. From the stereo speakers in the corner, Patsy was still walking for miles along the highway.

Jillene poured purple drink into a tall glass. "Do you like ice?"

"I'm good without it." He took the cup.

She returned to the refrigerator decorated with drawings, a school lunch menu and photographs of the family dog. He could see her tattoo because she wore scuffed sneakers with no socks. She had a tiny bruise on her shin. She stood back and tucked her hands halfway into her pockets. If she felt uncomfortable with him standing in her kitchen, she didn't show it. He was the one who looked out of place among the soft wall colors and kids drawings.

"You're missing an ear," he observed, his gaze dropping to her ankle.

"I'm what?"

"Your rabbit tattoo is missing an ear."

"It's a rub-on. I'm surprised it's lasted this long."

"Here I thought you were into body art expression."

"Hardly." Then to his amazement, she said in a tone that hinted at a bit of mischief, "I should call the cops on you."

"Why is that?"

"You were sneaking around on my property."

"I wasn't sneaking. I came to the back door," he responded, spotting his book at the kitchen table with over-ripe bananas on top of it.

"The bananas are only there temporarily," she swiftly offered, noticing where his attention had fallen. "I'm still reading."

"You shouldn't if you don't like it."

"But I'm partial to the detectives investigating the case. I like the West Valley one in particular."

"He's a good guy."

"Yes. I can see that. I suppose that's how you make it work. You take a likable character and put him in the middle of the bad stuff."

That she'd understood he had to put heroes in his books was amazing—most readers didn't figure that out. And she didn't care for his genre.

"You describe some horrible things that happen," she said. "How do you do it?"

"I have to be careful about the stories I choose. Some cases are just too hard to live with, so I don't write them." Lentz seized his mind and Vince shoved him aside to the dark abyss of yet-to-be-complete pages. "If you study the Ramirez book, I don't actually describe his murders in detail—that's not what it's about. It's the psychological part of the crime, not the physical."

Jillene sighed heavily. "I've never looked at things like you do."

"Not many people do."

She swiped the black bananas off the book and plunged them into the trash can beneath the sink. Facing him, she returned her hands to her pockets. "What made you decide to investigate my woods?"

"I needed a change in scenery."

"So you walked over here from Al's?"

"Actually, I walked up from the marina. I'm staying on my dad's boat."

"You are? I assumed you were staying with Al."

"Normally I would. Not this time. I felt like being on the water. It's the place where I need to be right now."

Her brown eyes drew distant as if she were suddenly reliving memories. "I love the ocean. Sometimes I'll stand on the porch and watch it for hours and wish—" She looked down, then at him. "I think about a lot of things."

Quietly, he asked, "Did your husband live here with you?"

"Yes, he did."

Her gaze lowered. "Cerebral aneurysm. He was thirty-six. You don't think something like that could happen at that age. But it does. It did."

"Tell me." For reasons he didn't understand, it was important for him to know.

She turned away, rinsed a sponge and began to scrub the faucet handle with nothing but water. After a moment, she stopped to stare out the window above the sink. "We ate out that night. Chinese food. It was David's favorite. I went to bed early while he stayed up to watch the end of the Mariners game. I fell asleep and woke to find him thrashing in the bed. I thought he was having a nightmare. I tried to wake him up but I couldn't. The next thing I knew, he was on the floor.

"I started to panic and kept screaming his name. He

finally responded and asked me what was happening to him. He told me his head hurt. That it felt like liquid fire was burning holes into his brain. Then he began to vomit. I called 911.''

She slowly brought a hand to her cheek. The fourth finger was without a wedding band—something that had been there long enough that the circlet still made just the vaguest impression on her skin.

''It seemed like it took forever for the paramedics to get here. They took him by Airlift to Harborview. The neurologist told me he had an aneurysm. I didn't even know what that meant. He explained a blood vessel had burst inside his brain. He couldn't move his left arm. I remember all the tests. The CAT scan and the spinal tap. I kept thinking about Linda Blair—you know, in *The Exorcist*—how she had a spinal tap and it was horrible.

''The doctors had to operate. They explained the risks. No guarantees. They rated his chances at fifty percent. I gave my consent. Four hours later, I knew. I could feel it in my heart. Then I saw it in the looks on their faces. David had died.'' Her voice lowered to a nearly inaudible tone. ''And I gave my consent.''

As a detective, Vince had witnessed many painful scenes and had felt the acute anguish of strangers dealing with their grief. He'd connected with people who had counted on him for help. People who'd given him all of their assistance, hoping he could fix things. He'd had to be the bearer of bad news, offer his support during moments that families would never forget. The darkest hours. It had never gotten easy. He hadn't become immune to the devastation.

Listening to Jillene was no different. Her bereavement touched him beyond measure and he did what he always did as a comforter. He remained sympathetic in silence, giving Jillene his presence.

"God…I never talk about it." She faced him, her eyes shining. Combating her emotions, she forced herself to remain calm. "Maybe it's because you used to be a police officer. When it happened, I had to tell Sergeant Peck. He was one of the first people here to help me that night and he was incredibly wonderful. He drops by every so often to check on us and see if we need anything."

Vince's mind had trouble registering his boyhood friend's goodwill gesture. "Jerry does that?"

"He gave each girl a stuffed animal from the trunk of his police cruiser. He keeps them for traffic accidents if a child is involved. He brought the girls downstairs while the paramedics were with David. Jerry talked with the girls, coaxing them to give names to the animals so they wouldn't rush back upstairs."

Patsy Cline's song ended and the rotational click of a multidisk player moved to a different CD. Steady applause from a live concert sounded, then an announcer's voice introduced Mr. Peter Frampton whose guitar playing rose in decibels compared to Patsy's soft twang.

Jillene went to the player and turned down the volume.

Vince came to a realization. Her sharing the story about her husband's death had created an invisible but tangible connection between them that was something more than just sexual awareness. She'd let him see her emotional wounds. Her grief. And had made no attempt to hide the joy she'd lost.

"'Frampton Comes Alive'—double vinyl album," Vince said, turning the mood into one of youthful reflection. "I saw his concert at the Kingdome."

"June 27, 1977," Jillene supplied fondly, and the conversation went from bittersweet to fun reminiscences. "I remember the date because I got royally grounded for going. The acoustics were awful, but he was great.'' The worn thin cotton of her shirt was nearly transparent. The outline of her bra was visible where it cupped her full breasts. She put a hand on her hip. ''Wow. You were there, too?''

''Almost in the front row. And you're right about the acoustics being awful in the Kingdome. I hate to say this, but I wasn't all that sad to see it imploded. The Dome killed Zeppelin's concerts. I don't know how their sound crew dealt with the mixing boards.''

''Zeppelin rocked at the Seattle Center. I still have every vinyl they ever cut.''

''Me, too.''

''I wish I had a turntable that worked. When the girls were little, they broke the needles and I replaced too many to count. I think it was the rubber band around the penny that intrigued them.''

''I can't believe you put a penny on the needle arm. You might as well throw out the vinyl if it's scratched that bad.''

''Not if it's my Aerosmith *Rocks* album.''

''So you like Steven Tyler?''

''Mad crush. I slept with his poster over my bed.''

A contented warmth spread through him as he relived good memories from good times. In the late seventies, his only worries had been getting gigs for his garage band, attending college classes and making the payments on his '75 Chevy Camaro. Jillene pulled him to a simpler place. An era of rock and roll, hot guitars and kick-ass lyrics.

Giving her an easy grin, he asked, ''So why did you get grounded?''

She began to smile. ''Because I was fifteen years old and I snuck out with my girlfriend. Her brother drove us to the concert and I didn't come home until the next morning. We stayed after and watched the roadies load the buses. We were hoping we'd get to see Frampton up close."

"Did you?"

Her smile broadened. "I got his autograph on my ticket stub."

"No way."

"Seriously." Excitement caught in her voice, her face radiant. The style of her jeans shorts molded to her fine hips and thighs as she stood so casually. Like a silent invitation. His breath came fast. The blatant urge to hook his fingers in the belt loops and pull her flush against him hit with a hungry force. He shuddered at the charged thought of hotly settling his mouth over hers and kissing her until they were both out of control.

"I don't think my mom would have given me two weeks of hell to pay," she said, "if I'd gone with David. But he hated Frampton."

Fifteen. She'd been fifteen years old and David Mc-Dermott had been her boyfriend. She'd loved the man for a long time.

The back of her shorts lifted a little higher as she bent slightly, rearranging a sofa pillow. Her entire thigh was nearly visible, leading into the shapely swell of her buttocks. His hands wanted to acquaint themselves with her body.

"Did you go with Connie?" she asked.

Connie was the last thing on his mind and he sure didn't want to think about her now. "Why would I have gone with Connie?"

"Because she's very happy to see you again and the way she acts around you screams familiarity." Jillene flinched and her jaw went tight as if she'd said something she hadn't wanted to. Raising on tiptoes, she brushed a cobweb off the wall as if to give herself something to do. Her breasts were seductively accentuated against the thin fabric of that Felix the Cat top. "I mean, I heard the two of you talking over old times at the bank."

"We don't really have any." Vince had a flashing thought about putting his hands on her shoulders and crushing her to him. He nearly forgot what they were talking about. "Blue Heron High wasn't all that big when I graduated."

In an attempt to get his mind off the physical impulses that were blindsiding him, Vince moved to stand in front of the fireplace. His attention fell on a line of pictures. He recognized the girls when they were younger. There was a portrait of them wearing red Christmas dresses in front of a decorated tree. Sugar the dog had her own photo where she was curled up on the bed. And there was one of a couple on a beach. Hand in hand. Smiling at each other as if they'd just shared a special kiss. The man was good-looking with brown hair and strong features. The woman was familiar and yet she wasn't. Her hair was a lot darker than Jillene's, and while she wasn't overweight, she had ample and voluptuous curves that filled her summer dress.

"That's me and David." Jillene came over. "I used to weigh more than I do now."

Taking a longer study of the man in the photo with her, Vince wasn't sure what he was looking for—if anything. Maybe he just wanted to see the type of man Jillene was attracted to.

Damning himself, Vince made a comparison. He was taller than David and he was physically stronger. Her husband had clean-cut Redford-type good looks. Vince was

darker in coloring and too damn intense. If David Mc-
Dermott was what she liked, she would never—

He quit comparing and pulled his attention away.

Jillene's voice lowered to a whisper, losing its light
quality. "After he died, a lot of things changed. It's hard
to adjust, and I still struggle."

Beside him, she seemed delicate yet brave. It was a
natural instinct as a male to want to take care of her. But
from her stance, he sensed she was strong enough on her
own. Even so, an undiminished protectiveness welled to
life inside him when he saw the tears glittering in her
eyes.

He pulled her into his arms with a gentle ease, bringing
her snug against his shoulder. The top of her head slipped
comfortably beneath his chin as he smoothed her hair. He
held her, the wild beat of her heart slamming against his
as the wail of Frampton's electric guitar underscored the
electric chemistry between them.

Her body heat burned through his clothes as if nothing
separated them. He grew instantly hard in response. Holding on to his last shred of reserve, he stroked her cheek.
The soft roundness of her breasts flattened into his chest.
She fanned her hands across his shoulders, fisting the fabric of his shirt. The metal button on her shorts pressed at
the inside of his thighs, an unconscious prodding at his
sex.

Vince struggled with the insane urge to bring her to the
sofa.

The phone rang and Jillene jumped out of his arms.

Vince swore silently.

A second ring sounded but Jillene made no move to
answer it. As she breathed in small pants, her breasts rose
and fell with the effort.

The machine picked up, and Vince was barely able to

listen to her greeting as their eyes met in a burning exchange of arousal. After the beep, a man began to talk with noise in the background.

"Jillene," he enunciated seductively. "Jill-eeeeennne. If you're home, pick up. It's Moe, sweet thang. I know you want to talk to me. Quit playing games. You put the ad in because you wanted to meet me. Pick up."

Jillene's hands trembled.

The caller's connection clicked closed and a dial tone filled the room.

While Vince may not have had the right to ask, he did anyway. "Who was that guy?"

"Nobody. It's not important." She went to the sink and cranked the faucets on to fill the basin with floor cleaner, as if nothing had just happened. But the friction in the room hovered as if it were electrically charged.

"I think it was."

Her shoulders slumped, and he felt her determination faltering. "I can't get rid of him."

The phone rang once more. The machine picked up and the man began talking again.

"Jill-eeeeennne. It's Moe. Answer the phone."

Jillene stood still.

But Vince didn't. He purposefully snagged the cordless and spoke into the receiver. "Hey, buddy. Who's this?"

"*Moe. Who the hell is this?*"

"A guy you don't want to piss off."

"*Where's Jillene?*"

"None of your business."

"*Who's this?*"

Vince tucked the phone beneath his chin as he pushed opened the screen door and stepped outside. "This is her boyfriend."

That was the last Jillene heard. Vince walked into the

backyard. His facial muscles were a taut mask as he spoke into the receiver. Whatever he was saying, he meant it.

She anxiously waited, having the same feelings she had had when she first saw him standing on her porch. A collision of surprise and anticipation.

Slumping against the door frame, she wondered what had compelled her to tell Vince the details of David's death. Perhaps she was afraid to assess why. Just as she had feared he would kiss her, yet had wanted him to.

When he'd enfolded her in his arms, holding her close, all sanity had left her. She'd stopped thinking and had begun reacting, her body coming alive. She'd grown weak. The few dates she'd gone on had ended platonically. The plastic surgeon had tried to kiss her but she'd dodged him as if he'd come at her with a tetanus shot. The men she'd seen socially had left her cold.

Vince had gotten her attention with his intensity and intelligence. His touch and his sheer masculinity. She felt like falling headlong into the heat and letting it ignite. She was tired of making excuses. She needed. She felt. She longed.

She wanted to let go. Have a fling. An affair. Something meaningless and purely sexually driven that would satisfy her as a woman.

But she wouldn't. She was afraid to.

Even knowing she was doing the right thing by staying focused on what was important, she couldn't take her gaze off Vince. His powerful presence in her backyard was unsettling. Sunlight gleamed off his thick black hair, the color of dark-roasted espresso. The breadth of his broad chest was defined in a navy pullover polo shirt.

Vince returned to the house and hung up the phone. His demeanor was completely calm, but his smoky eyes were very direct. He reached for something to write on, coming up with his book opened to the blank front page. "If he calls again, let me know." He wrote down a phone number. "That's my cell. But I think you'll be fine now."

Jillene was comforted by his presence. He'd offered his protection, and the full impact of his gesture left her nearly speechless. "You said you were my boyfriend."

"Right."

"What else did you tell him?"

"Let's just say I made it clear he shouldn't call again. So, how did this guy get your phone number?"

She grimaced and answered faintly. "My daughters put a personal ad in the newspaper for me."

Surprise registered on his face, followed by a penetrating stare as if he were disappointed. "You're looking for a guy in the personals?"

"No," she shot back. "Absolutely not. The girls just thought that I was lonely and wanted to date."

"Why did they think that? You must have hinted."

"I never—that is, I went out a few times. Nothing happened. Jeez, why are we talking about this?"

A lock of hair fell over his forehead, and she wanted so badly to brush it back. He stared into her face, his eyes probing. "Are you lonely, Jillene?"

Lies formed on her lips but none came forward. And as before when she had talked about David, she inexplicably found herself being honest. "Claire and Faye are wonderful kids and I adore them. I honestly do. But I have moments when I desperately want to talk to somebody else and have it count."

"Count, how so?"

"I mean, not talking about the weather with the UPS guy as I'm signing for a package. Real conversation. I can't explain it. I guess I don't even know what I'm trying to say."

His deep voice gentled. "You miss intimate words, Jillene. You miss a man telling you how beautiful you are." The timbre in his tone lowered to a rasp. "How much you make him ache for you. You need to hear words that aren't empty. We all need them every now and then."

She wanted to tell him he was wrong, but he was so right.

A yearning in her heart pulsed to the point of aching. She wasn't sure she could make the needy sensation go away.

Because she was so shaken by his observations, she needed something—anything—to break the spell. "I have to tell you something," she said hoarsely.

"What?"

"You kind of have a Kool-Aid mustache."

As soon as she said the words, she wanted to take them back. But if she hadn't commented on something trivial, she was afraid she'd throw herself at him, cry into his shirt and beg him to make love to her.

His reaction was still and silent, and it lasted several seconds before he burst into a low rumble of laughter. "As long as it's purple and not blue."

"I shouldn't have—"

"I better go."

She'd wanted to apologize, but he was already at the front door and the moment was lost. Her composure was hanging by a thread. "Thanks for taking care of Moe for me."

The blue of his eyes grew dark like the storms of November. "Not a problem."

Fourteen

The St. Mary's Catholic Church white elephant sale took place on the second Saturday in June. Just as the annual event could be counted on for delicious baked goods and unusual household items, so could it be counted on for rain. When Father Pofelski and his parishioners met the night before to set up the tents, the long tables were always arranged beneath a plastic shelter.

On the afternoon of the sale, the weatherman didn't disappoint. Rain slipped from the white canopy and fell into noisy puddles onto the asphalt parking lot.

Al Tremonti wore a brown coat, with a lamb's wool lining to ward off the dampness, as he circled the tables. He'd made the rounds at least a dozen times to do inventory. But there was only one item that interested him.

Ianella Sofrone.

She sat at a table with a spread of delectable offerings in front of her. Coffee cake, cookies, Napoleons and muffins.

As he blended into the crowd and kept his distance, he thought *she* was pretty delectable looking. Her hair rivaled the brilliance of autumn leaves, all afire with shades of red. The arch of her eyebrows and the slant of her eyes were goddesslike. The fullness of her lovely mouth, softly colored with lipstick, vitalized his blood and made him too hot for his coat.

Whenever he saw her, he didn't feel his sixty-plus years. She snatched his breath away. She was the epitome of Woman.

To kiss those lips, to taste the warm skin behind her ear—

"Got your eyes on the pastry, do you, Al?"

Al's blood pressure suddenly strained every vein in his body to the point where he could feel his rapid pulse in the back of his eyes. Father Pofelski had drawn up beside him without his knowing it. The priest's observation threw his mind into guilty turmoil.

He would *never* call Ianella a pastry.

"I'm watching my waistline or I'd be tempted by the brownies," the priest said, patting his stomach where there were no outward signs of flab. The suit coat he wore was austere over a black shirt with a white cleric's collar. "But you're in good shape, Al. Go on. Indulge yourself."

If Father Pofelski had only known his thoughts but a minute ago, he wouldn't be saying that.

"I, ah…no, Father. I already made a contribution." Al had donated his barbering services and the proceeds went to the church.

"And St. Mary's appreciates your generosity. But I think you deserve a little home baking. You probably don't get much of that. Come on."

Unable to argue, Al followed Father Pofelski's lead and went to Ianella's table.

Up close, she was even more beautiful. He could hardly look her in the eyes without feeling his face grow warm. She wore one of those powder-blue Doris Day suits he liked, with braiding around the jacket and a silk bow at the neckline of her blouse.

"I'd like to thank you, Mrs. Sofrone," the Father said earnestly. "The church appreciates the time you spent baking everything. So much so that I'll be coming by your house later to have some of your famous ziti.''

If Al's blood had been hot before, it now hardened into ice.

Ianella needed spiritual guidance, after hours, with the Father at her house? Just the two of them?

Father Pofelski was a lot younger than her, in his early fifties, with a bald spot that wouldn't have been noticeable if he'd been a rabbi. The frames of his glasses were coal black with large rectangular lenses. He didn't possess Cary Grant allure, he was a priest for Holy Sweet Jesus. Fellas who wore the collar were supposed to have control of their urges and not invite themselves over to widows' houses.

Ianella countered frankly. ''I've told you that HBO Father Phil act doesn't go over on me, Father Pofelski. The ladies in the Guild get a kick out of it, but you just aren't the Lothario type.''

''I guess that's why I'm a priest. Aside from the fact that Christ called on me.''

Al had been so rattled about the idea of the Father going to Ianella's for pasta, he'd failed to detect the humor in his tone.

''I'm glad Edie Falco told that mooch off,'' Ianella remarked. ''Father Phil was a disgrace to the priesthood, and shame on you for making fun.'' Ianella gave Father Pofelski a frown, but her brown eyes simmered with amusement. ''Besides, I don't bake ziti anymore. Ever since *The Sopranos,* I got tired of it. It's always 'ziti this' and 'ziti that.' I'd rather eat lobster.'' Her gaze lifted to Al and lingered for a moment.

His tongue instantly felt thick and his throat closed. Remembering himself, he snagged the fedora from his head and held it loosely in both hands. "Hello, Mrs. So-frone."

She smiled at him, and what few cognizant thoughts he had, fled.

"Al here is in need of some sugar," Father Pofelski said.

The double meaning caused Al to blush.

"Perhaps you could offer some assistance, Mrs. So-frone, and pick out a treat for him."

"I'd be happy to, Father," she replied, her voice like an angel's.

"Bless you." Father Pofelski moved on and left Al alone with Ianella.

Self-consciously, Al's gaze roamed over the cookies and pastries that were neatly arranged and covered with plastic wrap. Some had a bow on the top and others had a smiley face drawn in black marker. He could imagine her delicate hand fluidly moving to mark the eyes and the curve of the mouths. The aroma of vanilla and chocolate made the air smell good.

"Are you partial to anything in particular, Al?" Ianella asked with eager expectancy on her face.

I'm partial to you, Ianella. Would you like to have a lobster supper with me?

"Let's see." She thoughtfully pointed to the goodies. "I have brownies and cinnamon coffee cakes here." The skin on top of her hand was as creamy in color as the vanilla filling in the Napoleons. "Oatmeal cookies, blue-berry muffins and butter brickle cookies there." As she rearranged the plates, he could swear the fragrance of her honey-and-almond hand lotion mingled with the smell of cocoa. "The pastries are a dollar apiece or a dozen for ten dollars."

"I'll take two of everything," he blurted.

"Really?"

He reached into his back trouser pocket for his wallet, then willed his hand to be still as he sorted through the bills. "It's for a good cause."

"It certainly is." She began tallying up what he'd purchased and packing it in a bag. "This is an awful lot. You can freeze the cookies and brownies, but I wouldn't try it with the custard pastry."

"My son is visiting. He'll help me eat them."

He paid her and took the bag.

"I saw Vince the other day. He's a good-looking man like his father."

Ianella thought he was good-looking?

Al's heart beat double time.

He couldn't trust himself to reply without babbling, so he nodded, fumbled with his fedora, then mixed back into the crowd. But not three steps away, a grim furrow set into his brow. He realized she could have taken his nod to mean he agreed with her assessment—that he thought he was good-looking, too. He'd meant the nod to be for Vinnie. Christ All Jesus. He'd just come across as being full of himself.

Al spent the rest of the afternoon unnerved.

When the sale was over, he stayed behind to help clean up. To both his dismay and delight, Ianella stayed as well. The Knights of Columbus took down the awning and poles while the Ladies Guild folded the chairs and stored the table linens. It was dark by the time everything was put away.

When the last volunteers closed up the church, they stepped into a deluge. Ianella dashed for her Cutlass and turned over the engine. A whining protest came from underneath the hood. The car wouldn't start. She tried once more and met with the same result.

Ianella Sofrone's battery was dead.

Thanking God for providing opportunities, Al propelled himself into action and rapped on the window, mindless of the rain pelting his shoulders.

Opening the door a crack, Ianella said, "The window won't work."

"You've got a dead battery."

"Oh, damn."

The curse took him by surprise, as had the thought of her watching a cable program as violent as *The Sopranos*. The language on it was pretty harsh. He'd seen every episode and, in fact, thought Father Pofelski's eyeglasses resembled Uncle Junior's. Al wasn't put off that Ianella had uttered a mild swear word, although it did make him wonder if her hair wasn't the only fiery thing about her.

"I'll have to call for a tow." She sighed with exasperation.

Raindrops slid down the smooth front of his coat. "I can do that for you. I'll have the car taken to the auto shop so Rupert can install a new battery first thing Monday morning."

"That would be lovely, Al. Thank you."

"Let me take you home," he said politely, disguising the rush of shallow breaths that assailed him.

She left the Cutlass and he opened the door to his Impala for her. He quickly rounded the front end and positioned himself behind the wheel.

The sweet smell of pastries filled the car's interior. Earlier, he'd set the bag on the back seat. His hands gripped the wheel as he gazed first out the windshield, then at Ianella.

She looked like she belonged in the passenger seat. She kept her knees together and her pocketbook on her lap. Her skirt wasn't too short but it wasn't too long, either.

Her knees were exposed. And those legs! Her high-heeled shoes had a strap at the back of the ankle and the toes were enclosed.

The downpour hammered on the Impala, bouncing off the hood and flooding the blacktop. But Al didn't care. He could have sat in the parking lot with Ianella forever.

Pulling his attention away from her, he started the car.

Regrettably, the drive to Ianella's house was short. He parked next to her curb and felt beneath the seat for his compact umbrella. Helping her out, he shielded her against the rain as they walked to the door side by side.

He would have kept enough distance between them so they wouldn't bump into one another, but he couldn't do that and keep her sheltered, so he moved in closer. His arm touched the side of her breast and he jerked back as if he'd just gotten an electrical jolt. Unbalanced, he almost tripped in a walkway crack.

He hoped he hadn't offended her. A cheap stunt to feel a woman up was something he'd have done when he was in his teens. But he was too far along in life to pull something like that now.

Once on the porch, she opened her purse to find her house keys. "It was nice of you to give me a ride."

He snapped the umbrella closed.

"It was my pleasure," he replied, the beat of his heart deafening in his ears. Al had felt so much enjoyment from having her beside him in his car—thoughts of the drive to her house scampered vaguely around in his head. The red seat upholstery and her shapely nylon-clad legs had looked great together.

Her hand paused. "Oh dear. You know what—I don't have a ride to church for tomorrow. I'll have to call Gladys and see if she can pick me up."

Al wished he could force his nerves to be steady and

offer his assistance, but she quickly rectified the dilemma herself.

Perhaps too quickly.

A look of disappointment passed over her features.

"Yes…I'll call Gladys," she said.

He didn't say anything.

Ianella found her keys, glanced at his car and then at him. She smiled with those scrumptiously full lips of hers. Never had there been a woman more dazzling than Ianella. Grace, God rest her, had been sensible and beautiful, and he'd loved her with everything in his soul.

But Ianella—she was sexy and stunning and feminine. Looking at her made his body burn with desire.

A raindrop glistened on her hair. His finger itched to brush it away. To kiss the place the bead of moisture touched.

"Thanks again for the ride," she murmured into his wayward thoughts. Her cat-shaped eyes were sultry and magnificent, the lids almost half closed as her voice lowered. "I like your car. I've always admired it and wondered what the inside was like."

He'd been so entranced by her, he needed a moment to reorient himself. "You have?"

"Oh, yes. Your car has pizzazz. Leo thought his Cadillac was so keen. I never did like the clunky old thing."

Anxiety gripped Al when she mentioned The Louse. Selfishly, he hoped she didn't harbor feelings for her dead husband. If she were to ask him to forget about his feelings for Grace, he couldn't do it. But the difference was that he and Grace had honored their wedding vows.

Sounding wistful, Ianella commented, "He left the car to *her*. Which is fine with me. Leo and I weren't exactly on speaking terms when I received the telephone call informing me of…well, informing me he was gone."

She smiled with a trace of sadness. Perhaps she was acknowledging that her marriage had not been a fairy tale, and maybe she was still hoping to find a Prince Charming. At least, that's what Al liked to think.

The rain brought out a florist-shop scent from the flowers that covered the overhang. He and Ianella stood in a sanctuary of clematis and roses, with glossy green vines curling down a trellis by her front door. In a mere moment, she would be going inside and he would be left to return home. A place of empty longing.

Each second that ticked by made him less accepting of the niche his life had fallen into. He had struggled for a long time to keep a respectful distance because of her married status. But that was then—when Leo had been alive. This was now. Al had to seize his chance, take the risk of being turned down. Move forward.

"Ianella..." he said, speaking her name aloud for the first time to her, "would you have dinner with me this Friday night?"

His heart thudded against his rib cage.

A corner of her mouth lifted.

He hastened to go on, perspiration dampening his forehead at the snug crown of his fedora. "We could go to the Lobster King. And take a walk out on the pier afterward. Or if you'd rather—"

"I would love to."

He dared to breathe, barely realizing he'd been holding his breath. "You would?"

"Yes, Al."

No words could define his elation. In the midst of romancing her in the flowers to the serenade of cool rain, he uttered the unthinkable admittance. "I can't wait!"

Ianella's laughter was breezy and sweet. "Me, neither.'' She slipped the key into the door. ''I'll look forward to Friday. See you tomorrow at Mass.''

He nodded.

Al walked to the curb, his mind going in a thousand directions.

She'd said yes. *She'd said yes!*

He had to send his best suit to the dry cleaners, shine his shoes, iron his dress shirt, pick out a tie and break out his special aftershave.

Climbing into the car, he realized his trouser legs were spattered with rain and his socks were soaking wet.

He'd forgotten to open his umbrella.

Fifteen

After Sunday Mass, Vince asked his dad to go out for coffee at Java the Hut. In the late morning, the coffee bar was moderately full with customers. Jillene had brought her daughters to work as helpers. The girls appeared to have been assigned jobs as the official greeters. They stood behind the entrance door wearing aprons that were slightly too large for them.

"You guys don't have to wait in line," Faye said, as he and Pop came through the door. "We'll bring you your orders today."

His dad got a kick out of that and headed directly for a table. "Let's see, young lady. I'd like a cup of coffee."

Faye positioned her hands behind her back, showing that she didn't need to write down the order. "Cream and sugar, sir?"

"No, dear. Just black."

Claire asked Vince what he wanted to drink, and he replied with his usual. "Caffe Americano."

"What size? Piccolo, media or grande?"

"Grande."

"The coffees will be coming right up," Faye cheerfully said.

The girls went to the counter and relayed the orders to their mom.

Vince's gaze met Jillene's and she acknowledged him

with a nod of hello. Most of her body was hidden behind the big espresso machine so he couldn't see her very well. But he knew she'd have on her white blouse with its open collar that showed a wedge of bare skin. At the hollow of her throat would be her heart necklace. He didn't think he'd ever seen her without it. Curiosity about who had given it to her crossed his mind.

Pop removed his fedora. The sleek glossiness of his neatly combed black hair was accented by silver threads at his temples. His smile was white and his brows had no hint of gray. He didn't have many wrinkles, just character lines that gave him a facial personality that was pleasing. He looked good for a guy his age. Not that he was over the hill. But something about him today was different—different from the day when Vince had come home. And for that matter, different even from when they'd been on the boat together a week ago—which had been a difficult time.

The expression in his dad's eyes was livelier, and he'd walked out of the church with a lighter step. Vince didn't think the lift in his spirits was due to Father Pofelski's sermon. No disrespect to the Father.

"What's going on, Pop?"

His dad innocently shrugged. "I'm having some coffee with my son."

Vince had seen the way Pop talked with Mrs. Sofrone in the St. Mary's receiving line. Pop had stood next to her, smiling and making sure she wasn't bumped by a group of teenagers who were leaving ahead of them in a rowdy burst of energy.

"Okay." Vince settled into his chair, affectionately staring at Pop.

But the teasing quality between them sobered when his

father then questioned, "How are you doing? With everything."

There was no need to define *everything*. Vince knew exactly what he was talking about. For days Vince had been grappling with the outline and was making little progress. Each sentence and thought was a hard-fought battle, to the point where he just wasn't sure if the words would ever come. "I called my agent and told him this was a difficult case."

"Can I help you out with anything?"

"I'm fine, Pop. Having you to listen was good."

"All right, Vinnie. You know the best way you have to go. But if you need anything—it doesn't matter what it is—you come to me. That's what a pop is for. To sit and talk with his kid."

And Vince appreciated that. Today he was pushing all thought of the outline from his head. He was taking the day off and concentrating on bringing his mind to a place where he could think better.

The girls came back to the table with the order.

"Here you go, sir." Faye was careful not to spill the coffee.

Vince took his from Claire. "Thanks."

"You young ladies are very good servers." Pop reached into his billfold and gave each girl a buck tip.

Their gleeful eyes widened and they shared secret smiles. Maybe they were saving for another Barbie doll whose hair they could cut off. That thought made Vince smile.

"Thanks, Uncle Al," they said in unison.

"You're quite welcome. You girls will have to go and buy some ice cream after you get off work."

"We can't." Claire wore blue eyeshadow and large hoop earrings reminiscent of the seventies. A lot Vince knew about the styles of teenagers. "We're going over to our friend Trudy's house to spend the night."

"So our mom can have the whole night to herself and take a bath without anyone bugging her."

Vince worked to keep from broadening his smile as he glanced over at Jillene. She stepped away from the espresso machine to rinse out the blender in the sink. Her motions were efficient and quick, that beautiful blond hair of hers piled on top of her head with small sexy wisps escaping.

The longer he stared, the more he saw her filling up a bathtub and sinking bare legs and breasts into a mound of scented bubbles.

When she caught him looking at her, she lifted her brows.

"Excuse me," he said to his dad and headed for the counter.

Jillene desperately tried to quell the instant trip in her heart as Vince approached.

He had just looked at her as if he were imagining her naked.

"Hey," he said in greeting. He wore a white shirt, sports coat and a pair of dark slacks, coming across as neither too dressy nor too casual.

"Hello." She stood tall, knowing perfectly well she was fully clothed. His imagination would have to have been pretty vivid for him to conjure up an image that said otherwise.

She had exchanged casual words with Vince in the past few days but that was the extent of things. It was as if that day in her living room had never happened. They hadn't almost kissed. She hadn't wanted to lose herself in his arms. But his face had haunted her just the same. She saw his smile, sensuous and then serious. She couldn't think about what might have been. It was bad enough that she'd been tempted to dial his phone number just to hear his voice.

"Has Moe called you back?" he asked.

Nobody aside from the girls' friends and bill collectors had called the house. "Nope. You got rid of him."

She was no longer being harassed because the personal ad had been removed from the newspaper. Everything was back to normal. But she still wasn't sleeping well.

Whenever she heard Sugar's collar tags jingling in the middle of the night, Jillene bolted awake and listened fearfully for sounds outside. Even though she didn't detect anyone prowling in the yard, she still had a hard time falling back to sleep. She finally dozed off short hours before her alarm went off. When the buzzer sounded in the morning, it took a great effort to drag herself out of bed.

"Good." Vince selected a tin of coffee mints and laid a couple of dollars on the counter.

She rang up his charge and he put the change in the tip box. She wasn't sure why it rattled her when he did that. It never bothered her when other customers gave the baristas a tip.

Jillene placed her hands on the countertop as the brew timer went off behind her. "Can I fix you another coffee?"

"I haven't finished the one you just made." His gaze roamed over her at a leisurely rate.

She felt her cheeks grow as hot as the steam began rising from the large percolator. "Yes...right. Well, mochas are on special. You could try something out of your comfort zone," she suggested, her nerves slightly jerking with foolish wonder. Sometimes when Vince looked at her, she hadn't a clue as to what he was thinking.

"Not today."

Remembering the solid warmth of him as he'd held her in his arms, she repressed a sudden shiver of longing. She had a hard time not staring at the set of his square-cut jaw. The lower half of his face had been precisely shaved; his tanned skin was smooth.

She struggled to tell him something—not wanting to give away the plight of her business, but needing him to know how much he'd helped her.

She spoke carefully. "Vince, I want to thank you for coming in here to order coffee. I know there are other places you could go and I do appreciate your bringing attention to Java. When you're in here, my sales improve because of the extra customers wanting to talk with you."

The understated but rich laughter that rose from his throat made her heart contract. "I don't think you're selling more coffee because of me. I'm just a regular guy who happens to enjoy a good cup of joe."

Vince Tremonti was anything but regular.

Standing well over six feet tall, he towered over most men. His athletic body was perfectly proportioned. The definition of his shoulders was powerful. The way he carried himself had a sexuality that was rugged and explosive. He dressed simply, but with excellent taste. His black hair was smooth and was cut close to his ears. The color of his eyes could appear either blue or gray depending on his thoughts, and the sexy curve of his mouth could weaken even the most hardened woman's defenses.

Dragging herself out of her thoughts, she managed to say, "However you want to look at it. Thanks."

"Sure."

Returning to his chair, he talked with the girls before they went on to wipe tables. They sent more crumbs flying onto the floor tiles than they caught in the dishcloth. Their sloppy method was purposeful—they could then take turns sweeping up.

Vince engaged in conversation with his father. The two of them had a loving rapport that was quite evident. Vince smiled, nodding and taking a drink of his coffee.

His hands drew her attention. They were so strong. And they had felt so nice against her skin.

Suddenly, having the house all to herself tonight seemed very lonely.

The Cinema cost a dollar on Sunday nights. Its silver screen was literally just that. A screen hand-painted with silver metallic paint that probably dated back to when Harry Newton loaded Sinatra reels on the projector.

Nowadays on dollar nights, films like *Harry Met Sally* and *Jaws* played in their original wide-screen formats. Tonight, John Travolta and the Bee Gees' music were being featured in *Saturday Night Fever*.

Jillene sat in a middle row on the very right, in an aisle seat. The pull-down chair was uncomfortable and its hinges squeaked every time she so much as blinked. The crushed red velour armrests had lost their plushness a long time ago, but she didn't get up and move her seat for a better one. There weren't any much better and the theater was nearly full.

Who would have thought that Tony Manero would be so popular this many years later?

The houselights dimmed and Jillene sighed contentedly, allowing herself to relax for the film. Hopefully she'd be able to wind down more than she had in her bubble bath. Unfortunately, she hadn't enjoyed it very much, and not even wearing the fuzzy white mules had lightened her mood.

When she'd filled the tub and sunk down into the warm

water, she'd braced herself for the girls to barge in and disrupt her. But they never came and, oddly, she found herself let down. A favorite book she'd brought into the sudsy water didn't capture her attention the way it normally did; and even the hazelnut-flavored coffee in her favorite rose-patterned coffee cup didn't taste as good.

The girls had gone to the home of Trudy, a mutual friend they knew from their school in Issaquah—the one they attended before moving to Blue Heron Beach. Trudy's mom took the ferry to the island and picked up the girls for a sleepover since there was no school tomorrow due to a teacher's in-service day.

Jillene had anticipated wandering happily through the house, luxuriating in the peace and quiet. Instead, she'd been restless. Nothing held her interest. She wasn't in the mood to read Vince's book. Besides, then she would start to think about him—and it was bad enough that he was almost constantly on her mind anyway. The television programs were dull, and not even a box of chocolate candy was tempting. So she'd changed out of her nightie and put on her clothes to come to the movies.

Since she had been the only one working at Java today, all the tips had gone to her. Taking a dollar out of the box didn't make her feel guilty. She was going to divide the rest of the money and present it to the girls. She couldn't wait to see their faces when she said they could spend it on whatever they wanted.

For Jillene, a movie was just the splurge she needed to rejuvenate herself. And lucky for her, she loved this movie.

Saturday Night Fever was a trip back to the days of disco. She was going to let the movie sweep her away. She promised not to let Vince occupy a single one of her thoughts for a single second of the movie. She would only focus on Travolta and the white polyester suit she'd once thought of as a major foxy turn-on. Now, not even a Halloween party could entice a man to wear it—unless he was the kind who thought the *Miami Vice* wardrobe was still hip.

Jillene cracked a smile at her own joke, but it quickly fell flat on her lips. She could swear she smelled Vince's aftershave. She moved to turn her head, but the chair made an awful squeak and the person two seats over glared at her.

She faced forward, telling herself she'd only conjured up the barely discernible whiff of his aftershave. Because he was not here. Why would he be? Connie had probably sunk her claws into the back of his shirt and meowed her way into spending the evening with him.

Oh God, what if he'd brought Connie to the movies?

Slowly turning in her seat, Jillene tried to see if she could spot a sassy blond haircut in the silhouettes of movie watchers. The lighting was too obscure and the projector's harsh beam made it difficult to see. When she turned her body further to investigate, the chair protested.

Squeak.

"Shhh!"

Freezing, she carefully faced front once more.

As the movie played out, she had no energy to follow the dialogue or the story. Her concentration was taxed. Why had Vince Tremonti's aftershave lingered so strongly in her head that she imagined smelling it? She could swear he was sitting right behind her and all she had to do was lean back, tilt her head and he could kiss her in the dark.

She brought her hand over her mouth.

Jillene, you are in serious trouble.

She almost didn't make it to the end of the movie, and

when the credits were rolling, she jumped out of her seat and walked up the aisle. Again she caught just the vaguest hint of that heavenly scent of aftershave, but he was no-where in sight.

That did it. She was going directly home, taking two aspirin and crawling beneath her bedcovers. A sensible plan. She'd be better in the morning.

But entering the brightly lit lobby, she stopped dead in her tracks.

"It *was* you," she blurted.

Vince stood at the concession counter with an open box of candy in his hand. He popped one into his mouth, then gave her a bad-boy smile. Lots of flashing white teeth and even a slight dimple in his cheek.

"Where were you sitting?" Her question was more an accusation than a question. The man had driven her to distraction for two hours. She'd missed the whole damn movie. She bit firmly on her back teeth, convinced he had known exactly what he was doing.

"In the row behind you," he drawled.

"Thanks a lot."

"Why are you so hot about it?"

She gasped in horror. Was she so transparent? Her heart was beating so fast, he could probably see her pulse points. Or maybe the uncontrolled blush on her cheeks came across as a sultry invitation.

"I'm not hot." Her body began to awaken in dangerous places, betraying her with a liquid warmth moving through her bloodstream. Her breasts tingled and her knees grew weak. "Didn't you know it was me in front of you?"

"Not until you turned around. I came in a few minutes late."

"I hate when people do that," she snapped, irritated

with herself. Every time she was near him things around her became hazy, and she focused so fully on him that she saw nothing else.

"I thought you were taking a bath."

"W-what?" His statement practically buckled her unstable legs.

"Your girls said you were going to take a bath tonight without anyone bothering you."

She smothered a groan. "Did they? I'm going to have a talk with them."

He suppressed a muffled laugh, but she heard a sliver of it before he chewed another candy. He held the box out to her. "Want one?"

"No, thank you."

She didn't appreciate the way he ate that candy. All slow and savoring-like, his mouth so divine as he tossed a white licorice piece between his lips.

Since she was all out of furious words, and they had no affect on him anyway, she asked, "What are you doing here?"

"Watching my man Vinnie Barbarino."

She took her time to think about it, then ventured to ask, "Do you get that a lot?"

"The Vinnie thing? Naw." He shrugged. "Sometimes."

"I never think of you in that way."

"Most everyone I associate with calls me Vince, so it doesn't really come up much."

She became aware they'd started walking out the theater doors together. Vince had either left Connie behind in the ladies' lounge or he'd come to the movies alone, too.

"How about you?" he asked. "Your name is unusual."

"I was named after my dad's sister, my aunt Jill Ellen."

The movie crowd merged with passersby on the sidewalk. The vanity lights from the theater's awning twinkled above them. Without thought, Jillene kept walking beside Vince, until she realized her car was parked in the opposite direction.

She stopped. "My car is that way. So, I guess I'll see you around."

"Have an ice cream with me. Chocolate dip."

She hadn't had one of those in years.

"It's early." His voice was deep and sensual. "Don't go home yet."

"I have to…" The excuse trailed because there was no excuse.

"The Silverwater Diner is open and last time I sat at the soda fountain, they served dipped cones."

"They still do."

A couple walked passed them, holding hands and whispering while they shared a kiss while keeping their footsteps in sync. Their intimate laughter mingled with the motor noise of a pickup truck packed with high school boys. The boys whistled at a group of girls gathered across the street.

Vince briefly laid his hand on her shoulder, the masculine weight of his palm appealing. "Let's go."

She didn't resist, realizing full well she'd wanted to go with him the second she'd seen him in the lobby.

They headed down the sidewalk toward the center of town. It had rained while they were in the movies and the pavement had a pungent asphalt smell that rose upward into the night.

"Are you sure you don't want a candy?"

"I'm sure." At the moment, that was the one thing she

was sure of. Her heartbeat was pumping in overdrive, but she was unsure about this romantic game of checkers they seemed to be playing. Move and jump. Jump and move. She didn't know the rules.

"I quit smoking not too long ago. Candy, gum and mints help me with the nicotine cravings." Vince slipped the flat licorice box into his shirt pocket.

"My husband smoked. It was the one thing we argued about." She wasn't in the habit of divulging personal things about her marriage, but it felt natural to take Vince into her confidence. "I used to smoke when we first got married, but I quit. Then we had the girls and David wouldn't smoke in the house, but I still hated that he kept on with it."

"How long were you married?"

"Seventeen years."

"That's a long time."

They walked at a leisurely pace, blending into the light foot traffic on the sidewalk. Sol Slobodkin from the video store drove by and waved. A plush purple Barney was stuck in the grill of his car as if he'd hit the stuffed animal head-on.

"What about you?" she asked. "Have you ever been married?"

"Nope."

"Girlfriends?"

"I've lived with a couple."

"At the same time?" She couldn't help teasing.

"Of course. Every man's delight," he said as he held open the door to the Silverwater for her.

They sat at the soda fountain and ordered two dipped cones. The waitress was so excited to see Vince that she made them extra-large ice creams. She chatted up a storm before reluctantly moving on to take plates of burgers to a table, but not before making him promise to autograph a book to her before he left.

"You didn't really live with two women at the same time," Jillene said, biting into a piece of hard chocolate shell.

"No. But I have lived with two women. The last one moved out on me."

"Why?"

"Incompatibility."

"How so?"

"We were both writers."

"I would think that would be a match."

"You'd think." He licked his ice cream, and she watched how his tongue swirled over the soft vanilla inside. Her stomach tightened and she felt too full to eat. Heat brushed against her nerve endings. "The day she left, she told me I was a total waste of her makeup."

"Are you that hard to live with?" she asked, fascinated and trying to keep her thoughts anywhere but on his mouth.

"She was referring to my using her lipstick."

Jillene's laugh was loud, and she quickly muffled her voice. "You're making that up." She never presumed a man as deeply intelligent and complex as Vince would have a sense of humor that could be so—so...silly.

She liked it.

She liked him.

They talked about why and when she'd moved to Blue Heron. She told him about the hard time City Hall loved to give her. Just to make a simple change of business name for Java the Hut from Coffee Time had required triplicate forms.

"I bet they'd make me fill out a form to have...you know, like, pink lawn flamingos in my yard."

Vince nodded. "This town can have some high expectations."

"I imagine you've had to live up to some."

"A few." The distant look that had sometimes possessed his expression came and took him away from her for a second. She hated to see him seem so burdened all of a sudden.

She changed the subject and they compared what it had been like to grow up as only children. They debated their favorite television shows from the seventies. *The Monkees* had been high on her list. Making a bland face, Vince shot her down with *The Rifleman*. Both speculated that a person had to be born to the Seattle climate to tolerate the rain and sunless days.

Before she knew it, the time was eleven o'clock and they were the last ones in the Silverwater. The Open-Closed sign was flipped on the door, but the waitress let them linger at the soda fountain stools after she handed Vince a copy of one of his books and a pen for him to use.

"I just loved it," she gushed. "True crime is my favorite and you write them so good." She was a seasoned woman who'd probably been waitressing at the diner for twenty years.

"Thanks," Vince replied, writing an inscription in the book and handing it back to her. She held it to her large breasts and sighed.

"This is so great! Thanks a bunch, hon."

It was only after she'd refilled the last salt and pepper shakers, that she reluctantly sent them on their way. She blew Vince a kiss and told him to come in again.

Vince and Jillene walked down the main street toward the theater parking lot, gazing in some of the store windows.

"How does that feel?" Jillene asked.

"Signing a book?"

"Yes. That woman was this close to giving you her underwear," she teased.

"I don't think so," he joked back, then grew serious. "It's a pretty good feeling—most of the time. But I don't consider myself a celebrity."

"You are in this town."

"But I can still go to the Seaview Market and not be bothered, for the most part."

"That would be weird to have people recognize you."

"I don't think too much about it."

"Did you get that scar on your chin from police work?" she asked.

"This?" He brought his hand to his chin. "Naw. I ran into Jerry Peck's P.F. Flyer. He plowed into me when he was on a park swing. My face happened to be in front of him."

"You never said why you 'retired' from the Seattle police department."

"I didn't want to go into details about it in front of your girls."

Jillene feared the reason was something horrible. Hesitantly, she asked, "What happened?"

"I got shot."

"Oh, Vince." She gentled her voice.

"A cop being shot isn't real common. It's blown out of proportion in the movies."

"What happened?"

"I sent a guy's brother to jail and he came after me at my house."

"How did he know where you lived?"

"It's not hard to track down an officer's residence. You can get followed home. Some guys never admit they're on the force because they don't want to be bothered during their off time by domestic disputes from their next-door neighbors. That's what 911 is for. It's usually the patrolmen on the beat who say they work for the city. It's not a lie, but it doesn't always assure them anonymity.''

''I had no idea policemen did that.''

''You learn. The first thing you learn as a cop is to keep your gun hand free. That's how he got at me. I had something in my hand. And it wasn't my Smith & Wesson.''

Jillene stared at the profile of his proud, hard face, knowing that this was a difficult story for him to relate. But he was going to do it for her sake. She wanted to understand the pieces of his past that had molded him into who he was today. A writer living with gruesome tales he was compelled to get down on paper.

''I was in my kitchen getting ready to leave for the station. It was dark outside at that hour and I had a light on. I was like a goldfish in a bowl—you could watch my every move through the window. While it's always in the back of your mind to be on guard, it takes more than balls for a shooter to stalk a cop. It's a death wish. Theirs. Because if we've drawn our weapon, we've made the decision to shoot.

''My revolver and shoulder holster were on the countertop by the coffeemaker. I'd just poured a cup, and in those few seconds, waiting for the steam to blow off, I heard a noise outside. Before I could set down the cup and reach for my .38, a bullet ripped through the window.''

Jillene felt everything slow. The speed of her pulse and the pace of her walk. She nearly stopped so she could lend him her full attention, but he kept walking. So she stayed with him.

"I must have been shielding myself with my arm because the slug nailed me in the left hand. I dropped on the floor to dodge the next round and I thought to myself—" He bit off the words in midsentence. "Let's just say I wasn't too happy about what had just happened to me.

"The perp is in my house now and I hear the front door slamming into the wall. I'm lunging for the counter and my life, but a bang goes off and I feel like I've just been kicked by a horse. I'm on the floor again. I'd been shot at point-blank range in the back."

"Oh my God." Jillene touched his sleeve, the cotton fabric warm from his skin.

"Anyway," he said in an easygoing tone, though it had to be a very hard thing for him to recall. "It was a morning I'll never forget." With the yellow haze of a streetlamp high over his shoulder, he glanced her way. "Hell, you don't want to hear about this."

"I don't want you to relive something that disturbs you. But if you want to go on, I would like to hear the rest."

Vince's gaze lowered to capture her face. If he could read her expression in the poor light, he would see it was one of deep awareness for his suffering, coupled with the wish to relieve it.

He must have seen something because he continued.

"The bullet went through the right side of my back and knocked out my lung. The only thing holding my chest together were my ribs. I never saw my shooter, but when I was laying on the cold floor of my kitchen he thought I was dead and he said something to me—and it wasn't hello."

The memory of the gunman's voice shot through Vince with the same force as his bullet had. *Goodbye, motherfucker.*

"I knew I was shot but I didn't know how bad. My body went into shock, and—this'll sound crazy—in my mind, I thought I had a really bad case of heartburn."

A reminiscent smile twitched on his mouth, and Jillene's throat ached for him. She had her own painful memories, but they'd all been emotional. Nothing physical such as this.

They'd come to the parking lot where her car was the only one left.

"I don't know how I made it to the bathroom, but I went to get some antacids. I was more than a little surprised," Vince went on with sarcastic humor, "when I took a look at my reflection in the mirror and saw my hand covering my bloody chest."

Stark and vivid thoughts kept her motionless beside her car.

"I stumbled into the bedroom, lay down and closed my eyes. I don't remember calling the operator. But I woke up on an ER gurney with an oxygen mask on. I was in the hospital nearly a month. Then I went into physical therapy. As an exercise for my wounded hand, they sat me in front of a keyboard. I had a lot of trial and conviction cases I'd worked on, so I just started writing about one of them. It turned into my first true crime book."

"What about the man who shot you?"

"They caught him. He's rehabilitated and claims he's born again. It doesn't do him any good if he's faking it because he's a lifer. And the brother he was avenging—he got out and was gunned down after twenty-four hours on the streets. Drug deal gone bad."

Vince exhaled, half sighing and half laughing. "And that's why I never hold a coffee cup in my right hand. Superstitious about it."

"I never noticed," she murmured.

The parking lot light above them flickered and burned out with a buzzing sound.

She could literally feel the tension surrounding Vince. As if it had sucked the energy right out of that streetlight and he'd taken it all in. A charged and darkly bound shadow of a man as ethereal as any dream.

He stood in front of her, his strong thighs mere inches away from being pressed into hers. The beat of her heart hammered in her chest. Staring down, he looked into her eyes. She didn't know what he was searching for. Maybe a friend. Maybe a lover. Which did she want to be?

She whispered, her words more mouthed than spoken, "Do you still own a gun?"

"Yes."

With a small step, he closed the distance that separated them and backed her up against her car fender. Her butt was crushed next to the cold metal frame, but Vince's body heat tugged at her like a blanket she greedily needed to wrap herself in. His moist breath skimmed her face—sweet and heady with licorice and chocolate. They were tempting flavors she wanted to taste on his mouth.

Shivers of desire scattered through her, burning in a low swoop of heat that put pressure between her legs. The liquid fire that pulsed was begging for release. Her arousal was instant and fiercely wanting. Years of denial unlocked in a floodgate of shameless encouragement.

The rough texture of his jeans rasped against the thin layer of her khakis like a hot iron. He rubbed himself over her ever so slowly, and in a whimper, she brought her hands to his shoulders.

On a ragged breath, she asked, "How long are you staying in Blue Heron?"

"I don't know."

Trying to sound level-headed, she said, "Then, we shouldn't start anything."

His face moved steadily downward toward hers. "Were we?"

A host of frantic tingling sensations danced through her breasts, centering at her nipples. They were beaded into tight knots against the cups of her bra.

"We've been starting something since the minute we met." She arched her neck. Feelings washed away thoughts.

She wanted to steal what she could of him.

On a guttural growl of possession, his hands came around the back of her head and brought her mouth to his.

Jillene softly moaned and closed her eyes.

The kiss was slow and hard, urgent and blazing.

She brought her hands around his neck to maximize the contact of his solidly built body. She kneaded his taut muscles, delving her hands into his hair.

She remembered how wonderful kissing had been. How good this could feel. But the mouth hungrily searching hers was unfamiliar. Initiating pleasure, it was sexy and exciting. Demanding and new.

Vince's fingers tangled into her unbound hair, and the empty ache inside her begged for more of him to fill her. She held his face close to keep him from leaving her.

The skin at his jaw was rough against her fingertips. He changed the slant of the kiss, toying and eliciting a deep shudder from her body. Making her push her hips into his. She felt the solid length of him at the fly of his jeans.

His mouth burned and tortured. She wanted him so badly she couldn't see her way to stopping.

Pulling in a short breath, she parted her lips for him.

His tongue sought and found hers. He was so warm and wet. She welcomed the fiery invasion that wrapped her up in a sweetly draining anxiousness.

The dormant sexuality in her body had come fully alive. She felt consumed by him.

In surrendering moans, she rose to meet him fully. She kissed him with a sucking motion of her mouth, releasing and running her tongue silkily across his teeth and inside his lips. He probed into her mouth, darting over and around her tongue. She would have lost all sanity and inhibition and wrapped her legs around him for anyone to see in that near-dark parking lot.

She wanted to resist, but she was too lost to care.

A car drove by in the street causing a violent curse to abruptly tear from Vince's mouth; he pulled back from her with a moan. The chilled evening air took the place of his hot mouth.

A savage silence overpowered everything that had just happened.

Jillene was shaken by the long-dormant stirrings of a climax and the ecstatic moment of kissing. She tingled and felt aware of him in every pore of her body. How would she have responded to him with her clothes off?

She should have been shocked. At the very least, she should have been thinking about Vince as the first man she'd kissed since David. How did she feel? She'd thought about when or if it would happen, yet she had never imagined it. Now that it had happened, she wasn't thinking about anything aside from how badly she wanted Vince to do more than kiss her.

The blood in her veins seemed to flow slow and thick like honey, with a wondrous ache that made her feel as if she had no bones in her body to support her.

"I gotta go." Vince reached out and jerked her purse

from the hood of the car. He dug blindly inside its depths. His hand came up with her car key and stabbed it into the lock. He opened her door and without a word, positioned her to sit behind the wheel.

Then he slammed the door.

He pressed his wide hands on the window. The nostrils on his chiseled face were flared. His breath was uneven. "I'll be around long enough to do that again."

He staggered backward, raking his hands through his black hair.

The heat from his hands left prints on the glass long after he had left, swallowed up by the night.

Sixteen

By the time Friday came around, after a long week of struggling to write something viable, Vince was ready for the telecast of *Smackdown!* World Wrestling Federation television proved to be exactly what he needed.

Pyrotechnics, MTV-like blaring music, bravado, threats and an audience feeding into the hype. The flashes. The ceremony. Kane, Chris Jericho, The Big Show, and the Undertaker, who came onto the set riding a chrome motorcycle. Leather-clad and oiled wrestlers stood in the ring holding microphones, screaming about their pride and baiting the audience—claiming tonight they'd change the course of history when they knocked the lights out of a certain performer. Boos followed the challenges and it all promised to be a hell of a match-up. An expletive-hammered retaliation from the cocky guy who'd had his ass handed to him a week ago. A verbal threat shot back indicating he should get out of the ring while he still had his balls.

Vince sat in Pop's sedate living room with the television screen beaming a picture of Triple H being tromped to the mat by a colossal opponent. Metal folding chairs went flying. All the moves were given a play-by-play from a female announcer with triple-digit silicone breasts squeezed into an animal-print blouse.

Through the jeers and blows, Vince wondered how he

could justify watching such a violent sport when he had to deal with violence in his work.

While he was no psychoanalyst, he theorized that viewing guys slamming against each other stimulated his thoughts versus his emotions. Lentz had taken a hit at the latter. By tuning out his emotions Vince could regroup.

Dudes wearing spandex were amusing—and entertaining to some people, including him.

By the Federation's own admission, the WWF matches were stringently choreographed. In essence, it was controlled content. When he'd had enough, he could aim the remote and shut it off.

He couldn't do that in real life.

In an unintentional way, WrestleMania was therapy for overload and depression. Vince had battled that adversity after being gunned down in his own house. He knew of another true crimes author who couldn't survive without the new generation of antidepressants. Vince preferred to watch WWF television when a case pressed in on him, rather than rely on a pill.

Pop reclined in the big Barcalounger, but he was anything but relaxed. He kept looking at the clock on the wall above the set. His gaze seemed to be tracking the red second hand as it ticked past the numbers.

"You want a beer, Pop?"

"No." He lowered the footrest to the down position so he could sit straighter. "You go ahead."

Vince went into the kitchen and came back with a cold one. The malt taste was mild and quenching.

"What are you looking at?" Pop asked, repositioning himself and looking at the clock once again.

Sinking into the cushioned back of the sofa, Vince narrowed his eyes. "Wrestling." Something was definitely going on with his dad if he had to ask what men bashing in each other's skulls was doing on the tube.

"I don't mean the TV. The papers—what are they?"

Across the sofa armrests, on the coffee table and the floor, Vince had spread out every piece of information on Samuel Lentz that he had compiled so far. There was a mile-high pile of it and, with the papers fanned out in front of him, it looked like a small lake. His yellow legal pad was filled with handwritten pages containing a rambling, disjointed first draft, but it was nothing he'd submit.

The outline had been due on Tuesday. He'd missed the deadline. And he hadn't called anyone in New York to explain why. For the first time in his career, Vince had blown off a promise. Lentz was a huge part of it, but there was something else. Someone else.

Jillene McDermott.

He was so preoccupied with her that he couldn't think. Even if these had been the best of circumstances for him, he wouldn't have been able to compose a decent sentence, let alone an outline. He wanted her so badly he couldn't concentrate or focus on anything but the memory of her in his arms.

That night after the movies, when they'd talked, he had shared a part of himself that he normally kept tightly bottled up. But Jillene had cared to a degree that he felt her compassion inside his heart. She wanted to know. She understood his fear and she made him feel—

Hell.

He'd kissed her. Everything about that kiss had inflamed him. The taste of her tongue and the maddening crush of her breasts into his chest. The thrust of her nipples against his shirt. Raw sexuality had caught hold of them both. He could have taken her right there. In the parking lot. Made love to her on the hood of her car and not given a good damn about anything but her body taking the length of him, plunging himself deeper and deeper until they both came.

Without that sexual release, and with his mind so fully alive with the awareness of her, he'd had to stay away from Java this week. If he'd gone to see her, he'd have taken her from the counter to the back room. To hell with her customers. He was mad for her—he ached for her.

But Jillene was right. He would be leaving and going home to Los Angeles. Maybe tomorrow. Maybe next week. He wasn't used to sitting in one place. He was on the move a lot, following stories. How could they get involved? It would only be sex. Physical and nothing else. She deserved more than that. She should be loved and cherished, not taken to bed without promises.

Each day this week he had tried harder and harder to embed the book inside his head. That would be his mental release. He'd write the Lentz outline to prove to himself he could do it.

He'd written for endless hours, holed up on the boat trying to organize his notes in a meaningful way. But after more than a week of writing he wasn't much closer to finishing, even though he'd had his laptop sent to him and had been incorporating material on the computer.

He had been ready to call it quits for the day.

Al cleared his throat and said, "Vince?"

"Oh, sorry, Pop. Yeah, this is my Lentz outline," Vince replied belatedly, his gaze directed on the television.

"You look like hell."

Vince hadn't shaved today. In fact, he hadn't shaved for a couple of days. He'd let himself go, something very rare for him. "I ran out of razors."

"Take one of mine."

"Okay." Vince had a full box of blade cartridges on the boat, but he neglected to mention that.

Al was sitting on the edge of the recliner as if he were waiting for the smoke detector to go off any minute, ready to evacuate the house. He looked at the clock once more, the soles of his loafers flat on the rug and his legs bent. He was leaning forward, elbows on his knees. Classic body language indicating distraction.

"How come you have your good shoes on?" Vince asked.

"I do?" Pop looked down, brought his feet back as if to hide them, then shrugged. "I'm trying to break them in." The brown tassel loafers were his best church-going shoes. He wore dress socks, too.

"I thought you did that when you bought them."

"You never can get Italian leather too soft." Pop's tone was strained as he steered the conversation back to the outline. "So, do you think you'll finish it?"

"Maybe. Probably," Vince replied, not wanting to talk about the book or the case or anything associated with it.

Vince had come over to his dad's, hoping they could go out for dinner and do something afterward like bowling or hitting balls at the driving range.

"So, uh, Vinnie," Pop said, standing. "Didn't you say you had plans for tonight?"

"Yeah, I was going to ask—"

"Sorry you have to go."

"I don't have to leave."

Pop's expectant expression fell. "You don't?"

"No." Vince became suspicious when his dad paced in front of the coffee table. The scent of his special bay rum aftershave became distinct.

Studying Al, Vince noticed he was clean-shaven, when usually, about this time of day, he had a dark beard shadow. His jet-black hair was combed into place with Lucky Tiger. He wore his gold watch, not the Timex.

Curious, Vince folded his arms over his chest and said, "I was going to ask you out for some chow and then take you to the driving range, but it looks like you've already got plans."

"Nothing really."

Vince kept silent, waiting for an explanation.

Alphonzo Tremonti, in the scheme of personality profiling, couldn't lie his way out of a paper bag. The muscles in his jaw tensed and his eyes widened.

"Something big." Pop exhaled in a rush. Then all the pent-up restraint in him fell apart. He blurted, "Holy sweet Jesus. Vinnie—I have a date."

If Pop had been anticipating criticism, he was going to be let down. On a genuine nod of satisfaction, Vince heartily said, "Good for you."

His dad didn't appear to be any more at ease. "I didn't want to tell you in case you weren't okay with it."

"Why wouldn't I be?"

"Because of your mother."

"Pop, Mom's been gone a long time. I never thought you'd wait so long to search for someone special."

Vince had never questioned his dad's decision not to remarry, but when he went through puberty, he did wonder if his dad missed sex. Or maybe Pop had somebody he saw and he kept things discreet. That was clearly a subject Vince would never broach. Al had loved his wife with all his heart, but he had a large heart. Enough to share with somebody else.

Pushing the sleeves of his knit shirt higher on his arms, his dad nervously declared, "It's not easy for me. I didn't want to put away Grace's memory. I loved her, Vinnie. I still love her, and I can't ever forget what we had."

"You don't have to forget. And you're not disappointing her. She'd want you to keep living. I never pushed you, Pop, because it's your life. But I think this is really great." Vince clicked off the TV. "Who are you seeing?"

Al's neck flushed red. His Adam's apple bobbed when he swallowed in slow motion. "Ianella Sofrone."

"I kind of figured that's who you'd say." Vince knew there was a spark of something too bright to ignore. He'd witnessed Pop's infatuation over the years, but there was the matter of Mrs. Sofrone being married. Now she was a widow and available.

She was an exceptionally beautiful woman, not only on the outside but the inside. Vince would never forget the kindness she'd shown him at his mother's funeral, nor the home-cooked meals she'd brought to their house in the following months.

"She's...she's incredible." His dad shook his head, almost as if he couldn't believe he was actually taking the woman out on a date.

"So that explains why you have a freezer full of goodies," Vince teased. He remembered Pop bringing them home last week, tossing out some containers of his best spaghetti sauce to make room for the sweets labeled *Baked with love by Ianella.*

A smile broke out on Vince's mouth. "No wonder you stayed all day at the white elephant sale."

"I couldn't help myself."

"And you shouldn't, Pop. Go for it."

Al read the clock once again. "Vinnie, she's expecting me at seven. I don't know which tie to wear. I can't decide. I had everything cleaned and pressed. It's between the stripe and the paisley." His hands were almost trembling from excitement. "I have to look sharp."

Getting to his feet, Vince suggested, "Let's check them out."

"Would you mind, son?"

He slung his arm over his dad's wide shoulders. "No, Pop. Not at all."

The Lobster King was decorated with fishing paraphernalia. Heavy rope nets and blown-glass weights were arranged on the planked walls. Suspended from the ceiling, lobster cages hung over each table. Inside each of them were plastic lobsters.

By the reservation desk, a large saltwater tank was filled with the live crustaceans. Rubber bands kept their claws closed and they didn't do much in the way of swimming while waiting to end up on somebody's dinner plate.

Al and Ianella picked their selections from the tank and were shown to a table in the back corner. He had requested it specially when he'd phoned for their reservation. There was a quiet and secluded atmosphere to the area as well as a view of the ocean. He'd timed the evening so that they'd be sitting down just as the sun was setting.

A candle flickered on the table as he helped Ianella with her chair. Gently, he guided her forward, then sat down himself.

The softly wavering flame allowed him to view her without feeling self-conscious about it. When he'd picked her up, he had been trying hard not to make any wrong moves. But now that they were at the restaurant, he felt slightly more relaxed—one hurdle was over and he hadn't stumbled. It also helped that they'd had a glass of Chianti in the bar.

He said, "I hope this table is all right."

"It's very nice."

"You can watch the boats in the harbor." *I can watch you, Ianella.*

She wore a deep-green dress with a small bow at the rounded neckline. Like an emerald. That's how he'd describe the color. Ianella was a true jewel in it. The dress brought out the red in her hair, which she'd partially pinned up. Sparkling earrings with a little dangle to them set off her face to perfection.

He couldn't help sighing with pleasure.

She smiled at him, her lipstick shimmering.

He nearly lost every wit about him.

A waiter brought a basket of warm bread to the table, along with butter and two small plates.

Al immediately broke off two slices. Living out his fantasy, he buttered one for Ianella and put it on her plate. "For you, dear."

What had he just done? The endearment had slipped out!

Ianella's smile widened and her dark eyes grew more exotic than ever. "Thank you, Al."

His hands dropped onto his lap and his napkin shifted. He shoved the linen back into place over his brown slacks. Then the oddest thing happened. He got mad.

At himself.

He'd waited six years for this evening and he was starting to fumble through it like he was seventeen. He was sixty-four, a confident businessman, and a solid friend to those who knew him. He'd been through good times and bad. Paid his dues and learned his lessons. Life was moving on past without his catching a ride with romance. This was his second chance. If he walked away from tonight never having told his ladylove how he felt, he would regret it for the remainder of his days.

Al reached across the table and took each of Ianella's

hands in his. Her surprised reaction lasted a mere second before she surrendered her soft fingers to his hold.

"Ianella," he began, uttering her name with every feeling welling inside him, "I've always wanted to ask you to a lobster supper, but it was out of respect for your marriage vows and our belief in the church that I refrained. Now that Leo has departed, I can speak freely. Although he's only been gone for a month, I think you mourned his loss a long time ago. I understand that losing a spouse, no matter the circumstances, is difficult to go through. Your adult sons have been a comfort to you with their families and grandchildren. But when you're alone, everything seems challenging. You've managed just fine and I admire your strength and courage."

"Al." Her voice barely lifted above a whisper.

"Please, let me say this." Giving her hands a gentle squeeze, he went on. "The feelings I have for you go beyond high regard and friendship. They're romantic." He didn't dare gauge her reaction yet. "Ianella, I think you're one of the most wonderful women I've ever known. And it would be my honor if you'd allow me to come calling on you."

The pounding of his heartbeat was so strong it could have knocked his tie from its clip.

She bit her lip, then shook her head. She dug into her pocketbook for a handkerchief.

The spirit of his soul sank. Right down there with the *Titanic*. So deep it would never be salvaged.

"Oh, Al." She dabbed her eyes.

He'd made her cry. He felt a nauseating despair submerging him further.

"I've wanted to say the same things about you," she confessed.

Time stopped moving.

His gaze lifted to hers. He rose from the bottom and was floating again. "You have?"

She nodded. "I know how much you loved Grace. She was your heart. I could never replace her. I don't want to be that for you. I just didn't know that you were ready to find out what we could be."

Find out what we could be.

"I'm ready." He couldn't rally his affirmation quick enough. "And I have been for years."

Ianella brought her hand to her cheek in admiration. "Then, let's enjoy every minute. Tonight is a long way from being over."

Seventeen

When Vince didn't come into Java on the Monday morning after the movie, Jillene was relieved. On Tuesday, she was still trying to figure out what small talk she'd make when she saw him. Wednesday, her relief turned to slight annoyance that grew into chafing irritation by Thursday. Come Friday, she was outright angry he hadn't shown a little pursuit. After all, she'd all but screamed "Take me" at him in a dark parking lot.

The weekend came and went and she never saw him. Not at the Laundromat or at the Seaview. She assumed he'd gone back to L.A. and it killed her to admit she was devastated. He hadn't even said goodbye. But what had she expected? He owed her nothing. They weren't seeing each other. He had no obligation to inform her of his plans.

She had to buck up and move on. Claire and Faye would be going for a visit to her mom's soon and there were things to do to get ready for their trip. Jillene had also been busy reformatting her ongoing plans for Java. What she had done so far had the potential to be something big.

June could end up being her month for making a turn-around.

Mocha Madness and her bookstore coupons were proving to be a smart decision. Business at Java the Hut had improved. The customers—notably the locals—still weren't coming in large numbers unless Vince was inside the store. But tourist traffic was way up and the increased sales helped Jillene's unbalanced budget. Also, after making some phone calls, she'd changed pastry vendors. Her new supplier, Pastry Cart, was a fledgling company eager to gain clients. She was getting lower prices for the same, if not better, pastries.

As she worked behind the counter with Hannah, Jillene glanced at the dining area. She caught herself looking for Vince, knowing he wouldn't be there. Half of the tables were occupied—no small feat given it was a cloudless afternoon. Usually when the sun came out, people stayed outside to enjoy the clear skies while they lasted.

While she recognized some of the customers, others she did not. More vacationers were arriving daily, but they'd been slower to get out to the island this week because there were film crews in Seattle drawing everyone's attention. She'd heard a big Hollywood movie was being filmed over there. She wished the studios would film something on Blue Heron. Then her business would really get a shot in the arm.

Slipping into the back for a moment, Jillene took a sip of her iced Italian crema coffee. Her personal weakness. She was on her third one today and it was after noon. Her usual cutoff time.

She'd been drinking far too much caffeine. She wasn't sleeping soundly. There had been no nightmares or obscene phone calls. Just dreams. Vivid pictures that assaulted her sleep. She was naked in bed with Vince. Wrapped in clean sheets, a sea breeze floating in from an open window. Warm and soft kisses. Arms entwined. Stroking a hard place she hadn't touched in a very long while. Fingers skimming down her legs and an arm over her shoulder to pull her closer. Touching and exploring every inch of skin.

She wanted him so bad, she trembled. It all seemed so real. She could smell and taste him.

But when she woke, she was alone. And with an ache so needy it was unbearable. The intimate place between her legs was slick and warm. Unsatisfied. Stumbling into a cold shower, she willed herself to put the man out of her head so she could start her day.

She was appalled. She had to get a grip. If she didn't, she'd be asking Hannah where she could send away for a vibrator.

Beside her, Hannah pumped syrup into a cup, stirred in steamed milk and snapped a lid on top.

Velma Hicks took the cup. The wig on her head was synthetic cotton-candy pink piled in a four-inch-high bee-hive bubble. "What are these called again?"

Hannah replied, "A mocha."

"What's in it?"

"Espresso, milk and chocolate."

"Light or dark chocolate?"

"Dark syrup."

"I've never heard of such a thing." Her mouth twisted and she stared at the cup as if it were filled with fungicide. "The only reason I'm trying this is because of Mrs. P. J. Paulson. You wouldn't know her. She was born and buried on this island before you moved over. She used to live on Ninth but was killed by wasps. They were inside her chimney. She didn't know that when she went to clean it out with her rubber broom. She was attacked."

"That's awful," Jillene said, masking a shiver. She didn't like spiders, or anything that flew with a stinger, or most any variety of bug for that matter.

"Mrs. Paulson spoke to me on my Ouija board last

night. The letters *M-O-C-H-A* were spelled out, and I told her spirit she had to be more specific than that. Then my fingers were moving over to the *J* and the *A* and the *V* and the *A*. And I said, 'I know what that is. The hoity-toity coffee shop owned by that mainlander who charges ten dollars for one cup of coffee.'''

Jillene held on to her courteous smile, but it was brittle.

Velma continued, ''She had a message for my cat, too.''

Jillene and Hannah waited for an explanation. Velma didn't elaborate. But the expression on her face looked like it wasn't good news for the cat. She took her mocha to a table, rummaged through a tote bag and brought out a needlepoint project.

Several minutes before one o'clock, Rob Duniway walked through the door, the uniform khaki apron with Java the Hut on the bib thrown over his shoulder.

''Ladies.'' He greeted them as he stepped behind the counter.

''Hi, Rob.'' Jillene was pleased to see her new hired help show up for his second week on the job. When he'd appeared to submit an application, she'd never been so glad.

Wearing his blond hair in a neat buzz, Rob was nineteen with a heavily built body. A member of the high school wrestling team, he'd been a lead scorer. He'd just graduated and needed a summer job. Not only was he qualified, but he'd had experience at Tully's last year. After interviewing him, Jillene had given him the position on the spot.

No longer did she have to worry about Hannah or herself being alone in the store, because Rob would be around. While he was young, he was also strong.

Paying his salary would be a definite strain on her account, but Rob was worth it. She had money left over from the Chihuly sale, but her budget was stretched to the limit. Just another little pull to funnel a weekly check to Rob. She could do that with the help of peanut butter and jelly sandwiches every night for dinner.

"I saw Olde City Coffee pull up in back, Jillene. Do you want me to get the order?"

"That would be great."

Slipping his apron over his neck, he walked right on through to the back where the service door was located.

"I can't believe how lucky I am to have found him."

"I like him, but I was hoping you would hire somebody more my age," Hannah teased, dumping the tamped grounds from the porta filter. "I could have made out with him in the storeroom."

"Yes, right. Sorry about that." Jillene willed her mood to be buoyant. She was not going to waste another day moping around for Vince Tremonti, hoping he'd walk through the door. So she went along with Hannah. "Next time I'll hold out for Heath Ledger."

"There you go! He's *so* hot. I don't know what he ever saw in Heather Graham." Hannah ran water over the shot glasses. "I've seen *10 Things I Hate About You* at least seven times. I wonder what movie they're filming in Seattle. Somebody said that they saw Al Pacino."

"If Al Pacino stopped in here for a coffee, Blue Heron would never be the same."

Velma reappeared. She thunked her coffee cup down. "This hot chocolate is missing the marshmallows."

"You're not drinking a hot chocolate," Hannah corrected. "You ordered a mocha."

The burgundy lipstick Velma had poorly applied was emphasized when she frowned. "What's a mocha again?"

Jillene snuck another taste of her iced latte and explained, "It's a hot espresso with chocolate and milk."

"That's what I thought. I want marshmallows on this hot chocolate."

Shrugging, Hannah said, "We're all out."

"Well, shoot." The curls on her wig didn't move an inch as the ceiling fan blades rotated softly above her head. "Do you know what movie they're filming in Seattle?"

Hannah pushed her horn-rimmed glasses farther up her nose, the tiny silver ring glinting from her pierced nostril. "I'm not sure."

"I wonder if that Woody Harrelson is over there. He was at the Hempfest. I watched him play Larry Flynt in a movie." She made a face. "They should arrest all those potheads." The Myrtle Edwards Park Hempfest had drawn nearly a hundred thousand die-hard pot smokers rallying to legalize marijuana.

Velma grabbed her coffee and returned to the table.

"Larry Flint?" Hannah repeated, amusement dancing in her eyes. "Velma watched a movie about the king of raw porn?"

Jillene was caught between laughter and astonishment, trying to keep her expression blank in case Velma glanced back at them.

"That reminds me." Hannah's chain bracelet slid down her arm as she adjusted her glasses. "Velma reported that the ladies' rest room is out of paper towels."

"I'll go fill it." Jillene collected a stack of accordion-folded paper towels. She needed to move around and work off some of the caffeine charging through her or she'd fly through the roof.

After filling the dispenser, she dared to look at her reflection. She almost slumped against the wall. How could losing what she had never had show so much in her appearance? She might as well wear a sign that said: *I Am in Withdrawal from Vince Tremonti.*

She rolled her eyes and pushed the door open.

The corridor that led from the seating area to both rest rooms was closed off from the service area and she'd barely taken a step, when Vince appeared, heading directly for her.

Against her will, she faltered and a slow smile took possession of her face. Who had she been kidding about not caring? The second she saw him, her heart came alive.

He looked so handsome in a short-sleeved pale blue shirt, the collar a pleasant contrast next to his tan. He wore stone-washed jeans, and if she wasn't mistaken, they were the same pair he'd had on at the movies. She knew just how the texture felt. Worn and soft at his thighs. Hard in a certain place.

He'd had a haircut. The fringe across his forehead was more spiked and the sides above his ears were tapered back in a neat trim. The wind had blown a healthy color on his cheeks as if he'd been out boating. He slipped his sunglasses from his nose and stuck them into his pocket. His eyes were blue, so clear and cloudless she swore it almost seemed as if whatever darkness had colored them had disappeared. Or maybe not.

"Hi, Jillene."

She hated how he said her name like that. Silken and drowsy as if they'd just...

She loved how he said her name.

"Hello—"

Vince's lips burned into hers, his mouth widening to take in all of her. His tongue swept through her, slick and gliding. The kiss was fast and volatile. Stolen and hot. He knit his fingers through hers, raising her arms over her head. She felt herself being backed against the wall, his body fully covering hers. With their arms high and locked together, her breasts thrust against his chest. She'd been fantasizing about him, but nothing she'd conjured in her mind had come close to this.

The kiss was over just as abruptly as it began.

When he pulled back, his breath came out in a hot, ragged gasp. "I'm not the kind of man you're used to."

Completely stunned, all her words fled.

He took her by the shoulders, turned her toward the dining room and gave her a nudge. Woodenly, she walked back to Hannah with her entire consciousness rocked off-kilter.

Vince drew up to the counter seconds after her, his face and body so unshakably composed she had to wonder if what had just happened between them was something she'd fabricated in her head.

"I'll try a mocha today," he said, reaching for his wallet.

The riotous jump in her pulse couldn't be quelled. It felt as if the wind had been knocked out of her and she couldn't get enough air into her lungs. Her lips were parched, and licking them didn't help moisten the dryness because each time she did, she tasted Vince on her mouth. Then her rampant heartbeat went crazy again.

Jillene poised her hand over the cash register key. "A-and how would you like that?"

"However you think I would."

Their eyes clung.

She made a quick study of his face. His wide mouth, and his eyelashes, inky black and stubbed. The arch of his brows made a very subtle curve. The faint scar at his chin gave his face a rugged look. He was an unpredictable man.

Her brain was in a tumult. His unexpected appearance had thrown her off so badly, she couldn't think.

She felt a tremor in her fingers as she punched the price buttons on the machine. "Grande double-shot vanilla mocha, no whip."

Hannah repeated the order back as she wrote on the side of a cup with a black marker. "Double-shot vanilla mocha, no whip."

He paid and dropped a generous tip in the box.

"I thought you left town," she said, then instantly winced. She damned herself for speaking the foremost thought in her head. She'd sworn to herself that if she ever saw him again, she wouldn't discuss where he'd been or what he'd been doing. It was no concern of hers and she was out of line to question him.

But what did you call that kiss he'd given her? If that hadn't been out of line…right where anyone could have chanced upon them. But that had all been part of the thrill—being caught up in those scant minutes of ecstasy.

"I've been working."

"That's nice." No, it wasn't. It was a lame excuse. He could have come in for a coffee or just to say hello. People didn't shut themselves off like that when—

"How've you been?"

"Great," she automatically said. She wasn't going to let him know how much he could make her want him no matter the circumstance or the place. Although it was a little too late to pretend that kissing him was no big deal. "Really good."

He nodded. "Good."

"Grande vanilla mocha, no whip," Hannah called as she set the cup on the hand-off station.

"It was nice to see you, Jillene."

"Likewise…Vince." She would not hold back from

saying his name in reciprocation even if the sound of it teased the fine hairs at the nape of her neck like a caress.

He took his coffee and went to sit down. As was his custom, he blew softly across the hot liquid, then brought the cup to his mouth. Jillene observed him, desperately trying to tamp down the heat that flared low through her abdomen. A solemness sprang to life in her, taking the place of desire. A deeply felt understanding came as he held the drink.

In his left hand.

He lifted his head in her direction, as if to say the coffee was to his liking. Approval was in his eyes, both for the mocha and for—

"I think he's the one."

Jillene turned to Hannah. "He's the one what?"

"The one you should have sex with."

"Hannah!" Jillene hushed her, praying Vince didn't hear.

How could Hannah have hit so close to home?

"Why not? He's good-looking *and* intelligent. From the way he looked at you, he's interested."

When Jillene could breathe again, she replied, "But I'm not."

"You should be." Hannah glanced at the wall clock. "I'm off in a minute. Ask him to have dinner with you. I'll watch the girls. But not tonight. Wonder of wonders, *moi* has a date in the city with a fireman. Maybe he'll show me his fire hose. I can come over tomorrow and hang out with the girls while you and the writer go write some bedroom chapters."

"I'm not going to ask him to dinner," Jillene managed to say. "Tonight or tomorrow."

"Think it over." Hannah snatched her backpack from the back room. "See you later."

Jillene wanted to keep her attention on the counter and make coffees, but she messed up two orders in a row. She spilled hazelnut syrup when refilling the dispenser. She couldn't help staring at Vince. And every time she did, he was staring right back. She wondered if his eyes had ever left her. When she caught his gaze skimming her body, he silently dared her to break eye contact first.

Her stomach jumped like a kernel of popcorn on a hot griddle. She hated this nervousness…this infuriatingly basic element of wanting that had gotten hold of her. Maybe it was the way Hannah had spelled it out—she needed sex—or maybe it was all the coffee she'd consumed that was making her so jittery.

In either case, if she didn't get out of here right now, she'd hand Vince her heart and soul on a plate and ask him if he wanted a coffee to go with it.

"I'm going to run over to the Seaview," she said to Rob while standing in front of the open refrigerator. "For some reason, we didn't get nonfat in our milk delivery this morning. We've only got one carton left." She grabbed her purse. "I'll be back soon."

A headache from overindulging in caffeine throbbed at her temple. She really shouldn't have had that last coffee. Her hands were shaky.

On her way out the door, she gave Vince a parting glance. A cell phone was at his ear; his features were taut with concentration. Whomever he was talking to had his rapt attention. Java could be falling down around itself and he wouldn't have noticed her.

Vince locked his jaw tight and listened as Mel plainly stated, "You should have let me know what was going on. I represent you and your best interests, but I'm not a mind reader. You have to talk to me and keep me updated if you're going to bail. Gail said she just got the outline this morning from FedEx. A week late was something that I'm sure we could have smoothed over but nobody heard from you. Gail tried your cell, I tried it. We called your house and all we got was your voice mail." There was a constant ringing from another telephone in the background. "Do you have a problem I need to know about?"

"No, I don't." Vince stood and walked outside where he could talk freely. "I delivered the outline just like I said I would."

"A week late."

"So what the hell? I wrote it."

In the nine years Vince had been with Mel Herzl, he had never lost his temper with him. With his mind pushed to the breaking point, however, his stress overload impeded his ability to be civil. His effort had sucked the blood out of him until all that was left was sweat and hard work. He had completed those fifteen pages, but anyone who read them would never know how much they had cost him.

"I apologize, Mel." Deep remorse filled Vince. He was mentally sabotaged by the images Lentz had painted on those tapes.

A pause stagnated on the line.

"Accepted." Mel's reply came late, but it was what Vince needed to hear.

Mel went on. "Gail read everything and we're a go with the book. I'll get your check out to you as soon as I receive it."

Being paid for this project made Vince extremely uncomfortable. Out of habit, he fingered the inside of his shirt pocket for a pack of smokes. He came up with his Serengetis and cursed the fact he had no gum or mints. "About those phone messages, I knew what you and Gail wanted. There was nothing you could have said to me that would have made a difference." Vince gazed across Seaward Street, noticing that Pop needed to come out and wind the barber's pole. "I had to do this one my way."

"Keep yourself available, Vince. Your participation would have made a difference in the sales catalogue. The copy could have been sharper and more compelling."

"I'm sure it's not bad. Gail has an eye for that kind of thing." Vince went to the edge of the building and looked out at the marina. The boat sails resembled snow-white tuxedo shirts snapping in the wind.

Mel spoke away from the phone. "No, I can't. Take a message. Don't send through any calls. And close the door." Speaking more clearly into the receiver, he said, "You sound wound up, Vince. Are you having any trouble I need to know about? Level with me."

Changing the cell phone to his other ear, Vince squinted against the sunshine that brightened the expansive dome of Washington sky. Its gleaming radiance created deep black shadows across the pavement.

His peripheral vision registered movement, and he noticed Jillene sitting in her Altima with the driver's window rolled down. She couldn't have been there long; he'd stepped outside only a minute or so after she had.

Vince delayed his answer to Mel as he watched Jillene dig through her purse. In what was apparent irritation, she tossed the handbag on the seat and blew the blond bangs off her brows. Whatever she was looking for, she clearly couldn't find it. With a slap of her fingertips, she flipped down her visor, then started the car.

"I'm not having any trouble," Vince replied, his gaze fastened on Jillene. She didn't see him standing there.

The loud rumble of a clunker without a muffler filled the parking lot. Velma Hicks had started her emissions-failure Ford LTD Country Squire wagon. The top of her wigged head barely cleared the steering wheel. Stars and moonbeams hung off her rearview mirror.

"I had to ask, Vince. If it's personal, I'll stay out of it. You know that. But if it's something about the book or your career, it's my job to advise you." Mel's voice went from quietly emphatic to briskly businesslike. "So be available on your phone from now on."

"I will have my cell turned on, Mel. If I can't answer, I'll call you back."

"Good deal. I'll be in touch."

Vince clicked off the phone and shoved it into his pocket.

The chrome hood trim on the Country Squire caught a white ray of light and shot it through the parking lot like a flash of lightning, momentarily blinding Vince. Both Velma's and Jillene's vehicles must have shifted into gear at precisely the same time. Rather than rolling backward, the accelerator on the wagon was gunned and it jolted forward. The Country Squire plowed into the right side of Jillene's Altima with enough force to shove the compact car several feet out of its parking slot.

Red and white plastic headlights and glass littered the ground around the Altima's front bumper. The corner had crumpled like an aluminum can. On impact, the air bag deployed and the horn blared repeatedly before finally dying out.

Sprinting to Jillene's car, Vince latched his hands on to the door frame and leaned forward through the open driver's window. "Are you okay?"

She sat in a daze. Her eyes focused straight ahead and a bruise already welled on her forehead. The black clip she used to pull her hair back had slipped lower, sections of blond hair fell on either side of her center part.

"Jillene!"

"Huh?" She touched the base of her skull and winced. Softly shaking, she asked with a quaver in her voice, "W-what happened?"

"You had a car accident."

"I did?" Fumbling for the door lever, she attempted to get out of the battered car.

"Wait. Don't move. You might have broken something."

"I don't…think so. What is this?" She punched the air bag, trying to move it out of the way. Having moved too sharply, her breath caught and she gritted her teeth. "What happened?"

"You were in a car accident." Vince reached over her, unfastened her seat belt and opened the door from the outside. "All right, let's get you out. Come on, honey, hold on to my arm. That's right. I'm going to help you."

Once she was on her feet, she wobbled. "W-what happened?" she repeated, looking at the damage to her fender. "I couldn't find my sunglasses. Who hit me?"

Vince gazed across the lot. Velma came toward them without any noticeable injuries. The LTD wagon's blue body didn't appear to have any major damage. Just a slight ding on the grill. The glow-in-the-dark window ornaments in the back windows had a green tinge in the stark sunlight.

In the Pacific Northwest, a sunny day was responsible for more accidents than a gray one. People weren't used to clear skies and were unaccustomed to handling them— sunglasses had been lost during nine months of dreary weather, eyes strained to get used to summer and the warm pavement rippled in waves that distorted distances.

Velma's crooked cotton-candy wig covered one eyebrow as she looked over at Jillene. "You came at me from nowhere."

"What? I was just sitting here seeing if I had enough money in my wallet to buy some milk. Or did I already buy the milk?" Looking to Vince, she asked, "Have I been to the market?"

A crowd had gathered in the doorway of Java and the blond kid who'd come in earlier that afternoon ran over to them.

"Jillene! Are you okay?"

"Yeah, I'm…yeah…" She felt the purple-red lump on her forehead. "What happened?"

"She's got a concussion," Vince said, putting his arm around her. "Call for an ambulance."

"Am I hurt?" Jillene asked. "Where?"

Holding her tightly against him, he said, "I think you need to sit down."

"I don't want to sit down. I need to go to the store for nonfat milk. My head hurts. I told the girls not to play with my sunglasses. They weren't where I left them. Who hit me?"

Velma assessed the damage on Jillene's car. "My gracious, these imports aren't very safe."

"Velma, stuff a yarn ball in your mouth," Vince angrily shot back. "You can't drive for shit and you never have been safe on the road. You put the car in drive rather than reverse."

"I did no such thing." She snorted.

"The hell you didn't. This accident was your fault." He couldn't help blaming her, with Jillene sinking weakly against him. A surge of protectiveness fiercely welled inside him, strong and demanding.

Velma defiantly glowered at him, her cheeks pasty

white with dots of rouge. "It was not my fault, Vincenzo. *She* hit *me*."

Jillene pressed a trembling hand to her forehead. "I'm not feeling well."

"The ambulance will be here any minute, honey. They'll take you to the hospital and—"

"Wait!" Jillene suddenly stiffened, her muscles tensing as if they were poured out of a quick, ready-set mix. "What's the date? Is it the eighteenth? Say it is. Right? Am I right? It's got to be the eighteenth."

Vince glanced at the date on his watch dial just to make sure. His own days had been blending one into the other. "It's the nineteenth."

"Oh, shit. Oh, shit. *Oh, shit.*" With a moan, she pried herself free from Vince and wandered in a circle in the handicap space. "Forget the ambulance. I can't go to the hospital. I can't go. I *can't* go." The steady motion of moving clockwise had her lower lip quivering in pain. "Ow. Ow. Ow."

Vince laid an arm over her shoulder and made her stop. "You are going to go to the hospital. You need a doctor to look you over."

"Nooooo."

A siren sounded in the distance, the screech growing louder as it turned into the parking lot with its small crowd of onlookers from Java and the neighboring businesses. Pop came dashing across the street in his white barber's coat and was informed by one of Java's customers as to what had happened.

Velma kept declaring her innocence, and Pop took her off to the side to calm her down.

"No ambulance!" Jillene shouted. "Send it back. I'm not getting in. I *can't* get in. How many times do I have to tell you?"

The large white truck with its flashing red lights and beefy tires rolled up to the scene. The loud and smelly diesel motor vibrated while an EMT grabbed a clipboard from the dash.

Jillene took one look at the paramedic and said, "Turn around and go back. I don't have any medical insurance."

"We're a county hospital, ma'am, so you can work that out with them and the taxpayers," the medic said. "We don't deny anyone care."

With her brown eyes glazed from shock, Jillene glared at Velma. "Call the cops. I want her blood tested for pot! She smokes weed. She knows Larry Flynt. Call Woody Harrelson."

One of the EMTs wheeled a transport stretcher toward Jillene. Its white sheet and pillow were bleached and sterile looking. The black-and-silver straps buckled across the narrow mattress were locked in the restraining position. Another paramedic moved into action, attempting to subdue Jillene.

After a lot of convincing, they were able to coax her onto the transport bed. Vince stayed by her side. An IV line was started, and she latched on to his hand.

Her eyes were dark with emotion. "Where have you been, Vince? I missed you..."

He gently squeezed her fingers, rubbing his thumb soothingly over hers. "I'm here."

A sickness of heart and mind held Vince. Seeing Jillene on that gurney left him with a sense of helpless anguish. He could do nothing but be there and tell her she'd be all right, even though his heartfelt assurances sounded like hollow words.

"My girls...they'll be home from school soon. They'll wonder where I am—"

"I'll handle it," Vince said. "Don't worry about anything."

"I have to worry. I can't pay for this." With a gut-wrenching tenderness hard for him to identify, he caressed her hair and sifted the thick strands of it with his fingers. He carefully slid the hair claw from her hair so the hard comb wouldn't hurt her head.

As they were getting ready to roll her into the ambulance, she sleepily muttered, "What happened?"

"Mrs. McDermott, you've had a car accident," the EMT explained as he maneuvered her into the vehicle. "I'll be transporting you to Olympic View where the doctors can check you out."

The collapsible stretcher rails hit the floor of the ambulance and folded up. Vince kept a hold on her hand as long as he could, his fingers slipping from hers only after he could no longer lean toward her without getting in the ambulance too.

"I'll get your daughters for you, Jillene. I promise."

"Thanks..." she mumbled. Then her eyes fluttered closed and she lost consciousness.

Eighteen

The kitchen was a place Vince visited out of necessity—and not very often. He knew the basics, but cooking didn't particularly interest him. He could grill a steak and scramble eggs, toast English muffins and fry bacon. Breakfast for dinner worked for him—simple guy stuff Pop had taught him when he'd balk at time-consuming pasta dishes. He probably should have at least learned spaghetti, because fixing dinner for two girls was out of his recipe range.

The food in Jillene's refrigerator didn't help much. She had some milk and juice, a single egg, vanilla yogurt, lettuce and lots of condiments, a tub of margarine and apples. Lunch meat that looked promising was shot down on closer inspection. It had expired two days ago. Brown leftovers packed in a plastic container didn't inspire him to look inside.

He closed the refrigerator door and restlessly patted his thigh.

In the living room, Claire and Faye sat beside one another on the sofa. A *Seinfeld* rerun consumed the television screen, the volume up moderately loud. But the girls didn't stare at Jerry and Elaine. They stared at him. Waiting for him to do something.

Just like he'd promised Jillene, Vince had gone directly to her house and waited for her daughters to come home from school. The girls had stepped off the school bus, curious to discover him sitting on the front porch. As he'd had to do numerous times while a member of the police department, he chose his words carefully. He informed them that their mother had been in an automobile accident and had been taken to the hospital. Both girls immediately started crying. Through trembling sobs, they had asked to go see her.

Claire had a house key and she'd let them inside, where they tossed their backpacks down and gave the dog a moment to pee in the yard. Seeing their heart-shaped faces wet from crying tore through Vince's textbook reserve. Usually in those situations, he had been able to neutralize his feelings, but the McDermott girls had done a number on him. He'd floundered in a kind of despair he'd never experienced before. His control had been threatened.

After they had locked the house, they climbed into his Rover. Sniffling and shuddering, the girls sat in the back seat holding hands.

He understood the terror they felt.

They'd already lost one parent. The black fear of losing the other was petrifying. He'd had that same heart-pounding thought when growing up. What if something happened to Pop? Who would he live with? One of the relatives? He'd have to move and go to a new school. Or maybe it would be worse—maybe nobody would want him and he'd go to an orphanage.

At Olympic View hospital, they had gone to the emergency room desk and were told that Mrs. McDermott had been admitted overnight for observation. From there, they'd taken the elevator to the fifth floor and found her room.

Their attempts to compose themselves for their mother's sake hadn't lasted long. When the girls saw her, they broke down. Jillene still had an IV line, but the lump on her forehead didn't appear as swollen. It had gone down enough to reveal the small reddish abrasions on her skin. Dark circles beneath her eyes indicated she was taking in more than saline through the IV. The girls sat on either side of the bed and held her hands. The three hugged.

Vince had become invisible.

He felt completely useless, so he stepped into the hallway and sat in a chair to wait. *Wheel of Fortune* was on the television, but his concentration on the game was nil. Some time later, Faye peeked out the doorway curtain and called for him.

He went inside to see Jillene. She slurred her words slightly and was forgetful, yet relaxed and not in pain. She had a concussion. He'd asked her if there was anyone he could call for her. Her mother or her father. She'd told him no. Both lived out of state and there was no sense in upsetting them since there was nothing they could do. She had requested he try to get hold of Hannah Marshall, the girl who worked for her. But nobody had answered at the number when he called. Jillene mumbled something about forgetting that Hannah was out for the evening.

Jillene had given him an alternative number for a babysitter, but the woman had been unreachable. Two more calls and no luck. That left nobody to stay with the girls.

Except him.

He'd volunteered. Through half-closed eyes, Jillene had looked at him with amused wonder. He hadn't thought it was the medication that had made her give him a weak smile—at his expense. He knew a bachelor wasn't a prime baby-sitter candidate, but he wasn't a total stranger and he was dependable. The girls knew him, and he'd reassured her that he could handle things overnight. With a tired sigh, she'd told him to make sure they did their homework.

Now that the three of them were back at the house, reality set in. He was in charge of two children. The thought of such a responsibility after so many years of only being responsible for himself made him nervous.

"So." Self-conscious, Vince ran his fingertips beneath his chin, feeling his end-of-the-day beard. "You guys like *Seinfeld?*"

"Not really," Faye said. "We don't have cable."

Claire added, "We had to cancel it."

Obviously not having cable wasn't a good thing. "That's too bad."

"It stinks," Faye grumbled. "I want to call my mom again."

They'd already called the hospital once since arriving home. "She's all right." Vince spread his hands over the countertop. "I'm pretty sure she's sleeping for the night. The doctor gave her some, uh—night-night medicine. Remember how the nurse told you she was doing really well? She's coming home tomorrow."

"Are we going to have cereal for dinner?" Claire asked.

Faye rose from the couch. "I got dibs on the Rice Krispies."

For two kids who'd begged to have Taco Juan's, their knuckling under to Kellogg's surprised him. "Does anybody like Pisano's Pizza?"

Faye stopped midstride.

"Pizza?" Claire's fair complexion brightened. "I love Pisano's."

"Me, too." Faye appeared to be holding her breath, hopeful.

He grabbed the Yellow Pages. "So what do you like on yours?"

Claire hesitantly asked, "We can have it?"

"Yeah," he reiterated, thinking he'd already said that they could.

The girls shared excited, wide-eyed smiles.

"I like pepperoni and olives," Claire indicated.

Faye protested. "I like mine plain cheese."

"You always want plain cheese." Claire silently pleaded with her to change her mind.

"You always want pepperoni and olives."

"You could pick them off."

Vince didn't see any reason why they had to settle for something they didn't like. "I'll order one of each."

Incredulous, Claire said, "We can *each* get our own? Thanks!"

"Gee, thanks!" Faye went back to the sofa. "You sure are nice!"

Vince had no idea two separate pizzas could turn the three of them into best buddies. He got the idea that the pizza delivery boy didn't drive up this way much—if ever.

The state of Jillene's finances was apparent. A fridge that wasn't very full, and there was her distraught wail about having no medical coverage. There was no doubt she was having money problems. Hadn't her husband secured life insurance?

Her struggling to make ends meet was very apparent. He steeled his heart against emotions for which he had no outlet. What was he supposed to do? Give her money? He abandoned the thought. Maybe he was wrong. Her coffee bar seemed to be doing okay. But what was that she'd said about him being good for her business? Did she need help?

His thoughts were interrupted by the rapid click of TV

stations as Claire changed the channels. As they waited for the pizza to arrive, he took a seat in one of the wing chairs.

Every so often, he felt furtive glances land on him. He kept his eyes on the tube, but the canned sitcom laughter didn't keep his attention. In an unfamiliar setting, his senses were active. He watched the two girls laying on their stomachs on the carpet with chins propped in hands, heard the sound of a television program he had never watched, felt the furry weight of a yellow dog leaning against his knee, waiting for an ear scratch, smelled tuity-fruity shampoo, schoolyard chalk and mint construction paper paste.

Being in the house right now was different. Jillene wasn't here. He was in little girls' territory. *Unequipped* didn't begin to describe the way he felt. He caught himself drumming his fingers on the arm of the chair, then he gazed out the window for signs of the pizza man's head-lights.

Finally, he had to get up and move around. He couldn't stay sitting. He walked to the back porch to get some air. Within a few minutes, Sugar barked when the doorbell rang.

Answering the door, Vince was surprised to find Jerry Peck holding two Pisano boxes.

"Vinnie?" Jerry said, halting on the porch when he'd been ready to come in. "What are you doing here?"

Faye sat up. "He's baby-sitting us."

Jerry let himself inside and chuckled under his breath. "No shit?"

Vince held back from commenting.

Jerry didn't have his uniform on. He wore a Hawaiian shirt that strained at the middle. His comb-over had been slicked in place. Teva sandals and blue socks covered his feet. He was Vince's age, but Jerry looked older.

"I ran into the pizza guy in the driveway," he explained, heading for the kitchen. "Hey, girls." The aroma of oregano, tomato sauce and pepperoni from steaming cardboard boxes trailed behind him. Vince caught a whiff of basil and ignored the smell.

"Hi, Jerry," Claire said, going after him. "Our mom's in the hospital."

"Yeah, I heard about that." There wasn't a single note of false concern in his tone. In fact, he spoke with a butter-soft tenderness that Vince hadn't thought Peck capable of. "But don't worry. She'll be okay."

Faye poured a glass of milk. "She's coming home tomorrow but she's making us go to school. We have to wait all day to see her."

Jerry set the pizzas on the counter. The girls lifted the lids to check and see which was which. They licked their lips at the sight of grease swimming over mozzarella.

"Mmm." Faye picked up a slice.

Jerry motioned Vince to the other room where they could talk. "I heard what happened to Jillene. I was off duty today but Officer Nelson gave me a copy of the report. You're on the witness list." His eyes were direct and alert. He came across as a seasoned veteran, and determined. "So what in the hell is Velma's problem? This broad's big honkin' Ford has hit more people in town than Barry Bonds has hit home runs."

Vince clamped his jaw. "I saw the collision. It wasn't all Velma's fault." Nobody was more irked over that fact than Vince. "The accident was partially Jillene's fault. She pulled out without looking. The sun impaired her."

Jerry's stare drilled into him, his eyes hardened.

"Aren't you going to have some pizza?" Claire asked Vince, her voice carrying from the kitchen.

"In a minute."

Jerry grunted his disgust. "Aw, man. This bites. They'll both be given citations."

"That's procedure."

"So," Jerry said, gazing at the girls and then at him. "You're camping out here for the night?"

"Looks like it."

Dimples appeared in Jerry's round cheeks. "Never thought I'd see the day, Vinnie. You hanging out with kids."

Somewhat irritated, he replied, "I'm okay with kids."

He'd never had any trouble being around kids—he just wasn't around them very much. When he'd been living with Sheila, she'd talked about having a baby. But between his travel schedule and the fact that they weren't married, he'd been against it. He wasn't even clear on how he felt about it now. He was forty-two, not a young guy in his twenties. Whenever he thought about being sixty when his son or daughter graduated high school, the mental picture just didn't seem to gel.

Vince reflected on the years he and Jerry had grown up together. He had never figured they would grow apart. Jerry was always Jerry. A dopey kind of guy who made him laugh. He was a pain in the butt at times. He got carried away with the firecracker shit.

But the summers on Blue Heron wouldn't have been the same without him: Jerry in combat with their G.I. Joes, and riding Stingrays down to the marina to go fishing. With a fond smile, he remembered the time they'd rewired the doorbell in Jerry's house to sound like a fart whenever the button was pressed. Mrs. Peck never did figure out that the chime had been replaced by a Pull My Finger Fred winder.

There was no one thing to pinpoint why they'd gone their separate ways with chips on their shoulders. Or maybe there was and Vince didn't want to face it. It was easier to be a smart-ass with Jerry, and to have Jerry be a smart-ass in return.

"How's Jan?" Vince asked, inquiring after Jerry's wife.

"She's real good." Jerry folded his arms over his barrel-like chest. "You should see my son, Timmy. He's going to be a big guy like his dad. He's going out for the department when he graduates."

Vince nodded. "That's something."

"Well, I gotta go. I just wanted to check on the girls and make sure they were doing all right."

Jerry's hand froze on the doorknob when Vince said, "Jillene told me you swing by to see how she's doing."

Slowly lowering his arm, Jerry shrugged. "It's no big deal."

The Jerry standing before him wasn't the beer-drinking jokester who'd blown out his dad's inboard while chasing an imaginary marlin. Nor the lug who looked at panty ads.

Jerry Peck was being a man.

"It is a big deal, Jerry. And I'm sure she appreciates it."

"Yeah, well…" He self-consciously hitched the waistband of his Dockers so his pants were at flood length. "Okay, so I'll be seeing you, then."

"See you, Jerry."

Jerry paused before stepping off the porch. "Sorry I called you Vincenzo at your dad's shop. I was ticked about the squad car."

After closing the door, Vince tossed a slice of pizza onto a plate and sat at the table. But he didn't eat it. It dawned on him that Jerry had paid for the pizza.

The mood in the kitchen had definitely eased, but gone were the talkative girls from Taco Juan's. When dinner was over, they thanked him for the treat and sat on the sofa once more.

"Do you guys have any chores?" he asked, trying to remember the stuff Pop used to ask him.

"Faye fed Sugar when you were talking to Jerry."

After Vince stacked the dishes in the sink, he leaned against the breakfast counter. "How about homework?"

"I don't have any," Faye supplied.

"Me, either," Claire said.

"You're not yanking my chain?"

Claire put a pillow in her lap and leaned her elbows on its plush center. "What does that mean?"

Christ. "It means—like…not being truthful with me."

"We're being truthful."

There was a long, thick silence.

He looked at the clock. "What time do you girls go to bed?"

"Ten—"

"—Nine."

"So what is it?" he asked. "Nine or ten?"

"Nine," Faye said, to Claire's displeasure.

Vince checked the time. They had two hours. What was he supposed to do with them? They were basically old enough to take care of themselves. He was here just to be an adult in the house. They didn't really need him.

The dog came over and sat on her haunches. She looked at him through large brown eyes.

"Do you want to see Sugar do some tricks?" Faye asked.

"Sure."

Faye went to the cupboard and got a large box of dog biscuits. He watched as the dog performed: Sit. Stay. Speak. Spin. Down. Rollover. Beg.

Vince was impressed. "Who taught her to do all that?"

"Me and my sister," Faye said.

Claire added, "And our dad."

There were definitely things Vince wondered about David McDermott, but he withheld his inquiries. Jillene and her girls seemed to be coping.

The death of a husband or wife was very sad. Raising children added to an already devastating situation. His dad had done an excellent job, but Vince could look back and see how hard it had been for him. There were days when Pop broke down in the shower. No amount of running water could disguise the heartbreak of a grown man crying.

In Vince's experience, there was an unexplained guilt the child of a surviving parent had to bear. Sometimes he thought he was responsible for his mom getting cancer. It made no sense. He'd simply felt guilty during different periods of his childhood. When he began third grade, he hadn't wanted anyone to know he didn't have a mom. So he'd told his teacher that his mother was on assignment for *National Geographic* photographing elephants.

When his dad sat him down and asked him to explain himself he couldn't, because he didn't understand why he'd made up the elephant story. Years later, he realized he had lied because he didn't want to be different from the other kids.

"I know—we can bake some cookies."

Claire's suggestion landed in Vince's stomach like a lump of raw dough. He wasn't anxious to start a big production where something could go wrong. So far, there hadn't been any cuts or scrapes or burns. Nothing that could be construed by Jillene as him being incompetent or negligent as a supervisor. He wanted to keep it that way. "We shouldn't get all that mess out."

Pouting, Faye offered a dispute. "It's not a mess."

In an effort to deter them, he said, "I don't think you have all the stuff."

"For oatmeal cookies we do."

They apparently had him.

The kitchen counter became organized with baking ingredients. He was assigned the box of brown sugar. The granular block inside could have served as a paperweight.

"I think it's stale," he offered, tapping the bottom against the bowl Faye had shoved at him.

"You have to stick it in the microwave for eight, no ten seconds to get it soft again," Claire instructed.

He did as he was told, the hum of the micro blending with the sound of the mixer beaters.

"We need a half cup." Claire passed him a metal measuring cup.

He filled it and was promptly told he'd goofed up. He had to smash the sugar in hard. She took it and dumped it into the mixing bowl.

"I want to crack the egg," Faye said, holding on to the delicate oval.

"No." Her sister held out her hand. "I'd better."

"I can do it," she insisted, pulling her arm away. She knocked the egg against the bowl's edge and, rather than the shell cracking in half, it exploded in her fingers. Tiny white fragments fell into the sugar and margarine. The shell pieces were rapidly mixed in and became indiscernible.

"Faye!" Claire said sourly.

"I didn't mean to."

"That's okay." He tried to keep the peace. "I like my cookies crunchy."

Faye washed her hand. "Do you ever bake cookies with your family?"

"I live alone."

"How come?"

"Because I'm not married."

Claire stopped the mixer to dump in flour. "Why not?"

He should have known that question would follow. "I haven't met a woman who wants to marry me."

"How many have you asked?"

His skin flushed with heat. "None."

"Then, how can you get married if you don't ask?"

"I guess that's why I'm not married."

"Where's the raisins?" Claire stared into the pantry.

"I don't like raisins in my oatmeal cookies," Faye protested.

"But they won't turn out right without the raisins." Claire found the bag and the raisins went into the mixer.

In the end, the dough didn't turn out right anyway. When they baked, the cookies fanned out on the sheet and ran together. He didn't know what the problem was; nor did Claire who swore she'd measured all the ingredients properly.

Sugar the dog was the benefactor of their mistake, eating several of them. Even though the cookies looked funny, the girls put them on a plate with cling wrap on top. They created get-well cards for their mother and arranged them next to the plate.

The girls got ready for bed, and Vince was once again wondering what he was supposed to do. Should he read them a bedtime story?

He needn't have wondered.

They came down wearing T-shirts that hung to their

knees and told him to make sure he woke them up at six-thirty. Claire needed time to heat the curling iron, put on makeup and pick out her clothes. He got the distinct impression she was never satisfied with the first, or second, outfit she tried on. Faye had to apply eyeshadow and decide between two pairs of shoes.

As they clued him in on their routine, he thought they didn't seem like they were only ten and twelve years old.

It was true—boys matured more slowly.

While they seemed to have everything under control, just before lights-out, they made a blushing request for him to check their closets and beneath their beds. He obliged, finding nothing menacing on the floor amid the toys, bunched-up socks, pencils, gum wrappers, an earring, pennies and a dog's rawhide. And to Claire's bright red mortification, a forgotten bra under her desk.

Tucked beneath the covers, the two girls bade him quiet good-nights.

As he walked down the hallway illuminated by a night-light, he glimpsed the photo collages hanging on the walls. He saw birthdays, first steps, mountain vacations, parties and other windows into the McDermott family. Locked in those frames were memories of yesterday.

From an emotional place he didn't recognize, defined by shadows and the intangible, he felt as if he were missing out on something. Where were his yesterdays that mattered?

Life was short. Opportunities were fleeting. Chances rare. Judgment was questionable.

He'd second guessed his choices. The paths he'd taken. The career that was eating him alive right now. He wondered how things would have turned out if he'd been a machinist at Boeing. Or a software developer at Microsoft. None of those things had interested him, but he couldn't help the what-ifs.

After letting Sugar out for the last time, Vince made a bed on the sofa. Claire had given him a pillow and fleece blanket.

When he looked down at the polka-dot pillowcase, he noticed a Tootsie Pop with a note rested on it. In the muted light, he made out the message:

Sorry the cookies were no good. You can have my sucker. Faye

Lifting his chin, he expected to see her standing at the stairs.

Nobody was there.

Taking off his shoes, he laid down and tossed the blanket over himself. The dog jumped up on the couch and made herself at home. She crowded him, nudging his feet to wedge herself in. He undid the candy wrapper and sucked on the lollipop.

As he enjoyed the cherry flavor, he savored the feeling of being exhausted to the point where he felt he could fall asleep with no effort.

He pulled the blanket higher. The wool smelled like Jillene.

In the black stillness, it was his last waking thought as he drifted to sleep with the Tootsie Pop between his lips.

Nineteen

From the hospital, Jillene called the house at six-thirty, and Faye answered the phone.

"He slept with a sucker in his mouth."

"He what?"

"I woke up to go to the bathroom and I peeked at him on the couch. He was sleeping with the lollipop I gave him. You told me never to eat a sucker when I was in bed because I might fall asleep and choke on it."

"That's true."

"He didn't choke, though. He just came in and told us it was time to get up. Five minutes earlier than you do."

The glow of fluorescent lights at the nurse's station slipped into Jillene's room through the open crack in her door. "What did you do last night?"

"He ordered us pizza and we baked cookies."

"You did?" She couldn't envision Vince with a pot holder in his hand.

"Yep." A muffled noise erupted. A juggling of the phone in Faye's hand. "Claire wants to talk to you."

"Hi, Mom," Claire said. "How are you feeling?"

"Better."

"We had pizza last night."

"I heard."

"Can't we please stay home and wait for you?"

"No. You have to go to school. I don't want you to

miss a day." She tucked the thin blanket up to her chin, thinking it smelled like industrial laundry soap and not the brand she used at home. "Put Vince on."

There was a shuffling and then Claire called, "My mom wants to talk to you." To Jillene she said, "He's getting it downstairs. Bye, Mom. Love you."

"Love you, too. Tell Faye I love her."

The line clicked and Vince's voice filled her ear. "Hello?"

It seemed strange to hear him on the telephone in her house at this hour of the morning. Strange...yet decidedly reassuring. She'd slept a lot better than she had thought she would. She remembered neither the accident nor much about how she had gotten here.

"Hi," Jillene said into the receiver. "How did it go?"

"Good."

"You baked cookies."

"I participated in the measuring. Claire was in charge of the oven and timer."

"She likes to bake." Jillene's hand was cold from the IV line and she wished she was home snuggled into her own bed. With her girls and Sugar. And... "So there were no problems? The girls minded you all right?"

"They were fine. Really good." Vince's voice sounded husky and sleepy, as if he hadn't slept well on her sofa.

"Good."

"What time did you want me to come pick you up?"

Momentarily thrown, she replied, "I was going to call Hannah."

"I'll get you."

"You don't have to. You've done enough already."

He ignored her. "What time, Jillene?"

She guessed. "About ten."

"I'll see you then."

She lowered the receiver onto the cradle and closed her eyes. A painful awareness set in, knowing that she was without family in Blue Heron to count on in a crisis. If Vince hadn't made himself available, who would have been there for her last night? And this morning?

There had been times in the past two years when Jillene had thought about moving to California to be near her mother. But she wasn't keen on putting the girls in the L.A. Unified School District, or living in all that traffic and smog. Jillene loved it here, and Claire and Faye had only known Washington as their home. They had friends here. They were happy. This was where their father was buried.

She bit her lower lip to keep it from trembling. She had been strong for so long. For her girls. For herself. She had tried so hard after David died. She was doing her best, but her best was being tested—she just wasn't sure how to fight back. She'd been on her way to making Java turn around, and now this happened.

And Vince happened.

Her feelings for him were moving too quickly. She wasn't ready. That's why she substituted so many things in her life for intimacy—so she wouldn't miss it, or want it. In doing so, she had lost a part of herself.

All of a sudden, her world was spinning backward on its axis. Each revolution took her away from her past. She was beginning to forget how it had felt when another's mouth claimed hers. How another said her name in a morning voice.

She was borderline ready to declare defeat. Searing tears gathered in her eyes.

Just as panic was about to set in she bolted upright with a gasp. Breathless and burdened by confusion and self-reproach, she swiped the hair from her eyes.

No! She was strong.

I am woman. Hear me roar.

On that note, she pressed the call button for a chocolate pudding.

Misfortune was recorded on Jillene's book of fate. Signed, sealed and delivered: hospital billing, ambulance charge, auto insurance deductible, traffic citation and towing cost. No woman's debt should have to rise so high.

Thank God despair was free.

Quietly crying in pitiful misery, she curled into a ball on her side and yanked the blanket over her head. The pile of magazines on the bed slid to the floor in a slippery flow of paper. No wonder Olympic View hospital charged a hundred and sixteen bucks for drugs—they had subscriptions to every magazine in circulation. Being able to read the entire issue of *People* without having to flip through the pictures in the grocery checkout wasn't worth nine hundred dollars.

Nine hundred dollars.

She had never thought an overnight stay in the hospital could cost this much. She knew the bill would be expensive, but the Admiral Suite at the island's Outlook Inn was only $249 a night. And it came with a free Continental breakfast, HBO and a view of the water—not a four-story parking structure.

She made an arrangement with the hospital to pay twenty-five dollars a month toward her bill; her checkbook would feel the pinch as if she were paying two hundred and fifty a month.

Breathing fast, Jillene felt on the verge of hyperventilating.

If only she hadn't run out of milk, she wouldn't be lying here.

The accident played out in her head, and as much as she wanted to blame Velma Hicks for the whole thing, Jillene knew she was partially responsible. She'd had too much coffee. She'd been jittery. The sun had hindered her. She'd been blinded by it and she hadn't been able to find her sunglasses. One big disaster.

The changes in her life that she'd been feeling optimistic about yesterday didn't strike her the same way today. She was back where she'd started. At the bottom. Actually—in a deep hole. The hardware store didn't sell a shovel big enough for her to dig out. She might as well just let the walls cave in and declare...declare...

She gulped and tears trembled on her eyelids.

...declare bankruptcy.

Bitterness filled her mouth and her clamped lips imprisoned a sob. The shock of defeat held her immobile. Her anguish peaked to shatter the last shreds of her dignity. With jerky motions, she tugged the blanket off her head and kicked her legs to disentangle herself.

Numb, she sat up and stared at the sterile medical supplies on the counter. Then she yielded to the compulsive sobs that she'd been trying so hard to hold back.

Right in the middle of her good old-fashioned cry, Vince knocked on the door frame.

"Do you want me to get the doctor?" he asked.

Looking up, she caught sight of him through blurred eyes. His height, the jeans and T-shirt. She didn't know what it was about him that made her cry even harder. Maybe that he looked so handsome and confident, while she sat in her rumpled Java uniform with a coffee stain on her blouse. "Nooo," she said through a stuffy nose. "I don't want a doctor. I've met my quota of white-coated robbers and I'm tapped out."

She blew her nose and wondered if she'd be charged

234 Stef Ann Holm

for the box of tissues if she used them up. But the tears continued to come. The fragile crack in the dam had broken and nothing could hold them back.

Vince stepped inside the room and stopped at the foot of the bed. "Are you sure?"

"Yes, I'm sure," she snapped. "There's nothing wrong with me except that I'm a…loser." Then she uttered the unthinkable. "Just like my cousin Steve."

Vince reasoned, "Everybody has a loser cousin."

"Not as bad as Steve Frenchik. He schemes how to screw loan institutions instead of paying his bills. His sailboat takes up his front lawn and the rudder is secured to the porch by a steel cable and The Club." She bowed her head and murmured. "When he parks his car on the street, he keeps a nasty-looking monitor lizard on the front seat as a watchdog. Did you know repossessions are illegal with a person or live animal in the vehicle?"

"I have heard that, yes."

"At night," Jillene muttered, "he calls the locked garage for his silver Honda Prelude 'The Bat Cave.' The car has smoke-tinted windows and a license-plate frame that says *My Other Penis Is a Porsche*." Biting her lip to control a choking cry, she said, "I once bought a license-plate frame that said *I Have PMS and a Handgun*, but I never had the guts to put it on my car. Now I don't even have a car to put it on."

The floodgates had burst wide open and her feeble effort couldn't pull them back in place. She was doomed. "My life is in the toilet and I can't even afford to buy the good two-ply paper. You might as well call my money situation one big flush." She sucked in a shallow gasp of air and vented, "I sold that fabulous Chihuly for nothing. Here I thought I was doing the right thing and I am no better off. I'm worse. I'm—"

"I think I should get somebody for you," Vince said, his low voice and awkward.

"—not finished," she said, changing her train of thought. "I need a plan but I don't have a plan. All this business crap I read in *ROAR* is just another dead end. But if you look at Connie—" She petulantly snagged her lower lip with her teeth. Jillene might have been in the middle of a defeatist tirade, but she was no dummy. Connie Duluth didn't need any help looking perfect in the competent department. "No, don't look at Connie."

Vince's brow quirked.

She rubbed a tickle on the underside of her nose. "I don't know what to do."

Pulling a tissue from the box, Vince extended it to her.

"No!" she squeaked. "I can't afford that."

"A tissue?"

"Never mind. I know what I'm going to do."

"That was quick."

"I'm going to write for tickets to *The Price Is Right*. On this morning's show, a lady from Trenton, New Jersey, won twelve grand playing PLINKO."

"And this is your plan?"

"Do you have a better one?"

"I think you need to get out of here now," he suggested, grabbing her apron from the chrome chair. "The smell of latex gloves has got you acting loopy."

"They haven't signed me out yet. I have a good mind to stay and never leave, just to irritate them."

"I saw the doctor at the nurse's station. He said you were okay to go."

"Of course they'd say that."

The strap of her khaki work apron dangled in his hand. "Are you feeling worse and think you should stay?"

"No. Let's go." She slid off the bed. "Give me my apron. It's not your style."

On that, she walked out the door. Right after taking the tissue box with her. It wasn't even Kleenex. Some sandpaper brand.

Once they were in Vince's Range Rover, she shuddered in spite of her best efforts to regain her composure. Whenever she thought she was okay, she pathetically started crying again. A growing mound of used tissues filled her lap.

Drizzle misted the windshield. Every so often, the wiper slid across the glass. She kept her gaze averted from Vince. She didn't want him looking at her. Vanity aside, she could accept being "comfortable" in front of a man— no makeup or anything. But she knew she needed those eyedrops that could get the red out.

"Stop at the Mini Mart," she said in desperation. "I want to buy a lottery ticket. Can you spare me a dollar for a scratch ticket? I'll pay you back when we get to my house. I think I can scrounge up a few quarters in the floor heater vents."

Vince made no comment, and she was about to ask if he had heard her—when they neared Java.

Traveling on Seaward, she had been looking out the opposite window, but she shifted her attention when she saw the parking lot at her coffee bar. Not only were most of the slots taken, two by the UPS and FedEx trucks, but also Sergeant Jerry Peck's canine unit and another Blue Heron Beach squad car were angled right in front. All illegally parked.

"Oh my God," she breathed. "What's going on? Have I been robbed? That's it! Isn't it? Oh my God! Java's been vandalized. Oh, this is great. Wonderful. Oh God. Pull over. I can't believe this. No, wait. Don't pull over. I can't bear it. Take me home.''

He continued driving and she couldn't help turning her head to see all the cars. All the people probably gawking...it didn't really make sense that all those people would be there for a police report.

"I was waiting until you were done, uh 'letting it all out' before I told you.'' Vince's strong voice pulled her attention to his profile.

"Tell me what?'' Even to herself she sounded meek, as if she'd thrown in the towel.

"Early this morning, a movie star stopped by Java for coffee.''

Her mouth dropped open. Her heartbeat was a titanic *thud* in her ears.

"He caused quite a stir.'' Vince went on, turning up the road that led to her house. "Customers have been over at your place talking about it ever since.''

Elation made her hot and sweaty. Jillene put her hand over her heart, the box of tissues falling to her feet. "Al Pacino!'' she predicted.

Vince pulled into her drive and cut the engine.

"I've seen *Scent of a Woman* a hundred times.'' Pure joy erupted in her while she remembered his films. "He was wonderful in *Donnie Brasco*. I cried at the end. And *The Insider*. Oh! Fantastic. And *Any Given Sunday*—I don't even like football but I loved the movie.''

The passenger door opened, Vince having come around to let her out. "Actually, it wasn't Al Pacino.''

As she slid her bottom off the Rover's tall leather seat, she felt as if she'd fallen down five feet instead of two to hit the ground. "It wasn't?'' She thought about who'd be so great that they'd bring in a deluge of customers. "Bruce Willis?''

"No."

"Arnold Schwarzenegger?"

"Nope."

"Sylvester Stallone?" She went through the owner list of the defunct Plant Hollywood on Seattle's Sixth Street. Sly had to be the one who'd come over to the island for some R & R and a mocha.

"Not the one." Vince unlocked the front door.

She followed him inside. Sugar's tail wagged a mile a minute when she saw her mistress.

"Then, who?" Jillene asked, waiting in anticipation.

Vince set her keys on the breakfast nook. "Ernest Borgnine."

She made a face, scrunched her eyes, then her jaw went slack. "Who?"

"Ernest Borgnine."

"Ernest Borgnine?" No offense to the star, but she couldn't help saying his name without inflecting a sour note. The actor had been quite good in his time, but why would there be a stir over an aging man with winged eyebrows and a gap between his front teeth? "I could see Al Pacino getting two cop cars to park on the side-walk…but Ernest Borgnine?"

"Hey," Vince defended, as if he were a longtime fan, *"The Dirty Dozen* is a great flick. I wish I'd been over there myself. When I leave here, I'm going to swing by."

"What for?" She noticed a plate of cookies and two handmade cards on her kitchen table. "He's gone."

"But I hear he drew something on one of your napkins and there's a debate brewing about what it is. Sol even started a betting pool."

"Huh?" She shuddered at her own lackluster grunt.

"Money's on either the ocean liner from the *Poseidon Adventure* or the PT73 from *McHale's Navy*."

Jillene laid her hand on the hard swell of her bruise, trying to ignore the slow and steady pounding in her head. This all sounded crazy. ''I'd better go and check out the napkin.''

''You're staying here. Hannah and Rob have things covered.''

Since when was he on a first-name basis with her help? ''That's good to know, but I still have to go down there.''

''No, you don't. You just got out of the hospital.''

A spear of pain shot between her eyes at the innocent reminder. She let out a sigh. ''Maybe you're right. I'm tired and I need—''

Vince's large hand took her chin and tilted her face upward. The mere touch of his fingers sent a cascade of shivers across her skin. His mouth lowered over hers. Her eyes drifted shut as he gave her a tender kiss. Its warmth and gentleness caused her fragile emotions to whirl and skid to a screeching halt.

When he lifted his mouth, she felt dizzy.

Her lashes fluttered and she gazed at him.

''What you need is a fresh perspective. Tomorrow, after you've had a quiet evening at home with your family, you'll be able to put faith back into yourself.''

There was no mistaking that his optimism and hope for a brighter tomorrow was based on the energy of her character and the strength of her children. He would never know how badly she wanted to bury her face in the front of his shirt and tell him how much the words meant to her.

A straggler tear crept slowly down her cheek. He caught it with his thumb. She almost lost it again.

''Your girls will be coming home from school soon. They made you get-well cards.''

She nodded, not fully trusting her voice. She had to

pull herself together. It was not good to stand here with her heart wide open. With great effort she dragged in a deep and fortifying breath. ''I've got everything under control now.''

He went to the front door.

Pausing before he stepped outside, he said, ''Is that why you're wearing a Kleenex box on your foot?''

Twenty

High up in the tree house, Claire and Faye snacked on Cheez-Its. Every now and then, they tossed down an orange cracker to Sugar, who waited patiently for them to fall.

"What do you want to do?" Claire asked.

"I don't know." Faye dug her hand into the box, searching for crackers that had the most salt. She didn't like them when they were burnt without salt. "What do you want to do?"

Claire sighed and hugged her knees to her chest. She wore her favorite jeans but her tennis shoes were embarrassing. The leather used to be white, but they were gray now with the beginning of a hole at the toe. Mom had tried to whiten them with sponge-on polish. That didn't work out. Now it looked like she had the school nurse's orthopedic shoes.

Claire hated not having money to spend.

"Give me some," she said, reaching for the box. "I don't know why we have school tomorrow. It's only a half day." She'd already received her report card for the final semester. Only one C. In P.E. The rest of her marks had been B's. Faye, of course, had earned straight A's. *Again.* Mom thought it was easy to make that happen. It wasn't. Not when there were cute boys around.

"I know," Faye replied. "It's stupid to go to school on the last day. We don't do anything."

"Yeah. Pretty stupid." Claire dropped a cracker over the edge and saw Sugar nose around in the grass to find it.

Faye brushed crumbs onto her dry legs. Her shorts cut off at midthigh and she gazed at the baby-fine brown hair that had grown more visible since last summer. She decided she was going to shave her legs just like Claire and Mom.

Claire twisted a length of her hair. "If you could pick any car for us to have, what kind would you pick?"

"A Volkswagen Beetle like my Barbie car."

"Come on. Pick something good."

"I was."

"I'd pick a Mercedes or a BMW Roadster." Claire was awfully tired of having to ride her bike everyplace to run errands. When they had to buy groceries, if Hannah couldn't take their mom, all three of them had to get on their bikes with baskets to hold the bags. The last time, Tony Starkovich had been in front of the Seaview and she'd turned her head the other way so he wouldn't recognize her.

Why couldn't her mom just get a new car? Or get theirs fixed?

Or drive Dad's? It was in the garage.

Maybe her mom could ask Vince for a loan to buy a car. Claire liked Vince. He wasn't sappy. When he'd spent the night, he hadn't tried to make her and Faye laugh when they didn't feel like it. He wasn't strange. He was normal. And he didn't try too hard to impress them. He talked to them like they weren't dumb kids.

"Do you like Vince?" Claire asked.

Rubbing two Cheez-Its together, Faye made crumbs. "Do you?"

"Yeah."

"Me, too." Claire examined her hair to see if it was getting any blonder. "You know when we put the ad in the newspaper?"

"Yeah."

"We were a couple of goofs to do it."

Faye turned her head. "How come?"

"Because we didn't think it out. A lot of losers called the house."

"Chopper."

"No, that was Moe."

"Oh, yeah. We sure had tons of phone calls."

Claire had been thinking about this a lot. The weirdos that had called were desperate. Once, she'd answered the phone and the man had thought she was her mom and had said something nasty to her. Their mom would never meet another true love through the telephone. She'd end up with her heart broken.

Faye's stomach hurt deep in the bottom, as if she'd swallowed a Jolly Rancher, whenever she thought about how upset her mom had been when she found out about the ad.

"How can we make it up to her?" she asked.

Claire sat straighter, not paying attention to the outline of her boobs in her bra like she usually did. Sometimes a bra just wasn't important. "Set her up with Vince."

"Oh!" Faye loved the idea. "How should we get them together?"

"We'll figure something out. We've barely got a week before we go to Grandma's, so we'll have to think fast."

Twenty-One

With a book deadline that seemed far away, Vince thrust all his energies into an overhaul of the Chris-Craft. He took the *Gracie* out of the water and put her in the shop at Eugene's Boat Works. Eugene let him use his mechanic's tools and sleep on the office cot. After pulling the engine, it took Vince two days to install the new one. While he had everything torn apart, he added a new set of plugs and a water pump, and had the hull cleaned and revarnished.

Pop thought he'd gotten a little too obsessed about it, but Vince had to immerse himself in an activity to keep his thoughts safe. Overhauling a boat engine was just the thing to occupy him. He worked almost around the clock, mainly because he didn't have time to be undertaking such a project in the first place.

When he felt like this in Los Angeles, he climbed into his Rover and just drove and drove to disconnect from all the stuff cluttering his thoughts. He knew the road to Palm Springs by heart, and could have driven with a blindfold over his eyes.

He had no problem secluding himself at Eugene's morning, noon and night. His profession required that he spend a lot of time working alone. So he was used to being isolated.

The circle of friends he had were fellow genre writers.

Everything they talked about had to do with the business. Discussions of what was happening with what publisher, which author was working on which case, and speculative conversations on what the outcome would be if a trial was wrapping up. His life revolved around publishing, investigations and conclusions.

But last week when he'd brought Jillene home from the hospital, being with her had changed him. Catching and wiping away that one tear falling down her cheek had been a mistake.

In that instant with Jillene, something more came alive inside him. He could understand that looking at her aroused him physically. But how had it happened that touching her face like that had fanned a tender flame in his soul that he had thought Lentz snuffed out?

Vince could deal with seductive encounters and spontaneity in the short-term. Kissing her in Java was different from the understated kiss in her living room. Those few seconds without careful thought or consequence had been a mistake. The feelings that had welled inside him were tenderness, leaving him susceptible to his own tormented emotions. If he gave way to them, he would dissolve.

Contending with his own problems, he wasn't in a position for her to count on him—because he couldn't be counted on. The Moe thing had had an easy solution. Being a baby-sitter for the night—he'd handled that all right. But those were one-time-only situations. He kept telling himself that what he'd done was simple and basic. But they were turning into a big deal to him. He was drawn to wanting to do things for Jillene.

Maybe because he'd seen so much of the bad side of life, goodness became more conspicuous when he found it. Jillene's house was comfortable and inviting—her daughters, the innocence of baking cookies, even the dog leaning against his leg. He wanted to grab hold of it, but he couldn't.

So he had to try to drive her out of his head.

Rebuilding a 400hp Chrysler engine had been a start. And at present, Connie Ronco—formerly Duluth—wearing a bikini had been a decent enough follow-up.

About two hours ago, Connie came down to the marina carrying a lunch hamper and wearing stylish mules on her feet. Her bathing suit was probably dry-clean-only with its intricate beading and gold threads. A see-through wrap was tied around her waist and not very modest. The small pieces of fabric covering her breasts and hips were accentuated by her hip-swinging walk. He had a pair of eyes and was looking, to her delight. She had an appealing figure and firm skin with perfectly manicured pink polish on her fingernails and toenails.

She brought beers and a bottle of gin with tonic, a tin of caviar, a box of butter crackers and some coconut-smelling suntan oil that she handed over to him. He performed her "Rub some on me, hon" request, but hadn't felt his groin stir in response when his hand ran over her exposed skin, even when she subtly scooted her behind next to his crotch.

He'd taken the *Gracie* out for several test runs, but Connie had opted to stay on dry ground. She told him she didn't want to get her hair wet with marine spray. She had to be at an open house at one o'clock.

While he made some final adjustments to the engine, she sat on a dockside chaise with a cocktail in her hand, her gaze burning into him. He hadn't paid her the attention she was seeking, but was more interested in the engine hatch and the tools spread out in front of him.

Crouched on the boat's deck, he rose and went to the

cooler to grab a chilled beer. He twisted the cap and swallowed a long and quenching pull.

Wiping his mouth with the back of his hand, he slanted a smile her way that was filled with mixed admiration. "Connie, so how is it you've got your shit so together?"

"Ambition, Vince. And the love of money. You should know, you have enough of it to do whatever you want."

"I could live without it."

"No, you couldn't." Connie bent her legs. Her skin glistened with the sheen of oil and without a single blemish in her perfect Bronze Bed UV tan. "We're alike. We could do really well together."

Taking another ice-cold drink, he made no immediate comment. She knew the answer without him having to respond.

Connie grew candid, exposing a vulnerable side of herself he had rarely seen. "I'm offering myself to you on a beach blanket, Vince, but you're not interested."

"Got a lot on my mind."

"I'll take your mind off your troubles."

"Connie—"

"I don't give up easy. I'm not a quitter, but I don't have a chance with you and I don't think it has anything to do with me." She gave him a million-dollar smile and held her arms wide open as if to say, *Check me out, honey.* "There's nothing wrong with this body. I could have anyone in town."

He gave her a wink. "Go for it, baby."

The teasing tone in her voice faltered. "Gawd, but you're good-looking when you do that." She sighed. "Hell, you haven't lived in Hollywood too long have you? Is that why?"

"Sorry, Connie." Vince half smiled in return. "But my sexual preferences haven't changed since high school."

The side of the boat was level with the rubber dock bumpers, and Vince hopped out of the fifty-foot Catalina and stood beside Connie. His tall shadow fell over her as she tilted her head back to look up.

"It's almost one, darlin'. You have to go."

"I could cancel my open house."

"I'm not worth it." He held out his hand to her and pulled her to her feet. "You'll find some guy who drives a Jaguar and has more money than he can burn. That's who you want, Connie. Not me."

She gave him a wistful shake of her head. "I think you're wrong, Vince." She brushed her lips against his. "Very wrong."

For four days, Jillene had resisted the urge to walk down the trail down to the marina, but on Sunday afternoon she gave in to temptation. What she saw when she got there slowed the blood flowing in her veins.

Connie and Vince stood on the dock kissing.

Even though Connie wore a sheer sarong over the bottom of her bathing suit, the bikini was so skimpy a panty liner would have given her more coverage.

Jillene was halfway to turning around and heading home, when Vince and Connie saw her. If she left now, she'd look like a coward. She had little choice but to proceed with a friendly expression and a lightness to her steps that she did not feel at all.

By the time she arrived at the boat slip, Connie had packed up a chair and basket and was leaving.

"The mocha was good with raspberry syrup, Jillene, but I'll stick with my lattes," she said as she went past. "Great sales concept. See you around, Vince."

Unable to trust her voice, Jillene remained quiet. Her gaze fell to the captain's helm on the boat. She took in the empty beer bottles and the cocktail glass with its lipstick imprint on the rim.

So this is what he had been doing for four days. No wonder she hadn't seen him. How stupid of her to worry she hadn't thanked him properly for all he'd done for her and the girls. When he had brought her home from the hospital, she'd been a mess. In the days that followed, he didn't appear in Java and she realized he probably thought she was a lunatic to stay clear of. But her assumption about why Vince had stayed away was obviously wrong.

Finally gathering her words, she stiffly said, "I just came down here to say thanks for everything. I'm sorry I was so emotional when you picked me up from the hospital."

That night of her crying jag she had had a lot to think over. The way she saw it, she had two choices. Either make it on her own or go back to the kind of life she had—a woman in the dark without the spunk to stand up for herself.

Jillene McDermott wasn't going to retreat because of a major financial setback. Thanks, in part, to a napkin with a drawing on it.

"Business is really turning around for me," she mentioned, trying hard to sound enthusiastic though her mind kept replaying his kiss with Connie.

In truth, small strategy pieces were falling into place for her even though her debt had gone up from that hospital bill. The plan she'd put into effect for her life and for her business was slowly working out. All her ideas were starting to improve her revenues. So much so that she'd had to do some major debit and credit ledger shuffling after her accident and hire another employee for two to three hours a day during their peak rush time. A seventeen-year-old girl named Gabby whose name suited her well—she could gab with any customer and make him or her feel right at home—was now on the payroll as well.

But it was that celebrity napkin that had really made sales take off. Everyone in Blue Heron had been over to Java to see the Ernest Borgnine doodle of the ship. Even Al Tremonti had put money into the betting pool, and she knew that he had never really warmed up to the fact that her building blocked his view of the marina.

While there would never be a way to determine what the drawing actually was—the PT73 or the *Poseidon*—its presence in her coffee café had turned Java the Hut into a cult hangout. She'd had the napkin framed in a shadowbox and had hung it on the wall. Those who'd been in Java the day the actor had stopped by, loved to retell the story. Island locals and vacationers were filling her tables each day.

Vince stepped onto the boat. He wiped his hands on a rag, the metal of his watch flashing. The sleeves of his small geometric-print shirt had been rolled to his elbows and he wore navy shorts.

She could see he'd been working on the boat engine.

He bent down to put the hatch cover back in the boat's floor and gazed over his shoulder at her. "My dad said you were doing well."

With bad grace, she replied, "You could have dropped by to see for yourself."

His focus was on a set of tools. "I've been busy."

Once more, her eyes moved in the direction of the discarded beer bottles and that lipstick-marked glass. "I can see that."

She grimaced over her caustic remark. She hated that she was burning with jealousy over his affair with Connie. Seeing them kiss had cut her to the quick but she'd be damned if she'd reveal just how deeply.

He gathered the wrenches and put them in a metal tool chest. Then he rose and looked directly at her. She stood, unmoving and guarding her emotions, as he freely took in the details of her face.

"You look good, Jillene."

She held back from replying in turn, gritting her teeth to keep from opening her mouth. She wouldn't let his gentled voice destroy the mettle she had fought to regain. She kept her composure as cool as spring rain.

Since the accident, the bump on her forehead had disappeared. What pale yellowish traces of the bruise were left could be hidden by a light application of foundation.

A slight wind ruffled Vince's hair. "I've seen you riding your bike with the girls."

She hadn't thought he'd seen her at all.

"It's good exercise." Her current method of transportation wasn't great, but that was all she had available.

"What's the word on your car?"

The Altima. A subject she couldn't concentrate on without remembering the time his body had been next to hers with his kiss burning an imprint on her lips.

"Five hundred dollars from my insurance company had to go to Velma's insurance. Velma's insurance gave mine five hundred dollars on our collision claim. The two checks canceled one another." Now all she had to do was pay the deductible to the auto shop and she could get her car. The front axle had been knocked off-kilter from the impact and needed to be replaced entirely. That was the easy part. Getting the five hundred dollars was not. She didn't have it. So there was no point in glossing over details. He'd seen her at her worst and heard her admission that she wasn't rolling in revenues. "It'll be a while before everything's in order on my part."

Shifting his weight, he rested his foot on a deck cleat. "Why don't you drive the car in your garage?"

Her gaze jumped to his and shock made the tendons on her neck tighten. How did he know about the car? Maybe he'd seen it in the garage. Maybe the girls had told him. It really didn't matter. Because she wasn't driving the car.

Not now. Not ever.

"That car is my business," she snapped.

The Karmann Ghia was David's legacy. It wasn't that she thought the vintage Volkswagen was so wonderful she feared damaging it on the road. If only that were why.

For his thirty-fifth birthday, her husband had bought the sports car. Seven thousand dollars had been an enormous bankroll for them during a time when signs of their financial instability were coming to light. David had driven to Shoreline *promising* only to look. But he'd come home with a broken promise and had traded her old but reliable car into the bargain.

She got his Altima. He got his show car. He spent forever buying new parts, revamping the motor, restoring the interior and having the exterior professionally painted with the original color.

A 1963 Karmann Ghia wasn't exactly the kind of car you just advertised in the newspaper and then received numerous calls for. A convertible wasn't a hot-selling item in a city that averaged eighty clear-sky days a year. She'd never regain close to what David had sunk into it. To her, its worth was next to nothing. The white coupe represented David's selfishness and goaded her resentment.

Instantly, guilt flared. Jillene didn't want to feel resentful toward her husband. But whenever she saw that stupid car in her garage she got angry. She didn't like that reaction.

Her biting remark to Vince came from disappointment in herself because she couldn't face the facts. The hard truth was—she did have a solution to her transportation problem. For once, she didn't have to struggle to make something progress. She had the means right at her disposal. But she was afraid—with a stark fear so dark and gripping it paralyzed her.

She'd never once sat in that Ghia.

If she did now, the memories of David would come flooding back and maybe prevent her from moving on with her life—and she couldn't bear that. She couldn't.

Not conscious of what she was doing, she narrowed the space between them and boarded the boat. She came close to him but held her hands out to ward him off. She measured the hue of his eyes, trying to read his thoughts. "What are you doing to me? You come into Java and practically slam me against the wall for a kiss that I wasn't expecting. I don't see you for days, and when I do, you're laying one on Connie. Well, I'm not like her. I don't go after men. You...we both—I never prepared for anything like this to happen to me." She was flustered, her hands trembling as she took a step back. "I can't do it."

He came toward her and she panicked, backing into the red captain's bench until she could go no farther. Bending his head to hers, he said in a murmur, "There's nothing between me and Connie."

"Ever?" Her tone raised in pitch, as if the answer mattered.

"Once." The proximity of his towering height and wide shoulders discomfited her. "A long time ago."

"She wants you back and I don't see you resisting." The heat of him saturated her every pore. An irregular sigh passed through her lips. He looked thoroughly handsome even though he needed to shave, and an assessing blue colored his eyes. Her body couldn't help responding to him. A pull tightened through her breasts, centering at her nipples. It was all she could do to say, "Never mind. It's none of my business."

"No, it's not."

Caught between arousal and anger, she was determined she had something to prove. To herself and to Vince.

With deliberate manipulation, she brought her arms around his neck and settled her lips over his. She kissed him, opening her mouth and seeking him with her tongue. His breath hissed with a harsh rasp but he didn't stop her from moving deeply inside. To the contrary, his hands gripped her arms and he pulled her fully next to him.

A spear of fire shot to the core of her body, taking her swiftly from the blatant kiss to a hunger demanding to be quenched. Scorching heat fanned across her skin as she disregarded everything and yielded to the pleasure that consumed reason.

Vince's hands splayed across her back. A low groan flowed from her throat, dissolving against his mouth. She shook, not anticipating the torment of need and the weakness buckling her knees.

In an instant of sheer power, she recovered with a will she hadn't known she possessed. Her mouth burned a final brand on his. It was a kiss she was in control of and would relinquish when she was ready.

Now.

With a gasp that ripped from her chest, she pulled away. Breathless, she swiped the wisps of hair from her eyes. She'd surprised him. This time with sexual power that belonged to her. She'd wreaked havoc on his adrenaline. The beat of his pulse pounded through the vein at the side of his neck.

"See?" Her heart clamored hard and she felt victorious. "I can kiss you and walk away, too."

Then she turned and ran up the boat ramp.

Jillene white-knuckled the steering wheel of David's car. She painfully acknowledged the rustling sound of her breathing.

He was here. She knew it. She felt him, she smelled him in the ocean air that caressed her cheeks. The worn-in shape of the seat fit his body where he'd molded it with time and use. Whether it was imagination or reality, his scent was all around her and invaded her senses.

God, how could she intrude?

The sand-colored vinyl was cold against the back of her bare legs. Her flip-flops weren't very secure on her feet as they rested over the two floor pedals. An afternoon breeze whipped up in the driveway, stirring the light bloodred blossoms on her Elizabeth rhododendrons. She should have changed her shorts for jeans, but she'd left the marina, come home and recklessly made a phone call to Java. Now she regretted being so impulsive.

The idling engine purred, waiting to be engaged.

Saliva thickened in the back of her throat.

David, I'm so sorry I was never interested in this car when you wanted me to be.

A layer of dust coated two round instrument dials in the dash, and she rubbed a clear spot on them with her fingertips. The plastic ivory knobs on the Saphire AM/FM radio remained tuned to the station David had last played. No sound came from the speakers.

Every one of her bones felt brittle and her teeth clenched as she worked up her courage. She could do this. She *would* do this.

Since David had last driven it, the car hadn't been

started. The battery was presumably dead—even she knew that about automobiles, German or not. She'd called Java and asked Rob to come over and give her a jump.

Pacing in the driveway, she'd waited for him. Several times, she almost went inside to call him back to say forget it. But he'd shown up a couple of minutes later.

When he saw the Ghia in the garage, he had been so taken by its classic sportiness she encouraged him to back it out. She stayed with him, walking alongside the car, absorbing every move he made with the floor pedals and the gear shifter.

As soon as she was alone, she sat in the car that was now facing down the street. The steep hill on which she lived grew overwhelmingly daunting and dangerous. The road had no curves, but she couldn't see to the bottom where the parking lot for the marina was located.

She closed her eyes to the insidious temptation to cut the engine and get out.

She'd never driven a stick shift in her life.

David had wanted to show her, but she'd always said no out of wounded pride and aversion to the Karmann Ghia. Having observed Rob maneuvering it into this position, she noticed there seemed to be a massive amount of coordination required. Clutch pedal in and out. Shifter backward and forward.

Only the certainty that if she didn't do this right now, she would never be able to, kept her from quitting.

Opening her eyes, she stared down the road. With her palms moist and her underarms damp in spite of the chill, she placed her hand on the gear stick. Biting her lip, she shoved the rod forward.

The most godawful noise whined from beneath the hood, scaring the daylights out of her.

Oh, shit.

Her heartbeat surged.

She tried again.

Same fingernails-on-a-chalkboard result.

Once more. This time, fiddling with her foot on the far left pedal.

Then, suddenly—she was moving. Slowly.

The weight of the car rolled the wheels forward. The odometer needle jumped up. Higher. Faster. She didn't have to accelerate. Her foot was still pressed into that funny floor pedal. She kept a tight hold on the steering wheel so she wouldn't hop up a curb as she increased speed.

She ended up coasting all the way down the hill.

Once at the bottom of the road, she swerved into the marina's lot with the tires screeching and an odious smell of burning rubber.

From out of nowhere, Vince Tremonti was in her way. He just seemed to appear.

She screamed.

She slammed down hard on the brake, but as soon as she did the car jerked—*really jerked*—to a dead stop. And stalled.

She couldn't hear anything over her heartbeat's thundering roar.

Oh my God.

She'd nearly clipped Vince and knocked his lights out.

Suddenly appearing next to the car, he shouted, "Dammit, Jillene! I told you. I'm not sleeping with Connie."

Twenty-Two

Vince felt as if he'd just narrowly been missed by a wrecking ball. He almost had to look to see if he was still standing on his legs or if they'd been clipped right out from under him.

Jillene sputtered, "I— That's not why…I—"

"What in the hell are you doing?" With an angry jerk, he braced his hands on the opening of the driver's window.

She slouched into the seat. "Driving?"

"That wasn't driving—that was a mission to kill."

"I didn't mean to get so close to you."

"Close? Another inch and I'd be flat out in the handicap spot."

"I didn't mean to!" she repeated.

He studied her a moment as the wind knocked long blond hair at her throat, teasing against the rounded neckline of her charcoal-gray shirt. He rarely saw her with her hair down. The strands danced over her shoulders, making his hands itch to sink into the silky depths. Her eyes were dark and filled with waning fear. He could see how badly she had been shaken.

Since she'd left the boat, his mind had been replaying what had happened and the heated words they'd exchanged. The suggestive scene at the dock with him and Connie couldn't have given a worse impression.

After Connie's departure, Jillene had shown an assertive side of herself that took no prisoners. *Damn*. Her assault on his mouth with a dominating kiss had gotten him so hard—he'd never experienced such a raw sexual ache. Lust sank bone-deep into his body. When she'd pulled away, a harsh groan had torn at the inside of his chest. He'd broken out in a sweat so hot, he'd had to inhale through his teeth to keep from uttering a low roar of frustration.

When she was gone, he seriously considered taking a swim in the icy water to obliterate the memory of her tongue scorching through his mouth, and the potency of wanting to hike her legs over his hips so he could drive himself deeply inside her.

Instead, he had turned his Range Rover upside down searching for a stray smoke. To hell with quitting. Emerging without even a butt, he had been on his way to buy a pack of cigarettes—when Jillene came out of nowhere in the car.

He didn't think running him down in a classic Karmann Ghia was her style. Then again, devouring his mouth with cruel intentions hadn't been, either.

"I'm sorry I almost hit you." Jillene emphasized her regret, sitting taller now as if she'd recovered from the incident. "A, uh…a squirrel jumped out in front of me and I had to swerve so I wouldn't hit it."

"Next time flatten the squirrel," he suggested with just as much mocking reproach as cautionary advice. "There are a hell of a lot more of them than there are of me."

"That's right." She swung her head and gave him a withering glare. "There is only one Vince Tremonti and so many women."

The ambivalent observation caused him to lean into the car and gaze directly into her unblinking eyes. "You've

got an underlying fire in you, honey, that makes me hot.''
His fingertips swept over the fullness of her mouth with
unsettling intent. He didn't miss the quick flicker of her
lashes. "And every time you show me more of it, I'm
this much closer to—''

Vince cut himself short and swore beneath his breath.
His biceps strained as he held tight to both the window
frame and his self-control, even though his resolve was
crumbling beneath him like the foundation of a house that
couldn't take another gust in a storm.

Backing away, he lifted his hands and held up his palms
in a way that would keep him from capturing her face in
his hands and grinding his mouth onto hers. "Goodbye,
Jillene."

After fragmented seconds, she said, "See ya."

"Okay, see ya."

"Bye." She dismissed him but didn't drive off.

He wasn't moving. "Go on, then."

She didn't do anything but bite her lower lip until she
stemmed the blood flow and paled the flesh.

A thought occurred to him. "Start the car."

Anxious and deliberate, she reached for the key dangling in the left corner of a flat metal dash. She turned it,
and panel lights flashed but the engine didn't catch. She
tried again with the same result.

Because she didn't have the clutch in.

"You don't know how to drive a stick," he accused.

Splotches of humiliation tinged her cheeks. "No."

"Then, getting up that hill is going to be tough."

Vince wondered why she hadn't just told him she
couldn't drive the car. The Karmann Ghia apparently had
some significance in her life. Either that or she had never
been interested in learning a stick. He couldn't guess, and
right now he didn't want to figure it out.

As he ran his hand across the back of his head, his skull prickled under the abrasion of his fingertips. He should walk before he changed his mind. The best thing he could do was dial roadside assistance so they could help her out of this predicament.

She didn't need him.

Dammit, but she looked so small and utterly defenseless sitting in the convertible with the breeze catching her hair. He wanted to shrug off an uncomfortable thought.

Maybe he needed *her.*

Wordlessly, he opened the passenger door and sat beside Jillene. She didn't shout at him to get out, neither did she look at him. She gazed at her hands resting on her lap.

The sound of his voice broke the dead silence. "We'll practice in the parking lot and a few side streets, then we'll get the car home."

"You don't have to do this."

"Put your left foot on the clutch and press down," he instructed, disregarding the option she gave him. "Then turn the key." He made sure the stick was in neutral. "Okay. You're all set."

"Vince..."

"Start the car, Jillene."

She stared out the windshield, then did as he said.

Once she kept the clutch in when she turned over the ignition, Jillene could get the car started. She just couldn't keep it in gear to drive. Irritation over her blunders marked her brow each time she popped the clutch when she tried to accelerate. He made her go through the motions until she got it right.

He had her turn left and right, stop and accelerate in the marina parking lot. When she was getting fairly confident, he showed her how to put the gears in reverse.

That took almost as long as it had to show her first through third. Once she managed that, he told her to go onto Seaward Street and around the block behind his dad's barbershop. Handling traffic wasn't too bad for her as long as she didn't have to brake for a red light. She stalled out at Seaward and Fifth. He saw her panic but, with determination, she restarted the car and got it going again.

A few minutes later, motioning for her to pull back into the marina, he gave her some pointers on driving up a steep hill. Since her street wasn't heavily used, he told her to take it slow and not to leave first gear.

Keeping watch on the hillside road with her, he said, "If you have to suddenly brake—whatever you do—*do not* take your foot off the brake pedal until I tell you to, unless you want to roll out of control backward and hit somebody."

They exchanged glances over his unintentional reminder.

She made it to the top of the hill, and turned into her driveway. She carefully drove the car into the garage. The German engine hummed in the confined enclosure.

"Leave the stick engaged in first gear," he said, motioning to the position on the shifter. "Some people leave it in neutral, but that's a bad idea if you're parked on a hill and forget to put yourself in first when you turn over the ignition. It's better to be in gear and get into the habit of it all the time."

The trembling in Jillene's knees had quit on Seaward, but a spasm visibly twitched her thigh muscle as she eased her foot from the clutch for the final time. She turned off the ignition. "I did it."

"Yeah. You did good."

She pushed herself from the interior and checked the

space in front of the car to make sure she'd pulled in far enough to close the garage door without hitting the car's rear fender.

She let out a sigh, and he could see the relief washing over her face.

She stood at the workbench that smelled like years of varnish and glue. The mustiness coming from wooden shelves filled the space along with the tin smell of paint cans and a metallic odor of nails in open jars.

The garage was disorganized, and he wondered if that was how her husband had left things. Or if Jillene had intruded and neglected to put things away. He saw her bicycle leaning against a stack of boxes marked "Christmas," but her daughters' bikes were missing and that implied they were riding them.

Jillene combed her hair loosely with her fingers, undoing some of the tangles. "Vince...I...I'm sorry about everything. Almost hitting you with the car and the—" She stopped midsentence.

"Boat?" he finished.

Silently, she nodded.

"Jillene," he murmured, drawing closer. "There really is nothing between me and Connie. The kiss you saw— it was her idea, not mine." He stood directly in front of Jillene, smelling the clean freshness of her skin and spindrift in her hair.

He filled his gaze with every detail of her face. The liquid brown of her eyes, her nose and smooth complexion, the quiver that caught on her mouth and the longing in her expression. He shouldn't have, but he couldn't help cradling her face in his hands.

Her lips parted and her breath came to him in a sweet puff. He wanted to lose himself in all that she silently offered.

"Are we still mad at each other?" The tentative pull of her smile and the gentle whisper of her voice clung to his heart.

"No." He willed himself to ignore the tension coiling in his belly.

"I don't know what came over me. You make me crazy. I want to forget about everything except you. The way you touch me and look at me. You have me missing...sex." She uttered the word so quietly that he shuddered, knowing how difficult that must have been for her to say.

It was only because of an ironclad control that he allowed himself to press a light kiss to her forehead, rather than on her mouth. But no amount of effort could keep him from burying his face in the soft curtain of her hair.

"Jillene." He breathed hotly next to her ear. "You'll hate yourself more than you'll hate me. It's easy to fall into bed. You don't just want sex. You want a man who—"

"How do you know what I want—" her voice was thin, delicate like a fragile thread "—when I don't?"

The sound of girlish laughter coming up the driveway signaled the arrival of her daughters.

Vince's shoulders heaved as he stepped away from their mother more reluctantly than he could have imagined. When the girls pulled into the garage and saw them together, their faces brightened to match the red apples of color on their cheeks from having pedaled up the hill.

"Hi, Vince!" Claire called, hopping off her bike and engaging the kickstand.

Faye was fast on her sister's heels. "Hi, Vince!"

"Hey, girls. How are you?"

"Good!" they said in unison, trading conspiring smiles.

"Stay for dinner," Claire said. "We're having hot cats."

Vince repeated, "Hot cats?"

"We can't say 'hot dogs' around Sugar," Faye confided, looking to see if the dog was nearby. "It hurts her feelings. We don't eat dogs in our house. Only cats."

That made sense—not really.

"So what do you say?" Claire's face eagerly awaited his answer.

"No, girls. I have to be going."

"Oh," Faye groaned. "Are you sure? We have brownies." Along with the enticement of gooey chocolate squares, a broad smile lit her face, showing nearly every one of her teeth.

"Sounds good, but I can't."

"Mom," Claire said, almost desperately. "You ask him to stay. I'm sure he will if you ask."

All eyes were on Jillene. A surprising shyness passed across her face. "You're more than welcome to stay for dinner."

His heart rate increased, but oddly his heart only ached for scant seconds. Because he reminded himself of the book he was supposed to be writing. From that turmoil, his answer came, black and affirming. "I can't."

As he walked back down the trail, he forced himself not to look back.

Twenty-Three

Al went to his barbershop very early on Monday, two hours before Sol and Mu would open their businesses for the day. While Al liked the two men just fine, he couldn't be distracted by gossiping conversations about what had gone on in Blue Heron Beach over the weekend. He needed the shop all to himself because he had to make sure everything was set up exactly right.

This morning was special. He'd invited Ianella to come over for a private tour of the barbershop. The foremost thought in his mind was making the best impression. Presenting himself as a businessman who was maturely sound and successful. He was a man who could offer her financial stability and security.

Getting right to work, he gave the barber's chair a complete spit and polish. Every last inch of chrome gleamed like the trim on his car. Then he applied lanolin conditioner to the seat leather.

He organized his workstation and lined up the Markham bottles with the labels facing forward like a line of soldiers. When he had the request, usually from a mainlander, he used Glacier Blue styling lotion. He aligned the bottle directly next to the shampoos. His Oster clipper and accompanying eight blades rested on the charger base by the Sanek dispenser for neck strips. Each one of his professional scissors were flawlessly maintained and sharpened.

After he swept the last piece of hair from the floor, he arranged all his magazines. *Sea and Marina, Time, The Outdoor Life* and *Newsweek* made a precision fan of glossy front covers. Lastly, he inserted the CD of ''The Marriage of Figaro'' into his stereo. An operatic overture and a soprano voice drifted from the corner speakers in the ceiling.

He stood inside the front door and pressed his back into the long handle so he could have the most panoramic view. He closed his eyes for a few seconds, and when he opened them he examined the area as if he were seeing it for the first time.

The room was perfect. Not one thing out of place.

Satisfaction caused him to smile, but that smile was soon knocked off his face when he heard the rap of knuckles against the glass behind him. Not a good damn time for Mu and Sol to stop by for a social visit before store hours. He'd have to get rid of them.

Turning with anxiousness, he paused.

Claire and Faye McDermott stood on the sidewalk and waved at him to let them inside. He glanced at his wristwatch. He had fifteen minutes to spare before Ianella was due to arrive.

He flipped the lock and opened the door. The girls came in and made their greetings.

''Hi, Uncle Al.''

''Hiya, Uncle Al.''

He thought he'd cut to the chase by reaching for his wallet. ''Girls, did you need some ice cream money?''

''Heck, no,'' Claire replied.

''We wouldn't be that rude to ask you for it.'' Faye

shook her head. "Besides, the ice-cream parlor doesn't open until ten."

Stuffing his wallet back into his rear trouser pocket he settled his hands on his hips. "What can I do for you?"

Claire nonchalantly said, "We just wanted to say hi."

"Yeah, we saw you in here and thought we'd say good morning."

"Good morning." Al consulted his watch once more. "If that's all, girls, I've got some tidying to do around here."

"Don't let us stop you." Claire sighed a little too forcefully.

Faye examined the shop with an admiring gaze. "If my bedroom was as clean as this, I'd know where I lost all my homework."

"Don't you girls have any school papers to do right now?"

They both laughed and Claire said, "School's out for the summer. Our last day was Friday."

"Then, you ladies need to go enjoy your first day of freedom. Why not head over to the marina and go dock fishing?"

They both grimaced. "Like, with worms and squirmy things?"

"I'm sure Vince could get you set up with a couple of poles. Why not go ask him?" Al again noted the time. *Please don't be early, darling.*

Claire and Faye silently communicated with one another, but Al was too distracted to notice.

Uncle Al was making it easier for Claire to bring up Vince than she and Faye had planned. They could skip right over Plan A and go directly to Plan B. "So-o-o." She drew the word out, thinking it sounded a lot more casual that way. "When your son was little, how did you get him to go somewhere if he didn't want to be there?"

Al rubbed the back of his ear and gave both her and Faye a funny look. "What do you mean?"

Faye blurted, "Like, if you wanted him to go—"

"Anywhere." Claire quickly took over. They couldn't just come out and mention the dinner! "No place special."

Faye glowered at Claire because she was being a big, bossy brat. Who had made her in charge? Faye wanted to go right to the question so they could leave and start to put Plan C into effect.

Talking fast, Al said, "If it was school or the dentist, I made him go. A social visit to a relative's house was a little different."

The latter part interested Claire. "What did you do to make him go to that?"

"It depended on whose house." Al wiped an invisible spot of lint off his white barber's coat.

Claire thought he looked more spiffy today than usual. His hair was combed without a single hair out of place.

"If it was his aunt Rosemary's," he went on, "I reminded him how much he liked her spaghetti."

"Ragu or Prego?" Faye quickly asked.

Al frowned. "Nothing from a jar. Always homemade."

"Oh." She pursed her lips. "What else does Vince like to eat?"

"Now, girls—I've really got to—"

"Doesn't he have a favorite food?"

"Swiss steak with tomatoes.'

"Anything else?"

"Crispy fried chicken."

Faye and Claire shook their heads.

Al grew a mite short. "Cheese enchiladas. Now girls, really—"

"That's the one," Faye exclaimed. "Our mom can make that."

Claire didn't realize they were being scooted to the door until they were there. "Uncle Al, did Vince ever not want to go to his aunt Rosemary's, even for the spaghetti?"

"Lots of times."

"Then what did you do?" Al opened the door, but they didn't step out.

Quickly he explained, "I sat him in the car and told him to be a man about it. But I do remember one time when Rosemary had the gout and she was on crutches. Vinnie didn't put up a fight that time, and I'm guessing it was because he felt sorry for her."

Claire didn't know what the gout was and she didn't care. She had the information they needed. "Bye, Uncle Al!"

"Yeah, bye!" Faye added in a rush as she followed her sister.

Moments later, Ianella appeared and Al had composed himself enough to invite her in and show her around without stepping on her toes.

"Al, you have such a nice shop." Under the intense vanity lights and the reflection of the mirrors, her skin resembled pure alabaster—so soft and pale he longed to caress her cheek. She held on to white gloves and the handle of her pocketbook. Her hourglass figure was molded by a deep-rose knit dress in a simple but classic style.

She gave his antique chair an admiring nod. "I've never been able to see the details by walking past. My goodness, but everything is so organized." With the muffled click of her shoe heels, Ianella wandered around and looked at the countertop with all its barbering appliances.

His heart swelled with pride. "I'm glad you approve."

"Of course. It's wonderful."

He followed her, smelling the incredible fragrance of flowers that always floated through the air in her wake. Today the scent was roses, as if to match the color of her dress. A deep longing filled his soul. How he loved her with everything he had. He hadn't fully realized just how much until that night over dinner at the Lobster King.

They'd been seeing each other for nearly two weeks. One night they went to the movies and another they took a short harbor cruise at dusk, then went out for pizza. Last Thursday after he closed for the evening, he rented a bicycle surrey—with a fringe on top—and they made delightful fools of themselves pedaling the four wheels over the bumpy marina boardwalk. Her company brought him an indescribable joy. He couldn't remember being so happy.

"Where does that lead to?" she asked, motioning to a door.

The louvered door separated his stockroom from the customer area. Aside from a bathroom cubicle, which was private, the space was cramped but orderly. He had shelves for shampoo and other inventory. There was a Formica counter with a working sink, a microwave, and a minifridge below where he kept his sack lunch if he was inclined to bring one and not eat out with Sol or Mu.

"Just a kitchenette and storage," Al replied. "I take my breaks in there."

"May I?"

"It's nothing fancy."

"I want to see everything that's important to you, Al. If that's all right." She gazed at him with those enchanting eyes and lacy eyelashes. How could he ever deny her anything, this woman of his heart?

Moving ahead, he opened the door and stepped inside behind her. In the small space, her presence bloomed; she was an exquisite flower with vibrant petals. Her beauty gave him a thrill that trembled through his blood, and he imagined what it would be like to kiss her angelic mouth.

After an interested examination of the area, she turned with a misstep that accidentally pushed her body against his. The bliss that came into his heart was endless. He had no thought of reinforcing his gentlemanly manners. All he knew was that she felt supple and lush next to his arm. And neither of them was moving.

"Ianella," he breathed, the sharpest pang of desire exploding in him like a thousand stars.

Al slipped his arms around her and brought her close, looking into her face. He watched her, waiting for any sign of protest. But all he saw was the reflection of his eyes in hers. The same emotions and feelings, desires and heartfelt wanting.

How long had it been since he'd held a woman in such a way? It felt so natural to stand together. Close and warm, body to body with the echo of pulses. A trail of fire seared to the pit of his belly and lower.

Unable to resist any longer, he lifted his hand to her hair and luxuriated in the soft texture. Slowly gliding his touch to her nape, he marveled in the lustrous feel of her skin. He stroked the column of her neck with his thumb, then the base of her ear with gentle swirls. He was drowning in her eyes, the pools of rich brown chocolate.

The fullness of her mouth beckoned as he spoke her name in a caress. "Ianella..."

"Al, my sweet darling."

Every sense he possessed was heightened by awareness

of this special woman in his arms. His stomach flip-flopped and passion raced through him with the speed of a freight train. She was so pliant and so feminine and curvaceous. He brought her closer, fitting her against his chest. Their hearts beat as one.

He tilted her head, then lowered his mouth to hers with a kiss. At long last, he experienced the velvet sweetness of her lips. Paradise. Her slender arms came around his neck and she went up on tiptoe, returning the kiss. It was a welcoming marriage of souls and a union of faith and trust. The promise of joy and the receipt of fulfillment.

The taste of her rosy mouth was like sun-kissed dew and infinitely beyond his best daydream.

For Al Tremonti, things didn't get any better than this.

Twenty-Four

Mist kept the overcast sky company. Jillene wished the moisture would drop in a massive downpour instead of hanging around as a gloomy vapor. She didn't usually have problems with the weather; it was something unavoidable and had to be dealt with in Washington State. But as the summer pushed forward and the Fourth of July approached, she could have used some sun.

Perhaps it was her mood that was increasing her feeling of discontentment. Her days were marked by a lack of repose and thoughts of a man who had stolen the rules of conduct she'd set for herself. Reason existed only if she enforced it. And when she was near him, she could never think wisely. It was best that he stayed away.

She'd worked a full day in Java and was tired at four o'clock when Rob came in to take over for the evening. Claire and Faye had visited for a couple of hours in the morning, then had gone home. Alone. This day had been inevitable and she knew she would have to deal with it.

She had debated about whether or not she should let them stay home alone for a short period of time during daylight hours. This was the first summer she had opted to give it a small test. The girls could stay in the house by themselves so long as they kept the doors locked, let the phone machine pick up, didn't answer the doorbell, and called her if they had the slightest problem.

Today had been their test run. She'd called every hour to check on them and see what they were doing. Their reply was the same each time: Playing Barbies and having snacks.

The house was still standing as she walked toward the front porch. The girls seemed to have passed day one without a hitch.

As soon as she'd come through the door with her apron over her shoulder and her feet aching, they charged forward.

"Hello, Mommy-O!" Faye said with a tickled smile.

Claire hopefully asked, "Can you *please* make cheese enchiladas for dinner?"

This was the third day in a row they'd requested that particular meal. She'd begged off before, too tired to go through such an ordeal.

She groaned. "Can't we have macaroni and cheese? You love it."

"I'm sick of mac." Faye held on to her Skipper by its hair and gave the doll a twirl. "We haven't had Mexican food since Taco Juan's, and I'm really in the mood for enchiladas."

Taco Juan's. That seemed so long ago...

"We could help you make them, Mom," Claire offered quite sincerely. "I'll grate the cheese."

"Do we have any cheese or tortillas?" Jillene hoped to get out of it if they didn't have the ingredients. She knew she had the sauce. On her last trip to the Seaview she'd bought a few cans because they'd been on sale.

"Actually, yes we do." Claire opened the refrigerator and took out a plastic-wrapped block of cheddar. "Me and Faye went to the store and bought some when you said we could ride our bikes."

Faye rifled through the crisper drawer and produced a package of corn tortillas. "We got these, too."

Jillene frowned. "Where did you get the money for that?"

"Tips."

"You spent your tip money on groceries?"

Claire said, "Yep."

"Not all of it," Faye clarified. "We got some super magic bubbles, stickers and tropical Starburst."

The candy and novelties sounded more like them.

"So, what do you say, Mommy? Can you?"

Claire was using the childish endearment to plead her case. They were up to something. But Jillene was starved and cheese enchiladas did sound good.

Setting her purse and apron on the counter, she relented. "Okay. Let me change my clothes."

"Yippee!"

Jillene went upstairs and stripped out of her Java uniform. She unhooked her bra, tossing it aside. She slipped a comfy turquoise cable-knit sweater over her head then stepped into white leggings. The fuzzy pink slippers that were her favorite went on her feet. Leaning over the bathroom sink, she washed off her makeup and brushed her hair into a ponytail.

After putting together the cheese enchiladas with the girls' help, she got a second wind. While the enchiladas were baking, in a renewed stream of energy, she ended up doing some housecleaning. Upstairs, her bedsheets came off the bed to be washed at the Laundromat tomorrow. For now, she tossed them on the carpet by her bureau. She went to the linen closet to get a fresh set, but got sidetracked when she saw the unsightly mess in the bathroom. She kicked off her slippers and scrubbed the tub.

As she cleaned, the girls rushed by the doorway with their eyes forward. They had come from the direction of her bedroom. It dawned on her that they were acting a little strangely. She paused with a soapy sponge in her hand. "Did you do something?"

Claire answered. "No."

"Well, you look guilty."

"We're playing a game with our Barbies," Faye said, then bolted down the stairs with Claire.

Jillene finished the bathroom and remembered her sheets. Once she was in the bedroom, she made up the bed, then bent to collect the dirty linens. They were spread in a lumpy mass on the floor and she had to step on them to collect the edges with both hands. When she did, a hidden object thrust into the bottom of her foot, and her ankle pivoted on its joint.

"Oww!" She staggered back, wincing in pain and hopping on one leg. *"Dammit!"*

She knew what she'd nailed before she saw it. From the numbing throb in her instep, she could tell that plastic boobs had jammed into her tender flesh.

How many times had she told the girls not to leave their Barbies on the floor where she could step on them?

With a jerk, she swept away the sheets and discovered there was a minefield of the dolls. A dozen of them. All naked and facing upward with those double-D conical breasts, and hard pointed hands and feet tauntingly positioned for warfare.

"You guys!" Jillene called as she sat on the edge of the bed and massaged her stockinged foot.

They came running and butted up to the door frame.

Claire took a particular interest in the foot resting atop her knee.

"I stepped on one of your Barbies," Jillene wailed with

irritation. "Haven't I warned you about leaving them on the floor? I almost broke my ankle."

"Did you hurt yourself, Mom?" Faye gave her sore foot a cursory exam.

"Yes, I hurt myself. I twisted my ankle and it's agony."

Claire exclaimed, "We'll get the crutches!"

Then they ran off.

"I don't need any crutches," she called after them, but she was talking to the walls.

Claire and Faye streaked like lightning through the living room and, on their way out the front door to the garage, Claire grabbed the cordless phone. Sugar barked and chased them in a blur of energetic fur.

Inside the garage, Faye climbed on the step stool and unhooked the crutches from the peg on the wall. "Got 'em."

"I'm dialing." Claire had memorized Vince's phone number from where he'd written it in her mom's book. She punched in the numbers, then held her breath. He just *had* to answer.

On the third ring, she heard his voice. "Vince Tremonti."

Her heartbeat leaped. "Hi, Vince. This is Claire McDermott."

"Claire?" The concern in his voice came across right away. "Is everything all right?"

Catching her breath, she said, "My mom—she twisted her ankle and she's on crutches. She said it hurts really bad." Claire kept right on talking and didn't give him the chance to say anything. "So tonight we'll serve the cheese enchiladas for dinner to help her feel better. They sure smell *yummy*."

Faye bumped into her shoulder and leaned toward the

receiver to add, "And she's got *agony* and I bet you could cheer her up."

The girls smiled at one another as Claire pressed the off button on the phone. Now all they had to do was wait for him to get here.

Vince didn't expect Jillene to answer the door. When she did, he knew right away he'd swallowed the bait—hook, line and sinker. The girls were nowhere in sight. He stood in his hastily thrown-on leather jacket, feeling like a complete idiot for having gotten here minutes after Claire called him.

Jillene looked great in a pullover sweater that hung loosely on her shoulders. The brilliant bluish-green color was striking with her sunny blond hair. She wore leggings that hugged her thighs and calves. He liked her pink mop-like slippers.

But he liked her mouth more. It was agape with surprise.

He said the first thing that came to his mind. "I heard you were on crutches."

"No."

"Then, you didn't twist your ankle?"

"Yes, but—how did you know?"

"Claire called me."

Jillene folded her arms over her breasts. "Oh. That's just great."

A set of crutches were in plain view, staged against the sofa arm. The delicious aroma of a Mexican dish came from the oven. Holding on to the railing, the girls appeared at the base of the stairs.

"Claire, why did you call Vince?" Jillene demanded. "I'm not on crutches."

"You were rubbing your foot and you said it hurt."

"Yeah, you yelled 'ouch' when you stepped on my Barbie." Faye brought her finger to her mouth and chewed on the nail.

Jillene gave each of them a harsh frown of comprehension, then faced Vince and shifted uncomfortably. "I'm sorry about this. I don't know what got into them. I mean, I know and I will talk to them about it. I feel bad you came over here for nothing."

With sudden efficient speed, the girls bolted for the kitchen and grabbed a stack of plates and some glasses. Claire sprinted in front of Faye as they made a circle around the table and set four places in ten seconds.

"Dinner's ready," Claire announced, using pot holders to take a foil-covered baking pan out of the oven. "Let's eat, everybody. We're having cheese enchiladas—nice and cheesy."

Faye pulled out a chair for him. "Come on, Vince. They're your favorite. Your dad told us." On a gasp, she cupped a hand over her mouth.

Vince shook his head with a wry smile. Damn, he had been so set up. But he wasn't angry at them for their deception. To the contrary. His emotions were affected beyond measure that they thought enough of him to instigate a relationship with their mother. "You girls have been talking to my dad."

"We might have said hello to him." Claire poured a glass of milk and set it by the plate where Faye was standing.

Turning to Vince, Jillene held on to the door's edge. Abashed, she stood stiffly. "You don't have to stay. The last thing I want is for you to feel manipulated. I never—"

"My dad's right. Cheese enchiladas are my favorite."

Vince let himself inside and shrugged out of his jacket. He laid it on the back of the couch and went to the table.

The absolute truth was that he was glad to be here. More than he dared to acknowledge. The simple and unpretentious environment instantly lured him, as did the aromatic smell of a real homemade meal. Tonight he'd planned to eat alone at the Silverwater Diner. He'd spent the entire day working on the boat, then he'd gone fishing late in the afternoon. There was a cove on the opposite side of the island he had fished at when he was younger. Revisiting it, he hadn't caught a thing, but that hadn't been the purpose of his excursion.

He had needed to seclude himself from everything that drew him to Blue Heron Beach. When he left the marina and motored out to sea, he became a solitary man on a vast ocean with its endless swells and whitecaps that rippled toward the horizon.

The steady mist hadn't bothered him as he cast and recast his fishing line. He'd been grateful for the dampness that seeped through his clothes, and the chill that crept into his bones. Elements and wind wore him down. Anything to numb his thoughts and reduce the knot that had formed in his stomach since he'd learned of a killer's planned prophecy. Every time he tried to make sense of the events, he failed to produce words worthy of publication.

Vince sat and Jillene nervously followed suit. She took a place on the other side of the table with the girls in between them. Most of the conversation was taken up with talk of their upcoming trip to California to see their grandmother. He ate, listened and smiled. Every so often, he added his own stories of trips he'd taken with Pop in the past few years.

When the meal was over, Claire scooted her chair back and said, "Come on, Faye. Sugar wants to play Frisbee."

"No, she doesn't," Faye replied, twisting in her seat to observe the dog sitting by Vince's knee. She'd parked herself there at the beginning of the dinner.

"Yes, she does." Claire's reiteration was spoken through tight lips.

"Oh, yeah! That's right. She does."

The girls left the table, grabbing a chewed-up Frisbee and going out the back door with the dog close behind. With their departure, a heavy silence unfolded over the room like a thick blanket.

"This was really good," he said, absently sliding his unused knife over the table space in front of him.

"You don't have to stay." Jillene rose and collected the dirty dishes. "It was very nice of you to go along with everything, but you can leave now. I'll tell them you said goodbye."

He got to his feet, took a handful of dishes himself and met her by the sink. "Do you want me to say goodbye?"

She tilted her head and studied him. Her eyes were a rich, deep color made all the more appealing by a slow sweep of her lashes. If ever there was a time when he wished he could read thoughts, it was now. "I want you to—" on a half sigh, she turned to the window "—do what you want."

Jillene braced her hands on the edge of the counter. Her mind was pulled back to the scene at dinner. The four of them together, sitting at the table. She could barely deal with it. What that moment had represented.

"I want to help you clean up." The sound of Vince's voice came through her thoughts with a deep and sensual quality.

An unconscious smile formed on her mouth as she drew

herself to the present. "You could have gotten out of here without getting your hands wet."

"I'll wash, you dry."

The summer days were getting longer and she hadn't turned on the kitchen light. She should now, as the room had grown darker. The billowy curtains above the sink were closed against the sunset that had suddenly sprung out of the parting clouds. The lighting in the kitchen was waxy, coming only from the light in the stove hood. But there was plenty to see by, and the shadowy atmosphere distorted the melancholy expression that had fit itself over Jillene's features.

The sink was filled with soap, and Vince removed his watch. He set it on the windowsill. She watched in fascination as he rolled up his sleeves and dipped his hands into the bubbly water to wash and rinse the dishes. The house was too old to have ever had a dishwasher, and she had seen no reason to modernize the kitchen that way. It was an inconvenience, but at this moment, she was happy to be without one.

She and Vince worked in a companionable quiet. Not having to make small talk was nice. He stacked the plates and cups while she selected pieces to dry.

The rectangular baking dish went into the cupboard above his left shoulder. "Excuse me," she murmured.

He leaned right, while she reached up to put it away on the lower shelf. As her arms raised, the bottom of her sweater lifted. A draft of air sluiced over the wedge of bare skin as she situated the dish. Then she felt the arresting warmth of sudsy hands as they grasped the circumference of her midriff. Vince's palms spread across her exposed skin, bringing with them shards of pleasure that tingled over her flesh.

Lowering her arms, she let him tuck her next to the

solid wall of his chest. His chest to her back. The curve of his chin settled at the back of her head. Tilting her head, she leaned in to him and strands of her pulled-back hair caught in the short bristle of his beard. He held her close in a snug embrace, his wet hands pressed tightly against her rib cage. She laid her arms over his as warmth began to pool low and deep, a total upheaval in her body. Pulling, taking her—

Not now…not this. Not here. She couldn't…

Then she remembered.

She brought his strong hand up toward the waning light to study the grooves and creases of his palm. He splayed it for her inspection, the beauty of bone and muscle that made fingers lean and powerful.

"You won't find the scar." He spoke next to her ear. "It's in my lifeline crease. Maybe that's what saved me."

He caught her shoulder, turned her to him and lifted her onto the counter. Startled, a streak of wildness made her curl her fingers into his broad shoulders as he ran his hands up her thighs. Higher still to her waist.

Then his mouth was crushing hers with a play of lips and tongue. Kissing her thoroughly, his hands slipped beneath her sweater, and her nipples tightened to heated points as prickles erupted across her skin. She kissed him back, laving her tongue through his mouth as his hands cupped the underside of her breasts.

In a strangled tone, he said, "You're not wearing a bra."

He held her breasts in his large hands, his thumbs striking a hot fire at the tips where they strained toward his touch. She gripped his hips with her thighs, the heavy bulge at his jeans hard against the thin cotton of her leggings.

She clung to him, mindless of everything but the pure

torture his fingertips gave her nipples—pulling and tugging and enticing them to their fullest erections. Her tongue swept through his mouth, licking and nibbling. Clinging to him, she lost all reason.

Without realizing, her hands were inside his shirt. Smooth skin met her touch in a hot sheet of muscle. Feeling the flatness of his abdomen and the rigid slabs of his taut belly she overcame her inhibitions. She worked her fingers across his nipples, dominating them with her own kind of coaxing, rubbing the pads of her thumbs across each one.

She raised her pelvis to feel him against her in the tightest fit. His hands cupped and kneaded her breasts, teasing her nipples between his fingers. The throb within her intensified.

But then she heard the laughter of her children in the yard and sobered so suddenly and completely that she felt dizzy. Pulling her mouth from his, she released her thighs and pushed him an arm's length away. But not without a moment's indecision.

God help her. The woman in her wanted to go on; the mother in her could not. She battled her raging sexual desires, both ashamed and almost sickened by her lack of restraint in her own kitchen.

"I can't." She put her fingertips over her mouth, a mouth bruised from kisses. Shoving herself off the counter she shook her head—a burning embarrassment on her face. Her speech stumbled and was just as unsteady as her legs. "Not with my girls just outside the door. I can't believe I let this happen. They'd never approve of what we were doing."

Vince didn't try to touch her further, but his voice was low and quiet. "They're the ones who threw us together, Jillene."

"Not for this." She buried her face in her hands but with no inclination to cry. "Don't you understand? They don't want a lover for their mother. They want a new dad."

The tick of his wristwatch on the windowsill was the only noise in the room for long, drawn-out seconds.

"I can't be that."

Her chin shot up. "Of course not."

"There will be somebody for you. You're a wonderful—"

"I hate your bullshit, Vince." She surprised even herself with the outburst of indignation. "Why do you do this? I can hardly think when you're around me. You came running up here when you thought I was hurt."

"Yes."

"You care about me."

"Yes."

She raised her tone to a frustrated level. "Why?"

"Because I'm your friend, Jillene."

"Friend? Maybe I don't need a friend." Yanking out her ponytail elastic, she dragged her hands through her hair. "I've got Hannah and Joe. And I know a lot of people in this town."

"But do any of them know you?"

"Of course they do. What does it matter?"

Coming close, he tucked a wisp of hair behind her ear. There was nothing sexual to his ministration. Just a gentleness. And perhaps that bothered her more than if he'd tried to kiss her again. "Do they know you sing to Patsy Cline?"

"Um…" Her breath came harder and harder. "I don't know."

"Do they watch you smooth your hair when you're nervous?"

"I... Maybe."

Everything about him triggered her emotions to dangerous levels, sending them to places they ought not go.

"Do they notice you always wear this necklace?" His fingertip touched the enamel heart pendant on her gold chain.

"Probably," she whispered, shivering under his light touch.

The roughness of his knuckles caught the underside of her chin. He tilted her head and made her look at him. "Do they understand why you go out on your porch at sunset?"

She gulped in air. "No."

"I do. Because I'm like you. I'm searching for the right answers, too. And that's why I came."

There was the barest constriction of her throat muscles before she candidly said, "Every time we're together, I forget. I'm used to one man. My husband. The way he sounded in the morning. But now I hear you. The way he drove with a hand on the steering wheel and an arm draped over the back of my seat. But now I see you beside me. I won't even be able to sit at my table anymore the same way. You don't understand. David and I were a couple for twenty-one years."

"I understand," he responded almost defensively. As if he warred with himself to not add something more.

Jillene moistened her lips with the tip of her tongue in an effort to conceal the quiver on her mouth. "When are you leaving town?"

"If you see me, that means I'm still here, Jillene." As he walked through the living room, he retrieved his jacket and opened the front door. "No promises."

He let himself out, and she wondered if things had ended between them before they had ever begun.

* * *

The hour was late, perhaps nearing midnight. Vince laid on the Chris-Craft bed with pillows propping up his back. The motion of water softly lapped against the hull beneath him. Papers were strewn over the bedspread; piles of catastrophic events and interview recollections from family members. Sleep eluded him. Every night wrapped him in its darkness, and he knew he would live forever with the deaths Samuel Lentz had inflicted on his victims. They were the prey, but he was the pawn.

He had taken a walk an hour ago, but he still didn't feel able to tackle the endless pages and documents any more that night. Playing some Jimi Hendrix on his Fender hadn't helped either.

A pale moon sliced through the open, louvered window blinds to make a zebra pattern of light and dark on the drop-down table. Other than the clang of a buoy, it was eerily quiet in the marina.

Reaching for a paper on the top of the stack, Vince read the lines. What was written came at him like a fiery fist of injustice. He felt the burn of fault and blame testing his fortitude. Why was he surrounding himself with the pages if he hadn't determined to make use of their power? In an angry burst of temper, he knocked the folders off the bed.

He jerked to his feet and went to the refrigerator, leaning his arm on the top of the door to stare at the contents. The fridge was marginally stocked with food, but he wasn't hungry. Habit held him in place; just staring was enough. At length, he grabbed a beer and went on deck.

As if a siren's song beckoned him, his gaze was pulled up the hill. He searched for light and found a hazy cube of it, high on the ridge, through the pitch-black fringe of trees.

Jillene was awake, too.

Vince lifted his wrist to view the time, but the familiar band wasn't there. He'd left his watch at her house.

Turning away, he tried not to think about what it would be like if he'd left himself there, as well.

Twenty-Five

"**Y**ou know my sons, Rocky and Carmine." Ianella reintroduced the two men to Al as they congregated in her living room. He shook both their hands firmly, recalling when they barely came up to his knees. Now they were taller than him by several inches. They were handsome men. Their Italian features were the best of Ianella and Leonardo, but they had their father's hair and eye coloring.

"Nice to see you again," he said. In turn, he met their wives and Ianella's three grandchildren. Two boys, aged eight and twelve—the peewee player and a skateboarder, and a girl who was nine and who had recently started ballet lessons. Ianella's sons lived in the Seattle area, and she saw them and their families frequently.

A couple of days ago, he had brought Ianella onto the *Gracie* to spend the afternoon with Vinnie. Ianella loved to sail, but he was a little awkward at first—the boat having been named after his wife. Respectful that Grace had christened the Chris-Craft when she'd been alive, Ianella told him she was humbled to be included for an afternoon of boating. The day had gone really well and Vinnie had seemed relaxed around Ianella.

Tonight, Ianella had invited her sons to her house for a barbecue. It was a chance for Al to reacquaint himself with her family, and he was more than a little nervous, as she must have been with Vinnie. The evening had been her idea and he really wanted to make a good impression. He'd worn his best Bermuda shorts and an eggshell colored cotton shirt that Vinnie had bought for him years ago.

Throughout Ianella's house, a woman's touch was highly evident and not a trace of Leo remained. The colors were soft and inviting, and the paintings on the walls were soothing landscapes.

After everyone said hello, they mingled until it was time to start the barbecue and bring out the food. He followed Ianella into the kitchen to ask if he could help with anything. He was glad to have a minute alone with her.

"They like you, Al," she said, taking a plate of antipasto from the refrigerator. "Don't worry, sweetheart."

"I do worry, Ianella. I don't want them to think I'm trying to take over for Leo. It's so soon after his death."

She shook her head. "Never you mind about Leo. His sons knew who their father was, and they have to make their own peace with it. Be yourself, Al, and they'll adore you." She smiled tenderly. "Just as much as I do."

The hours passed with merriment and good humor. He fell into an easy dialogue with Carmine about the Seahawks, and he and Rocky shared a fondness for Puccini's operas. The food was great and the conversation pleasant. Her daughters-in-law were wonderful and smart. He liked her grandchildren and he mesmerized them by the only magic trick he knew: the disappearing quarter trick.

Much later, after everyone had left, Al was still smiling as he closed the lid on the backyard barbecue. Ianella was at the picnic table collecting the last few glasses. Lovingly, he caught her by the arms and turned her to him for a surprise kiss.

"This was wonderful, Nella," he murmured next to her mouth. "I love you."

The words were suddenly just there—he hadn't planned, he hadn't prepared. Many times, he'd rehearsed saying "I love you" in his head. He would give her a dozen red roses and take her out for a candlelight dinner; he had wanted it to be special and the mood just right. He knew he would take her hands, look into her eyes, then tell her everything in his heart. The perfume of the citronella candle, the smoky odor of the charcoal briquettes and the dirty dishes on the picnic table didn't suit the romantic declaration, but he'd said the special words all the same—and they came out without any preamble. At long last.

And he meant every word.

"I love you, Ianella," he said once more, this time with purposeful intent. "I've loved you for six years...more than I had the right."

"Al...you mean...even when I was...oh, Al." Kissing him lightly, her lips melted into his. "I love you, too. So much I could cry."

"Nella...Nella. Don't cry. Just love me."

He kissed her cheeks and eyelids. Then her mouth, deeply and passionately with a sealing of undying affection.

In the heavenly cloud of bliss cloaking them, Al could swear he either heard shooting stars flying through his head or somebody was setting off fireworks early.

He chose to believe it was the stars.

"Get the hose!" Jillene laughed as the loud *pop-pop-pop* of a Mad Dog fireworks fountain erupted in the front yard.

Claire unreeled the garden hose, ran through the bushes

and aimed water directly on the fireworks. It didn't stop the noise. She was laughing just as much as Jillene. "It's not working."

"Eeeeekkk!" Jillene took the hose as the ear-piercing screams and whistles of explosive powders deafened the night. "I told the kid at the stand I didn't want any of the loud ones. Just the pretty ones."

Jumping up and down, Faye giggled. "Don't hose it! Let it keep going!"

Jillene's neighbors were going to kill her for causing such a racket. The showers of white sparks fizzled to darkness, but the soggy cardboard cylinder didn't stop popping. She stood directly over it and shot water into it.

While the woods surrounding the homes helped buffer the noise, she shouldn't have set off the fireworks at this hour. But tonight was the girls' last night at home before flying out to her mom's tomorrow, and they were going to miss the Fourth. Staying within the confines of her budget, she'd selectively bought three fireworks. She had point-blank asked for colorful ones, not loud ones. She wanted a pretty show for the girls, not a series of cap-gun blasts.

So much for trusting a sixteen-year-old boy with a pimply grin who had thrown in a box of sparklers at no charge.

In the chaos of the hose, the water and the noise, Sugar streaked crazily through the yard. Snapping at the spray coming from the hose, she got hold of the empty plastic bag from the fireworks and took off with it in her mouth. The girls were laughing and running after her. Cutting the water to the hose, Jillene joined in. If anyone had come out to see what was going on, they would have got an eyeful.

The three of them were in their pajamas.

An hour later, they were back inside and getting ready to play a game of Trouble. They'd set up a slumber party in Jillene's room with popcorn and soda pop. Burning candles flickered from the bureau and sleeping bags were spread across the floor. Earlier, they'd painted their toenails with Pink Party polish and had given themselves facials in the tub.

Claire and Jillene waited for Faye so they could start the game, but she'd disappeared.

"Faye!" Claire shouted. "Hurry up. What are you doing?"

Muffled by the bathroom, Faye's voice carried into the bedroom. "I'm trying on my Disneyland outfit again."

"I hope you're not standing on the side of the tub," Jillene said in a cautionary tone.

The girls had a habit of using the bathroom mirror as a wardrobe check. They didn't have a full-length mirror and, as they got older, they wanted to see how they looked in an outfit from head to toe. So one of them had got the idea of standing on the edge of the tub to look in the bathroom sink mirror. On occasion their feet would slip, especially in socks, and Jillene's heart would stop. There was nothing more frightening than sitting downstairs and hearing a *boom* overhead followed by the shower curtain pole falling down. No flimsy plastic curtain was going to prevent a crash landing.

"Faye, you already tried that outfit on twice. Come on and play Trouble with us," Jillene called.

"In a minute. I'm checking something."

Faye had shaved her legs tonight for the first time, and Jillene supposed she wanted to see once more how her legs looked in the new shorts she'd picked out to wear.

"Faye!" Impatiently, Claire scrambled to her feet and went to see what was taking her sister so long.

Jillene lay on a sleeping bag and propped her chin in her hands. Butterflies flitted through her stomach and they weren't from worries about putting her daughters on a plane tomorrow. While that did always give her concern, the skittering of nerves was caused by something else— something she'd told herself she was going to do.

She couldn't believe what she'd done already to set it in motion. Whenever she thought about it, she wanted to bury her face in a cool pillow to relieve the heat in her cheeks.

Fireworks weren't the only thing she'd bought when she'd gone to a store in the town of Poulsbo. She could have bought the item in Blue Heron Beach, but she couldn't have faced Edith Schlichting at the drug counter and her big-as-a-barrel voice that might as well have announced the purchase over the Thrifty Nickel's P.A. system. Then everyone in Blue Heron Beach would know that Jillene McDermott had bought a box of condoms.

Oh dear…

Tension and nerves collided within her when she thought about them hidden in a Nike shoebox high on her bedroom closet shelf. She had never in her life bought condoms. Standing in a drugstore trying to figure out what kind to get had been awkward. She didn't have the daring to examine one of the boxes to read the fine print. Unaware there were so many varieties and types, she ended up grabbing a brand she'd heard of and piling a few other products on top. Toothpaste, a box of hair color for blond highlights, No. 9 envelopes and Roman prophylactics were bagged without a single comment from the elderly female clerk.

A month ago if anyone had told her that she'd buy such a thing, she would have told them they were nuts. And now she'd done the inconceivable. Because Vince Tremonti was still in town.

He'd come to Java every morning for a coffee since that night in her kitchen. Her skin burned whenever she thought of his bare hands on her breasts, his tongue tracking through her mouth.

Each day he appeared in the coffee bar for an Americano she held her breath. Wondering and waiting. She'd given him his watch back and they'd spoken, staying on safe subjects. But she was aware of him just as much as he was aware of her. Whenever she looked in his direction, he was watching her movements behind the counter. His eyes followed her as she wiped tables. The deeply sensual expression on his face was one of desire. He wanted her, and her own reaction was exactly the same. And that was why, for the first time, she was excited to be home alone when the girls left for the summer.

Jillene was going to seduce Vince on the Fourth of July.

Twenty-Six

"**S**amuel Lentz called three times for you." A woman's voice came through the receiver and Vince listened as his secretary updated him on his Los Angeles business. "And I accepted three times because I wasn't sure it was him at first."

Calls made from L.A. County jail were connected by an automated operator. When the person on the outside answered, a recording stated the incoming call was from a correctional facility. There was an option to reject the call, but he'd told his secretary she could accept them when he was out of the office. A correctional call wasn't unusual.

"He wants you to telephone him immediately," she went on. "He was quite anxious."

"Is that all he said? Just call him." Vince was alone at his dad's house. From the family room, he absently watched the activity of the birds at the backyard feeder.

"He wanted to make sure you got the envelope."

"What envelope?"

"I forwarded it to you last week. I put it in one of those brown manila envelopes, the padded kind, so his bulky envelope would fit inside it."

Moving through the room, Vince gazed at the mail his dad had set aside for him on the dining room table.

Among the letters his secretary had forwarded to him at Pop's was a large manila envelope on the bottom.

Vince's pulse snagged like a bad premonition as he replied, "It's here."

"Good." She paused, as if wondering whether or not to be frank with him about something. After a moment, she said, "Vince, this one creeps me out. There's something in his voice that gives me the chills. He's just too polite and chatty. It's almost like he's watching what I'm doing. Which I know is impossible, but the hair on the back of my neck stands up whenever I hear his voice on the phone."

"If you get another call from a prison, reject it."

"Thank you. Normally this kind of thing doesn't bother me, but he just…he's weird."

Vince's eyes remained on the envelope. Distaste filled his mouth as he contemplated the contents.

He concluded his call with his secretary after she briefed him on other details he needed to handle. When he clicked off his cell, he stared, long and hard, at the envelope.

Picking it up, he undid the seal and pulled out Lentz's large envelope. Vince had a business address he used for his mail rather than a post office box. It was a physical street address where multiple mailboxes were rented in a high-rise. That Century City Boulevard address was below his name. The penmanship seemed feminine and had been written with a fine-point marker.

The *Department of Corrections* censorship stamp and prisoner identification number weren't in the upper left corner. This envelope hadn't come out of L.A. County jail. Lentz was printed in the return address area and the postmark cancellation said Anaheim and was dated a week ago.

Someone on the outside had mailed this for Lentz.

Vince slowly peeled back the string closure. Cold sweat broke out on his palms as he tipped the open envelope onto the desk and twelve sealed letters tumbled out. Each letter was for Samuel Lentz and each letter had the same address. Vince knew it well. The address was the one where he'd finally been arrested.

There was a note that went with the letters.

Happy reading. Check the postmarks so you know where to start.

While Lentz's lawyer had been less than stellar in the courtroom, Vince was doubtful he'd written the note. Maybe a friend. A relative. Where had these letters been all this time?

Vince's gaze landed on the red circle postmarks. Sickening fear went through him as he mentally correlated the dates, beginning with the oldest to the most recent.

The first date was the night of the first murder. The second date was the night of the second murder and so on. Twelve murders. Twelve envelopes.

Stepping away from the desk, Vince rubbed his hand across his jaw, then exhaled sharply. His chest felt as if he'd been hit with a sledgehammer and his bones were so tense they ached.

What was the sick bastard up to?

Who had collaborated with him on this and why?

Vince didn't know if he should open the letters or not. Were they some kind of evidence that would have altered the outcome of the trial? Why had Lentz sent them through the post office to himself? Were they a kind of record of the days he had killed?

Then Vince remembered something—an old copyright

law that writers sometimes used. Even he had gone through the archaic steps with his first manuscript. He'd addressed a large envelope to himself, slipped his finished manuscript inside and mailed it to his house. He'd received the envelope days later and had never opened it. The U.S. Government postal cancellation was documentation that the enclosed material was from the author. This was to protect him from plagiarism.

As far as Vince knew, the "send and receive" practice wasn't done anymore. But he concluded that the documentation could still stand in a court of law. Lentz must have been going for some kind of proof that he had done something on those days.

Holding the first envelope up to the window light, Vince tried to read what was inside. He couldn't make out any text. By his estimation, it contained about three pieces of full-size paper.

Christ Almighty... Should he open one? He had an attorney he used for advisement, but it was the Fourth of July. He'd never find the guy on a holiday week.

Relying on what he knew about the law, Vince determined there was nothing that prevented a person from opening correspondence sent by a death row inmate. He received prisoner letters all the time from men who told him their stories and wanted his help.

Indecisively rubbing his chin once more, Vince relented and got a knife from the utility drawer. He slipped the sharp tip of the blade inside the seal. Slowly, he sliced it open and removed the first letter.

It was addressed to *him.*

Dear Vince:
Here it is, finally time for number one and I've made sure that everything...

He sat down in one of the chairs because his legs were about to snap beneath him, and read on. Lentz noted every move he'd made before and after the murder. The information was presented like a journal entry. A diary of the events—what happened and how he felt about it. The pages covered details that pertained to the five senses— something a writer would be interested in. The smell of blood, the sight of cut skin.

Spasms of repulsion gripped Vince. While he wrote about such scenes, he never used graphic illustrations of violence. He went into the mind of the killer; he didn't present a macabre itinerary of the crime.

Vince read the second letter, then the third and the fourth. All the letters were the same. What got him the most was that they had been calculated down to the last minute detail.

Samuel Lentz had known from the moment he selected his first victim that his goal was to have a book written about himself. He had made sure all the particulars were documented. These letters were shocking if not wholly bizarre. Vince had never encountered anything like them.

He felt as though Lentz had just closed his hands around his throat and was choking the life out of him. Vince felt as if he were being dragged back to a place he didn't want to revisit. It was as if he were reliving it.

Needing to erect a wall of defense around himself, Vince grabbed his car keys and the stack of mail. Walking outside, he got into his Range Rover and turned over the engine. He began to drive with no conscious thought about a destination.

After turning the corner, he'd gone two blocks when he was sent on a detour by a Blue Heron patrol officer standing beside a squad car flashing its red and yellow lights. He'd forgotten about the Independence Day parade. Seaward Street was closed off to through traffic.

With a curse, he turned left, then right. He had to wait for a fleet of Mary Kay Cadillacs to move into position behind the Fire Department trucks. There were seven of the pink luxury cars in a slow caravan. He impatiently drummed his hand on the steering wheel, thinking he hadn't realized the island had that many cosmetic distributors. The ladies driving them honked and waved.

Looking over his shoulder, he put the Rover in reverse and went off in another direction rather than wait. Cutting through an alley behind the Seaview Market, he rounded the street corner.

A group of parade watchers walking with folding chairs were getting ready to cross the street. He recognized the cropped black hair of Hannah Marshall and noticed she was with Rob from Java the Hut. Then he saw a woman beside them. His eyes and mind didn't readily register that it was Jillene.

She wore a paisley sundress in hot pink with a ruffled hem that rode several inches above her knees. Her shapely legs didn't quit—all the way down to her slide-on heeled sandals. Cat's-eye sunglasses hid her eyes and rose lipstick enhanced her mouth. Her hair was unbound. Long and blond and gorgeous. She'd slung an oversize straw purse over her bare shoulder.

Looking at her made his body burn.

The slight display of her cleavage pulled his attention. The valley of skin where her breasts pushed next to each other was exposed just enough to make his imagination run carnally wild. He recalled the night in her kitchen— the tight beads her nipples had made beneath his stimulating fingers. She hadn't been wearing a bra then and it looked questionable now.

The window on the Rover was already rolled down when she approached the passenger side.

"Hi, Vince." She leaned slightly forward to clear the door frame and connect with his gaze. The roundness of her breasts pressed next to her neckline while her necklace dangled away from her tan skin. He couldn't read the expression in her eyes because they were covered by dark lenses, just like his own.

"Are you going to watch the parade?"

"Get in." He uttered the command without thought, grabbing the mail from the seat and carelessly tossing it onto the back floor. Leaning over, he pulled the door handle and opened it. "I'm going for a ride. Come with me."

"Oh...a ride?"

Jillene looked over at Hannah, who waved goodbye with a grin on her face. Rob kept on going, pulling a blue cooler on wheels.

Jillene got into the Rover and the door had barely closed when Vince knocked the gear into reverse again. He took the alley to Sixth, then proceeded out of town on Gull Way.

"Where are we going?" she asked, placing her purse at her feet as the ruffled hem of her dress danced against her thighs in the breeze.

He didn't reply. Once on the highway, he turned on the radio. A Rod Stewart tune blared through the speakers. Wind flew inside the open windows to catch Jillene's mane of hair. She held on to most of it but wisps teased her face.

She looked great. Smelled great with a perfume that was spicy and sweet. He was fiercely aroused—more than he'd ever been in his life. The intensity of his response made him forget about the letters, Lentz and the twelve women.

Passing the busy ferry terminal, Vince drove to the opposite side of the island highway. He turned onto a two-lane road that lead to the west shores. Tall pines shadowed the asphalt in spiky patches of gray and black. He came to a graveled turnout where the only services were a pre-war filling station and a tackle store.

Vince cut the motor. "I'll be right back."

He got out of the Rover and returned a moment later with a key stuck through a fishing-lure key ring.

"Where are we going?" Jillene asked again, this time with a little more firmness.

Pulling out onto the road once more, he said, "A fishing cabin."

"We're going fishing?"

A dirt road became visible to the left. He took it, and in a few minutes he parked in front of a log cabin. Ferns and blackberries grew around the property along with sumac. Moss slanted down the tree trunks of the evergreens.

"That gas station back there is owned by an old friend of mine." He viewed the peaceful setting, feeling its strange attraction once again. He'd spent a long time in these woods. "He's a retired Seattle cop. I stayed here when I wrote my first book, and he said I could make myself at home whenever I wanted."

"It's pretty," Jillene said, slipping her sunglasses off and dropping them into her bag.

They got out of the Rover and walked to the porch together.

At the wood-framed screen door he wedged himself between it and the entry. Using the key to gain access, he swung the door inward and waited for Jillene to pass through ahead of him.

The interior was large and rustic. There were no walls

aside from the exterior, and the built-on bathroom was the size of a closet. A living room, bedroom and kitchen blended into one common space.

Hunting memorabilia, elk and deer heads were mounted on the wall beside a rainbow trout that had been preserved in a way Vince couldn't fathom. Stuffed ducks and geese were suspended in time on the deep windowsills. Hanging above the earth-tone sofa was a historical saloon painting of a bare-breasted woman with flowing hair and a ribbon of filmy gauze wrapped around her pubic area.

His gaze traveled the room. The bed was small. A double. Meant for one person. Solitude. Reflection. He'd done so much of that when he'd come here after being shot. If the calendar pages could flip back, he wouldn't make the same choices again. There would have been no books, no redirection.

No Lentz.

The very thought was like a flash of blinding light. He squeezed his eyelids together to ward off the knife-hot sensations. But the reality of his situation remained in his mind, chaotic and turbulent. He felt as if he had somehow directly caused the death of twelve women...even though he had never met any of them.

"Vince...what's the matter?"

He slowly gazed into Jillene's face as she searched his expression in vain. He knew his Serengetis made it impossible for her to read his thoughts. Which is precisely why he wore them.

Holding on to the sides of his sunglasses, she slipped them from his face. "I think you hide behind these."

He didn't reply. He was fixated on her mouth.

Vince's forehead lowered, nearly touching her smooth skin and the fringe of her windblown bangs.

The muffled *thud* of her purse resounded through the room as it fell to the floor.

His arm passed around her waist, capturing her and tucking her next to the throb low and deep in his belly. The heat coursing through him was a relentless molten river. The sweet smell of her skin filled his nostrils, and his longing was so sharp it consumed all his thoughts.

He positioned his mouth fully over hers, kissing and tasting her with a guttural moan climbing up his throat. He had never been this overcome by the need to sink himself inside a woman. Not just any woman.

Jillene.

He loved the sound of her name, so feminine and beautiful.

His hands were filled by the silkiness of her hair and his mouth was seduced by the sweep of her tongue. She kissed him back, hot and responsive. She pushed herself next to his erection and it was all he could do not to hike up her dress, slide her panties from her legs and bury himself inside her.

She was right.

This moment had been coming for a long time.

On the day they met, he'd wanted her. And not just for the physical release. He'd wanted to become a part of everything inside her body and mind. He knew the union would be explosive. Something he'd never experienced.

Sexual urgency took over the kiss; he felt it coming from her as well. His hands skimmed over her sun-warmed shoulders, bringing her close and delving his tongue deeper into her mouth.

She trembled from the force of their kiss but didn't back away. If anything, she became more uninhibited in his arms. Her hands roamed across the tight cords of muscle at his neck and sifted through his short hair. Then the flat of her palms descended lower and lower to his waist. The gesture was suggestive and taunting.

A jolt of breath escaped him as she jerked the tail of his shirt from his shorts, then slid her hands beneath the freed fabric. Her hands were warm; her slender fingers were soft and searching. The slight length of her fingernails gently dug into his flesh.

She kissed him, sucking on his tongue and at the same time discovering his nipple. She took it between her fingers and brought it to a knotted peak.

On a muffled growl against her mouth, he hooked his finger into the spaghetti strap of her dress and brought it down over her shoulder.

Pulling back, he gazed at her. She did wear a bra. The nothing kind without the straps and with demi-cups so the tops of her breasts were just barely covered. The rosy crescent of her areola peeked out at the lacy edge. With a downward pull of the lace, he released her breast. Its perfect roundness quivered, and he sought the extended nipple with his fingertips.

He bent his head to take her into his mouth, pulling and sucking, swirling his tongue around her as he breathed in the alluring fragrance of her perfume. Its scent took over his head, his body. Consumed him. She tasted so sweet. Her skin was soft and warm.

She leaned back, arching and offering herself more readily to his mouth. Her legs bobbled, and he caught her with the back of his arm and brought her closer to his thigh to support her. She straddled the length of his thigh, and while he sucked on her nipple, his hand reached beneath her dress to her sex.

The thin silk of her panties was wet and hot where her legs met. He moved aside the band and slid his fingers inside. He stroked the sensitive folds of her with his thumb, and she shuddered, raising her pelvis to him.

She flicked open the button to his shorts and fumbled to unzip his fly. Through the ribbed cotton of his underwear, her hand slowly rubbed over the length of his erect penis.

The friction jerked him to life. Lust slammed into his chest. He tilted his head back with a feral gritting of his teeth. Still partially supported on his upper leg, she reached into the band of his underwear and flagrantly touched him. The heat from her fingers curled around his shaft and she gently squeezed. She knew just how to stroke him, how to make him fight to hold back his release as she applied pressure to the base where his testicles had tightened. She held back from bringing him over the edge, kissing him as he claimed her mouth once more.

Swiftly, he hooked his hand around her panty elastic and brought the panties down her legs. She stepped out of the silk scrap, and he kicked off his shorts. His shirt hung open. Her dress was on with one strap off her shoulder. The pale globe of her breast lightly jiggled with her rapid breathing. The rosy nipple glistened from the soft bites of his teeth and suckle of his mouth.

She took a second to dig through her big straw purse. Her hand emerged, holding a box. The next thing he knew, he was opening a wrapper.

There was no thought of the bed. He began to kiss her, nudging her backward toward the wall. When his hands were on either side of her face, and she was pressed against the rough wood, he gave her plump lower lip a nip with his teeth. Then he hiked her leg over his arm and supported her buttock with his other hand. The tip of his penis pushed at the core of her slick and ready entrance. He guided himself deep inside her body. The first scorching heat of her sheathing him and squeezing his hard penis created a delirious fever that dampened his skin.

Her arm curled around his neck, holding him close. She let him carry her weight in the strength of his arm. Her head dropped against his chest as he moved, stimulated by her soft hair next to his bare skin.

The only sounds were those of their raw breathing as he pumped her hard and fast. She moved her slim hips to the tempo of his, urging him to move faster. His erection pushed deep inside her, becoming more intense, heading to the brink of completion. He held back, focusing on bringing her pleasure. He heard her cry of release against his mouth. Only then did he give over his control to a shattering orgasm.

He felt her contractions as she swelled around him, giving him every second of total fulfillment.

She grew limp against him, her leg still hooked through his arm and her face buried in the separation of his shirt. Warmth pooled low and he was still semi-hard. Sated, but still hungry.

Kissing her swollen mouth softly, he traced the seam of her lips with his tongue.

"Jillene..." He breathed her name, their bodies linked. "Can you stand on your own?"

"I think so."

Reluctantly, he pulled himself out from her as she lowered her leg to the floor. Neither of them moved, except for her slight quaver as she balanced herself. Each of them stood in half nakedness.

He with his pulse beating through every inch of his body.

She with something new and untried filling her senses.

The rippling orgasm that gripped Jillene had given her a need that would never be erased. She wanted more.

Needed more. The fire-hot spear of penetration into her body made her feel as if she was a virgin all over again. She'd been stretched to a point of slight discomfort but she had taken him. Welcomed him. Vince was large and thick, beautiful in his male anatomy. Under the rhythmic force of his thrusts, he'd awakened desires long ago buried and forgotten. In her memory, and more recent imagination and fantasies, she had not really remembered how good making love could feel.

Vince's powerful masculinity and sexual expertise had shown her a primitive release she'd never felt before. Something untried and wild. She hadn't been self-conscious. In fact, her lack of inhibition surprised her. While she had only known one man and her experience was based on that relationship's long-term creativity, she hadn't been resistant to this new lesson in sex…against a cabin wall.

"You're so beautiful," Vince murmured, his eyes a deep blue.

He held her captive with his voice. The sound of it caressed her, bringing forth a series of tingles across her skin. She shivered with an uncontrollable tremor. Her breasts grew heavy and rose high, the nipples sensitive and tightened to hard points.

She silently unbuttoned Vince's shirt and pulled the curtain of fabric apart, slowly slipping it from his powerful shoulders. She wanted to feel every inch of him— naked against her.

When the shirt was free, she took in every ridge of his bare chest. A washboard stomach that stretched taut across his middle, the whorl of hair that made a line from his navel to his groin.

He turned away only for a moment, then presented himself to her. The hard length of his arousal jutted from a patch of dark hair, elongated away from his flat belly. Looking at him made her mouth go dry. He was all sinew and muscle and bone—and the definition of a perfect male.

Daring and desire manifested themselves inside her. She reached out and grazed her fingertips over the pink, clefted head of his penis. The length of him bobbed under her touch. It was amazing to have such power over him, such sexual control.

She stepped out of her sandals as he slid his feet from the boat shoes he'd been wearing.

Vince came to her and reached around behind her to unzip her dress. The chiffon fabric fell to the floor in a puddle of hot pink. The lacy white of her bra came off next. She was fully naked now, too. His hands fit beneath her breasts while his thumbs fondled her nipples. She languished as the suction of his lips circled each areola. He took as much of her into his mouth as he could, licking and teasing the nub as he had done before.

She took his hand and led him to the bed, where she pushed him down onto the mattress. Leaning over him, she brought her knees down on either side of his thighs. The crisp feel of his body hair made her dizzy.

His full lips turned into a slight grin, his eyes closed halfway. She almost couldn't breathe, the air in her lungs coming out in ragged gasps. She didn't touch him except for the slight tension of her inner thighs wrapped on the outside of his. She seductively leaned over the steady rise and fall of his ribs as he breathed. The weight of her breasts came forward, falling in the shapes of pears above his mouth. She offered herself to him like sweet fruit—something he hungrily sampled and tasted.

She could feel the pulsating swirl of his tongue and that in itself almost brought her to a climax. The need was there to arch her back and bring down her hips. Unintentionally, when she moved she pulled free of his mouth—and instantly missed him.

He brushed back her hair from her shoulders, stroking her temple and tracing the shell of her ear. Then he brought her head down to his and kissed her lips. Tenderly.

She kissed him back, slipping her tongue into his mouth, enjoying the torment of their leisurely pace. Her breasts crushed into him as he kissed her neck, then her collarbone and the high curve of her breast's plump roundness. Her pelvis strained and she raised herself up, wanting him to enter her.

His hands slid down her waist to her navel, then lower to catch in the curls between her legs. She'd never been so wet, so ready. One of his fingers slipped into her sex, opening the wet folds with a gentle rub. He found her clitoris, exciting her as she moved to the rhythm of his hand. Wanting him again badly, she spread her legs wide open to take him.

She braced herself on her elbows and brought her hand between her legs, encircling him and stroking lightly. When she couldn't stand to be disconnected from him any longer, she slowly rolled protection over him, his gaze taking in the gentle movement of her hand; then she lowered herself onto his penis.

The penetration was just as shocking this time, filling her as she slowly mounted the entire length of him. He held on to her waist with his wide hands, splaying his fingers across her skin. And that was the end of her seduction as Vince manipulated her hips to his liking.

He withdrew himself from her a little at a time, retreating and tormenting her until she cried out. He'd suddenly go deeper, then partially hold back once more without completely pulling out.

She whimpered when at last he plunged hard into her and buried himself as far as he could. She met his strokes with a frantic energy. He moved faster and harder until she was gasping and on the border of complete release.

A sheen of moisture collected on his skin, igniting her senses with a musky scent. His biceps rippled with inordinate strength as his hands gripped her buttocks, kneading the flesh as she ground herself on top of him. Every driving stroke of her body into his depleted all thoughts but one demanding need. The feeling was intoxicating and fervent. When she came, she said his name in a trembling voice. Only then did he empty himself inside her, the hot stream of his climax blazing as her inner thighs clamped around him.

She quivered in the aftermath, the pounding of her heartbeat a roar in her ears, and felt every bit a woman.

"You ruined my plan to seduce you," Jillene announced in a tone that was light and airy.

The outdoor deck they sat on overlooked a dense hillside, and in the short distance beyond, the ocean glimmered in rich golden waves under a July sunset. The sky had already begun to turn a deep purple hue. They had been at the cabin for almost half the day.

Vince was beside her, in a matching Adirondack chair, wearing his shorts and no shirt. The smooth breadth of his chest was tan and solid with muscles. He gazed across at her with mock surprise.

"You had a plan?"

Wearing only his shirt and her panties, her legs weren't covered. She rested her feet on the rustic porch railing.

The color of her toenail polish seemed out of place in such a woodsy setting.

"I don't just happen to have that particular *item* in my purse. I have never in my life bought them before."

"Stepping out of your comfort zone, Jillene?" he teased, and she recalled how she'd tempted him into a mocha with similar words.

"Way major out of my comfort zone." She turned to face him, her thoughtful expression ebbing to serious. "But I knew we'd be together. I *wanted* that…so very much. You did, too."

He slowly swallowed, the tendons of his neck tight with guarded emotion. When he replied, his voice hit a reverent note that cascaded through her. "Yes."

Their being together was no reckless moment without thought. A consummation had been brewing for a long time. But what she'd seen in his eyes when she'd taken off his sunglasses was acute pain. A smoke screen for something dark and turbulent clutching his mind. Touching his arm, she searched his face. "You were upset when you picked me up. What happened?"

His body, tall and powerful, bent and stretched into the wood-slatted chair. The smile he returned to her was soft, seductive and sure. "I got my IRS bill in the mail." Then, with a rakish grin, he handed her a shrink-wrapped package. "Twinkie?"

She frowned at his detraction tactic, but held out her hand.

He'd just returned from the gas station store and had brought back a bag of snacks. She was starved and would eat whatever he had to offer. Jillene had learned Vince suffered from a perpetual case of sweet tooth and had expected him to stock up on junk sugar. But the cellophane bag of dyed yellow popcorn and a fruity wine cooler surprised her. Even though she was more of a cream-filled chocolate cupcake girl, a spongy Twinkie sounded delicious.

Cracking the cap of his beer and opening her wine cooler, he ate his Twinkie in two bites, while she nibbled at the whipped white center of hers.

"Enjoying that?" Vince asked, his eyes suddenly bright and clear, as if at long last he could let the tension ease from his muscles.

"Definitely."

"There's a movie I once saw where the guy wouldn't let the woman eat a Twinkie," Vince mentioned, after taking a drink of beer. "She wanted the Twinkie, but he took it and squished it into the railing of a ferry and told her it would still be there in a hundred years. Or something like that."

"*Paternity* with Burt Reynolds and Beverly D'Angelo." Jillene ate a bite. "He didn't want her to eat it because of all the preservatives. I loved that movie."

"I saw it years ago. I'd probably hate it now."

Sampling the effervescent texture of the cooler against her tongue, she asked, "Why?"

"Because I'm older."

"And?"

"I might see some of myself in Burt Reynolds."

"You mean his desire to have a child so his name would be passed down to the next generation."

"Not the name aspect. I've never thought about kids like that—as namesakes. Hell, I could have a girl and she'd get married and then her last name wouldn't be Tremonti anyway." Vince leaned deeper into the chair. "It's more like kids are too late for me. I'm forty-two. I had my chances years ago but it wasn't what I wanted for myself. And now…"

He shrugged, playing down the bevy of emotions that had to be hitting him.

The soft quality of her voice drifted through the pine-scented air when she said, "You would be a good dad, Vince. Never say never."

"Just like you say never again, Jillene?" he said, reminding her about her declaration that she was finished with motherhood.

She couldn't begin to imagine being pregnant again. Changing a diaper was something she'd need a refresher on. The feedings and all the long nights. Stuffed animals, crib mobiles and the hassle of car seats... The baby-powder sweetness of a chubby cheek next to her breast. A first smile and first step. The sound of "I love you" in a tiny voice.

Jillene shook herself out of her wayward musings, ignoring the reminiscent shiver that brought gooseflesh to her arms.

"So," she said in her best smart and sophisticated tone. "Should we set up the terms for our summer fling? Or just wing it?"

The corner of his mouth lifted into a smile as he parroted, "Our fling?"

"Yes. Sex. Cut-and-dried. You and me."

His laughter was rich with seductive humor. "Sweetheart, what makes you think I'd go along with that?"

"You're a guy?" she answered with a grin.

He shook his head with a smile of amusement. Then he took her wine cooler from her and set it down.

"Come here."

He pulled her onto his lap so her legs dangled over the side of the chair. Her bottom pressed against him, her panties a next-to-nothing barrier. The contact was warm and exciting, and a heavy ache began inside her once more.

His arms came snugly around her waist. He shifted her position to settle the center of her most intimate part on top of him. She felt his hardness straining against his fly. He dipped to kiss her mouth, his tongue slipping inside.

The agony of wanting yet needing to savor clashed in a cascade of fiery sparks in her mind. His hands were on her breasts, pulling on her nipples with gentle tugs. She brought the edge of his shirt up and over her head so she sat nearly naked on his lap. Then his mouth came around her nipple, tracing the edge of its center until he finally took all of her. Every nerve ending inside her jumped and she drew in her breath. She brought her hands around the back of his neck and held his head immobile as his tongue and lips pleasured her.

Through the darkness of nightfall, Blue Heron's Fourth of July fireworks display erupted in a patriotic bloom of Red Phantoms, Blue Fountains and White Fireflies. The skies were alight with color and shooting stars. Everyone agreed the evening was City Hall's best show ever.

Vince and Jillene didn't see a single minute of it.

Twenty-Seven

If it hadn't been for Jillene, Vince would have driven out of Blue Heron. Habits were hard to break and the need to clear his head with a change of scenery always beckoned. But this time, he hadn't left.

He had seen her in that pink dress and he had stayed. To be with her. To make love to her and forget the hell that was burning beneath him in an unquenchable fire.

Standing at the bar in the Oyster Shell Lounge, Vince waited for Jerry Peck. He'd called his boyhood friend and asked if he could meet him.

Twenty minutes passed before Jerry showed up with a lit cigarette in his mouth. The outline of an antacid roll was unmistakable in the breast pocket of his outdated shirt.

"Hey, Vinnie," he said, taking a place beside him and ordering a Bud. "Sorry it took me so long. I had to take Duke out for a walk."

"That's okay, Jerry."

Jerry's beer arrived, and Vince had the bartender put it on his tab. "That's for what I owe you on the pizzas delivered to Jillene's house."

"Yeah, that's right. Twenty-two fifty."

"Start drinking." Vince raised his glass to Jerry, then drank his tonic water with a twist of lime.

"Her kids are out of town for a while," Jerry reported. "They went to their grandmother's in California for a few weeks."

"I know that."

"I guess you would."

"They're doing Disneyland and the whole nine yards." He smoothed his comb-over and took a drag on his cigarette. "My kids are always on my case to take them down there and see Mickey Mouse. But on a cop's salary you can't afford a trip like that."

"Going out on a limb here, Jerry, but if you quit smoking you could save up what you're giving to the tobacco companies every year. What's that add up to—maybe a grand or so?"

Exhaling a stream of smoke, Jerry asked, "How come you don't smoke anymore? Did the California liberals get to you?"

"Can't smoke in any of the restaurants down there, and I eat out a lot. It just didn't fit my lifestyle."

"How'd you do it?"

"Cold turkey."

"Damn. No patch? That takes some balls, Vinnie."

Vince smiled. "Don't think that I don't think about it. I do. I'm always just a step away from going back."

They shared a reflective moment, the noise from the bar all around them. It was ladies night and drinks for women were half price. Octogenarian Harry Newton and his sixty-year-old girlfriend, Wanda VanHorn, were cutting it up on the dance floor.

In the corner, a live band played some modern tunes. The bubble-gum stuff from trendy stations. Not like the rock and roll he and Jerry used to play in their band.

Leaning his forearms on the edge of the bar, Vince kept

his gaze forward when he asked, "Jerry—how does it feel to have everything?"

"What?"

Facing his friend, he clarified. "The wife and kids and dog and the minivan?"

Skewing his face into an outrageous frown, Jerry said, "I don't have a minivan. Jan drives a Cavalier and I've got a Saturn."

"I was being figurative." Vince cocked his hip and put the ball of his foot on the brass rail beneath him. "How does it feel when you go to bed at night and your wife's there with you and you know she's going to be there in the morning?"

Jerry's expression was puzzled, as if he were deciding whether or not he'd been handed a trick question. "It feels good, Vinnie."

"Yeah, that's what I figured. And the kids? You like having them?"

"Not when they're driving me up the wall, but...yeah, I like having them around. Timmy plays shortstop on his Little League team. Hey, I'm one of the assistant coaches. And Stacy, she's in the school band. Plays the clarinet. She sucks at it but she tries. The monthly rental on that instrument busts my balls. But you know how it is—you gotta do what you gotta do."

No, he didn't know.

For so long, the only person he'd been responsible for was himself. His girlfriends had remained independent even though they'd lived together. There had never been a legal commitment that was binding. No merging of finances or co-ownership of a house.

"Why do you ask me such a question, Vinnie?" Jerry held on to his beer, his forehead creased by a frown. "You've had more success with your careers than I'll ever know. You're rich and single. You could do anything you want. You can have anything you want.''

"I want to apologize for how things turned out between us.''

"Where's this coming from?'' Jerry nervously lit a fresh cigarette from the one he was ready to stub out in the ashtray. "What are you talking about?''

"I'm talking about the Seattle P.D. How I made it and you didn't.''

Angrily, Jerry spat, "Screw that. Water under the bridge.''

"It's not.'' Vince had no intention of letting Jerry downplay the past. Settling everything had been too long in coming. "I had an advantage—my pop could send me to a university.''

"I went, too,'' Jerry pointed out. "Junior college. It took me longer because money was tight for my old man, but I graduated.'' He took a long pull of beer, then slapped the glass on the bar. "Let me tell you something, Mr. Best-seller—I'm happy about how things turned out. I've got a life here with friends and family. I'm important. Kids at the elementary school love when I pull up with my K-9 unit and let them pet Duke.'' He raised his hands in a defensive manner. "So I haven't made Lieutenant, but I'm still trying. And I will keep trying. Hell, yes, I was disappointed not to make a bigger force, a better one…be a *detective*…but damn…it's okay. I'm okay.'' He nodded. "Yeah, I'm okay.''

Vince replied with an uncompromising edge in his voice. "I'm glad to hear that.''

"Well, don't say it so damn sanctimoniously. You've got a hell of a life. Fame and prestige. I saw the black Range Rover you drive.'' He scooped up a handful of salted peanuts. "Does it have heated seats?''

Vince made no comment.

Smoothing his hair again, Jerry breathed unevenly. "Jesus, Vinnie. You called me over here to tell me all this? You have to know that I respect you. I'm proud of you. I tell strangers in Anchor Books that I know you and to buy your books. Yeah, I do…aw, hell." A fistful of peanuts fell into his open mouth again, then he grimaced and brought out his roll of Rolaids.

"You've got it all wrong, Jerry. It's me who respects you. You've got the world, buddy. I mean that. I'd trade you if I could."

"Yeah, right." Jerry's undiluted laughter jiggled his belly, testing the security of his shirt buttons. "I'll bet you'd get no protest from Jan. She hasn't seen what a guy looks like without a tire around his gut in a long time."

"Seriously, Jerry." Vince didn't let up. "You've got a good thing."

Jerry sobered. "I know." Chewing on a chalky tablet, he added, "I was sorry when you got shot, Vince. It was a hell of a thing."

"Yes."

"It changed you."

And once again, Vince was changing. He was being shaped and remolded by the people he touched and came in contact with. He was who he was because of them, and whatever journey he had planned for himself was now veering off course.

Things were happening. He hadn't anticipated the emotions he was feeling. All around him, the people he knew had a focus. Jerry Peck was trying for Lieutenant. Sol had expanded his store. Even Connie, recently divorced, was focused on goals and knew what she wanted. Pop was getting older but he was making progress on a comfortable retirement. He ran a solid business and was starting a new life with Ianella Sofrone. And Jillene, she was the most determined of all of them, exploring everything she could be.

Everybody seemed to be organized and focused but Vince.

Jerry's voice came into his thoughts. "So I guess we're good friends again, huh?"

"No guessing, Jerry. I'd say we always were, only we didn't take the time to know it."

Vince gazed across the bar and saw Velma Hicks headed their way. Her daisy wig fluttered and her lipstick was on crooked. Aside from the usual, there was something quite prominent about her features that had never been there before.

A pair of purple plastic-rimmed eyeglasses.

"Hello, Sergeant Peck," she said with a courteous smile.

The lenses were a half-inch thick and magnified her eyes. It was kind of freaky, like she was looking at them with eyes twice the normal size.

"Hey, Velma. How are they working out?"

"Wonderfully. I resisted, you know that. But I'm so glad the department did this for me." Then she ordered, "Bartender, I'll take a highball." Sitting down, she set her pocketbook on her lap.

Leaning sideways so she could get a good look at Vince, she blandly uttered, "Vincenzo."

"Velma."

"I have glasses now. Did you notice?"

"Yeah, I noticed."

"Jerry and the boys down at the station paid for my eye exam and it turns out that I have a severe eyesight problem."

Shrugging, Jerry explained, "She's been driving on an

expired license all this time. Since nineteen sixty-three. A paperwork glitch never caught it for renewal. So no driving test. It looked current in the computer.''

"Wasn't that nice of Blue Heron's finest?'' Vince said. He had a strong suspicion the only reason the error had been found was that Jerry dug around in the files after Jillene's accident.

"Awfully nice.'' Velma pushed the glasses up her nose and took a long, hard look at him. "Did anyone ever tell you that you look like George Clooney?''

"Uh…no.''

"Humph.''

"Jerry, I have to go.'' Vince extended his arm and shook his friend's hand. "See you around.''

"That would be good, Vinnie.''

Vince left a bill on the counter for the tab. "Your drink's on me, Velma. Cheers to the glasses.''

Leaving the Oyster Shell Lounge, Vince drove up the hill to Jillene's house. Whenever he thought about her, his spirits lifted.

She called what they were doing a "fling.'' He didn't care to call it anything. If he put a label on their time in bed, he would be grounded by a sense of obligation. She was fine with the sex. And so was he. When he was with her, he felt almost exonerated. Not for his part in Lentz's crimes, but for the choices he had made and their consequences.

There was still the problem of what to do about the book. He'd had no contact with his editor, and only one call with Mel during which they had discussed details on another matter. By appearances, Vince was going ahead with the project.

Pulling into Jillene's driveway, he popped a stick of spearmint gum in his mouth and stepped out of the Rover.

Earlier this morning, he had told her he would take a look at her broken washing machine. He actually liked motors. Disassembling them and figuring out what made them work or why they didn't. He could fix pretty much anything.

He rang her doorbell and when she answered, he greeted, "Lady, did you call for service?"

Holding on to a giggle, she said, "Ah, yes. I need servicing. Very badly."

He gave her a swift kiss, then let himself inside.

It took him only a half hour to figure out the problem. The utility room was small and confining, and Jillene stood over him.

"You had a tweaked piece of thin metal in your water pump," he said, holding up the item and stretching to his feet.

"What—" Jillene's mouth dropped open. "That's a bobby pin." She took it, then muttered, "Claire. She never takes the bobby pins out of her pockets and I end up washing them. This one must have slipped through and got caught in the pump."

Vince turned on the fill dial to start the machine, and water splashed into the tub. "I think it'll work okay for you now."

Jillene moved close behind him and encircled his waist with her arms. She laid her cheek on his back. He loved the feel of her next to him, the feel of her body pulsing around him as they found their release in sexual pleasure.

"Thank you," she whispered.

The gratefulness in her tone went straight to his heart. Whether it was the sentiment or the softness, he didn't know, but he combated the dangerous feelings by flipping down the washer lid.

"We have to test it just to make sure it's running smooth."

Lifting her under her arms, he sat her on top of the white enamel washer. Then he nudged her legs apart and stood between them.

"It sounds okay to me," she playfully responded.

"Nope. We have to see how it does on the spin cycle."

"Ah, the spin cycle." She hooked her arms over his shoulders and smiled. "What do we do while we're waiting for it to engage?"

Grinning, he said, "We engage in activities of our own."

"Would what we're doing be ethical for a service repairman?"

He unbuttoned her blouse. "Definitely not. So I quit."

Then their mouths sought one another and came together in a kiss.

Twenty-Eight

Ianella dabbed her eyes with a delicate handkerchief. A piece of Al's heart tore, listening to the soft whisper of her crying.

"Ianella, my sweet angel. If I'd known you were going to get upset, I wouldn't have asked you."

"Oh, Al." She hugged him and pressed her cheek to his. "I'm crying because I'm so happy. I've dreamed about this moment, and you asked better than I ever imagined."

His spirits lifted. "Then, will you? Will you marry me, Ianella?"

"Yes. Oh, yes!"

They kissed one another to seal the promise, and he felt it all the way to his soul.

She'd said yes!

For now and forever, Ianella would be his bride. He had waited so long for her and he still couldn't believe this was all happening to him. He loved her so.

They sat in his red Impala, facing the sunset on the beach. He'd brought her to the old vista view, a turnout in the road on the north shore.

Reaching over her, he popped down the glove box and took out the tiny black velvet box he'd secreted in there before he'd left home. He'd checked three times to make sure everything was in order. And now, he held on to the soft edges and lifted the tiny lid.

"Al…" Ianella put a slender hand over her heart.

Nestled in a satin bed was a single two-carat diamond on a gold band. His Ianella was so beautiful he'd wanted a simple but extravagant ring as a testament to his love. He took the ring and then her hand.

"I'd like to ask again, Nella. And this time maybe you won't cry."

She nodded, biting on her lower lip. Her fingers quivered as she extended them.

"Ianella, darling. I love you. Will you marry me?"

"Yes," she whispered.

He slipped the ring on her fourth finger and she kissed his cheek. "I love you, Al. You've made me very, very happy."

Their lips met in series of tender kisses and nibbles.

On a sigh, she leaned into his arms and slid next to him. He brought his arm over her shoulder and kept her close as the gulls flew overhead and the sea breeze drifted through the car.

She sighed in a heavenly voice. "I don't want to forget a single moment of this. Not ever."

"Me, either," he said. "I don't want to go back yet. I want to keep this special. Just for us."

"Hmm." He could feel the curve of her lips against the side of his neck. She excited him and made him feel young. Vibrant and full of life.

Suddenly, sitting in the car like this transported him back to days gone by when coming up to the viewpoint meant friskiness.

"Nella…"

"Yes, darling?"

"Do you feel like necking in the car?"

Her laughter warmed him. "Necking?"

"Well, whatever it is they're calling it these days. Do you want to 'make out' for a little while?"

"No."

"No?"

Tilting her face, she murmured, "Let's make out for a long while."

Twenty-Nine

Jillene stirred to wakefulness in Vince's bed in the *Gracie*. She felt him beside her, warm and solid and aroused. Her head was pillowed on his shoulder and she rested a hand on his belly. Drowsy from the contented dreams she had only just awakened from, her fingers trailed lower.

How could it be that she'd become so insatiable? She'd always enjoyed sex and had missed it, but she'd convinced herself she could live without the complications of a relationship. What she and Vince had wasn't complicated…or so she'd thought. A fling was turning into something more. At least for her. She was both frightened and thrilled by the prospect of discovering the depth of her emotions for his man.

The days had blended into a week since they had first been together. When she dreamed, she saw Vince's face. Smelled his skin. Drowned in the color of his eyes. Gone were the imprinted images of David and the time when she had thought it would be devastating to replace old memories. Now she was comforted by the addition to them. She would always have a special place in her heart for David, and she acknowledged to herself that she was building one for Vince, too.

A light kiss fell on her temple as she slowly opened her eyes to find Vince's gaze on her. His hand bunched her hair as he caught her neck and brought her closer to him. Kissing him, she reached for his tongue. Warm and wet, she swept through his mouth. Under the exquisite pressure, everything inside her skittered. Hot and cold at the same time. She loved the feelings as they clashed and erupted in gooseflesh across her skin.

A fiery need sparked and desire wound its way through her blood. She hooked her leg over his to climb on top of him, but he shifted and pinned her against the mattress. He was heavy and almost more than she could bear as he positioned himself. But she welcomed the masculine feel of his strength as he kneed her legs open. Leaning over her, he reached for the sheath of protection on the table. She'd never imagined watching a man put on a condom would arouse her further, but it did. With one hand, he guided himself into her, sinking his length as far as she could take it.

The muscles in his thighs stood out as he moved deeply and swiftly to bring them both to fulfillment. She was vaguely aware of saying *"Please, oh please"* against his mouth. She drew him as tightly to her as possible, her hands gripping his muscular shoulders. Pleasure reverberated through her body with each of his thrusts, her nipples tight and sensitive. She crossed her ankles behind his buttocks, urging him to ride her harder.

At the brink of climax, she called out his name in a throaty sound of release. His body shook and tremored as he came into his own, then held her tightly, their hearts beating wildly together.

"Jillene," he breathed hotly against her ear. "You're going to kill me."

"I don't see your white flag waving." She nipped at his shoulder, her hands roaming down his back. The feel of his skin was like sleek, warm marble. "If you were ready to die, you'd surrender."

"Never."

He rolled onto his back, taking her with him. The instant they broke apart, she missed his fullness. Tucking her curves into the contours of his muscles, she snuggled, comfortable and satisfied, into his embrace.

Dangling from its chain, her heart necklace brushed at his collarbone. He touched the enameled ornament. "I never wanted to ask, but I've never seen you without this so I'm curious. You don't have to say."

She knew what he was wondering.

"My girls gave it to me for my thirtieth birthday. David took them to the jewelry store and they picked it out."

Was that an oddly placed sense of relief falling across his face? Perhaps he was jealous. She wanted him to understand. "Vince, I loved my husband. He's gone and nobody can replace him. But life goes forward. These days with you have been more than I ever could have imagined." She bit her lip, trying to form her next words. "I don't have to tell you this, but I want to." Looking into his eyes, she revealed, "I've only made love with two men in my life."

His face changed, softened. "I assumed that. But it was nice to hear. I can't explain why."

"You don't have to."

Vince stretched out his long legs and brought an arm behind his head.

"Ohhh, I don't want to leave. But I have to." Her protest was feeble, but she had lots to do at Java. Gabby was working the morning shift today and Rob was coming in an hour later, so Jillene had to make sure everything got done in his absence. She kissed Vince's neck and tasted the saltiness of sweat and his skin. "What time is it?"

"Five-thirty. When do you open Java?"

"Seven. I have to go home and..." Her sentence trailed. She had to shower and make herself look human and not like some sex-tousled woman with tangled hair and blushing lips from kissing half the night away. "...get my apron."

The soft dipping and rocking motion of the boat was soothing, a peaceful respite in the aftermath of their love-making. This was a great place to wrap up in intimacy. Sunlight barely slipped in through the Venetian blinds. The cabin was fully functional. The kitchen had all the amenities: a two-burner stove, a sink and icebox, plenty of cabinet space. Each cupboard door had a die-cut anchor carved in it. Vince had told her all the appliances were original and they still worked. Above them, two bunklike cabins at the bow flanked the living area. They lay on the double-wide sofa that turned into a bed. It was kind of like a fifties version of the futon.

"How long has your dad had this boat?" she asked, her toes fitting beneath his foot.

"He bought it when I was in elementary school. Jeez, that's back in the sixties."

"Oh, ancient times," she teased. "I remember them."

"Hmm." Vince threaded his fingers through her hair, catching a strand and wrapping it around his thumb over and over. The motion sent shivers across her skin. "Sometimes I think the world would be a better place if we could turn the clock back—even if that meant getting rid of the technology we know today."

"Why do you say that?"

"Back then we lived in a less complicated society. I remember moving into my apartment when I went to college. This guy came to our building going door-to-door trying to sell us cable television. I blew him off, telling him that nobody would ever go for that. Why pay for something when you could pick up ten channels for free? And now look. Hell, you can tune in almost anything you want twenty-four/seven. Nobody reads or talks to their neighbors anymore. Trust is a hard thing to find.

"The way things have changed is not necessarily a good thing. What was wrong with vinyl albums? There never used to be such things as CDs. No VHS players or DVDs. When I was little, I watched *The Jetsons* and was amazed by the fact that she could push a button and out would come this perfectly cooked dinner. I never thought that could really happen. It was a great fantasy. Now we have microwave ovens and we're our own Jetsons."

"That's a good thing. I couldn't live without my microwave."

Inhaling slowly, she felt the pull of his ribs next to her breast.

"The world is moving in such a direction that I question what's going to happen when man gets too smart. What's it going to do to the kids? Don't you worry about that, Jillene?"

She had never quite thought about it in those terms. While she had concerns and worries and desires for her girls, she was willing to let them learn to be the best they could. Whether they stumbled or achieved, they would be better for the experiences. "You have to put faith in your children. They know right from wrong today, just as we did in the sixties."

Vince was quiet for a long while. "They've got so much reality to deal with. I just don't remember life being as cruel as it is now."

She propped herself on her elbow and gazed into his face. "If life is so real for kids, then how come Pocahontas doesn't have armpit or leg hair?"

"What?"

''Pocahontas in the Disney movie. The girls and I were just talking about that.''

''Never saw the movie. Disney cartoons aren't my thing. But I will admit to watching wrestling—which can be cartoonish.'' His grin was disarming. White teeth flashed and the corner of his mouth curved.

She smiled at him and slyly added, ''Then, you haven't seen the *Little Mermaid* box.''

''Nope.''

''An artist at Disney studios decided to have some fun on the artwork for the VHS box. He drew a phallus in the castle.''

''No way.''

''Yes. We have it. They stopped printing the VHS box almost as soon as it was released—so I guess we have a collector's item.'' Jillene pushed off the bed. ''Come on, get dressed. I have to go, and you can walk me home. I'll show it to you.''

''If you're thinking it's going to turn me on,'' he taunted in a humorous tone as he rose from the bed gloriously naked and male, ''you'll be disappointed.''

She tossed a pillow at him and giggled when he came toward her with clear intent.

By the time they got to her house, she had twenty minutes to get ready for work. She handed Vince the Disney movie. ''See if you can find it.'' Then she punched the play button on her answering machine. She'd had seven messages overnight. A telemarketer must have been persistent.

''Jesus. It's right here,'' he said with disgust, his brows lifting as her first message beeped.

''Jillene, this is Mom. Now don't worry, but I had to take Faye to the hospital tonight...''

Fear gripped Jillene's heart and she froze, missing some of the message.

"...She'll be all right," Jodi-Lynn continued. "She was standing on the tub looking in the mirror, and Claire said she slipped. Her right eye is all right and thank goodness she landed the way she did. She had to have four stitches and she took it pretty good. She didn't like the numbing shot and cried a little bit. She wants to talk to you so we'll try again later."

"Oh my God," Jillene murmured.

The next message played. "Mom? Mom? Are you there?" It was Claire. "Faye wants to talk to you." There was a muffled sound. "She's not home yet." Then a click of disconnection.

Beep. Another message. "Jillene, it's your mother. Just trying again."

The last three messages were Faye. "Mommy. Where are you?" She was sniffling when she spoke. "I hurt myself. I got some stitches. Grandma bought me a chocolate sundae on the way home. I miss you, Mom."

"Mom? Where are you?"

"Mommy? Mommy? Mommy?" Then soft crying.

A sob tore free from Jillene's throat and her knees buckled. She gripped the counter's edge.

The last forlorn message had been recorded at one-eighteen in the morning.

Jillene hadn't been at home when her daughter needed her. If she had been with Faye, she could have cautioned her about the tub once again and maybe prevented the accident. But that was impossible. She hadn't been in Los Angeles and there was nothing she could have done. She couldn't have held Faye's hand or wiped her tears. But she could have listened to her fragile voice on the phone and given her reassurance.

Devastation worked through Jillene and a crushing realization immobilized her.

"I shouldn't have let them go," she said evenly.

"They deserved time with their grandmother." Vince came to her and reached out to hold her.

She backed away. "No." The hitch in her voice was sharp and jagged as tears filled her eyes. Guilt came crashing down on her. "I was excited to send them away so I could be alone with you."

He shook his head. "Don't do this to yourself, Jillene."

"You don't understand," she repeated. "My child needed me and I wasn't here. I was with you...I let my guard down. I got involved. I didn't mean to. If I'd been home like I should have been, I could have talked to Faye. I want to be here for her...I've always been here for them. And this time, I wasn't."

Frustration and blame welled up in her, almost choking her. She was lashing out at Vince for her own failure, but she didn't apologize. She couldn't. She needed to call Faye. That was what was important right now.

Reaching for the phone, she said, "You have to leave. I need to call my daughter. She comes first."

He didn't move immediately, as if hoping she'd change her mind. Then after several seconds and without another word, he let himself out the front door.

Thirty

Vince went to the barbershop, where he found his pop sweeping up after a customer who'd just left. Mu sat in one of the chairs reading the newspaper. The smell of Markham and Old Tiger lingered in the air.

"Hi, Vince." Mu greeted him in his Indian accent. "I have your clothes ready at the counter. Medium starch on the dress shirt."

"Thanks, Mu."

Pop set his broom and dustpan aside.

Sol opened the door and stuck his head inside. "Hey, Mu. I just saw that guy who did a *Crouching Tiger, Hidden Dragon* on your front-load washer go into the Laundromat."

Mu quickly set aside the paper and jerked to his feet. "Nice to have been talking with you, Al, but I have to be going now."

Striding swiftly, Sol and Mu went past the front window and disappeared down the sidewalk.

"Hey, Vinnie, I got my bank statement and there was a deposit on there I didn't make. I could guess who did it, seeing as the amount was close to the cost of the new Chrysler."

"Do you want to argue about it?"

"Not really. You'd win. You already won. Thanks, son. But I'll kick you in the keister if you pull a stunt like that again." Pop gave the warning in a cheerful tone. "So. How are you?"

How was he? Not good, considering Jillene had just asked him to leave her house after making love to her in a way that had elevated his enjoyment of sex to a whole new level. He didn't understand her self-reproach for not being there when her daughter called. Perhaps it was because he didn't have children. He viewed her situation as one where she had an enormous responsibility toward her daughters, but she also had an obligation to herself—to live her life and be happy. With their grandmother taking care of them, Claire and Faye were in good hands and there was nothing Jillene could have done last night. Instead, she was beating herself up over it. He didn't see that her being with him was any reason to alienate him, unless—

She was falling in love with him.

He could easily admit to himself that he had strong feelings for her. Dangerous feelings. He'd let his heart lead him all the way. He'd felt her anguish this morning as if it were his own. His need to comfort her was strong, but she'd pushed him away. Strangely, he hadn't wished for an out. He'd wanted to get involved and share more with her than sex, but maybe joy and grief weren't all that far apart.

"I'm all right," he replied.

"Son, I want to tell you something."

Al's face was alight with a happiness that Vince hadn't seen there for longer than he could remember. It wasn't as if Pop didn't have great moments, but whatever was going on with him now must be even better. To use Pop's description—better than drinking a mai tai on Maui with the surf crashing on the shore.

"What is it?"

His father adjusted the cordless trimmer at his station, as if pausing to collect just the right words. "Son, you know that I loved your mother. She was my heart, Vinnie. But my heart's still beating and it's beating faster. That's because I found a woman who makes me sing in the shower."

"You've always done that."

"But now I'm singing Luther Vandross." At the mention of the name, Pop's expression became serious. "Vinnie…" He gazed at his hand. The left. Where his wedding ring had been for so many years before he'd finally taken it off, long after Mom died. Looking up, he pressed his lips together. "I asked Ianella Sofrone to marry me and she said yes."

Vince had had a hunch this was going to happen the night Pop had taken Mrs. Sofrone out for a lobster dinner. But what Vince hadn't anticipated was the bittersweet rush that flooded into his heart. Pop had found true love twice in his life. Once was rare; a second time was precious. Vince had never been preoccupied with everlasting love, but the longer he stayed in Blue Heron Beach, the more he thought about it. About having it with Jillene.

"I'm happy for you, Pop." Vince embraced his father and gave him a few firm pats on the back. "I'm glad I was around so you could tell me in person."

"She's planning the wedding for October. Now that you know and she's telling her sons, we'll talk things over with Father Pofelski. Mu and Sol aren't going to believe this."

"I think they will."

"You don't know how much I love her, son. More than I could ever convey in words."

Vince nodded his understanding, thinking that he was

beginning to experience those same feelings himself. But unlike his father's situation, his had complications.

Vince didn't stay long at the barbershop before returning to the *Gracie*. Taking his fishing tackle and pole, he stood at the end of the pier and dropped his line.

The rattle of a rusty bicycle approaching grew louder. Duane Bobcock flicked the kickstand out and stared up at the orange Unocal 76 ball as it slowly rotated on its axis.

"How many times do you think that goes around in one day? I've tried to count but it messed up my head, man."

"I don't know, Duane. Probably a hundred or so."

"Shit, man. That's a lot." Duane brought out the makings for a joint and rolled one. He lit the end and took a deep drag. "Toke?"

"No, thanks."

Duane peered over the railing into the murky water. All that was visible sprouting up from the surface was the high-impact fluorescent line attached to Vince's pole. "Catch anything?"

"Nope."

"Bummer. That's because your line's got an up conversion on it." The heavy aroma of burning hemp clouded around Duane. "Ocean fish don't care about high energy. Freshwater trouts do, though. They're stimulated by the light source of one wavelength that emits radiation at another wavelength." He brought the joint to his mouth. "Let's say you've got—" he talked through a slow exhale "—a blue wavelength that's high energy and obtain a fluorescence at a longer wavelength like a green lower energy. It makes you glow like a Martian, man."

Duane must have been taking some hits all day because he wasn't making any sense.

"Some dyes have a shorter wavelength and they don't

fade," Duane added. "What are you using for bait, dude?"

"Squid."

"Far out, man. But you're still not going to hook one."

Vince wasn't following much of what Duane was saying until he mentioned "There are things in life that aren't meant to go together, but if you find out a way to make them connect, you've got something that works."

Vince turned his head to gaze directly at Duane. He wore scrub pants and a holey, tank-style undershirt. He needed a heavy dose of deodorant, and one of the straps on his huaraches was safety-pinned. The wiry hair of his beard was unruly and wild, but there was clarity in his eyes. He was really thinking hard.

"Like, if you could get earthworms to change color," he said in a nasal tone while keeping the smoke inside his lungs. "Turn them fluorescent green. You'd catch a shitload of trout. It's just a matter of figuring out how to get the worms to eat the dye. There's got to be some probability in that, man. I don't know what it is, but if I thought about it long enough and smoked enough reefer, I'd come up with something. It would save a lot of misery."

His curiosity piqued, Vince asked, "What do you mean by misery?"

"Getting wet in the rain. You know when the mist is going to turn into rain, but you can't leave your fishing spot 'cause you've only gotten bites all day but haven't nabbed one. So you wait it out and get wet. Then the rain fills the lake. The lake evaporates and fills the clouds again. Eventually, you'll get wet again by the same water. But you still go back to fishing even though you know you're going to get wet."

There was something in there that Vince pulled apart

and pieced back together. Duane was right. Life was an endless cycle of moisture. It filled the air, fell into the lakes and was claimed back by the sky.

If he didn't take a risk, he'd never know what it was like to stand in the rain with Jillene.

Jillene's heartbeat pumped double time as if she were next in line at the dentist. But at least she knew what she was up against with this damn clutch.

She was going to conquer the steepest road on the island and get Vince out of her head.

Shoving the Karmann Ghia's stick into gear, she began to climb Lighthouse Lane. It was a moderately winding hill with private drives leading to Blue Heron's most expensive homes. They were all secluded behind the lush, natural overgrowth of greenery and vines that wound over fences.

As a test, she stopped in the middle of the road. Her palms grew damp. The two-way lanes weren't heavily used and she hadn't passed a single car. With the nose of the Ghia aiming upward at a sixty-degree angle, she concentrated on moving her left and right foot at the same time so she wouldn't pop the clutch.

Easing into the maneuver, she stalled.

"Dammit."

Turning over the engine once more, she tried again. And again. She would keep at it until she got it right and could proceed through second and third gears before coming to the next stretch of road, where she'd try stopping again.

She blinked back the threatening tears, vowing not to let a single one escape down her cheek.

There was nothing to cry about.

She'd talked with both girls and her mother. Everything

was fine now, Faye was happy today, and Mom was spoiling her terribly for being such a good girl at the hospital. Claire reaped the benefits as well, being on the receiving end of an IHOP breakfast and a visit to the miniature golf course and arcade. Both girls had chattered about what they'd been doing. Then the inevitable question popped up: "Mom, where were you last night?"

She fibbed about her whereabouts. She said she'd worked late at Java and had fallen asleep at her desk doing some paperwork. The lie had tasted bitter on her tongue but she simply couldn't admit to spending the night with Vince. Not to her girls or her mother. What she had been doing with her time was private. But they wouldn't have to worry about her not being home anymore.

She'd sent Vince away.

On that thought, she shuddered. It was hard to accept.

After she'd spoken with the girls, she'd gone to Java and thrust herself into work so she wouldn't have time to be upset. And at the end of her shift, Jillene couldn't go home and face the empty house. So she just started driving.

Making another turn, she braked and gripped the steering wheel as if it were a lifeline and she were sinking. She could feel herself drowning in a knowledge that she wanted to both push away and welcome at the same time.

Determinedly, Jillene began to accelerate, trying to disassemble the potent realization from her mind. She couldn't accept it. Jamming her foot on the pedal, a soft popping noise sounded and then she felt the car sink low on the front end. She didn't have to get out to know what had happened.

A flat tire.

Great. Just great! She was in the middle of a hill with no way of calling anyone.

She opened the door and stepped out to assess the damage. It was flat all right. Any flatter and…whatever.

Brushing the hair away from her face, she tried to decide if she wanted to tackle changing it on her own or if she should ring the bell on one of the private gates and ask for help.

The purring engine of an automobile driving down the hill came to Jillene's ears like music. A godsend. She stepped off the shoulder to wave the driver to a stop.

Jillene lowered her hands when a silver Mercedes-Benz came into view with, of all people, Connie Ronco behind the wheel.

If Jillene could have, she would have shooed her away, but Connie had already stopped. The whir of her electric window sounded as she lowered the glass. A slender hand rested atop the door frame with gold bracelets flashing and a cocktail ring the size of a walnut winking in the sunshine.

"Car trouble?" Connie asked with a stunning smile. Her makeup was perfect and her blond hair had been put in an up-do with a gold clip. She had on huge diamond stud earrings.

"I have a flat," Jillene said in an equally flat tone.

"Too bad."

Jillene refrained from comment, figuring that Connie would relish leaving her stranded.

But what Connie did next surprised her. She got a cell phone from her purse. "I'll call a tow for you."

Folding her arms beneath her breasts, Jillene said, "I appreciate that."

The call was placed and Connie didn't leave. She pulled over to wait with Jillene, talking about a property she'd just had an open house for and was sure she'd have sold by the end of the evening.

All the while she rambled, Jillene didn't add much of anything to the conversation and had actually been tuning Connie out, when her next words brought her to the present with a hard crash.

"Do you want to call Vince and have him wait up here with you?"

"N-no," Jillene stuttered, completely thrown.

Crossing her legs at the ankles and leaning her thin frame into the flashy grill of her car, Connie said, "I've all but stood naked in front of him. He's not interested in me. He wants you."

The breath had been snatched from Jillene. She couldn't speak.

"Why aren't you happy about it? You should be gloating. I know I would be. I'm declaring defeat. You're the woman he wants. Gawd, but I hate to say it—maybe you're the woman he *needs.* Don't you see that? Or maybe it's him. Is he blind from all that California sun or what?"

The tears Jillene had fought earlier came back with a vengeance. She squeezed her eyelids closed so none would escape, but a few snuck through. Her emotions were on a dangerous precipice. She couldn't cry in front of Connie. She'd never live it down.

Struggling for composure, she discretely turned and wiped away the moisture from her eyes with the back of her hand. When she faced Connie once again, the realtor had the audacity to stand there, extending a tissue.

Silently, Jillene took it and blew her nose.

After a moment, Jillene managed to say, "I don't know what you're talking about with me and Vince."

"Then, you're turning your back on the best thing that could ever happen to you. I've known him forever. Vince is—" she sighed as if she'd missed out on the biggest clothing sale of the year "—really great. Wonderful."

If he was so wonderful, why had Jillene chased him away this morning at a time when she could have used his comfort and he had wanted to give it to her? Because she would have had to face more than she could handle.

But now she couldn't run.

"Oh…no," Jillene whimpered, "I *am* in love with him."

"Sold." Connie's summary was pithy but apropos.

"What am I going to do?"

"I'd start by telling him."

"I can't."

"Why not?"

"Because I don't want to be in love with him."

Jillene didn't see how falling into sex could have lead to falling in love. It made no sense. She wasn't prepared to face the truth. Because what could Jillene do about it? Nothing.

He had his life in Los Angeles.

She had her life in Blue Heron Beach.

The two lifestyles wouldn't work without major compromises, and she wouldn't sell Java. She was too close to success. She couldn't quit and move away.

And there were the girls to consider. They liked Vince and that was great. But they weren't thinking in the long-term. There wouldn't just be "dates" anymore if she gave in to her feelings. She'd want a permanence, men's clothes in the closet, sandy beach shoes in a size twelve on the back porch and silly sporting equipment in the garage. This was something she and Vince hadn't discussed. And what was there to discuss now?

Marriage?

The word brought a shiver across her skin, wondrous and scary.

"I can't help you there," Connie replied. "I don't know how to fall out of love with a good guy, only a bad one."

The tow service came and changed the Ghia's tire. Connie didn't hang around for that, but before she drove off her parting words were "If you and Vince get together, I'll list your house and fix you up with something fantastic." Then she pressed her card into Jillene's hand and waved, with a tinkle of bracelets, out the open window before she disappeared from sight.

Numbly, Jillene drove home. She had too much to think over. Pulling into her driveway, she slowed to a stop with her gaze fixed on the expanse of her front yard.

There were pink plastic lawn flamingos everywhere. Dozens of them.

She got out of the car and examined the display with amazement. Proceeding up to the front door, she saw the note, written with the girls' sidewalk chalk in large letters across her porch step.

You don't need a permit for pink flamingos.

She immediately recalled bemoaning to Vince that City Hall would probably make her get a permit for lawn flamingos.

"Hello, Jillene," Vince said, his voice resonant as he came from the side of the house.

"Hello." Seeing him made her heart turn over.

"What do you think?"

She swept her gaze over the pink flamingos. "I didn't think the hardware store had so many."

"They had an extra inventory box."

Smiling softly, she looked at him as if seeing him for the first time all over again. His height and strength. The broadness of his shoulders. The way he wore his watch. The smell of him, so sexy that it made her breathe faster. Windblown, the hem of his shirt flipped up around his waist. She marveled at his physique. The black hair that complemented his darker complexion. And those eyes. Incredible. The blue and smoky gray, a mix of so many things she'd come to know about him.

"If I could go back," she began, wetting her lips, "there are things I'd have done differently today."

He nodded, perhaps thinking the same.

"But I can't. Just like I can't help something that happened to me and maybe to us. I didn't expect it. I didn't want it. But it's here and I think I'm glad." The tattoo of her heart was like a drum, beating loudly in her ears to a deafening crescendo.

She should stop talking while she was safe. The discovery was too new and she'd barely had a chance to accept it.

He gave me pink lawn flamingos.

The intensity of his eyes held her still.

She opened her mouth but nothing came out. She pressed her fingertips over her lip, then blurted, "Vince, I love you."

Black silence fell over them.

He stood there, a little paralyzed and glancing down for a moment, then back up at her. He ran a hand down the underside of his jaw. The habit he had that she'd thought so handsome burned into her like a flame of mortification. He was looking for the words to tell her that he didn't feel the same way.

He didn't love her. It was all about sex. She knew it. Dammit...she'd known from the start that there was nothing more. She'd said that all she wanted was sex. She'd set herself up for hurt the second she'd said those three words.

She wanted to hide.

Vince said, "Jillene, I—" But the ring of his cell phone cut off his words.

Perfect timing to let him off the hook.

"Never mind," she said, pushing past him and going to the house. "I didn't mean what I said. I was caught up in all the sex. I mistook it for something else. I was wrong. So just...never mind."

The phone kept ringing, driving a wedge between them.

She rammed her key into the lock, opened the door and closed him out. Leaning her back against the panel, she felt the tears falling down her cheeks.

Staring at the front door, Vince felt as if he'd been slapped as the chirp of the cell phone filled the air, then finally quit. Hell, he should have been slapped. But he hadn't had a chance to form the words that he needed. It was complicated. Something he'd thought about at length after talking with Duane.

Before he told Jillene how he felt about her, he had to be honest with her about Lentz. The whole thing. The sick mess Vince found himself wrapped up in. He didn't know how things would turn out. For his career, for his peace of mind and for the lasting effects he would have to deal with. She had to know who she was loving and who wanted to love her and her family. If they accepted him as he was, they'd be accepting Lentz. It was something she'd have to live with if she lived with him.

But she'd slammed the door in his face and he'd had no time to explain why he'd held back.

He cut across the drive and walked to the door so they could talk.

The phone rang again. Whoever was calling was persistent, and he wanted to throw the phone across the lawn.

Dammit all to hell!

He took out his frustration on the cell and angrily punched the answer button, only to hear the hiss of an operator recording.

"You have a collect call from a California State Prison. If you wish to accept the charges, speak now. If not, hang up."

Vince's blood congealed in his veins. Nobody—*nobody*—on the inside had this number. Slowly he said, "Vince Tremonti."

"How professional." Subtle amusement caught in the man's voice on the other end. "Samuel Lentz here—from L.A. County jail."

Jerking his head around, Vince scanned the trees. He knew it couldn't be, but he expected to see Lentz. It was an eerie feeling he couldn't shake as the voice went on—keyed up and edgy.

"You made me work to find you, Vince."

Backing away from Jillene's house as if the call would contaminate her yard, he growled, "How the fuck did you get this number?"

"Why are you so angry? I'm the one who should be angry at you, Vince. You've ignored me and I don't like that. It concerns me. I want to know how my book is coming. Have you gotten to the good part? Have I sliced into any of the bitches yet?"

Vince debated between hanging up and going to Jillene.

"Well?" Lentz's voice was impatient. "I sent you the letters, I want to know what you thought."

The saliva in Vince's mouth thickened and the acrid taste of bile rose up his throat.

"I'm waiting, Tremonti. What do you have for us?"

Us? As if they were in this together.

The voice on the other end of the phone was the catalyst that had thrown Vince's life into hell. Lentz's demands were like a razor-edged sword slicing across skin just enough to draw a thin line of blood. Still, there was that feeling of being bled to death at the implication of Lentz's *us*. It was that word and all that had preceded it with Jillene—the hopelessness that now pressed in—that pushed Vince to the breaking point.

"Listen, you sick bastard, I am going to write your book," Vince hissed into the receiver. "You gave me all the information I need and I'm going to use every last bit of every damn thing you've given me. So don't call me again, you pathetic prick."

"Having a bad day—"

Vince fought off nausea as he punched the button to disconnect the call. Then he turned off the power entirely.

Seconds passed before he could breathe again.

Then he started walking. Away from Jillene, unaware that she had been watching him from the living room window. Unaware that she had seen the tension in his neck muscles, the terror on his face, and the angry gestures as he'd sliced into the air with his hand. He had no idea she'd touched the lock of the door, deciding to come out and see if he was all right—because he was already heading down the trail to the marina.

Loose rocks slipped beneath his shoes, raining down as he ran to the bottom. He was living a nightmare. He felt a jab like that of an ice pick tear at the back of his neck, chipping away at him until everything around him turned a dark color. The light had gone away. The hope. The brightness.

Just a moment before, he'd been ready to give in to the love and beauty and purity of caring for Jillene and her daughters. But that purity had just been ruined by one evil phone call. Vince's utopian thoughts had been demolished with a single swing of a wrecking ball.

He couldn't draw this woman and her children into his hell. How could he have hoped Jillene would accept the fact that a man had killed just to "impress" him? What about the next time? The next story?

He had a demon on his shoulder that he couldn't get rid of. He had no other career. Nothing else to offer but criminals like Lentz who would taint their lives. There would always be another trial. Another killer who was a hunter.

In his world, Vince would always look at ordinary things every day and see them differently. The knot in a shoelace would be analyzed as the type used to choke a victim. A blotch of ketchup on a restaurant menu would always resemble blood. For him, simple and mundane were challenges. He understood forensic science and criminal psychopathy.

Because Vince Tremonti was a true crime writer.

That was what he did.

He lived in the belly of the beast.

Thirty-One

Vince sat in front of his computer, the flat screen empty except for a blinking cursor. A commercial airliner making its final descent into LAX flew over his roof with a low whine of thrust. The roof tiles vibrated as the engine noise reverberated through his house. The windows were closed tight against the heat and smog, and his air-conditioning had been running nonstop since he'd arrived home late yesterday.

He'd said goodbye to Pop, had thrown his things in the Rover and headed down Interstate 5 in the same manner he'd driven north—nonstop driving and a single brief hotel stop. Just like that. No thinking. Just doing. He was back to his old life. His old ways.

This was home.

The summer day was hazy, the sky so thick you couldn't see the Hollywood Hills. The valley was like one big bowl of hundred-degree soup.

The cursor blinked like a lighthouse beacon, cautioning and constant. Waiting for Vince to acknowledge it and decide which way to go. Sometimes he thought of it as an important point on a coastline to steer toward—and sometimes it represented rocks in the shoals that could potentially sink him.

He had two courses he could navigate.

Ever since Vince's last visit to L.A. County, his apprehensions had grown in proportion to things unknown. The ferocity of his fear was as frightening as if he were staring into the barrel of a gun. His breathing grew absolutely still.

Years of writing about serial killers for the purpose of defining the various symptoms of crimes was not what it was about anymore. Samuel Lentz had changed all that, with his descriptions of deaths on tape, the warped personal ad announcing his intentions, and the letter diaries.

Vince's stomach clenched tight and the muscles of his forearms hardened. The premeditated terror was the real enemy and it was staring Vince in the face, taunting him, daring him.

With difficulty, he swallowed and slumped back in his chair.

Suddenly Vince realized he was part of the problem and not part of the solution. His fear was not about personal harm to himself or professional ruin. Regardless of how hard he might try, he could neither prevent nor change the things over which he had no control.

Vince now knew what he had to do.

Straightening, he let his fingertips hover over the keys. He paused and drew a deep breath into his burning lungs. Then his fingers began to fly over the keys, turning letters into words, words into sentences, sentences into paragraphs and paragraphs into pages.

Hour stacked upon hour, and he was aware of nothing but the sound of his hands possessively clipping across the keyboard.

When he heard the *thwack* of the *Los Angeles Times* hit his porch, he finally looked at the clock—five-forty a.m. Only then did he stop to make a pot of strong coffee. Memories of a woman with glossy blond hair handing him a Caffe Americano haunted him.

Before her taste, her smell and warmth could wrap around his heart, she evaporated from his mind and Lentz crept back inside.

There was no energy in Vince to think about anything or anyone aside from the book. The pages. The endless words that gripped his mind and consumed him such that the days rolled into each other with no beginning or end.

If one more person asked her when Vince was coming back to Blue Heron Beach, Jillene was going to scream. She kept telling herself she'd gotten over the stinging hurt of his departure.

The last she'd seen of him was when he'd walked down the wooded trail on the day he'd given her the lawn flamingos; the last she'd heard his voice was that night when he'd left a message on her machine. In hindsight, she questioned if she should have picked up. She'd been too numb to react quickly enough. She was so used to screening her calls that she'd remained on the sofa until it was too late. He'd hung up. But his words had remained in her mind.

Jillene, I'm sorry. I have to go back to L.A. and I'll be in touch.

But he had never gotten in touch with her again. He couldn't have spelled it out any more clearly.

She'd been heartbroken. But it was her own fault. She'd set up the terms and called it a "fling." She'd broken the rule of dating—at least, that's what a relationship counselor had said the other day on an afternoon talk show. Jillene had said "I love you" first. Women weren't supposed to, and especially not during an affair. It was the man's lead, like a dance, or so the therapist said. Jillene thought the point of view was lame and eventually discounted it. If you loved somebody, you had to tell them. In her case, it hadn't worked out.

But whenever Connie came into Java for her raspberry latte, her presence reminded Jillene all over again that Connie had told her not to turn her back on the best thing that could ever happen to her.

But it wasn't Jillene who'd left. It was Vince...

Maybe because she'd pushed him away. If only she'd opened the front door and followed him. Picked up her phone the night he'd called. She could call him now, but too much time had passed. She wouldn't know what to say. He'd clearly moved on—and she needed to do the same thing herself. She'd sunk herself into so many activities. She didn't allow herself even one moment to think about the way he'd once kissed her and made love...

The girls had come home from Jodi-Lynn's in early August and were disappointed to hear that Vince had returned to California. They often asked "Uncle Al" when Vince would come back, but Al Tremonti told them his son was working on a book and didn't have plans to visit at the moment.

Jillene saw the blighted hope on the girls' faces and knew they'd wanted to see her and Vince together. That wasn't to be, but it didn't prevent them from pestering Uncle Al about Vince. Faye and Claire filled the rest of their vacation with riding bikes, picnics in the tree house and Barbies. They'd be starting school in a few weeks and the old routine would begin again.

Jillene's summertime savior at Java, Rob Duniway, had begun classes at Washington State and was only working part-time now. She'd hired Gabby full-time and she was a great help. Hannah had found the man of her dreams and they'd been a hot-and-heavy item for a month—some guy named Glenn, who was the best lover she'd ever had in her bed.

Slowly, Jillene began to get a grip on commerce, and the concept of revenue numbers, policy and procedure manuals and business plans. She'd be able to reinstate her medical insurance soon. Optimism finally prevailed. Java was headed for good things. A Seattle-based magazine had come by to take pictures and write a feature piece on Java the Hut—for a "women who are succeeding in business" article. The issue was due to come out in December. This past May, Jillene wouldn't have believed such a possibility existed.

Just when she thought she was finally getting over him, Vince resurfaced in her life in a way she had never anticipated. It was the day she found out he'd paid off her hospital bill.

She'd made her August payment, only to have the check returned to her along with a closing statement. She'd been surprised to find out that she didn't have a balance anymore. It had been wiped clean by a VISA card. She knew she didn't have one. She'd called Olympic View to see what had happened and had been informed by the billing clerk that the town's local hero had phoned in his VISA number and had taken care of her charges. Then the woman had the nerve to ask how Jillene had gotten so lucky.

Astonished, Jillene had been at a loss over what to do. She'd been outraged, but in the end she hadn't confronted Vince. She'd been afraid that if she talked to him, she'd say things she'd regret. Whether they were words of anger or regret, it was best they never speak again. Instead, she saw his father and requested Vince's home address so she could mail him a check. Thankfully Al hadn't inquired about what had happened between her and his son. Surely he had to know that there had been something going on between them.

When Al came into Java he'd give her an update—as he did for everyone in Blue Heron—but she never asked him how Vince was doing, if he was happy, if he'd found somebody.

Jillene did some bill shuffling and decided to let a debt lapse into a late period in order to repay Vince. She'd mailed a personal check to his home. It had taken her hours to compose, but she'd finally settled on writing a curt note to him, telling him his generosity was not appreciated and that there was nothing more between them.

The score had been settled.

The second she'd popped the envelope into the mailbox, her heart had been mended. Well…not quite.

Now the skies were crowned with clouds and autumn had come to Blue Heron in a riot of golden fire. Leaves had changed. The season of her rebirth as a woman had come to an end. Sex and intimacy, and the close bond she had once shared with a special man were now over.

The summer days faded, but those moments with Vince Tremonti would remain eternal for Jillene.

"This isn't the book we contracted for, Vince." Gail Castellano's voice filled the phone line. "This isn't the Samuel Lentz story."

Vince had spent the past two months writing the manuscript in question without leaving his house. He had answered neither his telephone nor his mail. He left his office only to sleep or to take a swim in his pool at whatever hour possessed him. His secretary knew when to not talk to him, how to manage the cleaning service, and she made food appear somehow so he wouldn't perish. He'd been so consumed by the need to write that details such as those were unimportant.

The story that had formed inside his head was a piece of his soul, his heart. A very personal effort that, if published, could leave him wide open to ridicule and criticism from readers and critics alike.

Vince had no idea if he'd be ruined or not as an author. Every success he'd ever had was now clouded and forgotten. They didn't matter anymore—he knew he was taking a huge risk.

But the potential benefits of risk were far more important than ill-gotten gains.

His editor's pause was prolonged, then she said, "But it's the best damn thing you've ever written."

Until she spoke the words, Vince didn't realize how long he'd been waiting for her response to *Inside the Beast.*

He'd penned a cathartic book about how a serial killer had murdered women so he could be made famous by Vince Tremonti. Names were named. Real incidents written about. Everything was revealed. This was Vince's discovery of the beast, his time in the belly and subsequent journey out. The deeply personal book showed how he had changed. As an author. As a man.

The condemned man now sitting in San Quentin had not succeeded. His bid for glory and infamy was gone. The style of this book was not true crime, but rather an autobiography of an author who had once been devoured by the monster known as Samuel Lentz.

"That's what I'd hoped to hear, Gail." Vince felt strongly about having this book published so Lentz wouldn't win. Anyway, it was doubtful he'd get another author to touch the material after his sadistic plan was revealed.

The book was brutally honest and included a lot of detail, except for the letters written to Vince by Samuel Lentz. They were locked in a safety deposit box and would never see the light of day. There was no point in hurting the victims' families any further.

Aside from that, Vince wouldn't have to hide from the truths of the case. All the pieces to the Lentz case were public knowledge. He didn't have to fear. Didn't have to be ashamed.

"You're damn lucky the publisher loved this one, Vince. So did I. It's nothing short of amazing. And…very touching. I had no idea you were living with something like this. You could have been up front with me and we could have worked out something else. A different case."

Quietly, he said, "Then, you didn't read the epilogue."

"Oh, I read it. And I don't want to face it just yet. We have your option, you know. Don't show another publisher anything until we get first look."

He wasn't worried about that.

Vince would no longer be writing true crime or any kind of nonfiction. The books he had once written reflected aspects of the American way of life as face-value entertainment. He thought of the brutalities Lentz had committed, and he would never again be drawn to the questions that asked why criminals did the things they did. There was never an answer. Never a rational one, anyway.

Gail discussed the book's publication and publicity and wanted him to go on a tour. He declined. *Inside the Beast* wasn't a book he would promote. He had written it to cleanse his emotions. He had delivered it to fulfill an obligation, and how the book was received…he would leave to fate.

When he hung up after talking to his editor, Vince

smiled. Faintly at first. Then more widely—and he knew he was grinning.

Uncertainty still hovered. Destruction could be imminent. But this was his fresh beginning. And it seemed to be destiny that he would begin his new journey as the best man at his father's wedding.

Where he would see Jillene McDermott and explain why he had had to leave Blue Heron Beach.

Thirty-Two

Al Tremonti's bachelor party would be talked about for years to come by those who'd been there.

The festivities took place at Al's house. Sol Slobodkin brought over the video store's entire collection of Rodgers and Hammerstein musicals on DVD. Mujid Pantankar sprang for a state-of-the-art DVD player as Al and Ianella's early wedding present. Jerry Peck brought two keggers of Bud, and every customer who'd been patronizing Al's since he'd opened forty years ago, stopped by and brought him goodwill and gifts.

While Buddy Fontaine had never had his hair cut at Al's, he and some delinquent friends stopped by about midnight after hearing there was a kegger party. It didn't matter whose. In the ensuing scuffle between Buddy and Jerry Peck, Harry Newton switched *Oklahoma!* for *The Bridge Over the River Kwai,* then cranked up the volume. Amid the whistle of missiles and bombs, Jerry ran Buddy and his pals off with party ice tongs.

Things got further out of hand when Eugene, from the boat shop, and Jerry got into an argument over the best way to torch Al's illegal U-turn tickets. Jerry had brought them over, and in the nature of nuptial spirit, told Al he was no longer obligated to pay them.

Before Jerry was ready, Eugene flicked the spark on his Zippo and lit the tickets in Jerry's hand. He ran into the

backyard with a blazing fan of traffic violations and
dropped them on a piece of lawn furniture that went up
in flames. The fire department had to be called.

Al's best chaise lounge was in ashes.

But as Al stood at the altar of St. Mary's waiting for
his bride to come down the aisle, none of last night's party
was in his thoughts. His heartbeat chimed like wedding
bells. His breathing quickened as the organist began to
play the wedding march.

His son stood proud at his left side. The church was
packed with friends who looked upon him with smiles.
And then the double doors opened and his angel of love
appeared.

Slowly she came toward him, escorted by Rocky and
Carmine.

From this day forward, they would be husband and
wife.

Jillene hadn't been sure she would go to Al Tremonti
and Ianella Sofrone's wedding. She felt funny about it
knowing that Vince would be there. Ultimately, she decided she had to go in order to prove to herself that she
could. She would not be affected by him.

She'd been wrong.

She couldn't take her eyes off Vince during the entire
ceremony. He looked so handsome in his black tuxedo,
the starched white of his shirt contrasting against his tan
skin. The little buttons caught her eyes and she remembered how she had once taken pleasure in unfastening the
buttons on his shirt. Her fingers tingled at the thought.

He wore his hair longer. His eyes were focused as he
gave his father the gold wedding bands.

They hadn't had an opportunity to converse before the
ceremony. Not that she had made herself available. She'd

seen him in the chapel with his father and quickly retreated outside. In advance, she'd known he was the best man and that it would be inevitable that they'd run into each other. If they traded words, she didn't want them to be strained.

"Is he almost going to kiss her?" Faye asked in a whisper.

"Almost," Jillene whispered back to her daughter.

Claire demurely crossed her nylon-clad legs and patiently waited.

The girls sitting on either side of her had been excited about this wedding for weeks. It gave them the chance to dress up, apply sparkle body glitter and wear their hair curled.

As Father Pofelski pronounced the couple man and wife, Jillene was suddenly overcome with emotion. She fought against a sentimental cry. Her purse was full of tissues just in case, but she didn't want to get one out. Not in light of what the tears were over.

Was it possible she was still in love with Vince?

Here were all those feelings once again, rising up inside her in an admittance she couldn't deny. Their fling had been a charming romance that had intoxicated her like wine. She wanted another drink of its sweetness, to share the softly spoken reflections while they lay beside each other, skin to skin. It was an irresistible impulse, one she had to fight off.

As Alphonzo and Ianella Tremonti sealed their marriage vows with a kiss, there was no greater happiness this day in Blue Heron Beach. They dashed down the aisle to the cheers and applause of the congregation.

Jillene quickly gathered up the girls. They were the first to give their congratulations before leaving St. Mary's.

The time in the car on the way to the reception gave Jillene a moment to pull herself together.

This simply couldn't be happening. She couldn't let the shadow of regret fall across her. She had no false pity to spare on herself. The church had been a warning. Seeing Vince like that in such a setting made her think about a different wedding. One that had never taken place.

One that never would.

The reception was in the Mambo Room at the Lobster King. A tower of presents were stacked on a far table. Across from it, a three-tiered wedding cake sat beneath a beam of light aimed from the ceiling.

Soon, other wedding guests began to fill the room. Hannah came toward her on the arm of a man who was prematurely bald in front and who was five inches shorter than she was.

"Jillene, this is Glenn." She introduced him with a wispy sigh.

"Hello," Jillene said in return, shaking his hand. This was not the man she had pictured with Hannah, but if he made her happy, why not?

Yes…why not?

Jillene let the girls fetch their own punch and she listened to the musicians playing songs from the forties and fifties. When the wedding party arrived, she drifted outside.

The marine air was brisk, and the sky was overcast. She wished she had worn a coat but the girls had told her it ruined the outfit. They'd talked her into buying a black lace cocktail dress that had been on sale. The long sleeves were little more than lace. A scallop-edged low V made the neckline a little more plunging than she liked. The balls of her feet hurt in a pair of old high heels. She was used to tennis shoes. Her waist and hips were sucked into panty hose.

"Mom, can we—" Claire cut her question short. "Hi, Vince!"

Faye ran up to him and gave him a hug, one which he returned. "I'm so glad you're back. You're staying, right?"

Vince came toward them, and Jillene wanted to melt. It didn't take a genius to fall out of love, but it took a fool to fall headlong back into it. And with her eyes wide open.

God help her. She still loved him. Damn, damn and dammit.

It wasn't fair. He looked so composed and so collected, when her heart was breaking.

"Hey, girls," he said.

His smile was enough to send her pulse racing into first and then fourth gear—skipping the ones in between.

Faye replied, "So how are ya? Huh?"

"We never did get to tell you about our trip to Disneyland. And we saw Marilyn Monroe's star on the Hollywood Walk of Fame, too," Claire added.

When he spoke, he looked directly at Jillene. "I want to talk to your mom, girls. Is that all right?"

She willed her heartbeat to calm. It ignored her.

"Sure!" they both said.

"Jillene, will you take a walk with me?"

It was a little late to be asking, considering he'd already gotten the girls on his side. She nodded, and he took the initiative to descend the steps of the pier to the beach.

Her shoes sank into the sand so she took them off.

The chill wasn't so bad under the pilings, but she shivered just the same. He instantly shrugged out of his jacket and gave it to her. She would have protested, but it smelled so good wrapped around her, almost as if it were his arms. Warm and smelling wonderful. A combination she would forever associate with Vince.

Before she lost all reason and did something she'd regret, she asked quite bluntly, "Did you get my check?"

"Yes."

He stood next to her, facing the ocean as it swept up to the shore and then rolled back in churning foam. The squawk of seagulls overhead carried in the slight wind and the buoys clanged in the distance.

Pride bested her, and in a small voice she added, "Why did you do it, Vince? Why did you pay that bill for me?"

"Because I love you."

He couldn't have surprised her more. She reached out and braced herself against one of the roughhewn pilings. The loud drum of her heartbeat soared and lifted until she could barely hear herself speak. "Well, that's a funny way of showing it. Leave town, tell me you'll call from L.A. but don't, and pay a medical bill. Nice one."

Her cynicism couldn't be stifled. She was shocked to the core.

Vince stepped beside her, his presence and strength towering over her. "I'm sorry I didn't say goodbye properly. I left you a message and I meant to call again, but I got too involved in something and I had to finish it."

She could have lied but she saw no point. Surely her expression gave away everything she was thinking and feeling. "I got over not hearing from you."

"It was a tough time for me."

"Me, too," she quickly responded. "I told you I loved you and you didn't say it back. That devastated me. It's been hard to forgive myself for being so stupid."

"You weren't stupid, Jillene."

She bit her lip, a flicker of wind blowing a curl across

her brow. She felt him easing closer and she knew what he would do. Tossing the curl away, she thrust her shoulders back. If he touched her now she'd dissolve.

"You love me? Really?"

"Yes."

"God, why didn't you tell me when you knew?" Pulling in a much-needed breath, she went on. "When did you know?" Then unbidden, she reached out and socked him ineffectually in the arm. "You jerk."

"I am."

"At least you admit it," she meekly agreed. "So now I'll admit to something that I don't feel anymore, but I did at the time." She bucked up, licking her lips. "When I found out you paid that hospital bill, it was like you were paying for a summer of…sex."

"Not even close, Jillene." This time he did touch the curve of her cheek, and she battled valiantly to keep control.

"I wanted to help you and make your life easier."

"When you left, you made my life hell."

"Jillene…" The timbre of his voice as he spoke her name was like a caress, causing gooseflesh to tingle across her skin. "I've wanted to tell you this but I couldn't." The pain in his gaze was genuine and an honest sincerity infused itself into his words. "I came to Blue Heron to get away from a book I was working on about a man named Samuel Lentz. He did something because of me."

She listened as he told her a story so heartbreakingly horrible that she couldn't move. Her every breath hinged on what he was telling her. The pain he lived with, the guilt and self-inflicted censure. If she had watched Lentz's story on a movie screen she'd have been impressed by Hollywood's creativity, but unable to believe a person could be so calculated. So heinously barbaric and sick.

The criminal had called Vince the day he stuck all those pink flamingos in her yard. That was the reason he'd gone home. He'd written a book, but not about the crimes. It was a story about how the man had affected him. His life. His career. His hopes and dreams, and the job he was letting go of because he couldn't face it any longer.

"I don't know what's going to happen when the book comes out. I haven't spoken to Samuel Lentz since that day he called me on my cell phone. He's written me dozens of letters, but I've never replied to any of them. He has no idea what I've done since they transferred him out of L.A. County. I've contacted San Quentin and they'll be on the alert once the book is out."

"Vince...what a terrible thing to live with."

"It's all right. I can handle it now. Whatever happens, I'm good."

Jillene felt drained and relieved. "You could have told me, Vince. I would have listened."

"I didn't want to talk about it." He leaned over her face, tilting her head to his. "I was too caught up in falling in love. I was drawn to you from the beginning. Maybe because you added positive complications to my life that I thought I didn't need. Or maybe it was the way you served me coffee with a smudge of chocolate on your apron in a very sexy place."

Against her will, she blushed.

"You look incredible in this dress," he murmured above her lips. "So beautiful. I've missed you, Jillene. Missed everything about you."

His breath touched her face and she tingled as he gave her a kiss that reached into her very soul. Fluttering, her eyelids closed and she savored the contact of his mouth. His tongue flicked hotly over hers, teasing and reacquainting. Enticing nips of his teeth caught the fullness of her mouth and she moaned, pressing herself against him and wrapping her arms around his neck.

He lifted his head and gazed into her eyes. "Jillene, this isn't the ideal time and I'd hoped to say it when it would sound a little more romantic. But I can't wait. I love you. And I want to marry you."

Her entire being shivered with longing.

"I do love you, Vince. With all my heart." It would be so easy to just say yes without any more words. "But we never got this far before. This is the part where we have to bare everything."

Vince had to know what he was getting when he got her and the girls.

He replied, "I know what you're talking about, but details are just that, small things we can deal with."

"But I have a lot of debt and a second mortgage and a dog who likes to sleep on the bed. Java is on stronger legs, but it's still not quite there. I won't let you pay one dime to help me out of my mess, so you can forget that. My daughters are great and you know how much they mean to me. They're part of the package. You get them when you get me. I'm not ideal for a man who's never been married before."

"Jillene, I'm not so ideal, either. I don't have a promising income anymore and I don't know what I'm going to do." His hair fell over his brow and she lovingly brushed it back. "But I still want to marry you. To move back to Blue Heron and live here with you. I may not have any experience in parenting, but I want to be a dad to your daughters."

"And I think they'd like that," she said, her voice quivering. "I would like that. Oh, Vince…oh…"

"Marry me." He kissed her temple and held her close.

She clutched his neck and buried her face in the silk of his cravat. "Yes...yes. I'll marry you."

He held her, snug and safe in the cocoon of his arms. Music from above floated down to them. A ballad of the endurance of love.

"See the pyramids along the Nile..."

Vince and Jillene moved together, dancing to "You Belong to Me" with her hand in his, her shoes dangling from her fingertips and his arm around her waist.

This was the first dance of the rest of their lives.

Epilogue

One year later...

Vince's life had been incorporated into the world of Barbies and Miss America. During the television pageant, he'd had to keep tabs on his favorite contestant. Claire and Faye had instructed him to write down her name and the points he gave for personality and swimwear. He could have sworn Miss Texas was a shoe-in. He'd lost.

He'd been clued in to what "Girls Night" was and he stayed away from that female time. He didn't want a pedicure, although Faye had said she'd give him one.

Instead of crashing their girl time, he'd brought some "Boys Night" into the house. Tonight he was helping Claire and Faye build a couple of boss model car sets he'd bought for them. 1975 Camaros.

Faye glued while Claire painted.

He sat next to them at the kitchen table, watching their hands as they moved, steady and careful with the plastic pieces.

A crackling fire glowed from the fireplace. Photos were on the mantel. David's picture remained a centerpiece. Vince understood the importance of its placement and would always respect the fact that he was in their hearts. Next to it, there was a framed photograph from last Christ-

mas with Vince, Jillene, Claire and Faye, and Sugar sitting
in front of their decorated tree.

The home they had moved into after the wedding was
on the beachfront. This one was more modern than Jillene's cottage. They had talked a long time about whether
or not to move. After she had paid off the second mortgage and had cleared the equity, they'd decided it would
be best if they found a new place for themselves where
new memories could be created.

To Connie's credit, she'd found them the perfect house.
His and Jillene's bedroom, which would be a temporary
nursery, overlooked the beach, and the girls could go
down the balcony steps to play on the sand with Sugar.

In the living room, Jillene lay on the sofa with the dog
on her feet. She smiled at him from her bowl of ice cream.
He lovingly smiled in return. She shifted her weight, ad-
justing herself onto her side to settle more comfortably
against the pillows.

Her figure was bulky with their child.

The baby was due in three weeks. They didn't know
what they were having. It didn't matter if the baby was a
boy or a girl. Its arrival would be the completion of their
family.

The love Vince felt in his heart for this woman and her
children was profound and touching. It brought an ache
to his chest. Sometimes he couldn't believe how his life
had turned around.

A year ago, he hadn't known what was around the corner. But he had turned it anyway. Because he had faith
beside him. He had Jillene and her love.

Inside the Beast had been released and it hit every best-
seller list. It had been a blockbuster. Something Vince had
felt neither good nor bad about. He'd moved on from what
the book represented. Samuel Lentz would remain in San

Quentin awaiting execution. He had written Vince many more letters, but Vince returned them all to sender—unopened. He'd changed the number on his cell phone as soon as he returned to L.A. and hadn't been contacted by Lentz again. Vince had heard that Lentz denied the credibility of *Beast,* saying it was an outright lie. But no other journalists would touch the material, and the book stood on its own for the readers to judge.

As for his writing, Vince had fallen back into it with a new outlook and a new contract. He'd sold a novel about a police officer who lived on a small Washington island. Something like Blue Heron Beach.

And he had a dog named Duke.

"Dad, can you play us a song on your guitar?" Faye asked.

Dad.

The sound of it still brought him to his knees.

"Yeah, Dad," Claire said, holding on to a paintbrush. "Something really good."

Jillene felt her whole body smiling. Every time she heard the girls call Vince "Dad," her heart warmed. It had been an incredible year. Her new life had brought her everything she thought she'd never have again, as well as so much more.

Java the Hut was now a thriving business and doing well enough for her to have done the near impossible. She'd been able to buy back her Chihuly. The beautiful chandelier that she had so loved and admired was hanging in Java again. *ROAR,* the magazine she'd once been stymied about, was coming by this week to award her its "Businesswoman of the Year" award.

When she looked at her husband, she was so filled with love and peace that she couldn't stop smiling at him. He smiled back as he rose to get his Fender.

Vince positioned himself across from Jillene and gazed at the women in his life. Warmth and tenderness held him still. He thought of a song that would convey everything he felt in his heart.

Settling the guitar on his lap, he strummed the strings. A melody fell into time, and he began to sing with all that he was and with everything good that he had become.

And nobody could say it better than Jiminy Cricket.

Vince's voice carried through the room. "When you wish upon a star, makes no difference who you are."

Now Leaving Blue Heron Beach, WA
Population 3,562
Home of the Glowing Green Earthworm